Books by John Sayles

PRIDE OF THE BIMBOS
UNION DUES

Union
Dues

Union
Dues

JOHN SAYLES

An Atlantic Monthly Press Book
Little, Brown and Company — Boston–Toronto

FIRST EDITION

T06/77

LIBRARY OF CONGRESS CATALOGING IN PUBLICATION DATA

Sayles, John, 1950–
  Union dues.

  I. Title.
PZ4.S27534Un [PS3569.A95]   813'.5'4   77–914
ISBN 0–316–77231–3

ATLANTIC–LITTLE, BROWN BOOKS
ARE PUBLISHED BY
LITTLE, BROWN AND COMPANY
IN ASSOCIATION WITH
THE ATLANTIC MONTHLY PRESS

Designed by Susan Windheim

Published simultaneously in Canada
by Little, Brown & Company (Canada) Limited

PRINTED IN THE UNITED STATES OF AMERICA

Union
Dues

1

The boy leaned out from his porch to look down the long row of wooden-box houses. Nothing much stirring. He hopped onto the street lugging an overstuffed laundry sack and tried to look like everything was normal. A few women stared from their porch rockers as he passed, surprised to see him during practice hours.

The boy wore white and black three-striped running shoes, he walked quickly and hunched to balance the sack comfortably on his shoulder. One five-block row of identical frame houses faced another at the base of the hollow, the road then twisted up and around the butt of a ridge. Sloping above the first bend was a small cemetery. The boy paused and waved to an old man dragging a rake in between the headstones. The old man was trying to rake back the crumbling red dog that had spilled down onto the mown grass, spilled down past trunks of autumn trees, through yellows, reds and browns, past solid green stands of pine, spilled from the base of the spoil bank higher up where they'd begun to strip the ridge. The trees were all gray up by the dozer-scraped highwall, tilted at crazy angles with their roots poking into space. The boy stood where his mother was. MOLLY BUNTIN MCNATT, DEVOTED WIFE AND MOTHER, the dates. The red dog hadn't reached her yet.

Directly around the bend, on the downhill side of the road, was the Holiness Church of God. The boy could hear them singing before the whitewashed cross flashed into his view, could pick out Delia's strong, righteous soprano and picture the bright-eyed look she got when she was filled with the power.

> *Won't you join up with the faithful,*

they sang,

[3]

Let your spirit be restored?
And surrender worldly striving
To become our Maker's ward?

He could hear her daddy's bass and see the way he thumped time on the pulpit. He could feel the Preacher's strength in that bass, feel the crushing handshake he got whenever Delia had him for dinner.

Won't you walk the holy country where
Christ's blood and tears have poured?
Won't you offer up your life to the Lord?

The boy half-trotted past the church.

The road flattened for a bit and a side lane, paved with red dog, forked off behind tall white oak to the high school. The boy slowed a little to listen. Terry Blankenship was barking signals, running the two-minute drill most likely from the rhythm of the breakhuddle clap and shout. A whistle blew, the team let out a wavering, on-the-sprint roar — then silence. That would be Coach, tough and sincere with his day-before inspiration. Election Day classic, he would say, quoting the papers. Last and most important of the season, '69 should be our year. Beckley kids tough but human. Pants on one leg at a time. Proud to be Pioneers. He always said that, Coach, the day before the big one against Beckley, always finished by saying they should be proud to be Pioneers. The boy hiked on out of the whistle's range.

The wind picked up as he climbed higher. His brother's fatigue jacket flapped loosely around him. It was light cloth, summer issue with a big red 1 on the shoulder. The boy stopped to take a leak in the shelter of the little board-and-batten house the Appalachian Volunteer people had stayed in before they were run off. Thumbtacks dotted the front door where Preacher Cutlip had torn their literature down. The boy kicked at charred two-by-fours, broken glass. He had helped them put up their outhouse.

The road split again where the ridge fed into the side of a small mountain. A potholed, sparsely graveled path cut straight up toward the driftmouth of Number 7, up where his father would be working, where his uncle Lou and his cousins and Curt

Lockly who'd started at his position for the varsity last year would be working, would be digging underground. The boy looked to the top of the mountain, following the scattered glint of railroad tracks to where he knew the tipple stood, but the dust was too thick to see through. It hung gray and still, tinged dull red where the setting sun tried to break through. Night came early on this side of the mountain. The boy took a few steps up the mine road, as if testing how steep a climb it would be, then hurried back down. He stayed with the blacktop, dipping over into the next hollow.

The West Virginia Turnpike cut through the bottomland. The boy stood on an overpass and faced north. The way they'd driven on Dar's eighteenth birthday, taking him to the recruiting center in Charleston. Three of them, father and sons, hardly speaking the whole ride.

The boy left the Turnpike behind, shivering inside the fatigue jacket and punching his clothes deeper into the laundry sack. He saw the Blue Star bar and packette up ahead, where the eastbound Trailways would stop. Beyond that he didn't know the road, he'd never been.

2

When Hunter McNatt called at the front door, his arms full of groceries from the 7-11 store, there was no answer. He had to put the bags down and open up himself. Hobie was out. That was strange, it was dark already and Hobie knew he should be in early on the night before the Beckley game. Coach would have shitfits if he called and Hobie wasn't in.

Hunter piled the bags on the kitchen table. His right arm, the bent-up one, was all tingly the way it always got when he had to carry something heavy for any length of time. No, Hobie wasn't anywhere in the little house, not shut in the bathroom or asleep on his bed.

The note was in the refrigerator, wedged under the flip-top ring of the beer Hunter put aside every day to drink before bed. It helped him to sleep when he was sore, helped to bring the coal-gas bubbles up. He read the note first by the light of the open refrigerator door, then went to sit on Hobie's neatly made, empty bed and read it again.

He put the beer aside and made coffee. He read the note again. He untaped Darwin's last card from the refrigerator door and looked it over. A steaming bowl of baked beans in front of a city skyline. Postmark and return address, Boston. *Just staying with friends*, it said, *till something comes along.* Maybe Hobie was out to see Dar. The postcard was three months old.

Hunter looked through Hobie's closet and drawers to see what was gone, but realized he couldn't remember much of what his son had worn. The fatigue jacket was missing though, Darwin's jacket from Vietnam, he knew that much. First Dar and now Hobie.

Why would Hobie want to go? Now, of all times?

It hadn't been *bad* between them. Just a little — a little *awkward*. The two of them alone in the house. Not as easy as it had been before Dar went for the Army. Hey fellas, he'd say, why don't we — and Dar was always ready to play along, which meant Hobie would want in on it too. A lot easier when he could think of them as the boys, as hey fellas, and not as separate people.

With Dar overseas, the letters home always brought him together with Hobie. Like they were together when Molly was going out. They'd sit at the kitchen table and Hobie would read Dar's letter out loud and then they'd talk over what they thought it was like there, what they thought Darwin meant by some of the things he said. *I done some things here*, he wrote, *that I can't explain in a letter. Have to tell you when I get back. Hope you'll understand.* It was the only times he and Hobie really talked about anything more than his school or his sports.

Then with the trouble, with Dar come home and gone so quick, it got worse. They didn't talk much at all. Hobie had always kept his own counsel, he took after Molly that way, but with Dar at home there was at least a connection between them. With Dar sent away it was the two of them left alone in the house, making their own dinners and eating separate, thinking up things to say when they bumped into each other's space. But they got along. They did.

Why would Hobie want to go? The Beckley game was tomorrow, he'd been playing real well, coming into his own. Out of his brother's shadow. He had that Delia Cutlip who seemed to be just crazy about him. He had his last year of school to finish. Where had he gone? Why?

Curt Lockly had said just the other day up at the mine how Hobie was a real popular fella in his own quiet way. How he was the kind you couldn't close into one category or another, and how the other kids respected him for that. Why would he run off from his friends?

Hunter stood in the kitchen and began to put the groceries away. There were all the things he got special for Hobie, the RC Cola, the Fig Newtons, the crunchy peanut butter. It was one way they talked, thinking what each other liked when it was their turn to shop. They never made a list or spoke about it. Hunter's can of beer had gone warm on the table, Hobie's coffee ice cream was half melted.

He would call the Blue Star to see if Hobie had taken a bus out. No. Dolly Greaves was on tonight, let a word slip to her and everybody in the hollow would know it within minutes. He'd wait till tomorrow, Emma would be working the tickets. What would he tell people? Should he call the Sheriff's Office, have them watch the roads? Maybe. And call the Army recruiter in Charleston, make sure Hobie wasn't out to make right on what his brother done. You could lie about your age to get in, Hunter had done it himself way back when. The boy was seventeen years old. Not so young, really. Hunter had been to Anzio beach, he was seventeen. Lot of the fellas he worked with were already down in the holes by that age. But still —

He'd have to tell the school. He'd want to tell Ray and Lucille. Hobie was gone, he didn't know where. He'd go to work like nothing was wrong, go on about his business, and maybe Hobie'd think better of it and turn back. But if he didn't there'd be decisions to make.

Hunter finished putting the groceries away. He put the beer back in the refrigerator. He took Hobie's note and went to sit on his bed, the bed he'd built for himself when Molly went bad, with the sheet of plywood underneath for his back. It was too quiet, he turned his radio on. He set it between stations so there'd be noise but no words to distract his thinking. Distant noise. He was worried about his hearing lately. Even with the earplugs on, a full day at the face on the continuous miner took its toll. Everything sounded distant to him for hours after work, Hobie would speak and it was like he was a half mile away. He couldn't stand it, hearing that distance all the time.

He read the note. Hobie had run off.

Why?

3

Hobie hadn't realized the ride would be so long. Here it was deep into the night and they weren't even to Wilkes-Barre yet. He'd only brought the last of the Fig Newtons and two sandwiches and he'd eaten the ham one in four bites when they crossed the Shenandoah. Being nervous and jiggling over the highway had really brought up his appetite.

It was all black people on the bus now but for him and the driver. Nobody had their reading light on anymore but you could see them when someone used the little bathroom in the rear and the light came out from the door being opened. Hobie had gone in there back in Virginia and right in the middle if it, cramped and itchy in the little box, the bus had stopped. The engine shut off and the light went out. He was closed in there in the dark in the middle of his business and couldn't leave. He broke out in a sweat. He hated it, it was like the time after they beat Slab Fork last year when Verl Biggins stuffed him in the locker and wouldn't let him out till he was screaming and pounding and everyone was laughing at him. The closeness, the smell. Like his mother's room the last time she was sick. He hated it. The bus started up again and the light came on and he got out, but he decided he'd hold anything else until they got to a station.

He wasn't so nervous now. It was dark in the bus and only a few headlights passed outside. He was by the window with his stuff in the laundry bag on the seat next to him. Some of the black people around him were talking softly. Up ahead and across the aisle a little girl would start to whine to her mother every few minutes.

"Mama, I'm *hun*gry."

"Shhhhh. We'll eat when we get there."

"But I'm hungry *now*."

"You be quiet."

The little girl would get bored and walk down the aisle to the rear and then back up to her mother. She always peeked around the seat at Hobie when she passed. She was cute, big eyes and a little bump of a nose. She seemed a little scared of him.

Hobie wondered what Dar thought now when he saw little kids like her. What he thought about them, after that thing that happened in the Army. He wondered if Dar saw things all different now, like how he himself had suddenly begun to notice the nipples on girls and women, through no matter how many layers of cloth, after Delia let him see and touch hers that one time. When before he had been blind to the existence of nipples. He wondered how it made Dar see things, what he done.

He was awful hungry. The Fig Newtons were gone. He pulled out the peanut butter sandwich and unwrapped it as quietly as he could manage. There hadn't been much of anything to bring from home. It was the end of the week and it was his father's turn for the groceries. It would have looked too funny if he had offered to shop a day earlier. His father would be up from Number 7 now, would be home to see the note. Better not to think about that.

The little girl was staring at his sandwich. She had halted her trip down the aisle to stare at it.

"You want some?" Hobie tore it in half as best he could, a little jam plopping on the wax paper. The girl glanced up at his face

[9]

and then shied away. He laid one half of the sandwich on the outer armrest and gulped the other down.

He looked out the window but mostly got a dim reflection of himself. It would have been nice to have made the trip in the daytime, to see all this new country, but this was the only way he could get a head start on them all. It had been hard enough just keeping his nerve up. But now he was out. He was on his way.

The sandwich half was gone from the armrest. She was a quick one. He could have used it himself, he was still pretty hungry, but that was okay. Dar would have something around, in Boston. Dar was always a big eater. If he could find Dar right off it would be fine.

Delia would miss him tomorrow, she'd have to find someone else to sit by at lunch. Coach would break his chalk and go into a tirade against the youth of today. Mr. Hinkle would be concerned about him, about his grades. He was the type. His father —

Hobie leaned his seat back and rested his eyes until he sensed somebody by him. The little girl was standing in the aisle, staring at him. She gave a shy, flirting smile, then opened her mouth to show a hunk of sandwich on the back of her tongue, then was gone up to her mother. Hobie laughed to himself. Chew and show. Like he used to do at lunch period, in the second grade, when he was a boy, back home.

4

Blackness and high whining, metal shrieks, dust-choked light shafts tunneling blackness, glistening through a billion years of dark, the continuous miner squats to rip at the screaming face of coal. Top jaw discs tearing ahead into the seam, bottom jaw scooping glossy black, in through the gorge, through the flat body then shat black into the long-box shuttle cars. Blackness drilled by light, high whining constant at the coal face, the shuttle peels away immediately replaced by its twin, peels away from the flank of the continuous miner, hauling five tons of black, trailing wrist-thick power cable and fanning the walls of the vein in its speed to spill out onto the humming belt. Blackness blasted with light, tailpiece man caught leaping away in the shuttle's headlamp, flash of black glossy skin, man leaping back when the shuttle has dumped, back into whine and hum and roiling cloud of coal dust to shovel frantically at the spilloff around the belt before the next shuttle-beam blasts him aside. Whining, shrieking, humming and the power-grind of the roof-bolter steel-pinning the slate ceiling in the continuous miner's wake. Blackness, just blackness and machine noise as jagged lumps ride out through the section shaft, ride the humming belt away from face-whine and shuttle-lurch, ride inches from the seam top out into light again, rattling into the low coal cars that the boom boy switches forward as they fill.

A man in a white helmet talks with the boom boy, a man half squatting, half stooping to fit in the five-foot seam. He nods his headlamp beam down to his wristwatch, yanks a lever and a buzzer blats loudly in the section tunnel. The continuous miner's whine cuts dead. Coal hums out from the section for a while, the boom boy switches a new car into position and the man in the white helmet stoops away. There is empty belt then, puking constant black tongue from the section's mouth, then a round spot of light begins to grow. They spit out one at a time, beams from black helmets announcing them, spit out belly-to-the-belt into the main shaft. The boom boy counts heads and turns the belt off.

Identical black-covered men, clothes dull, skin glossy, shooting light from their helmets. Shocking white eyes ride down the beam to see. The walls here are blasted white with rock dust, the floor puddled with water and inches-thick in coal dust. Sounds of men now, labored breathing, footsteps, plastic ding of helmet on rock, they bend under the seam and walk to the dinner-hole. Identical black-covered men.

Hunter McNatt is last in line as they walk for the tunnel crosscut to eat. He can recognize each of the men from behind, black-covered or no. Old Woody Estill with but two fingers and a thumb left on his hand. Swung that shuttle just a bit too close to the wall, left em mashed along the side of the old north section. And Toleman Coombs there, by how his left shoulder hangs low, where the slate fell down and tored hell out of his collarbone. And Luther's knee from when the belt snapped, and young Lockly, easiest of all to spot with nothing out of place, still waiting for his first accident. Hunter has to stop for breath every several steps, his arm won't unbend all the way from the time he bit too deep in the wrong place operating the continuous miner and pulled the top down on himself. Black-covered men walking to lunch, cuffs and laces taped tight so the belt can't snag them, heads ducked, quiet.

"Hunter," said Woody Estill rooting through his metal lunch-pail, "you best ease up the *pace* a little. Luther or me is bound to snap a cable keepin up if you don't stop doin like that. God damned dyno-soar you run is gonna burry us all you don't slow down." Woody pulled out a dozen-box of glazed donuts and stuffed the first into his mouth. They sat on the floor with their backs against the wall, glugging from thermos bottles, feeding white bread to black faces. "Hate to see it happen, Hunt."

It was the same story every day, the people up top pushing for more production, the ones below wanting to go careful. "Got no control over the thing, you know that," said Hunter. "I back off and let it fan air to give you fellas a break old Ruppert'll be up there on my tail readin the God damned riot act. At's why it's called con*tin*uous, buddy, don't pause for man'r beast."

"Maybe so, but you won't find Ruppert or no other foreman nowhere's near your tail when you outrun the roof-bolter an that monster is got us burried alive in coal. He'll be up on the phone trying to tell the money people what the slowdown is for. 'Got a couple boys went in over their heads,' he'll say, 'gonna have to dig them out the way fore we can get back at that seam.' "

Hunter smiled a little. "Snot a foreman's *job* to die with the rest of us, Woody, haven't you read the contract? Somebody's got to keep the score. You know — Coal ten, Miners nothing."

"Never thought of it that way, Hunt."

"Sumbitch leaves *me* down here," said Luther Justice, "he

won't never hear the finish of it. Thell be a holler full of broke-hearted wimmin givin him the hard-eye for the rest of his days." Luther was a wrinkled, vulture-looking old-timer with the biggest collection of dirty stories in the mine. "Nosir, won't let the sumbitch forget what he done me."

"He *heeee!*" Donut crumbs sprayed out and Woody slapped the top of Luther's helmet. "Man sets here jawin about women like it aint a fact that the only place he'll ever make out is the Home for the Blind. And on a dark night at that. Face it, Uncle, down here covered in coal dust is as good-lookin as you *get*."

"Don't you Uncle me, you —"

"Man is so sorry-lookin, he goes home he's got to hang a pork-chop round his neck so's the dog will play with him."

"— little squirrelly-cheeked son of a —"

"Now gentlemen, let's not lock horns on this thing. We all know that Luther has got a way with women." Cletus Spicer pushed three Tums onto his surprising pink tongue. "Runs him fifteen, twenty dollars a roll, but it's a *way*."

"He *heeeeee!*"

"What you want to do, Luther, is cut out chewin them God damn ramps like some old back country ridge-runner. Woman takes one whiff an it's 'Whoo-eee, what mountain has *this* old goat been grazin on?' "

"He's got you there, Uncle, he does. Hell, cave-in is the least of your worries, what you got to watch for is you don't sphixiate to death. I can see the obitchiary headline — 'Luther Justice Succumbs to Own Fumes.' "

"You tell it, Woody. How any fella chews wild onions can call himself a ladies' man escapes me."

"Snot the worst thing excapes you, Cletus." Luther gulped down a hunk of peanut-butter-and-bacon sandwich. "You let off one of them whistlers from your business end near a methane pocket an we'll all be playin in the harp section. Hate to see the day you run out of them stomach mints."

"Swallow up that coal gas," said Cletus, "and it's got to come out somewheres."

"That's true, but we've all of us fellers got the same problem. McNatt here, he's a two-pack-a-shift man just like you."

"Rolaids," said Hunter.

"Right, we've all of us got the problem, but buddy, you're the only one I ever seen could make *sparks* fly."

"Ought to have a contest, Luther's breath against Cletus' wind. Tell you the truth, sparks or no I think Uncle here would take it hands down. Them ramps'd peel paint off a battleship."

It was the usual lunchtime talk, Hunter didn't need to pay much attention. He had packed some food but had no appetite. He'd called the Sheriff's Office before coming up, they said they'd look out for hitchhikers. He'd be at the Blue Star tonight if the meeting was still on, he'd ask Emma in person about the bus.

Luther was telling one of his stories. They were all pretty good fellas, Hunter liked them, but it wasn't like he could bring up Hobie here. You could bitch and moan in a general way and it was fine with the fellas, it was mostly what they did when they talked. But specific problems, personal things, you kept to yourself. You just did.

Woody was giving Luther grief about his age and the old man didn't like it. "Don't you Uncle me, Woody Estill," he said, "You aint but five years behind me."

"Them are a *long* five years from where I sit, Luther. Must be all them women wored you out before your time."

"All I know is, in my day a man farted like that would have his short hairs picked clean for a penalty before the breeze got past his pants."

"In your day they hadn't invented farts yet. Had to tap it with an arrowhead once a month."

"In your day! Hah!" said Curt Lockly. Curt was strong, could handle the tailpiece shoveling fine, but didn't yet need to shave his face. He wasn't but a year older than Hobie. "What you mean in your day? I'm still missing half of my pubies from the first day here and the ones I got left aren't but a half-inch long. Guys left me near bald down there."

"Muleshit," said Luther. "We pulled one apiece, welcome you to the club. Time was when it took a year before you were out of the woods, young feller like you'd go home smartin ever other day."

"You'll get your turn, son, they'll be some comin in under you soon enough. You go down the high school and look over the senior class, pick you out some fresh meat."

"Won't make em grow back."

"Speakin of high school," said Luther through a mouthful of Milky Way, "what's the word from that boy of yours, McNatt? We gonna take it in the ear again from Beckley or what?" He gave Curt an accusing look.

Hunter shrugged. He'd have to play along like usual, like everything was okay. They'd all know soon enough if Hobie was gone for good, and then he wouldn't be mentioned for a good while. "Haven't spoken with him on it," he said. "Don't see him but for weekends, what with school and this evening shift, and he's not much of a talker these days. You know how they can get."

"He got any word from colleges?"

"Nothing yet. And Coach, he told me straight, don't expect too much. Boy just hasn't got the size. He's built wiry like me."

"He sure does *run*, though," said Cletus Spicer. "Never seen a boy, a white boy, could run with your Hobie."

"Any chance of a scholarship if he doesn't get taken for his sports?"

Hunter shook his head very slightly. "Snot his studies so much as it is the school." He'd tried saving for both of them, but whenever he got a little ahead Molly would need her treatments again and he'd go in the hole. Coach had said that if the school could field a track team Hobie might have a chance for a full shot somewhere. But as it was, no hope.

"When I tried," said Curt Lockly, "they said it was like I still had two years of high school left to learn. It don't measure up, they said, the schooling here."

"And there damn well isn't any way I can go the price alone," said Hunter.

They chewed in silence for a moment.

"Your Darwin," said Woody, "he had the size without the speed. But Hobie —"

"That Dar was a bull he was."

Dar was fair game to talk about again, he'd been gone over a year now.

"— Hobie is a God damned *gazelle* at that flanker position. Boy can *run*."

"From what I hear," said Luther Justice, eye winking white

from his blackened face, "he won't be running any too far. Not if that Delia Cutlip has her way."

"He *heeeee!*" Woody thwacked his belly with the flat of his hand. "I heard the same myself. Boy is gonna need all the speed that's in him with that one. Cards is stacked awful high in her favor."

"Stacked is the exact right word for it, too."

"Hell, who else has got a daddy can hold the shotgun in one hand and the Book in th'other?"

"Wunt take no shotgun get me on top of that Delia."

"Luther, you are just a *dir*ty old man, you know that? Lord'd strike you stone cold dead if you so much as *breathed* in that little girl's direction."

"An if *He* missed, Preacher Cutlip would thump you to death with his thickest copy of the King James Version. Sides, she's already got her mind set."

They turned to Hunter to see how he was taking it.

"The girl," he said, "has got some strong ideas." It always bothered him some how she led Hobie around, how she was so taken with the religion at her young age.

"Don't know if I could bear it," said Cletus. "Hymn-singin, ladies' socials, no drink or colorful language, starched shirts every Sunday —"

"Well, now, everthing has got its price." Woody was half-way through his box of donuts. "And if a little hymn now and then is the price for what Delia's got locked up twixt them long pretty legs of hers, well —"

"Like they say, fellers," said Luther, "road to Heaven is fraught with many a peril."

"Wonder if Hobie's ever been to Heaven?"

Hunter hadn't ever worried much about that sort of thing. Had never done any talks with Dar or Hobie. All that generally took care of itself, like it had done when he was their age.

"Gotten far as Purgatory, I figured," said Curt Lockly, "but no Heaven yet. Preacher's daughter don't open up them pearly gates till she's got that ring."

"Got that ring and pinned it through the poor sumbitch's nose is what. Long legs like that is the kind don't never leave loose."

"Iron thighs do not a prison make."

"A *dirty* old man, Luther, ought to be kept on a leash."

Toleman Coombs spoke for the first time. "You fellas," he said softly, "want to watch what you say. Don't forget, He hears us even in this shaft."

"Didn't think you much cared for Cutlip, him bein a rival preacher and all."

"We are both His servants. Toilers in the same field."

"Sorry if we make you uneasy, Tole," said Hunter. "They just kiddin around."

"I'm not the One you have to answer to."

"You're right there, Toleman," said Cletus. "I think the One is coming up the tunnel this minute to join us."

The men saw the flash of white helmet and sobered a bit. Woody closed the top to his donuts.

"Lo fellas," said Ruppert when he reached them, stooping with his hands on his hips, "how's the appetites?"

"Not bad."

"Okay."

"Just fine, Owen."

"Movin em pretty good this evenin, fellas, we're ahead of ourselves for a change."

"Uh-huh."

"Keep the money people quiet for a while."

"Yuh."

Ruppert smiled at nothing as the men ate silently. "You fellas got any problems up in the section? Anything I ought to look at?"

Spicer sucked thoughtfully on his Tums. "Nothin I can think of."

"Nope," said Luther, "nothin we kin think of right off."

"Well, glad to hear it. You fellas mind if I sit down?"

"Though there is that smell," said Luther, catching the foreman halfway to the ground. "Not so much a smell really, as a, you know, *feel*ing in the air up at the face. You might best go up, Owen, en give it a read with your safety-flame lamp there. Check out the methane level fore we get back up there and juice the machinery."

"Oh."

"Can't be too careful, you know."

Ruppert straightened as much as he could and moved off toward the section entrance. "Five minutes," he called over his shoulder, the foreman coming out in his voice, "five minutes and we got to get em rolling."

They waited till he was on the belt before they spoke.

"Last we can eat in peace," grumbled Luther. "Man won't never learn he didn't make the guest list."

"He's a good foreman," said Hunter.

"Best one in the whole damn mine, for what that's worth. He's still a company suck."

"He's a *foreman*, Luther."

"Right. And as far as I'm concerned a foreman aint but the small end of nothing shaved to a fine point. Bad enough to be a company suck without makin it your life's work."

"So who doesn't kiss the brown end, one way or another?" said Cletus Spicer. He was a little rooster of a fella, who went red around the ears when his temper was up. "For instance, Luther, what's this I hear bout you biddin off that shuttle onto the powder car? How'd you work that one?"

"Union just figured a man of my seniority shouldn't ought to be racin round in them damn shuttles —"

"Up there in all that *nas*ty bug dust —"

"— so they looked the thing over and give the company the word. Ought to come through any day now."

"And what's the union think about a man your age heftin them fifty-pound sacks of rock dust onto a powder car?"

"Oh, thell be some young snot like you to do the mule work. I'll just steer and point out where it goes."

"So how'd you swing it?"

"Like they say, fellas, rank has got its privileges."

"You're rank all right, Luther, we never questioned that. Your first day in Hell you'll probably bid off for something that's air-conditioned."

"I just gone through accepted union procedure is all. Where's the ass-kissing in that?"

"I'll tell you where," Cletus raised his voice. "We didn't hear you kick one bit over them layoffs in August, that's where. You bein so tight with the union rep and all."

"There's good reason for that. Layoffs is layoffs. We don't tell the compny how to run their business, they don't tell us how to run our union. They either got the work for people or they don't."

"And when they don't get called back, like that last bunch didn't, are they gonna find they're not in the union anymore?"

"Now those were bad members, Clete, they gone out and joined up with these dogholes we been tryin to close down. Spect the union to keep men that go right ahead, buck headquarters like they done? You should be glad them deadbeats were cut off, it bein *your* dues that kept them floatin."

"All I know is, when people went to the mailbox for what they should have been drawin from the union it weren't there. Can't blame them if they're forced to work the dogholes —"

"Cletus, you got a finger to point you best save it for the God damn meetin Sunday, oughtn't to bitch about the leadership unless the district rep is there to hear it!"

"District rep, my ass! Talk about company sucks, if he —"

"Fellas!" called Hunter, raising his hands. "We have a rule, don't we, about no politics during lunch? So nobody won't say what he wished he hadn't? Right?" He shot a look to Spicer. They'd agreed, the handful that was in on the meeting tonight, to lie low in public for a while. It was past the point where you could come out on the union anytime you felt like. Cletus's ears were burning hot, he ignored Hunter and pointed at Luther Justice.

But Curt Lockly interrupted to break the tension. "If you old gents don't mind," he said rising and loosening his gear-loaded safety belt, "I'll retire to the sanitary facilities before we got to go back to the grind." He stepped over their stretched legs and headed for a nearby mined-out section that hadn't been cemented up. "Got to drop a load."

It was like a cue, the surest way to reroute a conversation there was.

"That's your story," said Woody, and the others chimed in after.

"They tell me it falls off, you keep whackin at it like that."

"Bet he'll be thinkin on that Delia Cutlip the whole while."

"Some men spill blood for their beloved, and then others spill —"

"Don't get lost son, there is rats big as razorbacks in there!"

"Probly gone to count his pubies, see how they're growin back. You know how they are at that age. 'Vanity, thy name is youth.' "

"Never heard that one before, Luther."

"Must be the other half of 'Women are wasted on the young.' "

The men slammed their lunchpail lids shut and capped their thermoses.

"Woody! My *God*, buddy, have you gone through that whole dozen donuts? And not a one for your poor workin partners?"

"Saved you the holes."

"Give em to Luther, that's just about his speed."

"Just about his *size*, too."

"He *heeeee!* Hey Needledick, checked anybody's oil lately?"

"Needledick the Bug-Fucker!"

"I think I hear the belt startin up."

"Think it's Ruppert giving us a hint?"

"Owen don't hint. He might be a lot of things but subtle int one of em."

"Hoooo, my legs my *legs!* Have to get the old lady a job, she can buy me a new pair. Good Lord, they stiffen up."

"Luther's got a job for her."

"Think I'd ruther keep these old legs than go sharesies with Needledick. Just don't know *where* it's been."

"Hey Lockly! Tuck it back in, son, and come join the team."

The men creaked to their feet and began to move back down to the section. They weren't bad fellas, on the whole. A good bunch to work with. Hunter would miss them, if it came to that.

Cletus Spicer lagged behind to talk with him.

"You in there for tonight, Hunt?"

"I suppose."

"The Blue Star, like we planned. Don't let nobody see you."

"I'll be there."

A buzzer blatted twice down the tunnel.

5

It was still raining, raining cold for the fourth night in a row. Dominic eased the patrol car past the Castle Square projects and down Tremont Street.

"Seven bucks an hour," he said. Vinnie slouched in the seat next to him with his hat pulled down to his nose. "Seven bucks an hour they're makin, some of them, overtime."

"That's Cambridge."

"That's Cambridge, that's the Tacticals from down here. Seven bucks an hour, they stand outside, keep their tempers, maybe push a few kids around. That MIT thing there, I asked one of the guys."

"That's good pay. Why don't you put in for it, next time they have one."

Dominic shrugged at the wheel. "I ought to, you know? It's not like you're outnumbered or anything. Just stand there."

"And keep your temper."

"And keep your temper," said Dominic, "when they come by with a Viet Cong flag there. When they come and call you names."

"All you got to do is stand there."

"In the rain."

Vinnie grunted and tilted his hat back from his eyes. "It rains, you stand in the rain. You got your leather jacket, your helmet. The kids, they get wet it rains."

"They got them too, though, some of them," said Dominic. "Helmets. They come prepared. When the word come down to pinch a few, that's who you go after, the ones with the helmets. Wise guys, think they can't be hurt they got a helmet. I asked one of the guys, this TP, he said that's what they do. Go after the ones bring the helmets."

"You should put in for it Dawm, it sounds like good money."

"Why don't *you* put in for it?"

"Me? I don't need the money." Vinnie was big, pale pink skin, pale blue eyes. He had a permanent wince, like there was something uncomfortable trapped inside him that he couldn't get out. He talked slowly. "I got other things to do."

"Everybody needs the money."

"I don't. Go out and stand in the rain for six hours, kids come up, call you names, call your mother names, finally the word comes down to move them, but not too *hod*, so you maybe get your nose pushed in by some little girl with a two-by-four and a Jew-lawyer father in Brookline. That I don't need."

"You think it's so bad, why're you telling me to put in for it?"

"I figure you need the money, Dawm."

"Of coss I need the money. Everybody needs the money."

"So put in for it."

"Ahhhh, I don't know. Maybe the weather clears up, I will."

Dom turned the car left on West Newton, plowed through a block-long puddle and turned left up Shawmut.

"Gonna be out here in a motorboat, this keeps up," said Vinnie.

"Good. Make our job a lot easier, keep the boogies inside." Dominic was small and thick, his eyes almost black in his dark face. He spoke rapid-fire, unable to keep his hands down on the wheel. "Have to do their deals through the post office. Send it Western Union."

"They don't take to water much, do they?"

"Nah. That's why, places it rains a lot, you don't find so many. You go up the Pacific Nawthwest there, Washington, Oregon and all, you don't find hodly any of em. You don't see too many boogie lumberjacks."

"Yeah, and another thing you don't see them," said Vinnie, "is frogmen. They can't swim."

"Yeah?"

"Sure. I was in the Navy, right? In basic it comes time to do the half-mile swim and everyone jumps in the tank. Everybody is doing okay, Irish, Poles, the ghinnies even, paddling along, all except the boogs. Right to the bottom. It's something to do with the way they're built, they sink."

"What do you mean, 'even the ghinnies'?"

"Well, Dawm, no ethnical offense intended, they weren't so great." Vinnie sighed. "Not like the boogs, I mean they stayed afloat and everything, but all in all not so great."

"Bullshit. What about Columbus? What about Venice, they got streets made out of water? It's got water on three sides, Italy, you *got* to know how to swim."

"Well now, maybe my memory fails me. And maybe it's cause the ghinnies, whenever they hit the water, they left an oil slick. Like a tanker going down."

"Don't stot it, Vinnie —"

"Did you hear —"

"I don't wanna hear —"

"Did you hear who put fifty bullets in Mussolini?"

Dom was silent. He slowed and turned right on East Brookline Street, skirting the edge of Blackstone Square. Vinnie rolled the window down to sweep the grass of the square with the searchlight. A little pond was forming at the center of the plot. Vinnie rolled the window back up and waited.

"Okay fucker," said Dom after two blocks. "Who?"

"Twenty thousand Italian shopshooters."

They both laughed, Dom with a high automatic burst and Vinnie with a long wheeze.

"You get any sleep today, Dawminic?"

"A little. The rain's good, it makes me drowsy. But I still hate this fuckin graveyod shift. Specially when it's slow like this, you got to fight just to keep awake."

"It's the rain, makes it slow," said Vinnie. "People don't get ideas so much."

"It keeps up like this any longer they'll get plenty ideas. They'll get fuckin cabin fever, being inside alla time."

"You were really wiped out last night."

"Tuesday I didn't get no sleep at all." Dominic white-knuckled the steering wheel. "The kids are home all day, it's Election Day, they're inside, the rain, she can't keep them quiet. I'm about to commit, what is it, you kill your own kids? Bratri-

[23]

cide. An then I got to take her an go pick up her mother so we can go vote."

"Where do you vote?"

"The Dante Alighieri school there. You know East Boston?"

"No, I never get over there anymore."

"She lives three blocks from it, the mother, she can't walk. She's scared to go out. Evil eye or something, she won't go out alone. It wasn't so bad, though, voting, I seen a couple guys I know, had a couple of pops, got something down on it."

"On the election?"

"Sure on the election. What's wrong with that?"

"Oh, nothing, nothing." Vinnie put up his big hands defensively. "It's only you're the guy who needs money so bad, he's got to go up Cambridge and chase hippies around, and here you are down on City Council elections. Dawminic, I swear, your own mother was on her deathbed, you'd have something down on whether she'd make the night or not."

"So what's it to you?"

"I just worry you're not gonna stay on top of it, is all."

"I stay on top of it. I never missed a payment when it was due in my life."

"You don't stay on top of it Dawm, you know, they don't care you're a cop. In fact they're glad, they think maybe you owe them some favors. You know how those guys think."

"I don't do favors."

"Sure, Dawm, sure."

"Okay, I do favors, but never cause I owe guys money. A guy comes to me, he needs a favor, I think he's a good guy, then okay. It's nothing gonna fuck me up, I'll help him out. Everybody does favors, don't hand me that. Fuckin Irish, you guys run the whole depottment on favors. Fuckin Irish."

Vinnie smiled. "You got to take care of your own, Dawminic. But you get in over your head, you got to take care of everybody else, too."

"I'm not over my head."

"Wonderful. So how'd you do?"

"Huh?"

"The election. How'd you make out?"

"I just missed. That guy Atkins, the Council, he fucked me up. You had to pick all nine seats, right, and I figure Atkins, he's a boogie, he doesn't stand a chance. Turns out he runs second, behind Louise Day Hicks there, I miss it by one seat."

"You had to figure. All the people don't like Mrs. Hicks, they prawbly voted for him."

"That's what I thought when I made the bet. I figure Mrs. Hicks for sixty, seventy percent, so Atkins, even if everybody else does vote for him, has got maybe thirty-five. But I guess that's not the way it works."

"I'm glad I didn't run into no guys when I went," said Vinnie. "Those kind of guys are expensive."

"Where do you vote?"

"The L Street bathhouse. You know Southie?"

"Nah, I never get over there. I mean I figured, who in hell is gonna vote the both of them, right?"

"I voted for both of them."

Dominic slammed his palms down on the wheel and closed his eyes. "Assholes. I forgot to figure in assholes."

"You gamble too much, Dawminic."

"I gamble too much? I show you the bundle I took on the Patriots Sunday and then you tell me that." Dom swerved to avoid a puddle.

"I thought you decided to lay off them after the beating you took beginning of the season."

"How long is a woman pregnant?" The rain stopped beating the roof of the patrol car as it headed up Washington under the shelter of the Orange Line elevated. "Nine months, right? Nine. Every week they keep losing, the Pats, every week I lay off. Even when they're being real generous with the line, I think I can beat the spread, I lay off. They're no fuckin good, I figure, every time I'm down on them I go to the cleaners. But finally it gets to me, it's been nine in a row they lost, I gotta think it's like a pregnant woman. They're overdue. So this Sunday they got the Oilers in there who are not one of your all-time dynamite football teams, I find a guy give me a little extra on the line, I put a hundred down on it. Taliaferro shows a little smots, don't throw interceptions all afternoon, Nance grinds it out like usual, and the defense, they're beautiful, a shutout. Five to one I had from this guy, you tell me I gamble too much."

Vinnie turned the searchlight on the backyards of the Cathedral project to their right. "The way I figure it, Dawminic, you gamble at all, it's too much. You work hod for your money, out here at night, maybe somebody shoots at you, it's no fuckin picnic. Why go hand it to some guy, he's prawbly the boss of the guy who tries to take a whack at you? I don't understand it."

"I win."

"You *don't* win, Dawm. What you win just goes to pay back what you lost already. I can't see why you do it."

"Hey, Vinnie, it's *fun*. You know? It makes it more fun, I watch the games Sunday, I got something down on them. And I'm not like some guys, bet on anything that moves. I pick my spots."

Vinnie spoke to an imaginary passenger in the back seat. "He bets on Council elections, got to hit nine out of nine, he tells me he picks spots."

"I just missed that one. And the football, well, I don't play the cods. Those cods, they're murder, maw fuckin guys go deep in the hole trying to hit big on those things. They're stupid. The Office, they got computers, the Office, help them figure out the line. It's all prawbability, like dice at Las Vegas, you get that many teams playing. They even give you a break on one or two, try to suck you into playing the whole cod. It's all prawbability, it's like gambling." Dom turned left on East Berkeley for a block, then headed down Albany.

"So what you do isn't gambling?"

"Naw."

"What is it then?"

"It's just putting a few bucks down on a team I got a feeling about."

"Stupid fuckin ghinny."

Albany Street was wide and deserted, small factories and warehouses to the right, the Fitzgerald Expressway rising to the left.

"So what were the kids there for, Dawm? MIT? You never finished the story. I heard they went in some building up there on the radio but I didn't listen to the rest of it. They're against scientists, or what?"

"Vinnie, I wisht I could figure out what it is they're against. This one had to do with missiles. The ones they shoot from submarines. They invent them up there."

"They're against missiles."

"Right. So they go in this labratory there this mawning, try to shut it down. There's only one way in or out, so they got the night shift trapped in and the day shift shut out."

"They go round the clock?"

"Just like us, three full ones. There's a war on, Vinnie. Anyhow, there was all these guys supposed to show up at the administration buildings where the kids were the day before, these guys pulling overtime, seven bucks an hour, and they sent them over to the lab instead. Six, seven hundred of them, they moved the kids right on outa there." Dominic was squirming in his seat with the telling. "This guy I talked to said it worked beautiful, they come from both ends of the street, quick motch, shouting cadence, and the kids see that, they break up and run. Only the brass, they say once it's away from the lab that's it, you don't follow up. You don't chase. So there's only a couple busts, couple scuffs and scrapes. I don't understand it."

"What?"

"You got them on the run, right? Why not finish the job? This thing this mawning, once the kids are scattered they call everybody off."

"It's like Nixon said in that speech the other night, Dawm. You withdrawr from strenth, not from weakness."

Dominic shook his head. "I don't get that either. If you got the strenth why not use it?"

"You don't understand?"

"Nope."

"That, my friend," said Vinnie turning his head to see out the rain-beaded window, "is why you are where you are and the brass is where they are."

"Four-three," said the voice from the radio, "are you clear?"

Vinnie lifted the microphone from its hook. "Go ahead."

"Union Park Street between Harrison and Albany. Prowler call."

"Got it."

Dominic swooshed into a U-turn, spraying water, and headed

back up Albany Street. "Patrolman Doggerty, my friend," he said, "what would you wager we got ourselfs here?"

"Patrolman Aiello, my friend, I do not care to wager."

"I figured that. I would say we got us some wino got caught in the rain, he's hackin his lungs out under somebody's front pawch."

"Most likely you're right. Anybody's gonna be out prowlin tonight in this shit is too dumb to worry much about. Still, we do it careful."

Dominic turned the headlights off, then swung onto Union Park Street. There were construction warehouses on the left of the street, old factory row-housing on the right. Dominic used the hand brake to slow down, so the backup lights wouldn't flash.

"If you were a wino," he said, "where would you pick to sack out?"

Vinnie rolled the window down slowly, then took aim with the searchlight at the third doorway to the right, his thumb tense on the switch.

"Ready?"

"Do it Vin."

The light blasted the top step of the porch, but where the wino should have been there were feet in three-striped running shoes. Up on the toes for a moment, ready to bolt, but then relaxing. Vinnie tilted the light up. It was a kid, a very wet kid in jeans and an Army jacket shivering under the porch awning. Dom flicked the outside mike on.

"Come on over here."

The kid stepped out into the rain and walked to the patrol car. He looked as if he had only just begun to have to shave. Maybe every third day or so. He looked tired and a little scared.

"Sir?"

Vinnie made a surprised face to Dom then turned to the kid. "What're you doing out here?"

"Trying to keep dry."

"You're doin a lousy job of it. You from around here?"

"No sir."

Dominic butted in. "You like to stand in the rain?"

"No."

"You're not from Boston even, are you?"

"No."

"Where from?"

"West Virginia."

"What are you doing here?"

The kid crouched so he could see in to Dom. "I'm supposed to meet my brother here. He's got a car and we're going on a trip. I got here a day early I guess."

"And you don't have anywhere to stay?"

"No sir."

"Where are you sposed to meet this brother?"

"At the bus station. At noon."

"Uh-huh. What's your name?"

"Hobie McNatt."

"How old are you?"

"Seventeen. Almost eighteen."

"You got any ID with you?"

The kid fished a card from his pocket and handed it through the window. Vinnie rolled the window up so the kid couldn't hear.

"What do you think?"

"I think," said Dominic, "maybe we scoop him."

"You think it's worth the paper?"

"Who knows? Maybe he's got a want out. We should call in."

"We call in his name we got to scoop him. He doesn't look like a bad kid, be a shame the city put him up for a week, he gets bumbusted by some hod case."

"You're gettin soft, Vinnie."

"You wanna scoop the whole fuckin South End."

"We did, I'd bet you there wouldn't be many we couldn't hold for something legitimate."

"My point exactly, why pick on this kid? He gave us the right name and all." Vinnie handed Dominic the card, which certified that Hobie McNatt was seventeen years old and had passed his senior Red Cross lifesaving test.

"Could have boosted it."

"This thing says West Virginia, Dawm. He sounds like he's from West Virginia."

[29]

"You been there?"

"No, but I known a guy in the Navy, he was from out there, Kentucky. It's the same thing. That's what he sounded like, sawt of."

"I don't know. We don't scoop him what do we do with him?"

Vinnie sighed and thought a moment. "Pine Street?"

"With all the alkies? I thought you liked the kid."

"Be a good lesson to him, see where he can end up. Maybe next time he goes on a trip he'll plan his calendar better."

"I still don't like it."

"He didn't run, Dawm. Most kids, you shine a light at them they take off and there we are out in the rain getting our shoes wet chasin him. This kid didn't run."

"He's an altar boy, he didn't run?"

"I say give him a shot."

"It's all yours, my friend. It turns out somebody's got a hod-on for this kid and you threw him back, it's all yours."

"Fine. Gimme the cod." Vinnie rolled the window back down. The kid's hair was plastered flat on his head, water streamed down his cheeks. He sniffled and took the lifesaving card from Vinnie. "Have you got any money?"

"A little."

"How much is a little?"

"Twenty-five dollars. I need to keep some for the trip though. Can't afford no hotel."

"You in the service?"

"No sir."

"Where'd you get that jacket?"

"It's my brother's, he was in the Army."

"Your brother that you're gonna go meet on this trip."

"Yes sir."

"You got any wants, kid?" Dom butted in again, leaning over Vinnie's huge lap to the window.

"Dawminic —"

"Do you?"

"Sir?"

"Wants, do you have any wants?"

"Is anybody looking for you?" said Vinnie.

"Oh." The kid thought for a moment. "No. I don't suppose anybody is."

"He don't suppose so."

Vinnie closed his eyes and winced a bit more than usual. "You gonna let me do this, Dawm, or not?"

"S'all yours." Dominic put his hands on the wheel and stared straight ahead through the windshield.

"Now what you want to do is this. You don't want to be inna rain all night, we can't have you out here making people nervous, right? I'm gonna send you up the Pine Street Inn. It's for winos mostly but you tell them your story, leave us out of it, leave out the twenty-five dollars, and they'll give you a bed for the night. No chodge. We'd run you up there ourselves only then we got to call in, make a repawt, it gets complicated all around. You go out the end of this street," Vinnie pointed, "take a right up Harrison, you keep going up, you cross over the turnpike there and the first thing you see on your left, that's Pine Street. Little narrow street, the Inn is on your right, you can't miss it. What you want to do, before you go in you take that twenty-five dollars or whatever it is and you roll it in a sock and you keep that sock between your legs when you get in bed. It's not a bad place, just winos is all, and you can't hold them responsible, you know? You got that?"

"Yes sir."

"Get going then."

The kid pulled a bulging laundry sack from the porch and hustled down around the corner. Vinnie called in no action on the prowler and they started back to Albany.

"I still say you're goin soft," grumbled Dominic.

"What, he didn't seem like a bad kid was all. When's the last time you had a kid call you sir?"

"That, I'll admit, that was weird."

"I figure give him the benefit of the doubt. He did us a favor, he didn't run, we do him a favor back."

"There you go with favors again."

"For a kid I did a favor." Vinnie spoke very deliberately. "I'm not talking about some guy wears three-hundred-dollar shoes and answers telephones all day. I'm not talking about some guy busts your legs you miss a couple payments. I'm talking bout a kid he's a long way from West Virginia. Do him a favor."

"We scoop him pushing shit on the Common inside the month," said Dominic. "I'll bet you ten-to-one."

6

They ride the man-trip out, shivering a little in the empty coal cars without work to warm them. Past a dozen old section entrances and up a long slight grade to the high-ceilinged waiting chamber. The men of the hoot-owl shift are already there on benches in coal-grimed work clothes, only their faces and ungloved white hands to set them off from the departing miners. A few nods and small waves pass between the groups.

The steel-cage elevator lifts seven men at a time, each section crew tending to stay together till they hit the surface. It is a very clear night, a very bright sky. Once they walk past the giant exhaust fan that sucks at the shaft opening, the men smell pine lacing the heavy coal air. They spread out through the yard, not talking for the most part, dwarfed by the tipple and the string of freight cars at its base, standing on tracks that lead down the mountain and out of state.

The bathhouse is a big drafty box of cinderblock, with wooden benches on a cement floor and a layer of coal soot on windows and walls. The men rack their helmet lamps and safety belts on an iron bar as they ease in, shift their magnetic name-squares to the OUT side of the metal roster board. If there is a blast now, no one will be panicking their next of kin.

Wire-mesh baskets hang by pulleys from the twenty-foot ceiling, held level with electric heaters to dry the damp work clothes. The men let their empty baskets down and begin to peel off layers. Steel-toed boots, shirts and overalls of blackened denim, gray-stained long underwear — all heavy with coal and sweat. They stand free of the sodden clothes, men with black faces, black wrists and gray-white bodies. All the kinds of bodies that men can have — hound ribs and swaybacks, spare tires and sagging breasts, patches of wild hair furrowed with scar tissue, muscles pumped erect or hanging heavy with age. The men move slowly at first, picking up speed, and when they begin to talk it is a little too loud, as if the showers are already on.

"S'at big holdup round nine all about? Budka had us sittin on our hands there an never did come back and say what it was we were waitin on."

"Well, first it was a rock caught in the belt —"

"Likely God damn story —"

"Then it was a coal car off the track, holdin up the whole line —"

"S'at new kid you got at boom boy up there. Don't know his ass from an avalanche."

"And what did you know, Luther, when you first started? Spose you never fucked up on the job?"

"I knew enough to hold my peace when elders was talkin, Lockly. Who give you the floor all of a sudden?"

"They get cranky at his age, son, don't pay no mind."

"Amatoors." Luther sits in his long underwear, fiddling the dial of his big battery-run radio. TONY BOYLE, UMW PRESIDENT, it reads indelibly, 1968 CONVENTION.

"Give it up, Luther," calls Clete Spicer, "it won't get naught but old speeches anyhow."

"Got to be something sounds better than you damn coal miners."

The men peel off clothes and shout and bitch to each other. Their hair stands up sweat-soaked and banded from the helmet rim. They belch and fart and spit black gobbets into the corners. They tell each other the same old jokes, they laugh and tease and pulley up their loaded baskets. They come to Hunter McNatt.

"Got this ten-gauge," says Dean Womblies, "figure I'll bore it down some, do the choke, and it'll have better spread when I'm out for bird. Hunt, you know a little about that, don't you?"

Sidling up, indirect but obvious, wanting his final opinion.

[33]

Hunter sits at the end of a bench, quieter than usual tonight, thinking. But when they come he looks up and listens as careful as ever.

"— so he tells me I might's well just let this loan ride, pick up interest," says Cletus Spicer. "Cause the way money is goin now, the longer you wait the less it's worth when you finally do fork it over. Said that the de-valuation almost cancels out the interest. But Hunter, what he didn't tell me is how I'm gonna be sure to have *any* money come the day of payoff, no matter how much it's worth or not worth."

"Hunter, maybe you can straighten this out for us," says Toleman Coombs. "Woody here says that there is such a thing as left-handed scissors, and I say that if they sell them at all it's meant as a joke. You want to talk some sense to the man for me?"

"Hunter, I been havin a problem with my boy," says Bert Blankenship.

Maybe it's that they remember him on the football field right before the war, or the way he didn't let on about the medal from France till someone read it in the Charleston paper, or how he turned down a foreman spot every year when the company made an offer till they gave up. Maybe it was how he stuck with Molly through the whole sad thing with the hospitals and didn't once squawk over the expense, or the way he handled himself in that ribroll last March, keeping calm and breathing on the self-rescuer till they could lift the wall off of him. Maybe just small things, but they come to Hunter.

"*I been havin a problem with my boy —*"

"I'll tell ya," he says, rubbing the back of his neck and wincing to show he sees what a tough problem he's been handed, "if you still think the rest of him is fine, then you got no real worry. You'll learn to live with it. You force his hand and tell him to cut it off or else, well, you just be makin trouble where it doesn't have to be. Course if there's something *else* between you and this hair thing is just the tip of the iceberg, then it's different, it's a whole nuther bucket of oats. But he's a pretty good boy you got there, I don't think his hair is gonna make him change into anybody you can't live with."

"Elections?" he says, grinning and shaking his head. "What do

I think? I think it's as good an excuse for a paid holiday as any, but you won't catch me walkin out of my way to help any of that damn courthouse gang stay on top. And I mean either party. As for the traditional five-dollar token of appreciation that people around here seem to expect, I figure that what they're selling off is their right to bitch about government for the next two years. You ask me that's a pretty sorry price for their discontent."

"The Beckley game?"

Hunter shrugs, looks to the floor.

"Oh, he'll do fine. I give him the word. He knows I'll have all you fellas up here on my back for a whole year if he messes up. He'll do fine, Hobie." He moves to change the subject.

The huge common shower room jumps with water, stinging hard onto the men as they squirt strong liquid soap and scrub for pink. Got to take a little skin off to be shed of the coal. Spritzing through teeth cracks, scouring into ears and noses, digging under nails, the water runs off dark gray to the central drain. The men work their sorest muscles almost fondly, they wince and groan, catch each other's eyes to shake heads and grin. Brother, they seem to say, don't I *know* it. Int nobody works like we do. And under the rush of water, like a refrain —

"Moved one shitload of coal tonight, buddy."

"Sure did, buddy, we sure did."

They scrub and soak to a hot red glow, yelling through the shower, songs, insults, jokes, yelling high above the whine of the exhaust fan outside, high above the clanking freight cars, above the mechanical racket of coal, yelling just for the sound of their own human voices.

Hunter coasted down the access road. The old Falcon needed all the rest it could get. It was a toss-up every morning whether it would make the climb up to Number 7 or not. Anything further than Charleston would be out of the question.

Emma was out in the back parking lot when Hunter got over to the Blue Star. The lights were off, a dozen cars were hidden behind the building.

"I thought it was a little funny, him leavin just before the game," said Emma. "And when I suggested he get the round-trip he said he'd worry bout the way home when he came to it."

"He bought it all the way through to Boston?"

"That's right. Said he was out to visit his brother. Would of got in sometime this afternoon."

Hunter thanked her.

"Most of the fellas are in already," she called, heading for her car. "You go around to the back, it's open there."

They were whispering in the storage room when Hunter walked into the Blue Star. Lights on only in one corner, racks of dusty bottles, gins and whiskeys and bourbons surrounding them. It reminded Hunter of the old county library. Most of the men smoked, sitting uneasily in a semicircle, not a back to the door. Some with their hair still wet from the showers, others just out of bed. They looked openly relieved to see Hunter. There were a dozen or so, mostly younger men or men new to the mine. Cletus was there squirming to get started, Woody Estill's brother Pratt, Curt Lockly, poor old Birdie Hawkes with his oxygen-breather and young Hinkle from the high school, the one they'd taken to calling "Pink" Hinkle during the lunch-program fight. So this was the conspiracy, thought Hunter. He was the oldest active miner in the room.

"Take a chair, Hunt. We been waitin on you."

"Looks like a thieves' convention in here." He nodded to the men.

"Worse than that, buddy, worse than that."

With Hunter seated they raised their voices a bit, as if now it were safe. Cletus and the teacher sat together, their backs to the wall. A copy of the *UMW Journal* lay on the table in front of them.

"You know why we're here," Cletus began. "The fact that we got to meet in secret like this is as good example of the problem as any. We got us a bullshit union and we're scared to buck it out in the open."

"God's truth," called Pratt Estill.

"It could be a good one," said Hinkle, "it used to be the finest one in the country. But it's been stolen away from its members. What we want to do here is try to get it back." Hinkle had his shirt-sleeves rolled up and collar pulled open the way he always did. He wasn't from the hollow and didn't try to hide the fact in his talk. "This year for the first time we have somebody to go against the old leadership with, somebody with the name and organization to have a real shot at it."

"Had ten long years of bullshit from Tough Tony Boyle," Cletus interrupted, waving the *Journal* with its half-dozen front page pictures of the union leader, "and we can't have no more. Time was when a miner had the company against him and the UMW to take his part. These days the company and the union, they wake up in the same bed and a miner has just got to scuffle for himself. Replace us with machines, cut off our breath and don't pay compensation, put us down in unsafe mines day after day while Tony and his people just look the other direction. Sweethearts. Say a wrong word about one and you got the other on your tail."

The men grumbled agreement.

"It isn't only Boyle," said Hinkle, "it started a long ways back. It started with John L. Lewis and his closed-session bargaining."

There was a sudden, shocked silence.

The men looked at Hinkle. Hinkle looked to Spicer for help.

"Mr. Lewis, God rest his soul," said Cletus quickly, "must have been badly advised. Tony Boyle was an assistant to him back then, if you remember. Wouldn't be the first time an ambitious fella used his tricks to bring down a great man."

"John L. — Lewis," said Hawkes, stopping to catch his breath as he spoke, "was for the miner — all the way. F'he hadn't stepped — down — wouldn't *have* no problem today."

"God's truth."

"Well we do have em, have em bad," said Cletus. "Boyle is a thief, you ask me, stealin miners' money and stealin elections and stealin *lives* for too damn long. We got to get behind our man and see there's a fair election and vote ourselves back into our union!"

"Damn straight."

"God's truth."

"Got to be *done!*"

"Now Cletus, you were at that '68 convention," said Hunter, speaking for the first time. "You told me yourself there wasn't an honest vote in the whole show. How you plan to smoke him out when he owns all the matches? And what guarantee is there that this Yablonski would be any better?"

"Right, why should we get behind some hunkie we don't even know?"

"We got to hope he means what he says, fellas, that's all we can go on. I've heard him speak and I come away impressed. He's given up a soft position with the union in Pittsburgh there to take this on, he's as good as dead with the brass if he loses. He's got no practical reason to rock the boat. Says he's fed up with the way we been done and I believe him."

"Okay, Clete, I'll give you that." Hunter had read some of Yablonski's handouts, had talked with people who knew more about him. The man wasn't perfect, not by a long shot. Better than Boyle, of course, a lot better, but there was no way he could win. Hunter was sure of that. "But you got to admit," he said, "the odds are awful long. Why should we hop on a sunk ship?"

"Yeah, what good can we do?"

"Just get ourselves fu — fucked — over is all."

"We can open up an office here," said Hinkle, "and try to reach the other men. You're not the only ones who are fed up."

"That they're fed up don't mean they'll go against Tough Tony," said Pratt. "Antiunion they'll call it, cause Tony *is* the union. A plot by big business and big government to break up the UMW, a bunch of scabs they'll call us. I can just hear old Luther's mouth —"

"Oh, he'll give it to us, he will."

"That man is typical of the whole breed they got down there to the union hall, fills up his own belly then the hell with the rest of you. Just out for the softest touch he can bid off for."

"Never done shit for the men, like some hound tick, suckin —"

"Fat old hypocritical self-servin —"

"Old lard-ass shouldn't be much trouble we put a scare in him though, we —"

"Hold it right *there*, now. Jump back a few." Hunter shook his head slowly. They were letting it get to them, letting the anger carry them too far. "You maybe don't know the whole story on Luther, you younger fellas. Let me tell you a little something about *that* one."

Hinkle made a face and began to say something but Cletus Spicer touched his arm for silence.

"This is back right around 1930 when Luther was a young fella and the union was down and out, just tryin to get back a toehold around here. This is before Consolidation and U.S. Steel had come in, most of the mines were owned by the McElhenny family that old Judge McElhenny was head of. That's right, a judge. So the miners had the law against them as well as the company's hired agents. These agents were riffraff brought down from Cincinnati to give the union people hell while the Sheriff either looked the other way or joined right in. It was mostly hill people like Luther back then in the mines, you push em and they push right back. So naturally it come to shooting and the shooting come to bloodshed.

"One night some of these agents killed a union organizer, blasted him right off'n his front porch from their car while Luther and the other folks that lived by him looked on. They brought it to the Sheriff, said they could recognize faces and name names and all, but Sheriff said no, it was too dark to see. Wouldn't make an arrest. Well, people expected as much, so Luther and some of the other fellas who was tryin to bring the union in, they took it on themselves. Laid out all night with their rifles, waitin for a couple of the agents to come by this tavern used to be up the hill a piece from here. Eye for an eye they figured.

"Only there was spies in amongst them. The Sheriff and the agents got word and come down out of the pines round midnight, catching these miners from behind. Luther, he took one in the meat of the shoulder and one half-tored his buttock off but he managed to get hid under some brush. Lay there all the rest of the night bleedin, Sheriff and his people passing with dogs and lanterns and every now and then there'd be another couple shots. Couldn't whimper, couldn't cry, just lay there and felt his life playin out. Mornin come he's half dead, but he drags himself over to where he's got cousins living. Needs attention bad but all there is is the company doctor, fella they call the Butcher, who would of let him bleed to death or turned him in, and the Red Cross people. Now the Red Cross had come in to help all the people was starvin, giving handouts and medicine, but back then it was in cahoots, the Red Cross, they had a list the company give them. Your name is on that list of union supporters, the Red Cross don't want any part of you or your family."

Hunter stopped dead. The men listened. Gravel crunching in the front parking lot, an engine running. Idling for a moment, then rolling away. Hunter picked up the story immediately, gave them no time to panic.

"So his cousins, they carry Luther up to relatives on what used to be Rossum's Hill — over where they stripped the whole top off the mountain there? Country people. They done him up with herbs and poultices and whatnot while he lay back to heal and build up new blood. The company and the Sheriff they figured he was dead or run off for good.

"Then three months from the day, he come stridin down out of them hills big as life an tellin everyone he meets he was just off paying his union dues. Old Luther. And he stuck it all the way after that, stuck it till they come back in and made the company recognize them, broke the McElhennys' back."

The men chewed on that for a moment, trying to match the story with the potbellied, ramp-smelling Luther Justice who they saw at work.

"What I mean is, these are no pushovers you want to take on. They built the union up from nothing, dug the foundation with their fingernails, and there int no *way* they'll give it up thout a terrible big fight. Luther and those like him might have gotten a little fat over the years, let their positions go to their heads, but you best believe they are still some awful tough fellas."

"And that's why," said Cletus Spicer, "we need you to head us up, Hunt. Somebody out of the same mold as the people founded the union. The men will sit up and listen if it's comin from you."

"Hold *on* now! You way ahead of yourself, buddy. I haven't even joined the race and you got me leadin the pack."

"You're not in?"

He couldn't tell them about Hobie. He wasn't sure about it yet. Just like he wasn't sure about Yablonski. "Nope."

"What are you here for then?"

"Thought I'd come see what you people had in mind, then make up my decision. Think I'm onna buy the mule sight unseen? I mean this might end up doin nothing but bad to the people's in it."

The miners untensed and shifted, glad that someone had said it for them.

"Hunter has got a point there," said Verlan Strode. "It's not like if we lose this thing it's gonna be 'Too bad, fellas, better luck next time and glad you exercised your democratic rights.' Most likely those of us with seniority will be put back in some hump-and-jump job and those of us that don't will be down on the relief line. Union won't stand still for treason and that's just how they see even the slightest opposition. Treason."

"Right. Look what happened to Ray Wilcox."

"The way I see it, Boyle has got all the cards." Curt Lockly pointed to the front page of the *Journal*. "He's got the only news organ, he controls all the funds and all the voting machinery, plus he's still got most of the men behind him. By hook or crook. I got a great-uncle lives over to Kentucky, he's in one of them bogey locals. Bunch of old miners drawin from the retirement fund but somehow they still got a vote. Sposed to have at least ten active miners but they don't have a one. Still they got a local carries as much weight as ours does. Who do we complain to, Tony Boyle? Them old men know there isn't a penny they draw doesn't have Boyle's fingerprints on it. Spect them to make waves when they got a good thing goin? And there's hundreds of them all over, locals with old men paid direct from the union headquarters. This other fella got the money to buy all those votes away?"

"He wants to win it fair, Curt. He needs men, not money."

"Well he's gonna have himsef a time of it. Men can be scared, money can't. The men are scared, Cletus. Not me so much, but that's only because I just started, don't have a family or any responsibility. But other fellas, they wouldn't know where to turn they were run out of the mine. When you don't have much you come to be pretty careful with it, and all that most of us men here *have* is a job. We lose that, buddy, and we're between the rock and the hard place. And the old-timers, all they get is that pension check, which the union people in Washington know a hundred ways to take it away if you don't cooperate."

"They stoled mine — away from me," said Birdie Hawkes, reddening as he leaned forward to talk. "Worked twenty year —

in the union mines, last two — in a doghole. Things was hard, I couldn't h — help it. Cause of them two years they say I'm not — eligible. They stoled it right from me."

"Like Ray Wilcox."

"Right. Just like Raymond." Curt was talking hot, his throat raw with the hour and the cigarette smoke. "I only been up there eight months now, only just met the fella before it happened, but I can vouch for him. Hell of a hard worker, knew what he was doin, helped me out when I couldn't tell which end was up. Taught me how not to get hurt and I haven't been hurt yet.

"Now all he did, Raymond, was tell the foreman he wasn't going to move on till the roof-bolter shored things up some more. Said he didn't like the way the top looked, didn't trust it. Foreman was that son of a bitch Budka, he says to get going, roof-bolter would catch up when he could. Ray refuses to move on and Budka threatens to have him transferred to the labor gang. Now Raymond is about the best continuous-miner operator we got and Budka knows it. He's also got a back injury and Budka knows that too. Raymond can't *work* no labor gang." Lockly talked straight at Hinkle.

"All during the argument, the roof-bolter, it was Garvus Lilly I think, he was hustling to it and things are a bit safer. Raymond agrees to start up the miner again, but he's gonna file a grievance anyways. 'Just you go right ahead,' says Budka, 'see where it lands you.'

"Now this Budka is notorious, worst accident record in the mine and pictures himself as a real nutcracker. Always on your back for chickenshit while the important stuff goes right past him. You'd think the union would give a grievance against a guy like him some weight. Just the opposite. Old Luther and that union rep, the worthless son of a bitch, they call Raymond in to try and get him to withdraw the grievance. 'Don't get yourself tagged as a troublemaker,' they tell him, 'we got to keep that production up or we're all of us in the poorhouse.' Get that *we*. 'You already got a couple black marks with the company,' they said, 'so you shouldn't be after more trouble.'

"Raymond told them to go hang, he had a grievance and it was their job to see it through. Come to work on Monday and there's

[42]

Budka with a shovel, grinnin at him. 'You're the new tailpiece man,' he says, 'get to it.' Well, Ray goes straight for the union rep, he happened to be in that afternoon, and he says, 'Okay, here's your chance. Back me up.' Rep shrugs him off, tells him they need an experienced man at tailpiece, tells him that personnel assignments are the company's business, a whole load of bullshit like that.

"He tried as best he could to dig, Raymond, lasted out most the shift and then he just fell down with the pain. Just fell down. Couldn't unbend or get to his feet, shuttle car nearly run over him. He got that back problem years ago and the company doctor shafted him out of compensation, it's something doesn't show on the X-rays. Budka comes over and says, 'You can't do the work,' he says, 'you'll have to go home.' Raymond wouldn't lay still for help, he crawled onto the man-trip himself, hung on the back of a full-up coal car and rode out.

"He was laid up a month from that one night on the tailpiece. No compensation, no nothin. And while he's out they manage to drop him from the union. Rules infractions they said, though they never said which rules or how they were broken. That's what we got to face, Mr. Hinkle, and all that was over one tiny grievance. What you think they'll do if they're really threatened?"

"We got jobs on the line, Hinkle."

"Most of us got families."

"Ever try to make it on what the government gives out, teacher? They see what you need and give you half of it. The other half is your worry."

The men were angry and they had turned it toward Hinkle. Even Cletus Spicer was looking to see how he would try to recover the meeting.

"Hunter," said Hinkle finally, softly, "isn't Ray Wilcox your best friend?"

He had lived the whole story through with Ray. It had hurt to hear it told out like Curt had done. "We're pretty tight."

"And what did you do during all this grievance business, to help him?"

"Not a thing, really." Hunter shrugged. "He come to me when it started and told me to stay clear of the whole mess, that he had

[43]

finally had it and was going to push for the limit. He said there wasn't a thing I could do but get in trouble myself."

"So you watched while he was run out?"

"Yeah." Hunter shifted a little in his seat. "It's nothing I'm proud of but I don't think I could have done any good. They had him and they would of had me if I complained after he was gone." It was true. They *would* have.

"See, Hunter, that's just what we've got to end. The way they can pick you off one by one. That's the way the company worked before there was a union, before men could strike."

"Hah!" Cletus Spicer shook his head sorrowfully. "Don't even mention no strikes. When was the last official strike by the UMW? Sixteen, seventeen years ago? Seventeen years and if we want to walk out it's a wildcat. No law, no fund, we don't eat and we don't win. And the operators know it too damn well."

"Exactly my point," said Hinkle. "What kind of union is it that hasn't backed a strike in seventeen years? What kind of union works with management to fire a good man when it should be out fighting for him? How can you men let it go on like this?"

It was coming back into their laps and they didn't like it. The youngest-looking miner in the room, a boom boy on the evening shift, spoke in his high voice.

"And why should we stick our necks out if it's hopeless?"

"Number one," Hinkle ticked off fingers, "because it isn't hopeless. We just might win. If miners are fed up enough and this thing gets rolling maybe we can turn it all around. Okay, say we lose. Number two, the challenge itself is worth something, it makes it easier for the next try and it keeps the people in power a little more honest than they have to be otherwise. When did the UMW get moving for black lung compensation? Only after outside people and people way down in the ranks started making so much noise that the leadership was embarrassed into a commitment. Until then they acted like black lung was a myth. Just the fact that he's got a major opponent in this December election coming up is going to force Boyle into all kinds of programs to make himself look good, things he never had to bother with when there was no competition. There should be a lot of money spreading out from Washington in the next few months, but only if we make them worried enough.

"The third reason isn't a practical one, but it's something to consider. You can get shafted slowly, worn down year after year till you're beaten — or you can take your licks all at one time, all or nothing, and if you go down you go down fighting."

Cletus turned to Hunter. "You're right, buddy, it is a bad risk. But I'm going ahead with it, and I've got the word of a couple other of these fellas here. We could really use your help, but we'll do without it if we have to."

Hunter looked to Cletus a long moment, thinking. The men rubbed their eyes and waved at smoke but nobody yawned. "My Hobie," he said finally, "is likely to be down there with us pretty soon. It's something I've worked against my whole life but it hasn't turned out, I don't see any way out of it for him. All there is for a man to do around here is the mines and the welfare and he's not so sorry he'd go on the dole. He'll be down with us most likely, he'll need the money soon enough. Way I see it, if I can't keep him out of the mines least I can do is try to make them a decent way to live. I guess I'm in, fellas." Hobie would come back. He'd probably be home when Hunter got in tonight, full of apologies. He had to come back, what else could he do?

"I think we're all of us in, then," said Pratt Estill. "Cletus, you got yourself an organization here."

"Mind you," said Hunter, "I won't be nobody's leader. That's a hat I can't wear. If there's grief that comes I won't have on my mind that I brung a lot of other men to it. I'm with you all the way, you got my word, but I won't be nobody's leader."

"Once you people have declared your position," warned Hinkle, "you'll have to be totally committed. No turning back from here on in. We agreed?"

The men nodded and smiled and glanced around the room at each other. Sixteen of them. There was the brief flash that they were sort of an elite, founders of something that could prove to be important. Then the night train wailed, starting off from the tipple. Long and lonely. The night train wailed, chugging along the ridge. The men swiveled to listen and were aware of their number, aware that they were a handful of frightened miners holed up in a darkened barroom plotting way over their heads. "Totally committed," said Hinkle. "Now. We need a place to work out of. An office will help get people to take us seriously, make it look like we have a lot of support already. Any suggestions?"

Someone mentioned the shack the AVs used to stay in, but Hinkle said no, there were too many bad associations. People would connect them with outsiders, with dangerous new ideas. It wasn't right or good but that was how it was. Birdie Hawkes offered his place right in the middle of town and they agreed on it. Cletus was voted to head things up. One man's wife could type so he was made head of publications. Curt Lockly volunteered his pickup and Pratt Estill asked to handle food for the meetings. Cletus called a rally for the coming Sunday and told them to go get their sleep, details could wait awhile.

"It don't seem real, somehow," said Verlan Strode as they made their way to the door. "Don't seem official. Shunt we sing a song or something?"

Cletus and Birdie Hawkes had Hinkle backed against his little foreign car when Hunter joined them.

"— isn't nothin personal," Cletus was saying, "nothin personal atall. It's just what you said about people around here and associations and like that. I mean I sympathized with you people on that school lunch thing, buckin the board of education and the courthouse gang like you done. The more I think of it the more I see you were in the right. But people around here — that Pink Hinkle business and all — you understand? They see you in with us they'll holler red and scare everybody away. Dangerous new ideas and all that. Now we're awful grateful for your help so far, couldn't have brung it together without you, and we welcome your help in the future. But it will have to be kind of — like a silent partner? If somebody asks, you don't know a thing about it, you're a teacher, not a miner."

"Thed make a thing of it," said Birdie. "We can't be — be called out as Commonist or whatever, it'd finish — us off fore we got started. Sorry."

"Yuh."

"You understand why it's got to be? No hard feelings?"

Hinkle nodded and tried to smile. "No hard feelings, Cletus."

"Good. We'll keep in touch then."

They walked to their cars and drove off, leaving Hunter alone in the parking lot with the teacher.

"I should have known," Hinkle said to him, quietly. "In fact I should have suggested it myself, save them the embarrassment. Can't invite yourself into somebody else's fight." He was sweating heavily though it was a cool night.

"You still got your school."

Hinkle shook his head. "I'm gone after Christmas vacation. Board of education said there's been complaints."

"I'm sorry to hear that." Hunter kicked at the parking lot gravel. "My boy always speaks highly of you."

"You people here, I still don't understand you. The more you put in the less you seem to get out."

"Yeah, I suppose. It's like the mines. The easiest seams are the richest ones, while over at some little doghole operation you got to sweat blood and work on your knees for half the yield. Don't seem worth it, sometimes, does it?"

Hinkle shrugged.

"The men all preciate what you done. They just been fooled and tricked on so many time they don't give their trust away too easy. You got to keep that in mind." Hunter smiled and gave him a pat on the shoulder.

"Yuh."

"But they do preciate it. I preciate it. You should take some comfort from that."

"Thanks." Hinkle squeezed into the front seat of his car. He had a hard time getting it to turn over. "I hope your boy is feeling better," he said. "Coach has been having shitfits."

Hunter began to tell him that Hobie had gone, that there was problems, but held back and the moment passed. The teacher drove away down the mountain.

Hobie wasn't home when Hunter got back. The bed still neatly made, the lights off.

He had a beer. He had another. He heard the pump next door

[47]

come on, run for a while, click off. He heard the chipmunk that lived under the front porch rustling. He heard the defroster hum on in the kitchen, heard the house settling around him. It grew in his stomach, a sucking, empty feeling. He sat in the dark. It was the same empty he'd felt last March, trapped in a pocket of fallen rock, in total blackness. His headlamp broken, arm pinned by slate, measuring breaths through the self-rescuer. He didn't know the extent of the cave-in, didn't know if they would come for him. He lay in blackness and waited. At first there was only his arm, pulsing, the pain throbbing out till it filled the tiny crack of air, till it echoed back at him. He tried to muscle it back, failed. He tried to think it away. Tried to separate his mind from his body. That was when the emptiness began.

Spreading slowly from his stomach, up through his throat, numbness creeping till the pain was gone, till his arm was gone, till there was only the blackness and the sucking rhythm of the self-rescuer. He had no sense of time or direction left, only a hazy sense that there might be someone coming for him, trying to find his body. He lost the edge of the stone around him then, lost all his own edges to the blackness and was slipping away, the breathing device forgotten in his hand, till a random thought touched his mind. A slight, nagging thought, something that had been coming up all day at the face. Epsom salts. Hobie needed them, he'd been spiked badly in a game and Coach had recommended soaking in Epsom salts. Hobie had asked Hunter that morning if he would get some at the 7-11 on the way back from work. Hobie. Hunter found the self-rescuer in his hand, breathed. He flexed his crushed arm, flexed the pain back into it. The pain was better than the emptiness. The pain was better than nothing.

Hunter sat and tried to keep himself together in the empty house. He tried thinking about the meeting, about the men taking on the union, but it wasn't enough. They needed him, but not enough. He'd have to go. If Hobie wasn't back he'd have to go out after him.

It was lightening outside, more blue than black. Hunter put on a pot of coffee. Ray Wilcox would be getting home from work soon.

7

It was still dark when Hobie set off for Labor Power. The rain was light. All of his socks were wet now, except for the one he'd rolled the money up in. His running shoes were damp and smelled of wine vomit. His feet were cold.

He followed the directions the man at Pine Street gave him and was soon flanked by buildings covered in Chinese characters. Groceries, restaurants, imported-junk shops, even the banks and street signs were covered, even what was in English was done so it looked Chinese. The air came up sweet-and-sour from basement windows; one storefront displayed live chickens in crates. The telephone booths had plastic pagoda roofs on them.

The guy at the Shawmut Street address had said Darwin was gone to New Hampshire, didn't remember where, didn't remember when. Sort a hippie-lookin fella, he didn't seem to know much of anything. Permanently out-to-lunch, Darwin would say. Used to say.

Hobie hadn't figured on what he'd do if he couldn't find Dar. He hadn't let his thinking go any further. There had just been the feeling that he had to get out and Dar was the first thing he thought of. He didn't feel as bad as he thought he should that he'd missed his brother in Boston. He had made his move, he was out and he could do anything. It was kind of exciting, he could join the Army, go to sea, get his own apartment, take a job, get a drink in a bar, eat at a restaurant, do what he wanted with girls and not have the whole town knowing about it. Anything. It was like having the ball in the open field, you could run in any direction you wanted.

First, though, he'd have to make a little money. The twenty-five dollars he'd told the policeman about was really seven. He was afraid they'd arrest him for vagrancy. He'd have to make a little money, get himself started, then he'd go after Dar again.

Hobie walked down Beach Street in the light rain, wriggling wet toes inside his running shoes, carrying his sack over his shoulder. He left the Chinese writing behind for a more industrial-looking section, a lot of big, dirty buildings having something to do with clothes. Labor Power was on the bottom floor of one of these, on the right.

Nobody turned to look when Hobie entered the room. He went straight to the man behind the counter.

"I sign up for a job?"

The man slid a paper form and a pen at Hobie and went back to reading his newspaper. It was open to the sports section. A glass pot of coffee bubbled and spat like acid on a hotplate next to him, there was a stack of Styrofoam cups.

"Fuckin Brunes," he muttered to the paper. "Fuckin worthless."

The form had three sheets to it, you wrote on the top and it carboned through to the other two. It asked if Hobie had ever worked for a Labor Power office before. If he had any skills, if he preferred indoor or outdoor work. Hobie added two years to his age. He used Darwin's social security number. He would have gotten his own with working papers and all last summer, but when the Job Corps operation never panned out and the AVs were chased off it took all the summer work. Hobie slid the form back at the man.

"You can leave your bag behind here. Take a seat."

The men sat on metal folding chairs facing the counter, their backs to the street window. No one had a beard but no one had shaved for a couple days either. There seemed to be an awful lot of red noses but it was a step up from Pine Street.

EQUAL OPPORTUNITY, said an orange and black poster on the wall. FREE SITE DELIVERY, FULL PAY EVERY DAY. LABOR POWER. That's all there was — rows of metal folding chairs, a few posters on the cocoa-scum walls, a counter with two phones and several stacks of paper. A grid map of the area and a clock hung on the wall behind the counter. It was 6:45. Nobody talked. The coffee boiled and a few trucks clutched out on the street.

A few of the men slept in the chairs. One snored softly. They wore odds and ends mostly, though a couple had faded green work clothes and steel-toed high-cut shoes. One fella had a new denim jacket and there were two black kids, looked to be about Hobie's age, in skin-tight pastel pants, one red, one blue, and pointy black-shining shoes. They slouched with an empty chair between them, playing a silent card game. A little nut-colored man read a comic book with Spanish captions. *El Raton Fuerte.*

The phone rang a couple times and the dispatcher came out of his paper to listen and write things in a notebook. Around seven he began to call out names and men came up to have their forms written on. A few of them were handed money. There were ten men in the first group, mostly the ones wearing the work clothes. They left together. A few more men wandered in from outside. The dispatcher never looked up, he seemed to sense that they had arrived. Now and then someone went up to pour coffee. Hobie sat wishing he could dry his socks on the radiator.

Another group of ten was called up and sent off, some who had come later than Hobie. He looked around at who was left. He hadn't been able to track Darwin down and his money was nearly gone. The fella at Pine Street had said one night was okay but he should find a new place. His underwear was starting to itch.

"McNatt."

He hustled to the counter.

"Gonna send you out here, see how you do." The man was writing something on Hobie's form. "You need a couple bucks?"

"Huh?"

"A couple bucks for lunch or something?"

"Oh. No. Thank you."

"It's just an advance, it comes out your pay when you get back."

"No thanks." You never do anything on credit you can do straight up, his father would have said. That way you're never beholden.

"You want gloves?"

"Do I need them?"

"Who knows."

"I'd better take some then."

"You go out with this bunch, we get ten," said the man behind the counter. "Whenever the van comes back."

They crammed into a big orange and black van, ten of them plus the driver, and started out through the city. It was raining harder now and just as dark. Hobie was scrunched on the floor in a rear corner, not able to see anything but sky and the taller buildings through the windows. A few conversations drifted on and off, the only one he caught much of was about some fella who'd get drunk and hide his whiskey from his wife before he went to sleep, then wake up not remembering where he'd put it. He tried writing notes to himself but when he was sober he couldn't make out his drunken handwriting. So he decided to make a habit of never leaving a bottle unfinished once he'd opened it and became such an alcoholic his wife left him.

"What you call killin two birds with one stone," said the driver.

The van stopped to let people off at their work sites. They seemed to be driving out of the city. Pretty soon there was only the two black boys, Hobie and two wino-looking men left to go. One of the men had long legs that came nowhere near filling his baggy pants and a rash of little red pinprick marks all around his nose. The other looked like oatmeal, kind of boneless and grainy-skinned. The long one called him Donuts.

"The further out they send you, Donuts," he grumbled, "the later you stot. The later you stot the less you get paid. Then on the way back they pick up the furthest out first and work tawd home. So you spend most your time inside the van on the fuckin cuff."

"You got a point, Frank."

"On the other hand, you get your job close by in the city, they stot workin you seven shop and you do eight straight ones. Work your fuckin ass off. They got you comin, they got you goin."

"You work eight straight," said Donuts, "you get paid for eight straight."

"So? What good the money is, you roon your health workin too hod, you collapse with heat frustration? I got the strenth, got the health to work eight hours, I'd get a regular job."

"Don't worry," the driver interrupted. "We got a ways to go yet, we won't get there till eight-thirty, quatter of. Be lucky they get six an a half out of you."

"Sure, an I got to sit in the fuckin van all the way up an

[52]

breathe exhaust fumes. You know what that does to your brain cells?"

"If it kills one every ten minutes," said the driver, "you must be nearly tapped out."

"Thousands of em. They turn black an die, never to be heard from again. You be better off drinkin a gallon of crude whiskey than drive from here to Natick."

"Winos," said the driver.

"Don't mind him, he's just that way is all." Donuts jerked his thumb at his companion. "Frank the Crank. You give him a million dollars, he'd complain that green is his worst favorite color."

Hobie quietly asked where they were going.

"Medford, Bedford, Deadford, who knows? Somewheres clear off the map most likely, they got it in for us. Already we went by 128. All them brain cells."

"Forget your brains and pay attention, Frank." Donuts covered his mouth with his hand and spoke in a low voice. "We're gettin off the highway here. You take the left side, I'll take the right."

They traveled down a long strip of used-car lots and chain-bank branches and filling stations and fast-food huts. Donuts spotted a package store and gave Frank the Crank an elbow to the ribs. "Help me member the way."

The van left them off, Hobie and Donuts and Frank and the black boy in the pastel blue pants, left them under the awning of the loading dock of a warehouse in the middle of a huge industrial park. UNITREX CO. was stenciled every couple feet on the warehouse wall in thick black letters.

"You wait here for the foreman, guy named Ron," said the driver and took off with the lone black boy.

"Must have it in for that nigger," muttered Frank the Crank. "Go any further out you're in fuckin New Hampshire."

Ron arrived shaking his head at them and slapping a clipboard against his leg. He had shiny black hair combed straight back and a cigarette behind his ear. "Dammit. Goddam Labor Power. I ask for three, they send me four. Which one of you drives a fawk-lift?"

Nobody spoke up.

"Goddam Labor Power. Let's go, find youse somethin to do."

It was a huge cement-floored warehouse with stacks of boxes and wooden crates scattered about, men on forklifts zipping from stack to stack, barely missing each other in the rush. From the other side of the rear wall came a deep, powerful hum that vibrated the air around them. Beneath that was the sound of rain smacking the warehouse roof. Ron pointed to a man in white coveralls and told Donuts and Frank to report to him. Ron snapped his fingers at Hobie and the black boy then lit out across the floor. They had to jog every couple steps to keep up with him.

Ron led them to a head-high pile of brown cardboard slabs and a tape-roller machine mounted on a bench that lay within a narrow rectangle that had been laid out on the floor in adhesive tape. "You're McNatt, right? Right. And you're — what is it?"

"Wilsey."

"First name?"

"Theopolis."

"Right, Wilsey. Youse two are gonna make boxes for me. There's enough room here, the two of you, youse both can work. Only you got to stay inside the tape. You wander out on the floor one a these fawklifts'll shear your ass off. They go a couple tons, no suspension, they run over your toes it's pancake time, right? Okay. I'm gonna show you how to make boxes. I'm gonna show you one time, so pay attention. I can't be over here all morning jerkin off with you guys, I gotta keep the boys in line, keep it hoppin. They steal you fuckin blind you turn your back. You take one a these, right?" Ron pulled a slab of cardboard off the stack and slapped it on the bench. "It's all connected on the sides, folded up like this, all you got to do is unfold and tape the bottom." He picked the cardboard up. "You push like this fold here bend here fold here do this flap here take your tape not too long not too shot, slap it on, nother piece here and you got it. Simple, right?" Ron dropped the box onto a flat wooden loading platform that lay just outside the tape. It had spaces where the forklift tongues would fit. "You stack the boxes inside each other, eight to a stack, eight, an you hang this" — Ron flapped a strip of red cloth — "you hang this from the stacks where they can see it from the floor. Somebody'll come by with a lift, take the boxes and bring you back a loader. There's two of youse here on a one-man job, I want it should go twice as fast, right? No questions is there. Get to it." Ron trotted off.

Hobie and Theopolis Wilsey each took a slab of cardboard and unfolded it to make a hollow square with extra flaps hanging all over. Hobie folded the bottom flaps a couple different ways then went over to look at the box Ron had made. He rearranged the flaps once again, then pulled tape from the roller machine. It came out wet on the bottom and as soon as he tore it off the tape sprung into a circle and stuck to itself. He pulled another piece off, holding at both ends, then tried to center it to fasten down a flap. He got the thing nearly right on the third try. He taped the rest, having to tear off overlap on one side and patch in extra on the other. He laid his box inside of Ron's. Theopolis had torn one attempt apart and was having a hard time unsticking tape from his fingers. He went over and pulled Hobie's box out so he could look at Ron's. By the time he got his first one together Hobie had completed another. Theopolis started his own stack a couple feet from Hobie's.

They worked for a while like that, making their own boxes, squeezing around each other to get cardboard from the stack, waiting silently for the other to finish with the tape, being careful not to bump or meet eyes.

There were only two half-formed stacks of boxes when Ron buzzed by scowling and shaking his head. "Fuckin guys," he muttered in passing, "fuckin Labor Power."

"Hey," said Hobie after a while. "What if we split this thing up? One fella folds them into shape, the other tapes and stacks?"

Theopolis shrugged his shoulders.

"Whyunt we try it, see how it goes."

"Why not?" Theopolis was standing nearest the tape machine. They started.

It was much faster. Hobie found the exact way to grab the cardboard so it unfolded into a square as he took it off the pile, found the best rhythm and the right combination of left- and right-hand moves to fold the flaps with. Like a machine. On a five count. And when Theopolis asked after a while did he want to switch jobs for a bit, Hobie found the exact feeling his arm should have when the right length of tape was pulled out. Hobie and Theopolis made boxes till they hung the red cloth out and

[55]

had a stack and a half finished by the time the forklift brought a loader back. When Ron hurried by them he was still scowling but he didn't shake his head or say anything. It felt good, making boxes together so fast, so smooth.

A buzzer right above their head braaped for a full half-minute, making them both wince. The hum from beyond the back wall cut off. Forklifts stopped in mid-lurch and the drivers jumped down. Everybody seemed headed for a set of iron stairs at the rear of the warehouse.

"Think we're sposed to take breaks with the regular help?"

Theopolis shrugged. He pulled another slab of cardboard down and popped it into shape.

"Hey! Lunchtime!" One of the forklift drivers yelled from across the floor. "What the fuck's wrong widja?"

The cafeteria was up and into the adjoining building, orange and blue plastic scoop chairs and scattered low tables surrounded by three walls of vending machines. All the machines had out-of-order signs on them but the coffee vendor, and that took two whacks and a jiggle before it would pay off. Some kind of taped music played overhead but you could barely hear it through the men's voices.

Hobie and Theopolis sat in an empty corner by the out-of-order pastry machine. Neither of them had brought lunches. The men around them chomped into whitebread sandwiches, clamping fingers tight to keep the meat from pulling out, smacking and swallowing huge mouthfuls and picking their teeth. The men drank from their thermos tops and peeled oranges and shouted. They shouted across the room, they shouted point blank into each other's ears, they shouted sprays of whitebread crumbs through the air. Hobie and Theopolis slumped down in their scoop chairs and tried not to look hungry. Donuts and Frank the Crank were nowhere to be seen.

Ron poked his head into the room and a hunk of orange peel binged off the doorframe next to him. He gave the finger to the sniper, then used it to point at Hobie and gesture to the hall.

"So," he said when Hobie joined him. "How's he doin?"

"Huh?"

"The dinge. The colored kid. He goofin off on you?"

"No. He's doin okay."

"He's not layin down on you?"

"He's okay."

"Well you keep an eye on him for me. You let me know he stots fuckin off, right?"

"Yuh."

Ron smacked his clipboard and hustled down the stairs.

"So whud he say?" asked Theopolis when Hobie slid next to him. "We done sumn wrong?"

"Nah."

"So whud he say?"

"Just about the job."

"What about it?"

"Said I should keep an eye on you."

Theopolis looked at him for a moment, then smiled a little and shook his head. "That so."

"Make sure you don't fuck off."

"Hah! Man, you movin up. Half a day here an already you the sistant foreman."

"Yeah, well, I try to keep an eye on the boys." Hobie scowled a little. "I try to keep it hoppin, make sure they don't get any ideas."

"Make sure they don't cop you blind. Run off with no boxes."

"Sure they don't pocket a forklift, bring it home."

"Hah."

"But I don't ask em to do a thing I can't do myself."

"Oh no, I wouldn't do that."

"They just got to be fast as me puttin boxes together."

"An man, I got a Lympic medal for it —"

"The three-hundred-meter freestyle boxtape —"

"*Hah!* That's the man all right."

"Fuckin guys."

"Fuckin Labor Power."

It went even faster for a while after lunch ended. They worked at about the same speed but the time went faster with them able to talk. Theopolis told a griping story about a job counselor he'd been sent to who wouldn't get off his back but never had anything better than day labor to offer. Hobie told about spending a night at the Pine Street Inn.

"Booted his insides all over my God damn shoes and my last

[57]

pair of dry socks," said Hobie and Theopolis fell out laughing and broke up the rhythm of their box making. "Hate to think how it'd been if he'd had solid food in the last week."

The roller machine ran out of tape and an official-looking man yelled directions to Hobie. He crossed the floor in starts and stops, rushing from taped area to taped area dodging the speeding lifts. He passed Donuts, who was sitting brushing paste on labels and slapping them onto sealed boxes. In the far corner of the warehouse he found crowbars and staples and jars of glue, matte knives and baling wire and rolls of tape all laid out on a chest-high pile of wooden loading platforms. A pair of feet stuck out from behind the pile.

Hobie looked to see if anyone from the floor was watching, then peeked around the pile. Frank the Crank was asleep, lying on his belly where some cleanup man had swept all the chalkdust and tape stubs and wood shavings from the floor. An emptied pint bottle of something or other sat next to his ear.

"Wonder what they puts in the boxes," said Theopolis when they were back in operation. "They take em hind that back wall then bring em back all filled up and closed. You can't see what they puts in em."

"Smaller boxes."

"Naw man, I'm serious."

"So am I. You don't think so, ask somebody around here."

"Here come the man again. Why don't you ax him?"

"You're the one wants to know."

"Yeah, but you the sistant foreman. You axim."

Ron came up and kicked a stack of boxes.

"What goes inside these?"

Ron didn't seem to hear. Hobie spoke a little louder. "What goes in the boxes?"

Ron looked at Hobie like his mother had been insulted.

"I mean what do you make here?"

Theopolis stifled a nervous laugh.

"Does it fuckin matter? Listen, I been watching youse two. This aint a social club, you, it's a factory. You're not over here to jerk each other off. You let me catch you fuckin the dog again, so help me, you'll be some sorry characters. Now keep it hoppin."

The last hour and a half seemed to drag on forever. Theopolis got a moody look on his face and stopped talking. There was a clock on the far wall, Hobie could just barely make out the hands. The tape machine didn't seem to be rolling smoothly, Hobie and Theopolis kept getting out of sync so one would have to wait for the other. A few of the boxes weren't quite together, but once they were in the stack no one could tell. Hobie figured they were putting out twenty-five boxes every ten minutes and he started counting boxes toward three o'clock. That got boring. He tried to think of what Darwin was up to, of what he'd do after work, where he'd go, but he had no idea. He thought the words to all the songs he knew that had the word *cry* in their title. He thought as many words or verses as he could remember — to *I'm So Lonesome I Could Cry*, to *Big Girls Don't Cry*, *Crying Time*, *Cry Me a River*, to *Crying in the Chapel* and *It's My Party and I'll Cry if I Want To* and even hummed *96 Tears* for a while. That got boring. His feet were wet, hot and wet now and his arches hurt. His hands were growing clumsy with the tape. He had to force himself not to look at the clock.

"Gimme your slips."

Ron was there, scribbling what he decided their hours were and handing the slips back. He turned without a word and took off toward the back wall.

Donuts and Frank the Crank were already out on the loading ramp, standing just inside the stream of rainwater washing off the roof. It was pouring. Frank the Crank had chalk and sawdust smeared all over his front, he looked like he'd put in a tough day.

"Now I'll admit I was wrong to of finished the whole bottle," he said. "It's only right. I'm a fair man, I admit my mistakes. All I'm sayin is it wasn't worth it. That stuff, what was it, Franzia Brothers, it's too sweet. Now I'm not tryin to shift the blame" — Donuts stood mute with his arms folded over his chest, staring straight out into the rain — "it's just I'm sayin you should of listened to me and bought the Gallo. You got sugar, right? What the doctor is always tellin you? Now a full half-bottle of that stuff, that Franzia Brothers, could put you right out of the ball-game. Am I right?"

Donuts pretended Frank wasn't there.

"He's not always like this," said Frank the Crank to the boys. "He gets tempermental when he drinks."

Hobie and Theopolis compared their work slips. Hobie had been credited with seven hours while Theopolis was down for six and a half.

"Little bonus for the sistant foreman."

The Labor Power van swished in through the parking lot puddles. The black boy with the red pastel pants was sitting in the rear. They drove back slowly, the driver cursing his windshield wipers, the radio tuned to a disc jockey who laughed at his own jokes. Theopolis sat with the other black boy and didn't talk again to Hobie. The black boy bitched about the grease he'd gotten on his shoes and Frank bitched about how a workingman wasn't nothing but a slave and the driver bitched about the kamikazes on Route 1A. Hobie took his shoes and socks off and tried to wipe his feet dry with the gloves he'd been given.

The rain was lighter but the traffic worse in downtown Boston. The van was full up and stalled behind a major tangle on Tremont by the Common and somebody kept cutting killer farts that barely overpowered the smell of liquor. The driver suggested they get out and walk, it wasn't but a couple blocks away. Hobie hurried his shoes on.

They walked through the city in a loose formation, clearing a path on the sidewalk before them. They walked past Filene's, scattering women under umbrellas, walked down Chauncey giving hardeyes to the young office workers in their thin suits and bright ties. They were workingmen. Frank the Crank walked at the very front, strutting a little, showing off the filth on his clothes, pausing now and then to swat at it with his gloves. They walked down Harrison, staring back at the young punks who leaned in the doorways of the topless bars, walked through the tip of Chinatown like invading sailors, pointing and laughing and stomping their big feet through the puddles. They were workingmen and they walked all the way down Beach, a good deal more than a couple blocks, to find the van already parked out front and the driver inside drinking coffee.

They lined up in single file before the counter. The dispatcher was there, looking like he needed a shave. He read their work slips one by one, made some sort of mental calculation, and paid them. Hobie was at the very end of the line. There wasn't any change being given out, only bills. Only singles, the dispatcher licking his thumb and slapping down a little pile from the big roll he held close to his chest. He slapped the final bill of each payment down extra hard. The men left in ones and twos. Mostly ones. Hobie gave his slip over and was handed thirteen single dollar bills.

When he got to the door the street was empty but for someone under a hooded Army poncho holding a stack of paper.

Hobie decided to go to the Super Burger they had passed during the walk. He added the money to the sock in his bag and hurried out into the rain. He was handed a leaflet of some sort, Labor something it said, by the Army poncho. A few steps further there was a soggy pile of the leaflets strewn on the sidewalk. Hobie added his.

"*Hey!*"

The poncho was trotting up behind him.

"I wanted it on the fuckin sidewalk I would have dumped the whole lot there in the first place." It was a girl's voice. "You think I'm out here for my fuckin health?"

Hobie shrugged. It was a girl about his height, maybe a little older than he was, who had a big nose. He looked closer. He wasn't used to girls who said fuck.

"You think I like seeing twenty men in a row throw my stuff away? Hunh?"

Hobie shrugged again.

"Do you speak English?" She sounded a little apologetic.

"Uh-huh."

"I mean do you speak well enough to understand me?"

"Yeah. I'm an American."

"Fantastic." She was back to being pissed off. "You don't have to sound so fuckin proud of it."

"Sorry I threw your thing down. I was in a hurry."

"You didn't look at it. Where you going you can't even look at it?"

Hobie looked up at the rain a little impatiently, then to the girl. She had sort of neat-looking eyes. "Super Burger. Get something to eat."

"You *are* an American." The girl smiled. Hobie had never seen so many white, unfilled teeth in one mouth. "Do you work here a lot? Day labor?"

"It's my first time."

"You looking for a regular job?"

"Sort of. I spose I should be, anyhow."

"You're not from here, are you?"

"West Virginia."

"No shit." She smiled.

Hobie shrugged at her reaction. He felt shy about looking right at her now. She was pretty. No, pretty wasn't the word. High school girls were pretty, this one didn't look like a high school girl.

"So anyway," she said, businesslike but not mad anymore, "since you're so hot to trot, what you threw away says we're having a teaching rally for workers this Saturday and we're inviting everybody who's interested to come and talk."

"Uh-huh." Hobie started to ask who "we" meant, but was suddenly embarrassed to ask.

"Were you in the Army?"

"Pardon?"

"The Army. You know — salutes, marching, guns, napalm —"

"Oh. No. This jacket was my brother's."

Her face sobered. "Did he get killed there?"

"He was there but he didn't get killed. He's still alive."

"Good. So this rally is in Franklin Square — you know the South End?"

"Nope."

"I'll tell you how to get there. Where do you live?"

Hobie's feet were wet and tired. He was hungry. "You ask a lot of questions."

"You're right, I do. Everybody should ask questions. That's important, people should ask more questions. And with you it's like pulling teeth, you're not a very communicative boy. Now where do you live?"

Hobie didn't like it that she called him boy. "I don't live anywhere right now."

She seemed to look at him closer. She pushed the hood of her poncho back and shook her hair out. "No shit. You run away?"

She was older than him by some, you could tell. "No. Not exactly. I mean I left and all but no one is after me." Hobie wondered why he was standing in the rain telling personal stuff to some stranger when what he wanted was to get some food in his belly and find a cheap, dry place to spend the night. She had sort of Afro-looking curly hair, only it was honey-colored. "I come here to get in touch with my brother, see if he could put me up awhile, but nobody knows where he went to."

"Listen, you could come stay with us."

"I don't know." When he said it so quick he wished he hadn't, then again he didn't trust who "us" might be. It made him nervous that she would ask him so quick, without knowing him at all. The old fella who'd come over to his bed to talk last night had been that friendly right away and it had turned out to be monkey business he was after. Hands on the knee and winking and did he like the girls and all that.

"No strings attached, honest. You could even stay till you find a regular job or whatever. That's one of the things we're trying to do. Help working people."

Working people was a funny thing to call him but it was better than boy and she sounded like there was no trick behind her offer. "You got room enough?"

"Sure, loads of room. C'mon, let's get out of the rain."

She gave his arm a little tug in the direction she was heading.

She had light green eyes. Her nose wasn't so much big as there was this bump in the middle of it that was — was interesting. From certain angles. And there was all those white teeth when she smiled.

"Spose we ought to. Get out of the rain."

"We might even be able to find you something to eat better than Super Burger. You know what that stuff does to your brain cells?"

He turned to go with her. She smiled. "No strings attached."

As they walked down Beach toward Chinatown the girl handed Hobie half her stack of leaflets. Wouldn't hurt if he helped her spread the word.

[63]

8

Lucille spooned hard grease from the Maxwell House can onto the griddle. The round glob skated slowly.

"Won't be long now, Hunt, they got him workin a ten-to-six cat-eye over there. Damn people won't even run a regular shift." She dodged an old, disassembled bicycle on the floor and gently footed a chipped mixing bowl over by where Pappy Dan sat still as death in his rocker. A trickle of Mail Pouch ran down his chin. "See if maybe you could hit moren you miss today, all right?" she said to him. "Draws the ants."

Lucille's face was puffy with sleep, Hunter's drawn from the lack of it. Pappy Dan's face was all ridge and ravine, flesh caving in over the eyes and wattled at the throat. He spurted red tobacco juice every fifth time he rocked forward. Pappy Dan was a fast chewer and a slow rocker.

Lucille swirled the now-liquid grease, leaning back as it popped at her. She dropped in spoonfuls of buckwheat batter, holding it far away from the blue of her nurse's uniform. "Sure you don't want none?"

"No thankya. Don't feel up to it."

It was a very small kitchen. With Pappy Dan and the bicycle pieces and Hunter at the table it was tight for Lucille to move around. "I can see where you'd be upset. One of ours took off like that I'd just be *sick* with worrying. Probably a false alarm is all, he'll get up to Charleston or so and feel lost. Probably on his way back down home right now."

"Yeah. Probably."

"At's the trouble thall you people naow," said Pappy Dan through his big red broken nose, "won't finish what you start. Boy does turn around at Charleston en I wouldn't give you a nickel for im."

"I think you missing the point, Pappy. Hunter's son has run *off*. It's not like he's made a deal with anybody to stay away for so long. He'd be foolish to drop from school this late."

"Pigshit." Pappy Dan squirted juice toward the bowl on the floor.

"Pappy is worse than all the kids put together. Since I been filling in days it leaves just Ray to watch things and he's got to get his sleep sometime. Turn your back on this old goat and he's up on that hill by the graveyard."

"All my people is up there." The old man frowned. "All my friends. En the town, they don't keep it up proper."

"And what did the doctor say about you climbing up that hill? About your heart?"

"Hit's only just a little miner's asthma is all. Had it all my life, nothin to do with you heart. Besides, I kick off on the way up it'll save the pallbearers some steps. Always try to oblige people."

"Coffee, Hunt?"

"No thankya." Hunter sat with Hobie's note spread before him on the kitchen table. It was written on lined paper torn from a composition book, it had been folded and unfolded till the creases were soiled and fuzzy. There was a small mark, a crossout, where Hobie had considered how to head the letter. Dad? Daddy? Dear sir? He had left it blank. *I've thought about it alot*, he wrote, *and I really have to go. Tell Delia and Coach and everybody I'm sorry. It's not because I'm in trouble or anything like that and it's not anything you did. It's just me. I can't stay here. See you. Hobie.*

"He says it's not trouble."

"Of course it isn't, Hunter. He's an awful nice boy."

"Time was," said Pappy Dan, "young fella left town, he was about to be lawed or about to be a father."

"Pappy!"

"S'truth, damn it, what can I say? Godspeed to im. Don't think you haven't got your share of hafe-brothers en sisters all over this country. I done some runnin round afore your ma put salt on my tail."

"I hope none of them took after you." Lucille turned to flip the buckwheat cakes, then paused to shake her hair out and pop her eyes awake. Raymond was clumping up the back porch stairs to the kitchen door.

He didn't speak at first. He sat heavily in his chair with his eyes closed and took a deep breath. He held it in, worked his neck a bit, then let it go.

"Lo, honey. Hunter." He sat with his back to Pappy Dan and didn't bother to turn around.

"Man come to live in *my* house en he don't have the decency to say a good mornin. Kinda damned son-in-law is that?"

Ray ignored the old man. "What you up to this hour, buddy?"

"Hobie's run off," said Lucille. She laid a plate of warmed-over home fries in front of him and kissed the back of his neck. "Hunter got back night before last and Hobie was gone."

Hunter slid the note across to Ray. "I think he might have gone to Boston."

Raymond read slowly, holding a forkful of potato in midair all the while. He slid the note back. "Looks like he's gone all right. Why Boston?"

"Last we heard from Darwin he was there. We had a post-card."

"Long ways off, Boston."

"I'm hoping he'll find that out and turn back halfway there."

"Muleshit!" A gob splatted the linoleum.

Raymond sighed. "Luce, you have to get him up at this hour? Don't he need his sleep or something?"

"He gets himself up, Ray, int a thing I can do about it." She set a bottle of syrup next to his stack of cakes. "I come out this mornin he's here waitin on me."

"Man lives in his own house, he gits up when he damn well pleases."

Ray let it pass as he began to cough. Deep, dry, loose hacking, turning red in the face and holding to the edge of the table till he worked up a hunker from his lungs and spat it into Pappy Dan's bowl. It floated black within the dark red tobacco juice.

Ray took a deep composing breath and went on as if it hadn't happened. "What if he don't come back in a couple days, Hunt? What then?"

"I'll go after him."

"And leave everything you got here?"

Hunter gave a startled laugh. "Everything I got? Foor-room rented house and a six-thousand-dollar debt to the hospital people? Thout Hobie there isn't one thing to keep me here."

"What about the union?"

"Union, chickenshit." Pappy Dan tore off a fresh chaw. "Hasn't been no union since *he* give up the reins." He nodded to the wall where a portrait of John L. Lewis joined FDR and a sewing sampler of the two murdered Kennedy brothers. Each had a black mourning band cutting diagonally across the left corner. The band on John L. Lewis's picture was brand-new.

"Nobody asked you a thing, old man."

"What about the union?" said Hunter.

"You're with the fellas gonna try and take it back, aren't you?"

"You know about that?"

"C'mown buddy, this is miners we're talking about. Man don't but fart and everybody and his cousin feels the breeze. Gonna be a tough haul. It won't keep you here?"

"No. I don't believe it will."

"They could really use your help, Hunter. Luther and them can be some pretty tough people, you step on their tails. Can get awful revengeful."

"I know that."

"That Luther Justice makes one more smart comment to me on the street," said Lucille, "I'll knock his big horsey teeth down his throat."

"Luther thinks he's a ladies' man, is all."

"Cheats my husband out of a job then keeps on givin me the glad-eye ever time we pass. Big overgrown schoolboy is what he is, chasin after skirts with his jaw hung open."

"He was a good boy when I knew him," said Pappy Dan. "Never would back up wunst he made a stand. Wasn't sorry like a lot of them no-good loafers, like them that sucked around the Red Cross. A good, tough boy."

"Wonder what happens to a fella like that." Ray pushed his empty plates away. "I first come to the mine he seemed like he was all for the men. Back when that was a pretty dangerous thing to be. But now when the all-out war days is over — hell, you ask me the man lacks about ten ton of weighing a nickel."

"Things happen to change people," said Hunter. "It's hard to

[67]

tell exactly when a person starts to go wrong. You can be honest and brave without bein too smart, you know. People get to you, flatter you, turn you around a couple times and make your friends out to be your enemy and there you are, honest and brave for the wrong side. Oh, it can be a lot of things. Maybe you just turn sour on people. Luther wasn't so outa line with the women, winkin and leerin all the time, till after his wife lit out. People aren't a grateful bunch as a whole, it's easy to start to wonder why you should break your neck with so little return. And remember, Luther's got a few years on us, more time for life to wear on him. Oh, it can be a lot of things turn you bad," said Hunter. "Maybe he just got tired."

"And you're willing to leave the men in his hands?"

"I don't *want* to. Don't see as I got much of a choice."

"You always got a choice, buddy. Maybe a hard one, but you got a choice. Hobie's been pretty much on his own before."

"*Ray*mond! We're talking about Hunter's *son* run away. Of course he'll go after him if he has to. The men can take care of themselves."

"If only they could, Luce, there wouldn't be a problem. Hunter goes and an awful lot of fellas are gonna lose their nerve."

"Don't know about that, but —"

"Everybody wants to keep something." Ray had a grim look on his face. He was getting gray. Hunter had known him from grammar school and he was getting gray. "Everybody's got something they think they can't lose. That's how the others stay on top, they threaten to take away that precious something. One man it's his seniority, another it's his new car. Another guy can't part with the bonus he gets to go to a rigged convention. The next one, he's only got a year left for his pension, he's worried they'll screw him out of it. Have a heart guys, he says, see it my way. I'd like to be with you but — And then some fellas, well, they got family problems."

"You're not bein *fair*, honey. Put Hunter on a spot like that. Have you ever had to choose between your family and what you thought was right? Would you let me and the kids go for some union fight?"

"He'd let *me* go in an eye-blink, the ungrateful son —"

"Quiet Pappy. Would you, Ray?"

Ray shook his head slowly. "I don't know what I'd do. I hope I never get stuck where I have to make the choice. Hunter *does*, though, he's got it starin him straight in the eyes. I'm not saying what he should do, now, just makin sure he knows there is two ways he can go on it. People should always be faced with a choice if they got one. Right buddy?"

"Raymond, you're not an easy fella to be friends with."

"Probly why you're about the only friend I got. You never did aim for the easy way. You gonna stay and fight it?"

"Raymond, he's a little *boy* —"

"Now, Luce —"

"Little boy, cowflops. Looked full growed to me when I seen im off."

"You saw him?"

"Saw him leaving?"

"Stopped by the graveyard on his way. I's there tryin to keep the red dog off my people. Didn't put their lifes into this country to be covered by that shit."

"But what about Hobie?"

"Oh, he had a poke on his shoulder en waved me good-bye. Nice lookin boy, Hunter."

"Where was he headed?"

"Up the road. Bus station maybe, maybe to thumb on the turnpike."

"And you didn't stop him?"

"Hell. Boy is what — semteen, eighteen? Hit's time he was out on the world gettin his education. Fergit about this high school nonsense."

"He didn't say anything? Why he wanted to leave?"

Pappy Dan shook his head.

"I don't understand it. He said he wasn't in any trouble."

"One time I was workin this mine up to Kanawha County," said the old man, rocking even slower. "Seam wasn't but three-en-a-half feet en I was a pretty rangy young feller. Shrunk up since then. Now I'm from the picks, mind you, didn't have none of your modern-day machinery. It was a pooer land for farmin even back then en you got to eat. So we worked on our knees, pickin away, en we had to get it back from the face ourselves. We'd strap rags around our knees en wear clear through em by the end of the day. Hit were a gassy son of a bitch too, I remember, but it was the top pay around en we didn't have your welfare or stamps or like that. You worked if you were lucky.

"They'd hired a young bunch of fellers for our crew, a few married, but mostly not. Well, one day word comes that a recruiter for the American Expeditionry Force'll be through the next mornin, lookin after fresh meat for the Great War. It was volunteers they were after, conscription had mostly passed the area cause they needed the coal. You wanted to get kilt you had to ask for it.

"Now we'd heard stories bout the mustard gas en the disease en how the Hun treated his prisoners en all, but it was just *stories*. The real thing was a million miles off, it was unknown territory. It was also three squares a day and a clean barracks. I member this poster was down at the courthouse. This Frenchy-lookin woman kneeling, tryin to keep her baby offen some German's bayonet. Better to die on your feet than to live on your knees, it said.

"Day broke en I went down en the Lord strike me if there wasn't evry man-jack of our crew sittin on the steps, even a couple of the foremen. Thought they'd be made officers, I guess. Unknown territory. There was bullets in it maybe en maybe we'd end up in Flanders Field, but it was a choice for something different, it was unknown. We *knew* what was waitin for us down that mine, knew it too damn well, three-en-a-half feet of gassy air en not a winda in the joint.

"Recruiter made himself a killing that day."

Pappy Dan shook his head and fumbled for a fresh chaw.

"Old man gets these spells every so often," said Raymond. "He starts to make sense. You think the boy just felt things closin in on him?"

"It's got to be more than that, Ray. It's something I done, I know it." Hunter fingered the note as he talked. "When Molly was down with the cancer she always said how I should look out special for Hobie, he took things to heart so much. Now it was the *war* come between me and Darwin. We got along fine till they took him, sent him back a whole nuther person. But with Hobie — Ray, I got to go after him. I don't, he'll take it as a sign that I don't care. I can't be at peace wondering if there's something really wrong between us. Boys go away at his age, sure. I'd of lost him to something in another couple months anyways. But the feeling between us, I've got to get that straight."

"Then it's Boston?"

"Unless I hear different that's where I'll start. I don't want to go just when things are hot for the men, it looks like I run out. I know there's a kind of responsibility you got even if you're not an official leader. But there has to be something in it for me, something personal, or it's not worth staying for. With Hobie gone I'd feel like an outsider, my heart just wouldn't be in it."

Raymond pushed his chair slowly away from the table. He looked embarrassed. "Gimme a hand, Luce?"

Lucille came up behind and hooked him under the armpits. He braced his legs and shut his eyes tight. "Okay," he said, "let er rip."

Lucille took a deep breath and hefted him upward, kicking the chair away as he rose. Raymond stood with the color draining back into him and immediately began coughing. He hawked several times into the bowl Lucille held under his chin and was a little breathless when it subsided. "God damn inferior-grade coal we got over there," he muttered, "it don't cough as well as Number Seven's did."

"You need a rub honey?"

"I believe I do, it's all knotted up there. Join us in the front room, Hunter?"

They left Pappy Dan to chew and rock alone. "You just go to sleep with an ax handle under it," he called. "Swhat I always done for mine."

There were blankets on the little couch in the living room and Lucille's flannel nightgown hung from one arm.

"Welcome to my bood-wahr," she said. "It's been a little cramped since we lost the house."

Ray got to his knees gingerly, keeping his head stiff and aimed straight forward, then Lucille helped him ease onto the floor. She lifted his shirt up to his shoulderblades and went for some liniment.

"Pretty bad, int it buddy?"

"It's no funhouse, Hunter. Got misery in my back here but I

[71]

guess I got to live with it. There's no organization over there, you miss a week they tell you your job's been taken. Bad as it is, that damn union is better than no union at all. My God, buddy, if you could see the safety conditions. It's a joke is what. Other day the Man come down to tell us the Bureau of Mines inspector would be over in two days. Little tip-off somebody made to give us time to fake things up some."

"And the men lay down for it?"

"Got very little choice, Hunter. We thought the UMW was the least bit interested we'd turn over our water pails and wildcat on out of there. All we'd ask is some interest, under the table even, maybe a little strike fund.

"No way, though. They want it shut down, not unionized. The big companies they're in with, they tell the union we can't *have* these little dogholes underselling us. So you harass the men, you harass the operator, you give em all the trouble you want just as long as you never *set*tle with them. Union's like some little bootlicker puppy, sure nuff they say. The fella owns the doghole is in trouble, which don't break my heart, he'll survive. But the fella works in it, he's screwed from every direction there is. He's fucked over so many times and so many places they got to drill new *holes,* buddy."

"It's not fair —"

"Fair don't have a thing to do with it, you know that. I made my bed and here I am lyin in it. Face first. And I don't mean to be playin the martyr with you, Hunt, I really couldn't get out of that chair."

"If only we'd all of us gotten together when Budka started it, showed them we wouldn't stand for it —"

"Wouldn't have worked, Hunt. We'd of all been hung together."

Lucille returned to straddle Raymond's back and began to work Absorbine Jr. lotion into it.

"Wasn't any foundation for it. The fact is, I'm not a popular enough fella to get everybody out to bat for me. There has to be groundwork laid first. But there isn't any groundwork. There's just guys like you and me, want to earn their shift, bring home that thirty dollar a day and forget about it. No heroes, Hunter, just fellas who they stick together or they don't."

[72]

"You pretty hard-put for money? I mean if I don't have to keep up on the rent I could —"

"Pay is about two-thirds union scale and no benefits. But there's no dues wasted and no Luther Justice to bend my ear about his sex life, either. We'll make out. Lucille's been over to the hospital and that brings in some. Ought to see me get the kids off to school, regular little housewife. We're hurtin but it's been worse. You member during Ike's recession when there wasn't a thing doing at the mines? Cabbage-and-cornmeal days. Yeah, we'll make out." Ray smiled. "Luce honey, that is one *hell* of a back rub you give. Keep this up I'm onna have to give you a raise."

"You get better so's you can help me more around this God damned house and I'll be satisfied. Miners think there int a thing between the job and sleep but a six-pack of beer."

"Woman, if you only knew —"

"I know, I know, it's the hardest work a man can do." Lucille wrinkled her nose against the strong-smelling liniment. "All you miners do is bitch about your poor weary bodies and all the danger down there, but if they made it safer and easier, easy enough so *I* could do it too, I bet you wouldn't want no part of it. Sometimes I think you're *hap*py it's miserable and hard, gives you something to be proud of."

"Int she a beauty?" Ray reached back to give her thigh a blind squeeze. "Keeps me honest, she does, bettern a portrait of the Lamb a God over the doorsill. Better lookin too."

Hunter got up to leave. "Sorry I broke up your morning," he said, "but I had to talk it out with someone."

"No sweat, buddy. Listen, I had a friend in the Army, he lives in Boston somewheres. Brother is with the steelworkers. He offered to introduce me, maybe get me on somewheres, back when we thought we'd have to move out. I could write you a letter to him, case you have to set up shop in Boston awhile."

"I'd preciate it."

"Maybe he's home already, right while we been talking here." Lucille tried to sound convincing. "A cold night in a strange place can work wonders."

"Yeah," said Hunter, "maybe."

[73]

"Though you never can tell," said Ray Wilcox, wincing on the living room floor as his wife rubbed liniment into his back. "People get something in their heads they lible to go all the way with it. You know how people are."

9

Mark Remington met the girl on the front steps, showing her in from the rain, and made a quick appraisal. Younger than she sounded on the phone, probably a freshman or a sophomore, with a solemn little face and straight brown hair. Machine-faded baggy jeans, a yellow T-shirt and yes, a scuffed pair of Pappagallos. Needham? West Newton? Dover?

"West Newton," she said when Mark asked. "A real dump. That's one good thing about school, it got me out of the suburbs."

"I know how you feel," he said, leading her inside. "Most of our people are from the upper-middle-class towns around Boston. Got a few total outsiders though. I'm from New York. We had a kid come in from West Virginia a little while ago, looks like he might stay on."

The girl had called and Mark happened to be the one who answered the phone. Schenk probably would have told her to get lost. She was doing a project for her journalism class at BU, was supposed to interview someone high up in a radical political group. What the hell, he had figured.

"It's Ellen-something?"

"Ellenbogen," she said. "Debbie Ellenbogen."

"Debbie, right. How did you happen to pick Third Way for this thing?"

She shrugged. "My roommate got Michael Kazin and another girl picked Mark Dyen and somebody got Mike Albert from the November Action Coalition and Eric Mann was taken and even that guy Grossman was gone. I didn't think there was anyone left. Then I found one of your leaflets on the Green Line. About the Third Way."

"Very flattering," said Mark Remington. She was kind of a humorless kid, you could tell right off, into a heavy depressive thing. He'd have to work on that. "You thought there was no one left."

"Yeah. I'd never heard of you."

"Are you going to take notes?"

She looked concerned. "You think I should?" She had neither notebook nor tape recorder with her.

"It's up to you. It would be nice to know that I'll be quoted as accurately as possible."

The girl took a folded wad of paper and a pencil stub from her pocket. She asked if Mark was head of the organization.

"We don't really have a titular head or anything like that. I mean, I *was* instrumental in forming Third Way, in fact you might say it was my idea, and the others recognize that I have as much or more experience in the Movement as any of them. But I'm really just one voice in the chorus. We make all our decisions in group session and everybody speaks with equal weight."

"Oh."

She stood there waiting. It was clear that he could relax with this one, it was his show. "Listen," he said, "why don't I show you around the place, give you a physical feel for our operation while we talk?"

So it wasn't some lefty hotshot from *Rolling Stone*. What the hell, it would be good practice. He had been interviewed before, back in the early SDS days. He'd be interviewed again, interviewed all the time once Third Way got rolling. To communicate with the masses you had to be able to use the mass media.

Smallwood was collating pages of the newspaper in the parlor. The couch and floor were covered with reams of paper, were strewn with magazines and leaflets from other groups. Collating was the first job a new recruit was given after the hooks were pretty firmly in. It was important to learn that tedium was part of revolution.

Smallwood shuffled the papers faster when they entered. He was a reader, Smallwood, one of the few of the younger kids who was genuinely interested in theory.

"We use this mostly as a kind of reception room," said Mark. "When neighborhood people come over for help, this is where we meet with them. It's a little disorganized now cause we've got an issue of the paper coming out and we need the space to put it together. But usually it's for community access." Actually, not that many neighborhood people were showing up yet and the room was always full of paper. But when things got moving it would be used for meetings. When the people trusted them.

"We try to be as responsive as possible to the people in the neighborhood," he told the girl. "I mean, you can throw around a lot of words like radical and New Left and all that, but what it really boils down to, what we're trying to do here, is to give the neighborhood people, the working people, a hand. Help them out with job problems, housing problems, family problems — everyday things. It's pretty down to earth, but we think it's important."

He wished she had brought a tape recorder. It was much better when he could ask to hear himself played back, it always made him feel better about the interview.

"Let's go in the kitchen."

They had knocked a wall down to expand the kitchen into a huge eating area. There were two long picnic benches, made from the wood that King had boosted, the gas stove and a big trough-sink. Kitchen assignments were typed and tacked up on the wall. Tracy Anne and Rit DeRusso were by the food pantry trying to figure out how much soy-and-chickpea casserole it would take to feed twenty-five people. Tracy Anne was still in her sweatshirt and panties. If she didn't have leafleting duty or another reason to leave the house she stayed in her panties at least till noon. Sarah thought it was funny but some of the other women weren't so generous.

"We cook and eat communally," said Mark, "both out of principle and because it's much more efficient. A lot less wasted time over the stove. The food is nothing to write home about usually, but I don't imagine it's much at BU either."

"I don't really eat a whole lot," said the girl. "It doesn't interest me."

He believed her. She was long-boned and pale, with eyes held in sullen pouches. If she said that nothing much in the world interested her at the moment he would believe that too. There were so many of them, sad kids with nothing of value to hang on to, nothing to be positive about. The moaners and depressives, the Albert Camus freaks. The luxury of self-induced despair.

"Let's go upstairs."

He asked her why she had chosen to go into journalism. She went blank for a long moment and then said that you had to specialize in something. And her roommate was in journalism. That was it, they could share textbooks. He asked her if there was something else she would rather be doing than going to school. She couldn't think of anything. He asked her if she had any idea what she wanted to do after she was through with school. She said she didn't think that far ahead.

It was clear that he wasn't going to reach her through logical argument. Her defenses, all her years of numbing and denying, of being too cool to get involved, were too strong. But, when he stood close to her and looked down a little too steadily, when he sent out his testing, sexual vibes, he felt her tighten. He got a response. It was a tool like any other part of your personality. There were so many different ways to bring people in, to involve them. Charm and body English was only one of them.

"Originally we only had this second floor," he said when they had climbed the stairs. "Rented it. But the people on the first and third were just single families, they couldn't hack it when the rent went up and had to move out. With everybody putting in something, though, we can afford all three floors. The guy who owns it's an absentee, a real slumlord, so we don't worry about knocking down a wall here and there. Making improvements without his permission."

On the floor of the big meeting room you could see where the old walls had been, where the stove had been taken out. The room was absolutely bare except for a few stained mattresses and the big portable blackboard. Addresses of unemployment offices and day-labor outfits were chalked on it.

"This is where we have group meeting. No distractions. We make decisions about organization policy, have classes in history and political thought, talk over personal things, you know, group dynamics sort of stuff."

"Sounds like school."

Mark gave her a smile. Not his killer smile, he didn't want to shoot his wad too early, but a nice, flirting smile. "There is some education that goes on here. Re-education, actually. People un-learning some of the garbage they've been sold over the years, unlearning some of the more destructive fables they've been taught about America." He touched the girl's arm to lead her to the martial-arts room and saw her flush slightly.

"For instance, take your curriculum at BU. How many courses are offered there that really interest you? That you think are worth your parents' money?"

He saw that he'd struck a nerve with the parents'-money line. Good. It was more leverage he could use to pry her loose.

"Not many," she said. She shrugged. "There's none that I'm too excited about."

"You stay there another couple years and your answer will be the same. Oh, every once in a while a good course, a good teacher, will sneak through. But only till the word leaks out, and then whatever is honest and valuable about it will be forced under or co-opted. A university is in many ways just like any other busi-ness. It has to constantly be making compromises in order to survive. So you can hardly expect a place like BU to be especially interesting or challenging to someone who's bright enough to see what's coming down in the real world. Someone like yourself, for instance."

It was almost like an instinct with him, all the moves were natural, automatic. Schenk would be horrified at his method of course, Schenk was too much of a purist to admit the amount of soft-sell hype and ego-tickling that was necessary to build an organization. Schenk wanted everybody to choose sides and boogie on the basis of the plain facts. Schenk was a moralist, though he'd never admit it. But the fact was that there were a lot of angles to practical politics, and sex was one of them. Ira Wein could write a monograph on it some time, *Seduction and Ideol-ogy: The Personal/Political Dynamic in Peer-Group Formation.* Mark led the girl into the martial-arts room.

The floor was covered with old canvas wrestling mats, the radiator and windowsill were padded with towels. King was showing a couple of the younger kids, the shock troops, how to crush someone's windpipe with a forearm blow.

[78]

"We feel that for a mind to function at its proper level, the body has to be functioning too," said Mark.

"HEUAGGGGH!" King snapped his elbow up and followed with a hand slash.

"We use martial arts mostly for the kind of self-confidence and control they give you."

"HEUAGGGGGGGH!" went the line of kids behind King.

"We feel, somewhat like the Panthers, that we have the right, no, the responsi*bil*ity, to defend ourselves. Which unfortunately has become a necessity given the political climate these days."

"HWUUUUUUUNK! HRAAAAAAA! HWEEEEEEEEE!"

"I'll show you our printing press."

Mark wasn't so crazy about the whole martial-arts bit but Schenk had a case for it and it was good for the shock troops to blow off steam when they got antsy. And it was a way to get most of the Eastern mysticism crap that was floating around lately out of their systems. King gave them a little karate-is-a-thing-of-the-spirit rap and they seemed satisfied. The number of potential activists being sedated with that TM type of bullshit was appalling.

He asked the girl if there were a lot of people into Eastern religion at BU. She said she didn't know the numbers but it seemed very popular. Her roommate was doing Zen and had put burlap over all the mirrors in their room one night. A reminder of the insignificance of self.

Grant Parke was smeared with ink and oil, sitting on the floor in the little printing room. He was trying to fix the press, which had been choking on paper again.

"Say hey, buddy," he said, "whatcha got there? Some new blood for the Big Red Machine?"

"Never mind him," said Mark. "He thinks he's a comedian."

"Never mind him," said Grant Parke, "he thinks he's a socialist."

"This is where we turn out our newspaper and our pamphlets," said Mark. "Our information center. In order to help the people, often in order to make them see that they *need* help, we have to educate them. It sounds a little condescending, but it's not."

Schenk would say propaganda. Schenk would ignore twenty years of American conditioning against the word and slap it down on the table. Another reason why he'd never get to be a leader. "What it actually is," said Mark, "is just another form of aid to working people. Knowledge is power."

"And power corrupts," said Grant Parke. "You can figure out the rest of the equation for yourself."

Mark took the girl's arm and led her up to the top floor.

There were no doors on the third floor rooms. A Navaho blanket hung for privacy over the bathroom entrance. You hooked it up if the toilet was unoccupied. With twenty-five people and only one bathroom it was almost always full.

There were pots and bowls under the places where the roof leaked, they plinked in a complicated rhythm. Mattresses, sleeping bags, clothes and blankets lay scattered in small groupings in the rooms and hallways. People slept where they wanted, with who they wanted. There were no rules, no big deal was made about it like Weatherman was starting to do.

Sarah was up there working on the new kid, the hillbilly she pulled in out of the rain a while back. Mark had to smile to himself, he and Sarah both up there playing the same game at the same time. Recruiting. Between his young girls and Sarah's boys they had probably brought in half of the shock troops and a few of the older members. The only difference was that Sarah was almost totally unaware of what she was doing, she thought it was the politics, the ideals that she talked. The uses of seduction, Mark thought. Ends and means.

Not that he ended up sleeping with any of the girls. It wasn't necessary in order to hook them in, the come-on was enough, and now that he had Sarah he didn't personally need it anymore. There had been a time, a couple ego-tripping years, but that was over.

So he sat the girl down — he had forgotten her name, too bad, the name was always a nice touch, but he could glide around it easy enough — he sat the girl down just within earshot of Sarah and the West Virginian kid. Hobie, his name was, seemed like a nice enough kid. And it was refreshing not to have to listen to another set of middle-class suburban horror stories. Drifted in from coal-mining country. It was obvious the kid had a heavy case for Sarah, so he might stick.

The girl asked Mark what was in the cellar.

[80]

He smiled. "That's sort of our brain center," he said. Schenk would be down there. He'd just as soon not have to introduce her to Schenk. No use in upsetting him, in having to go through that no-personal-statements argument again.

"There's nothing really to see," said Mark, "just a bunch of New Lefties arguing over how many revisionists can dance on the head of a pin."

The girl forced a little laugh. Good, she didn't get the allusion but she was putting herself out for him. Easy pickings, ripe for the Movement, he'd known it the minute he saw her standing in the rain on the front steps.

She asked him if Third Way had a long-term goal.

He had taken her to the top floor. Let her have it. "We want to help make America into a socialist, humanist state. We want to change the existing order so that it works for the people instead of against them." He knew Sarah could hear him, knew she'd be listening, eating it up. "We want to help people win back control over their own lives."

"And how do you plan to do that?"

He gave her the killer smile then, sat on a mattress and patted it for her to sit beside him. She left her chair and sat, closer than he thought she would. Not much of a challenge. But the Movement needed them all, easy-come and hard-to-get. Though it wasn't a game there were elements of play, of sport even, and he was a natural.

"Maybe if I tell you some of the history of the Movement," said Mark Remington, "tell it through my own point of view and experience, it will help you to —"

Smiling, touching, reeling her in.

10

It was raining in Boston when Hunter pulled into the Greyhound, looked to have been raining for a good long while. The
man behind the counter gave him a once-over, then told directions. "The Courier," he said, "most of the transients go down
there." Hunter wished there'd been a chance to shave on the bus
trip.

There was a steady drizzle coming down as Hunter crossed
over head of the turnpike extension to where the Hotel Courier
stood dwarfing most everything around it at the mouth of Chandler Street. Its stone was dirty tan in a red-brick neighborhood,
lying directly across from the long warehouse of the Morgan
Memorial Goodwill. Clothes spilled out onto the front parking
lot from the Goodwill's big hangar doors, humps and tangles of
clothes muffling the rain's splat, harboring puddles. An old man
with a yellow slicker hat on was slowly tearing plastic trash-liner
bags into sheets and covering the clothes with them. He hadn't
gotten very far.

Hunter turned his face up for the rain, hoping it would wake
him some. They'd put the heat on the whole way in the bus and
all the windows were stuck shut. He'd always liked the rain
before, wet air kept the coal dust down in the shaft and there was
less chance for explosions. But the last couple years, with the
stripping, the rain washed red dog down on them, washed acid
into the streams. He didn't like it so much anymore.

ABSOLUTELY No, said the sign over the lobby desk, SMOKING,
COOKING, VISITORS ALLOWED IN ROOMS. A fat, foreign-looking man
got up from his little TV set to take the money and sign Hunter
in. Hunter thought a minute when he got to the space that said
Occupation, then wrote Coal Miner. He'd asked for a month and

they'd given him two weeks. There's a lot of fellas can do the work, they said. The union rep said there was no language in the contract to cover it. Hurry back.

The room was on the fourth floor, the elevator didn't work. Hunter was a little out of breath after the stairs.

There was a bed, a dresser with a scuffed mirror attached, a sink, a lamp and a wooden chair. The sink smelled like urine. Hunter sat in the bucket the center of the bed made and took a towel from his suitcase to dry his hair. It had been a while since he was in a hotel room. He hadn't been in many. He opened the top drawer of the dresser and found an old girlie magazine under the phone book. Black garter belts and mesh stockings. There was a small picture hung over the door, Jesus in a meadow with a flock of sheep. There was something written on it he couldn't make out from the bed. Jesus looked very young and smiling.

The first hotel Hunter'd been in he was just eighteen, gone into Beckley with Molly Buntin. They were married though — it was Molly McNatt. She was sixteen. When he explained the situation Ray had understood, had given him a loan from out his Army severance pay to have a weekend at the King Coal Hotel. They'd signed up under age together after Pearl, Hunter and Ray, thumbing up to Charleston, each afraid to back down in front of the other. It was no problem getting in, everybody knew those hill people didn't keep birth records. Besides, there was a war on.

The King Coal Hotel was pretty new then, in '47, the carpet was bright blue and the elevator run smooth and they even had little black boys in uniforms to carry your bags if you wanted. The rate was steep, but Hunter felt it was worth it. Knowing Molly and what she came from like he did, he didn't see any other way to get it done.

"Won't be long now," the fellas out front of the dry goods would call, "won't be long fore little Molly find out that it int only Jesus can rise again. Int only the Holy Light can make a woman speak in tongues."

But how could she, how could she with her mama and daddy just on the other side of the wall? With her little sisters out on the kitchen floor and all Ten Commandments done in samplers

[83]

hung around the house? With this or that local Hell-an-damnation preacher spearing chicken at the dinner table every Saturday night? It would be hard enough to live there till they got on their own feet, but no, not the first nights.

"One sure thing with that Molly," they'd say, winking and showing their gums, "you gonna be the one to get there first. Gon be openin up new territory there."

So he borrowed off Ray and took her from all her home and her religion into Beckley for the weekend. They sat by each other on the bus, Molly looking nice in the green dress Mrs. Buntin made for her graduation, hardly speaking till the outskirts of the city appeared.

"Hunter," said Molly then, "what if they don't believe us? That we're married?"

"We are."

"But what if when they see us, they don't believe us? What do we do?"

It hadn't occurred to Hunter. She looked like a dressed-up high school girl to him and he figured a desk clerk would see the same. He wished he had worn his uniform like so many of the other fellas were doing. They probably wouldn't question you if you had the uniform on.

"Maybe we could call back to the post office and they could run somebody down to fetch your mother, and she could tell the hotel people on the telephone."

"Oh Hunter, I *could*n't."

"What if we had them get Reverend Wattles?"

"*Hun*ter! Are you crazy? I'd just *die*."

"Well we *are* married. They have to believe us."

"And if they don't?"

"If they don't? If they don't, then I'll do something."

She was satisfied with that, she didn't need to know what he'd do. It wasn't her problem now.

His hand shook the slightest bit when he signed the register but there wasn't any fuss.

"I feel like we fooled em," said Molly in the elevator, "like we pulled somethin over." Then she covered her mouth because the little elevator boy was in with them. There were a lot of fellas in

[84]

uniform, walking with their girls in the lobby and halls and Molly guessed out loud which ones looked married and which didn't while Hunter told her to shush and she got to giggling. She giggled and held his hand and told how she hadn't ever been in a hotel before and was glad Hunter had been around and knew what he was doing. He didn't bother to set her straight on that.

The room was small but nice, with two beds and a dresser with a mirror attached and a sink and a lamp and an old Atwater Kent radio. And the bathroom, said the bellhop, was right next door. There was a Gideon Bible on the dresser that Hunter stuck in a drawer when Molly looked out their window. The boy left and shut the door behind him and Molly burst into giggles. Hunter had to smile but he couldn't come right out and laugh. He was supposed to be in charge. Molly plopped on the bed nearest the door and began to bounce up and down.

"They're real springy," she said. "Which one do you want?" She looked more like a little girl than ever, bouncing and grinning wide, and Hunter got the feeling that was exactly what she was trying for.

"I kind of figured we'd push them together."

"Oh." She stopped bouncing. "Sure. But which *side* do you want?"

"You pick. I'll take what's left."

Molly said she didn't want to have to decide anything yet.

Molly got real busy and real happy again, hanging their clothes on the little bar that served for a closet, testing the lamp, testing the hot and cold water, reading out loud the house rules tacked on the door. Hunter managed to kick the Bible behind the dresser before Molly came over to look in all the drawers. She talked mile-a-minute as she moved, about how her daddy always stayed in a hotel when he was up to Charleston and she'd always wondered what it was like, about how somebody they'd never know had been in here last night and who might they be and wasn't it a little spooky to think about. Molly talked too fast and her voice went too high and she flitted from object to object while Hunter sat on the bed and watched her.

She asked if he'd like to hear the radio and he said he didn't think he would. There was a silence then and she stood in the middle of the room, all moved in and nothing left to do. "I wonder," she said, "if maybe we shouldn't go look around town a bit. See where the churches are for tomorrow."

"We can take a look later. C'mere and sit down, Molly."

She sat by him with her hands folded on her lap. She looked like she expected to be spanked. "I promised Mama I wouldn't miss church."

"You won't. Don't worry."

She sat next to him on the hotel bed, thin and dark-haired in the graduation dress Mrs. Buntin had made. Hunter had to laugh to himself, thinking of stern Mrs. Buntin sewing the dress, never thinking it would end up here, that Hunter McNatt would be taking it off her daughter. He'd had Mrs. Buntin for eighth grade, the last year he'd gone to school, and he couldn't remember her smiling once. She'd rapped him with a yardstick a couple times. Taking Mrs. Buntin's daughter to bed in a hotel room. Hunter went hard in his pants thinking about it. He looked at Molly. Molly looked straight ahead. For a moment the idea of her being scared and shameful, maybe even fighting a little was exciting. Here she was with him, there was nothing she could do. No one — Mr. and Mrs. Buntin, Jesus, the law — no one could stop him. Hunter had never felt that kind of power over a female before and it made him hard in his pants. He could feel, just sitting there, how much stronger he was and thought of taking hold of her long hair and pulling her down under him, just doing it.

But she'd kept him company when he was lonely and admired him when he was sorry and out of work and she was brave against her parents when they'd forbid her to go out with him. He took her hand.

"I bet — I bet of all the rooms there are," he said, "hotel rooms are the happiest." It sounded like the start of a children's story, but he went on. "I'm sure that the people who go through them are the happiest so it figures that it must rub off on the rooms."

"You think so?"

"Uh-huh. In a hotel room you can put your feet up on the furniture. You can throw your clothes on the floor and not pick them up. You can play the radio after ten o'clock or yell as loud as you want to."

Molly smiled a little. "You can?"

"Sure." He tried to think of something else he wasn't allowed to do as a child. "You can eat crackers in bed."

"We don't have any crackers."

"We can get some. We can get anything we want and bring it up here and eat it and leave the crumbs on the sheets. We can pee in the sink if we want to."

"*Hunt*er!"

"We can. We can do anything we want and nobody sees us or knows us. That's why hotel rooms are so happy. People just come in and have a good time."

"People like us."

"Fellas and their girls. Like us."

"Married ones."

"Some of em. Some of em not. They all have a good time though."

"Who has a better time?"

"Oh, I'd say it's the ones that aren't married."

"Hunter! You teasin me."

"Why would I do that? Why couldn't it be more fun if they's not married? Anyhow, you'll never know."

Molly considered that a moment. "We could pretend," she said. "Pretend we didn't have the service."

"Pretend that I just slick-talked you into comin out with me —"

"But I didn't know what you had in mind —"

"That I knew your mama'd never have me so I tricked you away —"

"Took me off to a hotel, all *kinds* of wicked thoughts in your mind —"

"Lied to the desk clerk —"

"Fed me some story and took me up to the room —"

"Poo-er little innocent wide-eyed schoolgirl, tremblin and scared what's gonna happen next —"

"What he's gonna *do* me —"

"Settin defenseless on the bed in a hotel room miles from home."

"We could do that, Hunter. We could pretend."

"We could do anything we wanted to."

Molly was ready then when he touched her, and it was better than the other way because even though he felt her still being scared she smiled sometimes during it and held him so hard it left marks. The only hitch was when somebody went into the bathroom next door and you could hear every move they made and Molly stopped dead. Hunter thought he'd have to start from scratch but then Molly giggled. It was a different kind of giggle, not so little-girl as before, and they went on a little quieter.

By Sunday evening she'd begun to make extra noise when someone was in the bathroom, ignoring Hunter's shushing and getting them both laughing.

"It's the last I'll be able to make a racket for a while," she said. "Mamma'd call the Sheriff we did it at home like this." Molly missed church that morning and had stopped blushing when Hunter caught her looking at a part of him. "I want to live in a hotel all the time," she said, "I wisht we could afford it. Get over here Hunter, you're slidin down in the crack. That's one thing though, we live in a hotel, I want just one big bed instead of two you got pushed together."

"Like a duck to water," Hunter kept saying all weekend. "Like a duck to water."

It was quieter but just as fine living with the Buntins. In fact, holding in the sound added something to it, like they were kids trying to have an after-bedtime pillow fight without getting caught. They'd pet in the parlor till Mr. and Mrs. turned in, then tiptoe over Molly's sleeping sisters to their bed. Sometimes when they wanted to see each other and where things went they'd tent under the covers with a flashlight till it got too hard to breathe. Molly tried to get to their sheets before Mrs. Buntin's washday and do them herself. Especially the one with *King Coal Hotel* on it that they'd taken for a souvenir.

Later, with their own place and Hunter at the mine, with Darwin and then Hobie to be quiet for, it was even better. Not so often maybe, but better, more relaxed and giving, with the fact of the two sons adding something to it. Sometimes Hunter would come back so tired from the mine that she'd just take his head in her lap while she knitted in bed. He nuzzled his face into her belly now and then to kiss it and that would be their loving for the night. And then they figured out that Molly could go on

[88]

top, which was nice in its own way and saved him the muscle strain.

Three, four years it was good like that, but to Hunter it seemed a weekend's memory. And the other, the bad time, seemed to of lasted forever.

Hunter had to take a leak and went out to search for a bathroom, locking the door behind him. He followed his nose down the hall and to the left till he found a tiny closet with a toilet in it. The bowl was dry and jammed with a huge log of shit, the smell kept Hunter in the hallway. Finding nothing to poke it apart with, he held the doorframe and stretched his leg in to push the flush handle with his foot. No reaction. He kicked the lid down, shut the bathroom door and went back to his room.

"I was goin to exercise my squatters' rights," Woody Estill might have said, "when what should I find but the grandaddy of all turds a settin there before me. Looked to be a fifty-pounder, so old it had whiskers, grinnin up at me while the paint is peelin offen the walls."

They'd of all trooped in to see it, the fellas at the mine, and pretty soon someone would pin it on Luther.

"Only one man is got that much shit in im in the first place," they'd say. "Luther, you look like you lost some weight, buddy."

"Luther done shat his brains out."

"Hell, I don't see no peas in the bowl, do you?"

Hunter wondered how they were doing, the fellas, how they would make out with him gone. He missed them. Wasn't that something? Hadn't even considered it when he left. Bunch of sorry-lookin, garbage-mouth coal miners and he missed them. Oh, they'd do okay, as well as ever, without Hunter McNatt around. The world didn't stop for Ray getting canned, it wouldn't stop for him. The coal would get mined, the election played out. It didn't need him to go on.

Hunter locked himself in his hotel room. He ran both faucets and pissed in the sink.

Hmmmmm! said the cartoon-bubble scrawled above Jesus as he beamed at his flock, *lamb stew tonite*. The old keyhole was covered with a Band-Aid, a new brass lock system above it on the door. In the second drawer of the dresser there was a bloody

[89]

hunk of gauze pad gnarled in tape. Somebody in the next room was coughing.

The last time Hunter had been in a hotel room was two years ago. The King Coal Hotel in Beckley. The elevator clanked and shuddered, the carpet was worn gray and the hot water shut off for hours at a time. You carried your own bags. The doctors said it would be any day and there was a rule against sleeping over in the hospital. Hunter took a week's rate at the King Coal and called Hobie every day when the boy got out of school.

"She's fine," Hunter would say, "sleeping mostly, not in any pain." He was careful never to let the wrong tone into his voice, to let the impatience show. To let on that another day of it was the last thing on earth he wanted. "She doing just fine, son. You be by the phone tomorrow."

It had started with Hobie, or at least dated from him. Molly still recovering from the birth, complications, and the doctors saying it was just some normal female troubles. Hunter was surprised at how involved all that business was on a woman when they explained it to him. Molly losing weight. The bleeding. Like her monthlies but unpredictable, ruining their souvenir sheet one night she didn't even wake up. Then the first looks of accusation when he'd touch her a certain way, the first shift of her feelings.

"Maybe we shouldn't, Hunt."

"The doctor says it's okay. The bleedin's stopped."

"There's no babies in it anymore."

"Does that matter? The doctors said —"

"It's not the doctors I'm thinkin of, Hunt."

She'd brung out all the holiness pictures she'd stored away when they first got married and put them up on the bedroom walls. Hunter didn't say anything, but when she began to go back to church every Sunday he wouldn't go with her. "I keep my own faith," he said.

It wasn't perfect but it was livable. There was work and the boys growing up. Sometimes, maybe once a month or so, she'd turn to him if he touched. But even then she was careful not to let herself go, to enjoy it.

Sometimes it would be stinging bad and she'd sit in the middle of the bed with her knees drawn up tight and rock slowly while she sang.

> *Give me strength, O God, my savior,*
> *Make me deaf to Satan's lies.*
> *Strike me blind to evil visions,*
> *Save Thy kingdom for mine eyes.*

The more it hurt the louder she would sing, starting from a near whisper to the point where Hunter could hear her clear out on the front porch. It was like she thought the sound could keep the pain away. If he went in, those loud times, she would just stare at him dully and keep rocking, keep singing.

> *Help me feel not gross temptation,*
> *Let not lust within me dwell.*
> *Keep me pure, O Lord, I beg thee,*
> *Lest I join the damned in Hell.*

Molly lost weight. They had her into Beckley for tests and made the new diagnosis. It was the cancer, they said, but every day there was new ways found to treat it. Hunter and Molly went in separate to talk with the doctors cause it shamed her too much. All that talk about her private parts. The bleeding had started again and the smell, the smell appeared for the first time. Sort of like her monthlies had been but different, something else in it that was bad. You could only smell if you got right down close, which Hunter almost never did, or if it come onto the sheets at night. Molly always did the sheets separate from the rest of the wash, when the boys weren't around.

They never talked about it, she had closed up against him. But Hunter got the whole story from the looks she gave him at bedtime, from the prayers he overheard. It wasn't so much that she'd done it, there was a wife's duty and there was the boys to show for it, but she'd gone and enjoyed it. Thought about it when he wasn't even there, planned ways and times for it. Hunter, he'd encouraged her, led her into wickedness only feet away from her own mama and daddy, helped bring her to her present state of punishment. Oh, the punishment fit the crime all right.

"Forgive me Lord for my sinful pride and desire," she would whisper through tears when she thought Hunter was asleep. "Please have mercy and stop this burnin inside me. Make me clean again, Lord, make me clean."

Sometimes it made him hurt to see her so thin, to see her set her teeth against the pain, but he never showed her when he cried. He never showed the boys. Her looks and her prayers did make him feel guilty though he knew there'd been no sin. He never felt sorry for himself when he had to pay, when he had to work cleanup and extra overtime to pay for a new treatment all the way up in Charleston.

She had him get two separate beds, selling off the big double they'd bought when they moved from the Buntins'. She said she'd sleep better, and though he never told her, Hunter was just as happy. She was so thin he could feel her bones and the smell was worse now. Her breath held it, and her sweat, all her clothes smelled of her sickness. It was years of doctors, then, and years of preachers. If the gang at one hospital couldn't come up with a miracle soon enough she'd hop to another. There were remissions, months of peace and no bleeding, then it would come back even stronger. One cure left her with no hair on her privates, another made hair sprout from her chest. She lost weight and smelled bad. Finally she hopped so much that only the people in Beckley would take her, and with them it was a matter of "controlling the symptoms."

Years of preachers. Jesus returned to Molly's life with a vengeance. If Reverend Mooney at the Pentecostal Holiness Church couldn't cast out her devils, then maybe Reverend Tyrell at the Free Will Baptist could. Or maybe the power rested in Reverend Boggs at the Evangelist Full Gospel Tabernacle or maybe that new young fella they got at the Spiritual United Church of Christ Zion. She prayed and shouted and cried, she rolled on the floor with colored ladies while deacons draped white cloths to cover their naked kicking legs from mortal eyes. Hunter and the boys learned never to blaspheme under her roof, learned to tolerate whichever new Bible-thumper had become their regular Saturday night dinner guest.

Years of all that, Molly thin and bitter like a disease in the house. Filling it up with her pain and her Jesus till the boys stayed late as they could at sports and Hunter changed to evening shift at the mine. Molly rose at ten, went to bed at eight. They made their own meals, lots of fried eggs and potatoes, peanut-butter sandwiches. Talking was always hushed, lights always dim. Till the end, with Molly in the intensive care room and Hunter in the King Coal Hotel. Intensive care was to isolate the smell, there was nothing left to be done. The whole room smelled of it, thick and sweet, as if the room itself was some diseased chamber in a huge, dying woman. Molly lay shrunken in the middle of the smell, her face bony, dry. She looked to Hunter like an ancient monkey.

"Molly. You wake?"

Her eyes never quite focused anymore, milky with all the drugs they pumped into her. "Hunter."

"How you feeling?"

Her pupils were little pinspecks in the filmy blue. "Floatin. Only part of me I can feel is when it hurts. Down there."

"Hobie called, said hi." Hunter covered the knob of her shoulder with the blanket. "Are you scared?"

"No. Not anymore. Hunter? You do somethin for me?"

"Sure."

"You open the windas in here? I can't bear to be surrounded by it."

The windows were already wide open. "Sure honey."

"I don't want to die surrounded with all that sin in the air. That's what it smelt like, Hunter, that's what it smelt like to God the first time I done wrong. That bad. If I had only known. But we're only just mortals, we don't have the nose for sin the Lord does. Takes us so long to sense it. So long to die."

"That's nothin to worry about. You just having a bad spell. You've had them before."

"Oh Hunter, don't. Don't you fight the Lord's will. It's a blessing, it is. And we both need the rest."

She talked to him in a high, far-off-sounding voice, like she was lost deep in a fog and calling out. Hunter took shallow little mouth breaths to keep from gagging and sat by her till her eyes dropped shut. He stayed at the King Coal watching TV with the old men in the lobby and drinking warm beer in his room till one night she went out. Went out in a fog.

There was sand in the sheets when Hunter peeled the top cover down, he swatted it off with the side of his hand. In the third and last drawer of the dresser rolled an empty quart bottle of Thunderbird.

It was a man coughing in the next room and it hurt to hear him. Long wracking spasms from the bottom of his lungs. What the fellas at the mine called a twenty-year cough.

Hunter flipped through the phonebook. There were so many names, there looked to be more John J. Sheehans here than there were *people* back home. He took the address of the police headquarters and the number for Missing Persons. He would start in the morning. Hunter flipped through the pages, there was an off chance that Darwin had taken a number, that he had an address that could be tracked down. Hunter looked but there was nothing at all in the Boston phonebook between *McNary* and *McNaught.*

Hunter opened his window so he could smell the rain and began to unpack his suitcase. He spread the pictures out on top of the dresser. Last year's basketball team with Hobie circled in red, holding the ball. The picture Hinkle gave him from Hobie's ninth-grade file when he went to tell the high school. He didn't look too much older now. The snapshot Delia Cutlip had given him, Delia and Hobie holding hands on a field trip to Harpers Ferry. That was all he had to show. He had a picture of Darwin too just in case, boot-camp haircut and parade dress. He had his money.

The man in the next room coughed and choked. There was always somebody coughing. Back home it was like another language the men had in common, in a meeting or church service they could be heard hacking out their code over the words. Nobody thought a thing of it. But here it sounded different, the coughing, it was hopeless sounding. It was a man alone in a hotel room.

11

Hobie was in the parlor sorting leaflets when Mr. and Mrs. Ellenbogen knocked to ask if they could see daylight. The A. B. Dick
printing press was so old and abused that every fifth or sixth
leaflet came out illegible, and Hobie was assigned to glean the
smear-copies out before the new line hit the streets. They'd
begun to call the machine Sticky Dicky.

"Pardon?" The rule was that you didn't let anybody in without some kind of confirmation, no matter how revolutionary they
might look. The man was wearing a well-pressed baby-blue jean
suit with a brown, soft-covered coat over his arm. Suede, like
Hush Puppies were. He had bushy sideburns that were perfect
silver from the top of his ears down. The woman looked a couple
years older than the man, wearing a sort of grayish car coat.
Hobie only opened the door a crack.

"Daylight. We were told she was living here." The man spoke
from the top step of the porch. The woman stood on the sidewalk, looking grimly into space. "We're Mr. and Mrs. Ellenbogen. Her parents?"

"You mean *Deb*bie?"

The man, Mr. Ellenbogen, smiled and nodded his head a lot,
like he'd gotten something across to someone who didn't speak
his language. "She's Debbie again, that's good to hear." He called
down to the woman. "You hear that, honey? She's Debbie again."
He turned to Hobie. "All last year she decided she wanted to be
called Daylight." Mr. Ellenbogen's smile never quite left, the way
you'd do with a foreigner so that even if they didn't understand
the words they'd see you meant well. "She had a friend who
changed her name to Rain. Rain Abramowitz, and another who
decided to be Freedom. Freedom — what was her last name,
dear? The little blond girl?"

"Van Voorst." Mrs. Ellenbogen didn't look up.

"Right. Freedom Van Voorst. She just told us one morning to call her Daylight from then on out," he shrugged, "so what can you do? I had to reintroduce her to all of our friends. So. She's Debbie again?"

"She's here."

"Do you think we could see her?"

With the way he was smiling it was like he was asking Hobie permission. It was a funny feeling, an older fella like that. "I'll go see," said Hobie. And then, deciding that it couldn't hurt any, "Why don't you come on in and wait?"

Downstairs was pretty barren looking, no one used it for their actual living area. There were the piles of leaflets that Hobie had been working on, plus all the scattered back issues of Wein's underground-press collection on the floor. The *New Left Review* and *Ramparts* and *Black Panther* and *The Movement* and *The National Guardian* and *I. F. Stone's Weekly* and *Venture* and *Challenge* and *Old Mole* and *The Fire Next Time*. They had all been kicked against one plaster-crumbling wall to make way for the guerrilla-theater group Miriam had invited last week. The stuffed effigy of a policeman hung down in the center of the room. There was a meat cleaver stuck in its forehead.

The man stuffed his hands in his pockets and smiled and looked around.

"God give me strength," said Mrs. Ellenbogen.

Hobie started up the stairs.

"Say uh — could I ask a favor — could you hold on there a sec?" Mr. Ellenbogen had awfully good teeth for a man his age. There didn't seem to be a one of them discolored or out of place, and you could tell they were real when he smiled.

"Sir?"

"Uh — could you — uh, what's your name again?"

"Hobie."

"Hobie. Great. Hobie, do you think you could — when Debbie comes down, if she wants to come down — do you think —" he lowered his voice so much that Hobie had to step back down to floor level to hear, "— think you could, you know, sort of hang around? I mean just be here? Things can get pretty hot, parents and their kids and all, and maybe if you were here as sort of a — a — disinterested ob*serv*er, it would uh — help. Help keep things on a civil plane. Dayl — *Deb*bie — can get pretty upset. You probably know that, though, I don't have to tell you."

Hobie had never seen her do anything but listen and take orders.

"Are you the one?" Mrs. Ellenbogen had finally focused on something. On Hobie.

"M'am?"

"Are you the one she left for? Are you her —" She searched a long time for the word, then gave up. "Boyfriend?"

"No."

"I'd like to see him. Tell her I'd like to see him, whoever he is, who could make her walk away from her education. He must be something. I'd like to see him, he really must be something."

Debbie had come to the group on her own as far as he knew, alone off the street. Hobie decided she'd have to explain that to her mother herself and hurried up the stairs.

Debbie and Tracy Anne and Jennifer and a few of the other younger girls were sitting doing criticism/self-criticism. Hobie knelt to whisper in her ear.

"Oh shit. What do they want?"

Hobie shrugged.

Debbie stood up from the group. "Hobie, would you do me a favor? Would you sort of hover in the background for me? I don't want to have to go through a whole big scene or anything, and maybe if there's a stranger in the room they'll be embarrassed. Would you?"

"No sweat."

Debbie was wearing one of the men's flannel shirts and a crusted pair of jeans she hadn't changed since she'd been at the house. There were big blowouts where the back pockets used to be and you could see that she was getting zits on her bottom. She was a serious one and hadn't ever said much to Hobie.

Debbie stopped and stood firm three steps from the floor. Hobie had to squeeze past her to get down to the piles of leaflets. Mr. Ellenbogen smiled broadly and pulled his hands out of his pockets like he was going to go hug her. He settled for a little wave. "Debbie."

"What do you want?"

Debbie stood on her step with her arms crossed in front of her. Mr. was at the foot of the steps, shifting his weight from side to side. Mrs. stood by the door with her arms crossed in front of her, looking solemnly up at her daughter. Hobie went through the leaflets as quiet as he could manage.

"Just to talk, Debbie," said Mr., "just to talk. Your mother and I — we heard from your roommate where you were, and we came to talk."

"I told her not to say."

"She was worried about you. We're — your mother and I — we were worried about you too."

"I'm all right."

"We would have called — we tried to —"

"They turned it off."

"Oh."

"We voted not to pay the bill."

"Oh."

"And they voted to turn it off," said Mrs. Ellenbogen. "The telephone company."

"So what do you want? What do you want to talk about?"

"Where is he?" said Mrs. "I wanted to get a look at him."

Debbie looked to Hobie for a clue. Hobie sorted paper.

"He said he's not the one. I want to see the one you left for."

"I didn't leave for any*body*. I left for the Revolution."

Mrs. gave a little snorting laugh through her nose. "And which revolution is that?"

"If you don't know, it's too late to teach you." Debbie kept a perfect poker face.

"So you're the teacher now? Three months in college and already she's a teacher. Very impressive. College has come a long way."

"You never went."

"If I had I never would have left it for some boy."

"I didn't leave for a boy. You wouldn't understand but that's the way it is."

"You're right. I wouldn't understand. But of course *I* didn't go to college for three whole —"

"I don't think she means that as a putdown, dear, I —"

"Don't condescend to her!" Debbie barked it out at them. Mr.

[98]

Ellenbogen put his hands back in his pockets. "She can handle what I'm saying as well as you can. It's sickening the way you always do that."

"Don't talk that way to your father."

"And don't you defend him. There's no reason you should put up with that shit."

Mr. Ellenbogen winced.

"So there's not a boy?" said Mrs.

"There are a lot of men and a lot of women living here. We think of monogamy as an unnatural, counterrevolutionary state. We think it's a very destructive situation, that it only leads to misery. *That* you two should understand just fine. If you're interested in who I'm sleeping —"

"Your dog died," said Mr. Ellenbogen quickly. "We tried to call, but the phone — we thought you'd want to know."

"Oh."

"She was so old, it was best — her hind legs — we tried to phone. We decided she had to be taken, your mother took her, and we thought you'd want to be in on the decision." Debbie looked at him. "She was so old."

"It's okay," said Debbie.

"Your mother had to take her. I said I would but I just couldn't seem to — always one more day. Some days she could get up and move around the kitchen a little, and she could wag her tail and recognize your voice right to the end, even though her eyes were gone. I just couldn't do it, and the boys, they're too young yet — so I came home one day and she was gone. Your mother —"

"It's all right. Animals die. Everybody dies."

Mr. Ellenbogen nodded to himself like he'd never realized that before, like Debbie was real sharp for having figured it out.

"The boys miss you," said Mrs.

"We miss you," said Mr. "We worry about you."

"Don't. I don't belong to you anymore. I belong to the Revolution."

Mrs. Ellenbogen rolled her eyes to the ceiling and sighed out loud.

"Tell the boys to come and see me if they want. I'd like to talk with them, see what they're into."

"They're doing great," said Mr. "Stewie's probably going to be All-County."

Debbie took that bit of news in stride. "I'd like to talk with them," she said. "It might not be too late to save them."

"And it's too late for us I suppose? We're doomed. Who appointed *you* judge, jury and executioner?" Mrs. looked very tired, like she had been crying for a long time and had only just stopped to dry her eyes. "What did we do that all of a sudden you hate us?"

"It's not you," said Debbie. "It's what you represent. It's not even hate. You can't help what you are, that's too bad, but that doesn't change the fact that the whole class has to die."

"What class?"

"The whole white ruling class in this country. And that includes those of the white working class who can't get beyond their racism and see who their real oppressors are. It's the only way it's going to happen and it's happening right now. The people are going to win and you and the rest of the oppressors like you are going to have to go. A lot of people will have to die. It's the only way. I may have to die, all of us here may have to die, to participate in our own destruction, because we're too contaminated by our backgrounds to change. The Revolution will purge itself and we may have to go too. But it's inevitable."

"They've replaced her with a robot," said Mrs. "They took my daughter and they replaced her with a robot."

"Listen, you were always on my tail when I was growing up, do your homework, assert yourself, be a success, don't pass up opportunities, use your potential! Well I'm finally *using* my potential, using myself for something that matters. You ought to be happy. If you accomplished one thing in all those years of telling me not to end up like you did it was to make me unwilling to settle for anything but *win*ning. So I've joined the winning side, I've joined the people. You ought to be happy."

"But from a robot you wouldn't feel hate. From a robot —"

Debbie smiled and shook her head sadly. "I don't hate you. I don't even dislike you. I pity you."

"I don't have to listen to this," said Mrs. to Mr. "I'll be in the car." She turned and opened the door to the street. "And just you save your pity, Miss, for somebody who needs it. I don't want to be pitied by anyone I'm helping to support." She closed the door behind her.

"She uh — she *does* have a bit of a point there, Deb." Mr. Ellenbogen spoke in a reasonable tone of voice. Mr. Hinkle used to talk that way to fellas in school who hated each other's guts, used to try and make light of their fighting. "I mean, criticizing when you're still on the receiving end of all that — not that there's anything wrong with criticism, mind you, within certain bounds it's very healthy — but when you're still on the — the family payroll, so to speak, it's a little — well — hypo*crit*ical is not quite the word I want, but you *can* see her point, can't you Deb? I don't mean to put anything on a purely economical basis, I mean we're a family, we love you —"

"You can stop the checks," she said. "I won't be accepting them anymore. I've collected all the things I bought before, with your money. I'll bring them down."

"No, Deb, I didn't mean to — there's no need —" Debbie was gone up the stairs.

Mr. Ellenbogen sighed and took another glance around the room. He looked out on the street. He came over and stood by Hobie.

"So," he said. "How long have you been in the Revolution?"

"I been here a week or so."

"This organization, this Third Way — it's pretty radical?"

Hobie shrugged. "More than some. Less than others. I don't know the whole story on it."

"You're Communists?"

"I really can't speak for the group or anything. I'm not a leader. They're — we're — not connected to the Communist Party or anything." Hobie still had trouble with the word. Even with all Sarah's explaining about small-*c* communism and what it meant and that it didn't have to do with Russia at all, even with all that it was hard to say it out loud. An old habit. Like when he was off with King that time and King had the marijuana. It wasn't that it was drugs or that it was against group rules or that he was afraid what it would do to him or anything, it was that you had to *smoke* it. Like a cigarette. Old habits, so that all the while he smoked he was hearing a succession of coaches warning about stunting his growth and wrecking his wind and didn't feel anything but a little sick in his stomach. "What it is, is more like socialism. People gettin control over their own lives."

Mr. Ellenbogen nodded. "That's a very admirable goal. I mean, I'm as liberal as the next guy — of course you've probably heard that before, you probably don't — liberal." He laughed to himself. "We even voted for Stevenson. Debbie came home crying cause she told the class in Show-and-Tell and everybody called her names afterwards. I approve very strongly of your ends, your — idealism — it's great. But your *means*, you kids —" He shook his head. He stopped smiling.

"The thing is, I'm a regular tiger at the office. A troubleshooter, something comes up that nobody else can handle, they send it to Ellenbogen. I can cope. I can analyze, I can delegate. Somebody has to be laid off, to be fired, to be given bad news, they have me take care of it. It's not even my responsibility half the time. I don't miss a day, I enjoy, I *thrive* on it. The Iron Man, they call me. Iron Man Ellenbogen. None of this harried executive, none of this bland diet and fifteen minutes of meditation before a conference. I *give* people ulcers, I don't get them. I'm in control, and trouble is water off a duck's back —

"But at *home* — Debbie, her mother — useless. Helpless. I'm at a total loss, I give in, I throw up my hands. How can you deal with it, with everything going on in the world and family problems and personalities? Who has the know-how or the patience? So I defer. I pass the buck. Her mother is home all day, she's right next to the situation, she should know what's what. She has her ideas about things, how things should be. Very definite ideas. Like Debbie has ideas. They're both like that, definite ideas, won't give an inch, so when they cross swords what can I do? Do you fire a daughter? Do you pink-slip a wife? The boys, I can handle the boys. So far. I'm not making any promises, but so far so good. They've got school, they've got the sports —"

Mr. Ellenbogen sat by Hobie on a stack of leaflets. "You don't know," he said, almost to himself, "you have no idea, what it is like to hear from someone you've held in your arms, from someone you *love*, that they want you out of their life. You're not old enough. To have them talk to you like a stranger, like all of what you've lived together didn't happen, that all the past is *noth*ing to them. Like there's no feeling left." He shook his head.

"She wouldn't go anywhere without that dog. We had to get shots for it, quarantine, the whole thing when we spent the summer in the Caribbean. Used to feed it from her plate. You're too young to know, my friend, you have no idea."

If you really feel that way — his father sitting with elbows on the kitchen table, staring across at Darwin as the sun began to creep into the hollow, both of them hoarse from the night's talking — *if you really feel that way, feel no guilt or remorsefulness at all for what you done — then I don't think we'll ever be able to see eye to eye again. I think we come to a parting of the ways. I think you got to leave.*

"You play sports?"

"Sir?"

"I mean before you joined up here. Did you play sports?"

"Some. I played football mostly."

"My boys play sports, all three of em. Stewie, he's a shoo-in for All-County this year, and the others are coming along fine. It's some joke, the old man has been a total spaz since the year one, the coordination of a five-year-old, and here I've got these three — *jocks*. I didn't know a bounce pass from a bowling ball when they started and now I'm hooked. Season ticket for the Celtics, radio games when I'm driving home, on the banquet committee at the high school, all of a sudden I'm a fanatic. It's great. It's an escape, you know?

"They're cleaning up in their own league this year, no one can touch them. Stewie's averaging twenty-four, twenty-five a game. Of course when they come in here for the Christmas tournaments, run up against some of these all-black teams — I mean it's like a different game. I'm as liberal as the next guy, but —" He laughed. "I said that before, didn't I? I'll level with you, the next guy probably isn't all that liberal. I mean it's not that the *ideas* you kids have got aren't appealing, it's just that I'm sort of automatically — *elim*inated from your supporters. Automatically on the opposite side. She's probably right about that one, Debbie. What can I say? I'm a businessman, I own property, I have a family that I love and I have a big stake in the way things are. So we're on different sides of the fence. I admit it. There's nothing that can be done. I'll grant Debbie the courage of her convictions. It's a wonderful thing to think about other people's welfare, it's something we always tried to teach her. If only she didn't have to be so — she shouldn't hurt her mother that way. She shouldn't cut off her love like that."

Mr. Ellenbogen looked like he was going to cry. *If you really feel that way —*

"I wouldn't take it personal," said Hobie. "She maybe doesn't mean all those things the way they sounded." He felt a moment of disloyalty to Debbie, but went on. "She's pretty new here, and a lot of the ideas are — new. And sometimes you go overboard when you're all excited about something. And maybe — in front of me and all — she was afraid to act like she was glad to see you. There's a lot of that, you know, kids not wanting to show their feelings."

Mr. Ellenbogen brightened a bit. "I used to call my mother the Old Bat when I was out with the guys. I worshiped at her feet, the whole family did, but when I was with the guys it was the Old Bat."

"Yeah, maybe it's like that. She might be real glad inside that you come out but she can't let on for fear of what everybody else will think."

"I used to drive her home after dances in junior high," said Mr. Ellenbogen. "Only she'd make me park in the shadows a block away so nobody's see her getting a ride from her daddy. Once I almost got run in by a cop, he thought I was some pervert, waiting for the girls to come by. But she was afraid to walk home all by herself. It was a safe neighborhood, but kind of spooky if you were a kid. A block away in the shadows, like we were having an affair, meeting in secret. I'd stop by and get ice cream at a store on the way home. We couldn't go into a Friendly's or anything, somebody from school might see us together, but she could slump down in the car while I ran in to get a quart of butterscotch royale."

"Yeah, that's probably it. Kids." Mr. Ellenbogen worked up a pretty good smile and shook his head again.

Debbie came down the stairs hauling a large box full of junk and clothes. "Tell the boys to go through the records," she said, "see if there's anything they want. Give the clothes to the Unitarians, I guess, and —"

"Deb, honey, you don't really have to —"

"*Take* it! I don't want it. I don't need it. It came from your money, it's yours. I'll settle the first term bill as soon as I get a job. If they bill you don't pay —"

"Deb —"

"— and please don't come back here." She laid the box on the last step and backed away from it. "We don't have anything to talk about."

Mr. Ellenbogen tried to tell her that in ten years they probably would all be laughing over this little incident but Debbie had marched back upstairs to her self-criticism before he could finish. He turned to Hobie and smiled and shrugged as if to say, women, what can you do about them? Hobie offered to carry the box out to his car.

Mrs. was sitting in the passenger seat trying to ignore the neighborhood around her. Mr. opened the trunk for Hobie. Two black kids stopped and told him they hoped he wasn't moving in. He took it as a joke and told them not to worry. He smiled.

"You the one got to worry, Mista," said one of the kids. "We catch you out, we wipe up this street with your old gray ass." They weren't laughing. Hobie put the box in and slammed the trunk lid down and the two bopped away.

Mr. Ellenbogen stood by the door to his car. Some newsprint from the leaflets had smeared onto the rear of his jean suit. "What was it — Opie?"

"Hobie."

"Right. Hobie, it's been nice talking with you. I mean that sincerely." He peeked down at Mrs. and lowered his voice. "You strike me as a man I can trust —" He held out his hand and as they shook he pressed a bill into Hobie's palm. "See that this goes for groceries if things ever get lean for you folks. And look after my girl for me." He gave Hobie a wink and his sad, nervous grin and a solid man-to-man thump on the shoulder and then the Ellenbogens were gone.

It was a fifty-dollar bill.

12

The water was backing up on Clarendon, too much from too many places trying to flow down the same sewer grate. The center of the gutter stream moved ahead toward the grate, swirling bits of garbage, while the sides of the stream stood still or drifted back. There was a minor lake at the corner of Clarendon and Tremont, gray and cold-looking, its surface hissing with fine rain-circles. Hunter bent over to protect the slip of paper as he checked the directions the desk clerk had given him, checked the address he had for Darwin. He ducked out of the rain into a place called Central Lunch, to catch his breath. His lungs were acting up worse than usual with the air so full of water.

The window of the diner was crowded with what looked to be the prizes from a carnival skill game, a jungle of stuffed animals and plastic plant life. The stamped-tin ceiling was patterned in little white squares, with tiny Christmas ornaments dangling from each square. There were religious pictures on the walls, a lot of Jesus Christs with big bleeding red hearts and crowns of thorns. Taped to the inside of the door were several handwritten cards advertising furnished rooms for rent in the area. The two old women sitting at the counter and the old women behind it stared at Hunter. He tried to breathe through his nose. He turned his back to them and copied down a couple of the addresses. He couldn't keep up staying in a hotel and there was no way to know how long he would be.

Union Park surprised him a bit. It was just a cross-street off Tremont but it seemed like a totally different neighborhood. There were old, classy-looking, bow-front red-brick houses and a well-kept center island of trees and shrubbery. No traffic, you could barely hear what cars there were on Tremont passing. There were fancy black wrought-iron handrails on the front steps, swirls and spirals of metal vine. The basement windows were all secured behind thick iron bars.

Hunter turned down Shawmut, passing Greek and Lebanese diners, till the numbers seemed close to what he remembered. He checked the address from Darwin again.

He didn't expect them to be there. Darwin had said on the postcard that it was just a place he could connect with his mail, and that was almost a full year ago. He'd asked for his papers, all of them, for identification he said. Hunter had unlocked them from the fireproof box they kept all the important documents in and sent them along registered mail. If that was the way he wanted to do it. Military discharge, high-school-equivalency statement, birth certificate. If he wanted to take all traces of himself and disappear, Hunter had figured at the time, there was nothing to be done. The boy was of age. He'd been to a war.

The girl who answered the door was wearing jeans and a man's sleeveless undershirt with nothing under it. You could see her nipples right through it, you couldn't hardly help but see. Hunter didn't know where he should put his eyes. She was barefoot and had painted her toenails, each one a different color.

"He's not here. He doesn't live here," said the girl.

"But you know him?"

"I know who he is."

"I'm his father," said Hunter, then added, "he's not in trouble or anything."

The girl looked at Hunter. Hunter looked off over her shoulder somewhere. She moved to block his vision and pulled the door in a little more. Somebody in the room behind her was scrambling around and hissing whispers. Hunter tried to look her straight in the face. Her eyeballs were a bit on the yellow side. "Yeah, you talk sort of like him," she said. "Sort of."

"Do you know where he's living?"

The girl let the door swing open a little. "I think he's still in New Hampshire. Yeah, that's what I remember hearing. He went up there for some kind of construction thing they advertised. I think it was April or something, he wanted to be around some mountains."

"Do you have his address?"

"Nah. He didn't know where he was gonna stay I don't think. I didn't, don't know him very well, he was just around sometimes, you know. And he's, well, you must know how he is. He doesn't talk much."

"Uh-huh." The girl stretched her arms over her head. Hunter felt assaulted. She didn't seem to realize what she was doing, they were like two little fingers pointing at him.

"Spooky. He's kind of spooky, you know? The way he looks at you. Anyhow, that's where he was, New Hampshire. The last I heard. What do you want to see him for?"

He was Darwin's father, what other reason would he need? "Uh, I got this other boy, younger one, I'm trying to find him. I thought maybe he would of gotten in touch with his brother."

"Brother." The girl slapped her forehead with her hand. "Oh shit, that's right. His brother! He was here."

"When?"

"Musta been a week ago. Looking for Pfc., somebody talked to him I remember."

"Who? Looking for who?"

"Oh, Pfc. That's his nickname, that's what everybody calls him. Darwin. The Army and all. I remember somebody saying there was this guy here looking for Pfc., said he was his brother."

"Who was it that talked to him?"

"Jeez, I don't know. It was a week ago, like I said, and there's so many people, you know, in and out of here. I don't remember."

"Could you check? Please?" Hunter suddenly felt a great need to hurry, as if the boy were only a block away and escaping further with every wasted moment. "Could you ask somebody if they remember?"

"Sure. No sweat." The girl turned her head to call into the room. "Hey!"

A male voice answered. "Yeah?"

"You remember about a week ago, somebody said they talked to Pfc.'s brother? Who was it?"

"Who wants to know?"

"His father. Their father. Who was it talked to him?"

"Wolf."

"Nah, was it? You sure?"

"Yeah, remember, he went into this whole thing about how the

[108]

guy had on a Army jacket and how uniforms made him really paranoid and all. Remember? It was Wolf."

The girl turned back to Hunter. "It was Wolf."

"Does he live here? How can I get in touch with him?"

"Jeez, I really don't know. Wolf was just passing through, he's out on the Coast right now. It's not like you could send him a letter or anything either."

"Did he say whether he told the boy what you told me about Darwin? That he's in New Hampshire?"

"Oh no. No *way*. Wolf? You ask Wolf his name three times you'll get three different answers. Anyway, he wasn't here, I don't think, when Pfc. took off. He doesn't even know he went up there, probly. No, Wolf is pretty spaced out. You know? I'm surprised he even remembered to tell anybody that the brother had been here. Wish I could help you out, but that's all there is."

"You don't know anywhere else that somebody'd know Darwin?"

"Hey, like I said, there's a lot of people in and out of here, he was just another one of them. And he never talked. I heard him say two, maybe three things ever. He just sort of sat and looked at you with this smile like he knew something you didn't. It was spooky, it was like he could see through your clothes. X-ray eyes." The girl crossed her arms under her breasts and gave a little shiver. "No, I'm sorry, that's all there is." She shifted her weight and shrugged her shoulders. Hunter thanked her.

Hunter waited till he was halfway up Shawmut before he asked directions to the police station. It was right near his hotel. Hobie was here, he was sure of it, Hobie was here in Boston.

Mulcahy's feet were killing him and it wasn't nearly time for lunch. First he unlaced his shoes, then he wriggled his heels out, and then, when it got too bad, he took them out completely and nudged the shoes off to one side under his desk. Which meant he was stuck there until lunch cause his feet would swell too big to fit back in the shoes right away. Which meant, what with the way Rose was acting up, no coffee at all again this morning.

And all this morning guys bitching. Coming in and bitching over the weather. Coming in stomping their feet, making puddles on the floor, flicking rain-beads off their overcoats onto Mulcahy's paperwork. Just so he got the point they're out there pounding it in the rain. Like he should feel guilty he had a desk. Guys who hadn't come in for two, three years, they come all the way up the third floor to bitch and swipe raindrops on the paperwork.

"It's brutal out there, Mulcahy," they'd tell him. "Fawty days and fawty fuckin nights it looks like. There's some guy building a boat on top the Prudential Building." They'd look around and sigh and rub their hands like his office was the only warm spot in all of Boston. "Yeah," they'd say, "sure wisht I was on the tit like you."

That old business. Just cause his wife's brother happened to be tight with Fitzpatrick. On the tit, they said, like it wasn't work humping a typewriter all day and playing cop with the wives and asshole parents that come in. Like he should feel guilty he got a desk.

And if it wasn't the fucking rain it was the FBI. Guys all over the building cause of that thing with the draft boards last night, bitching about the FBI. Doyle especially, coming in and taking up half the fucking morning with his fat ass on Mulcahy's desk top, crumpling the paperwork every time he shifted, bitching about the FBI. How he got such a fat ass hustling around as much as he claimed to was a mystery. It wasn't like he had to stay by a desk all the time and never get any exercise. Another mystery was if he was so busy like he said, how come he's always in sitting on the desk top, keeping a guy from getting his paperwork done?

"They run me ragged, those guys," said Doyle. "Fuckin FBI. Get this, where's that, find out this, why didn't you do that. Like we work for them. Which isn't, isn't supposed to be, the case. We're supposed to work *with* them, not for them. Like the Lieutenant said."

"The Lieutenant," said Mulcahy. "That's what the Lieutenant tells *you* guys. To them it's 'My boys are at your disposal, give you anything you need.' Listen, Pauly, you wanna lift up over there? I need that fawm you're on. Got it, beautiful."

"It wasn't so bad yesterday. There was just a couple of em in town for that guy, what's his name, Rubin. Couple of em to take pictures of the crowd and all."

"Jerry Rubin. From the trial in Chicago there."

"Yeah, right, Jerry Rubin. You know all that stuff, don't you Mulcahy? Me, I can't keep up. I'm hustlin around all the time, I don't get a chance, keep up with events like you. Up here, on the fuckin tit, read the paper all day, it's nice I bet. It's good, keep up on things. Anyhow, this Jerry Rubin is up Copley Square yesterday afternoon making a speech in the fuckin rain and there's a couple these guys from the Federal taking pictures of the crowd and all and we're supposed to cooperate, which means bail out their asses if these kids get pissed off, having their fuckin pawtraits taken. But we can't look obvious they say, we just got to be around in case something flares up. It's a pain in the ass and the guys are snotty like they always are, like a working cop is a kind of disease they got to put up with, but it's not so bad, yesterday, there's only a couple.

"I was out there too, an it was a pisser. You know what he said? Jerry Rubin? He's in this trial, the Chicago Eight —"

"Seven."

"Huh?"

"It's the Chicago Seven. They're calling it seven now."

"Right. You're right, they chained the coon, what's his name, chained the coon up and took him off for a separate trial. Baby Seals."

"Baby Seals is some kind of vaudeville dancer, Pauly. Was. They don't have vaudeville no more. Bobby Seale."

"You prawbly start with the funnies, right, read the whole fuckin paper from back to front. Christ, my brother-in-law is a fuckin trash collector out to Mattapan. What good's that gonna do me, huh? Anyhow, he's in this Chicago Seven thing and he says it's the most impawtant trial since Jesus Christ. Direct quote. Can you imagine that? Jesus Christ he's calling himself, a guy looks like something even the cat wouldn't drag home. And this guy, this scumbag thinks he's Jesus Christ, has got us out in the rain playing nursemaid for the fuckin Federals. Some world.

"Then last night happens, with the draft bawds, it's like the fuckin Nawmandy invasion. They hit the local bawd over here on Huntington, they hit Roxbury, they hit Dawchester, they hit Jamaica fuckin Plain. All about the same time, files opened and thrown around, paint all over the place, like it was synchronize your watches and stawm the beach. A military operation. Then somebody calls up, says we done it. The Boston Eight they call themseaves. No names, just we take the credit, the Boston Eight. Maybe they haven't heard it's seven in Chicago now. I'm sure they're connected, it's all connected. And it's draft bawds, so naturally we got FBI up to our ears this morning, runnin us ragged and with that attitude they got, they don't have to say a thing, you can sense it, it's like okay, we gave you cops your chance and you fucked up, now let the grown-ups take over. Gets me so pissed off, I had to come in here, get away from it for a couple minutes. It's unbelievable out there."

"It's a bitch," said Mulcahy. "Listen, Pauly, could you lift up on the other side? I think my eraser's under there. Great. Yeah, it sounds like a real bitch out there."

He wouldn't leave. He sat there and griped and moaned like he always did, taking up half the desk top with his fat ass telling Mulcahy he should work out. You get stagnant on the tit, that's why so many desk guys got heart attacks. You should work out, do you wonders. And he cut farts. That's the other thing Doyle always did, he sat right there on the desk and cut farts, lifting up whichever mammoth cheek was furthest from Mulcahy like that made it okay and let out these whoppers. Like an elephant snoring, it sounded. Then he'd turn to Rose, who ignored him as best she could, who ignored most everything lately, and he said "Podden my French." That cracked him up every time, Doyle, he laughed his head off even when no one else cracked a smile. And he wouldn't leave until there were two customers waiting at the door and someone downstairs had called trying to locate him. He heaved himself off, scattering papers the way he always did, and said, "Oh well, back to the working world." Like Missing Persons was a fucking vacation or something.

And Rose, Jesus, it was getting worse with Rose. One morning she comes in, makes this announcement. No more coffee. He asked her really polite too, the way he always did when she got it. "Rose, honey, whenever you get a minute, we could use some coffee up here." Really polite. And it's like all of a sudden he stepped on a snake. "From now on, Jerry, you get your own damn coffee. And I'm not your honey." Which was bad enough, what with his feet how they were, but there was this whole new attitude of hers to boot. It wasn't like she was some young kid, gonna get caught up in all the women's ideas floating around and that stuff. Not Rose, she was nearly his age, they'd worked together almost twelve years now. She even had some gray starting that he kidded her about. Used to kid her about. You couldn't kid anymore, she wouldn't laugh at a joke. Used to be she'd even laugh at things Doyle said, and Doyle was a real pig. Maybe it was her change-of-life or something, he wished he knew. But there wasn't anyone else to ask about it, he was afraid of the gas he'd take if they found out. He took enough gas from that on-the-tit business, he didn't need any more. Mulcahy got to get his own coffee these days, they'd say, Rose cut him off. The gals down in Licenses still hustled around waiting on Kulik hand and fucking foot and they were all ten, fifteen years younger than Rose. And Kulik wasn't even fucking po*lite* for Christ sake, he chewed their asses off down there.

Of course, he *was* Rose's superior. If you wanted to get all technical about it. He could *or*der her to get it. But what if she refused? Press charges? Think of the gas he'd take for that, not to mention they wouldn't stand still for it. Whatever it was got into her, change-of-life or whatever, he wished it would blow over. It was torture, sitting there dry all day with his feet swelling up, nothing to wash his water pills down with, not daring to go down and get coffee himself for all the gas he'd take if they saw him and worrying everything he said whether it was going to offend her and set off something new. They did the same work and they were five feet from each other but they didn't even talk shop anymore, didn't talk much of anything and you could cut the air with a fucking machete. Not a word the whole morning, not a single word and all these guys tromping in bitching about the rain and Doyle with his fat farting ass bitching about the FBI and paperwork up to your ears and no wonder when the hillbilly or whatever he was come in Mulcahy wasn't in the mood. Just not in the mood.

"I'm looking for my boy."

They were all looking for their boy. Or for their girl. It used to be, four, five years ago, it was wives after their husbands gone off on a bender, or just sick of the bills and the crap they put up with at home and skipped town to try it somewheres else.

But these days it was the kids, everybody looking for their kids. From all over, from the suburbs around Boston, from New York, from the West Coast, all of them wanting their kids back. Though after you had the inside dope on these kids you got to wonder why.

They came in two kinds, the parents. The ones that were all "Where did I go wrong?" and wanted to cry on your shoulder, and the ones treated you like a servant. Like it was your fault the kid run off in the first place. It was a toss-up which kind was worst.

But this guy you couldn't figure out right off. He just sat there, breathing hard like he didn't wait for the elevator and ran up the stairs. The elevator was really slow, even on a Sunday. This guy sat there and didn't look like he was going to cry and didn't look like he was going to start giving orders to people and expecting snappy service. "I'm looking for my boy," he said.

Mulcahy rolled a form into his typewriter. "We have to fill this out first," he said, "it'll help us know if we got a line on him."

He was kind of a wiry guy, hard-looking though he didn't push it. One of his arms didn't hang right and his nose had been broken at least once. His sideburns were turning iron gray, his teeth had seen better days. He was dressed like a man who punched a clock and came home dirty. The guy answered all the questions about his boy directly, in the funny kind of accent he had. Name, sex, race, age, weight, height, hair, eyes, complexion, distinguishing physical marks, clothing and jewelry. The Army jacket was a good one, but if the kid was seriously on the lam he would have ditched it by now. A seventeen-year-old white male with brown hair and blue eyes, maybe 5'6", maybe 125 pounds. The guy had all the information written out with him, he had a couple pictures. He had no real idea why the boy split, he said. Mulcahy decided to leave that one alone for the time being. The guy told him about the other son, the veteran, and why he thought this one he was looking for had come to Boston.

"You don't want to fill one out for this older one, this Darwin?"

"No. I don't suppose I do."

"Why not?"

The guy thought on it a bit. "We had a falling out," he said. "You could call it that. We don't agree on a whole lot of things anymore. He wants to see me, he knows where home is."

"But you and Hobie, you still agree on most things?"

"I don't know," he said, "but I want the chance to find out."

Interesting, very interesting, but it didn't look so great for finding the kid. He didn't have any kind of record, he sounded bright enough to stay under for a long time if he wanted to, without coming to anyone's attention. It was too bad for the father. He talked funny but he didn't seem to be a bad guy. Most guys like him, working guys who came in, they wanted their kids found so they could be punished for something. Have the cops do what they couldn't manage themselves. But this guy, you got the feeling, he really just wanted to find his kid and talk it out. Most people come in you had a hundred you could remember just like them, but there was something extra going on here. Even Rose was listening in, but then Rose was a soft touch. Or else she used to be. But no, you couldn't worry yourself too much about it, get involved and all, or it would get to you and you'd be no good. And tit or no tit, Mulcahy was good at his job.

He went through the recent-arrests pile. He only had to go back two weeks to cover this kid so it didn't take too long. Nothing. There was an unidentified on the slab but he was the wrong color. When you came right down to it, if the kid didn't put himself in the phonebook or get caught at a crime, there wasn't much you could do. Mulcahy leveled with the guy.

"I'll tell you how it is. We got him on file now, so any time after this he gets picked up or is involved in a case, he'll get cross-referenced and we can send him your way. We really don't have the staff to go out looking for people don't want to be found. It's a big city, there's thousands of kids out there. But, there is a couple things you can do yourself. First, you want to go up to Cambridge Police, check out the missing persons there. Cambridge is where a lot of kids end up and it's not a pot of Boston. A lot of people, they're from out of town, they make that mistake. It's a different place. And while you're up there, Cambridge, you might want to just stand in Hovvid Square a bit, look around. Maybe, even, you feel like it, take that picture and show it to people. You never know. It's a place a lot of them hang out, kids with nowheres else to go. You could put an ad in some of the underground papers there. They'll be guys selling them on street-cawners, you could get a copy of each and they'll tell you how to put an ad in. In the personals, you know, like those 'all-is-fawgiven' things. He was older, I'd tell you to try welfare or unemployment, but I don't think he could swing that here. You don't have to check in with us except when you're changing addresses, we let you know the minute anything comes up. Other than that you just got to hope he decides it's not so wonderful out there and comes back on his own."

The guy just sat there then, like the wind had left him and he was all empty. He seemed to be waiting for more, only there wasn't any more to tell him. Nothing real, anyway. Mulcahy stuck the form on top of the Recent pile. Rose looked like she was going to say something, but then she just kept on typing.

"You never know though," said Mulcahy, out of the blue, surprising himself a little. "Sometimes they fool you. We had a case a couple of weeks ago maybe, was a beauty. Parents had money problems, right, always fighting over it, whether to send the oldest off to school or not. It's tearin em apot, this money business. You're a workin man, you know how it is. So the oldest, he takes off. They come in here, it's been faw months he's gone, they're afraid to come to the police, afraid maybe it's some drug thing he's messed up in like they read in the papers all the time, caused him to light out. They want to see him but not in jail. A lot of people are like that, afraid to come at first. We took down the infawmation, didn't find a thing. It looked hopeless, a cold trail. We can't do a thing for them, I felt lousy about it. Then, just a couple days after they come in here, they get a letter from him. And a check. The kid's been driving a taxi under phony papers, underage and all, but he's made enough to pay for a first year at school with some left over to send them to help out. Said he couldn't stand to hear them beatin on each other about money all the time, he figured he'd take some of the load off their hands. He was too proud to contact them until he was sure he had it made, to show them he could do it. Must have been doing twelve, fawteen hours a day, livin off other kids he met to cut down expenses. Last I heard, they worked out this thing where he's gonna be able to finish up what he missed of high school when he skipped and then get into UMass for the spring semester. You never know, sometimes, they can surprise you."

The guy looked a little better, he was at least breathing regular again.

"Yeah," said Mulcahy, "even when they run with no intention of coming back, they're relieved, deep inside, when you catch up with them. They got a lot of pride, some kids, sometimes instead of just admitting they shouldn't of left in the first place and going back on their own steam, they do some little thing, break a window maybe, so we'll pick em up and send them home. I'd wait awhile before I got too down on this thing, I was you. He's prawbly just as eager for you to find him as you are."

The guy seemed to have his breath all the way back then, and he thanked Mulcahy for his help and advice and said he'd be calling in a more permanent address in a day or so. Mulcahy listened to him wait in the hall awhile for an elevator, then give up and take the stairs.

Rose asked him where he got the story about the kid driving taxi to earn his tuition. He said what the hell, it couldn't hurt any, the guy seemed pretty depressed. Rose didn't say anything. Sometimes you didn't go by the book. Sometimes, even if it wasn't the case at all, you could hand out a little hope.

There was loads of paperwork to do then, he'd gotten behind with everybody and their brother holding him up all morning. He didn't even notice when Rose left. There was cross-referencing to do and fugitive reports to update and a couple letters from a private tracers company to be answered. One of the forms Doyle had sat on was crumpled enough so it had to be typed over. He didn't hear the elevator, didn't even hear her coming till she was right at his desk with a cup of coffee and one of the lemon twist pastries he liked so much from the machine downstairs. He stared at them on his desk top like they came from outer space.

"I was down there anyway," said Rose. "Don't get any ideas." And she went back to her paperwork.

Change-of-life, thought Mulcahy, it must be.

Cambridge was a city of children. After he left the Cambridge police Hunter stood under the awning of the news shed in the center of Harvard Square. The air was barely teeming with rain now, children passed him on all sides, shaking moisture from their hair. Children dressed in leather, in silk and velour, in denim work clothes. Children with hip-length hair and beards, with designs painted on their faces, with beads and boots and feathers. Too many children. They were like a different people here, a different race. They had their own stores, their own newspapers, their own radio stations playing from shop windows. The first time he saw an Army jacket Hunter was excited and jumped up to see over the crowd jaywalking at the light, but then he saw another, and another, and another, saw hundreds of children in their uniforms, children who walked like they knew it was their city. Hunter felt that there were too many, too many to ever pick one out as his own, and worse than that, felt if he saw Hobie right now, on this street, in this city, he wouldn't have an idea what to say to him. The children passed him, a cityful of them, and he had never felt so lost in his life.

13

"I think it's time we hacked out our position on the Panther issue." Wein paced slowly in front of the freestanding blackboard that King and Miriam had ripped off. The rest sat in a rough circle on the floor, backs against a wall wherever possible.

"Whether we're going to write them off as a devisive nationalist group like our friends at PL do, or to recognize them as a legitimate anti-imperialist force, the revolutionary arm of a colonized people."

"Like the Weathermen do."

"Exactly."

"Do we really have to get all judgmental about it?" Pinkstaff spoke from the radiator. "I mean couldn't we, you know, just coexist?"

"Value neutrality is a judgment in itself. We have to have a rational and consistent position to come from whenever we deal or decide not to deal with the Panthers. We can't rely on gut reactions for these things."

Hobie leaned back against the one mildew-smelling chair and tried to focus his attention. Group meeting happened every night and rarely ran out of gas short of two hours. It was hard to stay with when there weren't any breaks for class change like in high school. Even Mr. Hinkle's class, which he *liked*, even that always began to fade out toward the end.

The room was empty but for the cushionless chair and the blackboard. The walls were bare white plaster except where Miriam had stenciled DARE TO STRUGGLE, DARE TO WIN in thick block letters.

The other kids, the shock troops Schenk called them, lay flat and closed their eyes or fidgeted from uncomfortable position to uncomfortable position. Hobie practiced the deep breathing that King had shown them, filling his lungs, holding, exhaling slowly through the nose. His muscles were relaxing more each day, no more tight stomach all the time. He could vaguely feel where he'd been spiked on the ankle in the Slab Fork game.

"The primary argument against the Panthers now is that racism should be viewed as an economic and class problem." Wein had yellow-stained fingers from overlining in his texts with the Magic Marker. "That any isolation of blacks from the common class struggle is inherently divisive, diluting the energy of the workers. By promoting a black separatist movement, even though couched in Marxist-Leninist terms, the Panthers are playing along with the enemy's divide-and-conquer tactics."

"Sit down Wein."

Schenk cut through though he was clear across the room, way back against the hallway door.

"Excuse me?"

"You heard. Sit down. No one is supposed to be above group level unless he's using the blackboard. Remember?"

"Right." Wein grinned weakly. He turned full-circle like a

hunting dog, looking for his exact spot on the floor, then sat. "Sorry."

"Thank you." Schenk gave him a small bow. "You forgot to mention that they're hung up with this idea of fighting through the court system. Which is the same as recognizing that system as legitimate. Which it is not."

"Besides, they're pigs," said Miriam. "They treat their women like shit."

"Granted, the Panthers have their little internal contradictions." Wein waved and twisted his yellow fingers in front of himself. It was like playing cat's cradle without any string. "But our problem here is to ascertain what position they hold in the black community, what position they hold in the movement in general, and dependent on our findings, decide what our attitude toward them should be — all the time remembering that it's a question of political practicality as well as ideological foundation."

If Hobie leaned slightly to his left he could see around Tracy Anne and watch Sarah. Sarah sat Indian-legged, hands folded in her lap, listening carefully to every speaker. She sat next to Mark Remington. She was the only one who seemed to put energy into listening, who didn't either switch off and stare into space like King or seem to be preparing a counterargument the whole while, like Remington or Schenk or Miriam.

The first night she brought him to the group Sarah had listened that way. Just the two of them, talking in the kitchen while Schenk ran a class for the younger kids up in the parlor. The way she listened made him tell things he ordinarily wouldn't have, but afterwards, because it was her, it didn't seem like a mistake.

"I used to feel like just taking off myself," Sarah had said. "Lots of times. For no specific reason, really, just stuff with my parents and school, closing in. I never got up the nerve like you did though."

"It's different for a girl, I suppose."

"It doesn't have to be. Nerve is nerve. I mean coming to Boston when you don't know a soul here, it takes a lot of balls."

Didn't sound funny when she said it. When Delia tried to swear it sounded either really dirty or awkward or else cute.

Mostly cute, like how she said "oh phooey!" all the time.
"You probably feel like you landed in the middle of a *Time*-magazine cover story," said Sarah. "All this political talk."
"They got politics in West Virginia."
She laughed. "I'm sure they do, Hobie. But I mean like young people, you know, radical politics."
"No. Not much of that. We had the Appalachian Volunteers awhile but people run them out."
"I think I heard about that. I was in Vista when it first started up."
"Yeah, they had that, Vista, in some of the counties around us. They done some good things I guess, but the fellas in office don't like em. It's hard to buck the courthouse gang, and the people, they don't trust outside help."
"I know." Sarah was so regular, talking with him like they'd known each other a long time. "That's one of our big problems here, trying to become part of the community. In fact trying to be part of *any* community. There's no such thing where most of these kids come from, it's just separate little families in their ranch houses. Or else they're from communities that force the young people away. Like you."
"You got a lot of people here." Hobie nodded toward the parlor. Schenk's nasal voice was piercing through the wall. "It's like you got a boarding school."
"Well, people learn here, but I wouldn't call it a *school*. Everybody you see is here because they *want* to be, voluntarily. We do have, you know, *rules* and everything. But they're ones we made ourselves. So if you're told — asked — to do something, you always know *why* you're being asked."
"Where does everybody sleep?"
"Wherever they want to. There's bags and blankets all around, whenever you feel like you want to rack out just go ahead and find yourself a warm corner. You must be pretty tired, wandering around Boston all this time."
"A little."
"You say you couldn't find your brother?"
"No. There's a couple more places maybe I could try though."
"Feel free to stay here as long as it takes you."
"I'm not in the way or anything? I mean, with you doing your

political stuff, I'd probably make you feel uncomfortable. You probably have to do secret planning and all."

"What makes you think that?" She was laughing at him a bit but it wasn't sarcastic.

"Well, whenever there's gonna be a new gang trying to take over the Democrats, or when there's gonna be a wildcat at the mines, they always have a lot of secret planning to do."

"Everything we do here is wide open. We *want* people to know what we stand for, what we're working for. Anybody you see here, ask them what they're doing and you'll get a straight answer. It's not like we're trying to change things that other people haven't been trying to change for a long time. We just differ a little in our approach. Like the war. You said your brother was in the war, didn't you?"

"Yuh."

"And what's your status?"

"Pardon?"

"Your draft status."

"Oh, I don't know. I'm not old enough."

"But you will be —"

"In December."

"Do you want to go if they call you? Have you talked with your brother about what it's like?"

"He got really — messed up from it. It changed him a lot. Course, he en*list*ed, which I'm not gonna do. But if they call you up, you know, there's not much you can say about it." He wished she'd change the subject. He didn't want to get involved telling all about Dar. Not yet.

"That's one of the things we're trying to change."

"Good luck."

"And in order to do it we need more people like you —" Hobie began to speak and she motioned him quiet, "— not you spe*ci*fically, you've got your own business to look after here in Boston — but people like you who have a self-interest in the problem. We need kids from working-class families who know what it's like to live without choices, who have a self-interest in making a system where there *are* some choices."

"That sounds good."

"Listen, Hobie," she had said then, "why don't you take your socks off and put them on the radiator to dry? Make yourself at home."

Sarah talked with him till the class broke up, then introduced him around to anyone who seemed interested, then talked with him some more when the others wandered away. Nobody had ever talked with Hobie that long about anything important, not his father or his brother or the guidance counselors whose job it · was supposed to be or even Delia. All Delia seemed interested in was "us," the couple of Hobie and Delia and how it was faring in the world. Sarah talked and listened to him till the bus ride and the night at Pine Street and all the time in the rain and the day of box making caught up with him and she saw it and showed him to a warm place to sleep.

"So what you're saying is, we should wait to see what sort of following the local Panthers have attracted and how their immediate program complements or counteracts our own, rather than forming a policy based on national issues. Am I correct?"

Wein's voice startled Hobie a bit, tuning in at volume so quickly. He wondered what he'd missed, some sort of agreement seemed to have been reached.

"You're not only correct, Wein," said Grant Parke, "you're downright *prop*er. We just spent over a half hour traveling a full circle. We've decided to wait and check out what Paris Green and the local Panthers are into, which is where it stood before we started talking."

"But at least it's *con*scious indecision now," Wein gave his apology of a smile again. "Before it was just apathy. So. We're agreed, no action or public line regarding the Panthers for the present. And any action or public statement regarding them in the future must be first reviewed in group. Should we vote?"

"On what?" said Parke. "Is there a question?"

"Whether there is or not Wein can come up with one," said Mark Remington, smiling. "I don't think it needs to come to a vote. Not unless there's strong feeling for or against the Panthers here."

Hobie noticed a few of the younger kids looking back to Schenk. He shook his head no.

"Wonderful. Let's move on then." Wein stood and began to

pace in front of the board again. "The question has risen in class lately, in a general sort of way, just *where* we stand on student activism, given our community and our worker-oriented approach and the fact of working-class resentment toward students, but also recognizing the legitimacy of many student concerns —"

"Like the GE thing at BU," Pinkstaff called out. "Where do we stand on that?"

"Exactly."

Wein hadn't seemed too interested in Hobie when they were introduced. Not uninterested either, really, but more like — dis*tract*ed. He looked at Hobie and smiled and talked like one of those convention newsmen on TV listening to earphone instructions at the same time as they interviewed somebody. Sarah brought Hobie over and Wein said hello and shook his hand and asked what kind of schooling there had been in West Virginia. Just old regular high schooling, Hobie said, and Wein smiled and said he hoped Hobie would make himself at home. Then he went off to study. Funny, they didn't seem a bit alike but it was the exact same way Coach acted with the third-stringers on the team, the dinks he called them, when he ran into them in the halls and had to talk. Smiling and distracted, on his way to somewhere more important.

"We have to come out with some position on the BU disturbance."

"Why?" Grant Parke was right at Wein's feet.

"Because we live in a community that makes judgments on such actions, and, like it or not, which associates us with them."

"Why?"

"Because working people have been taught to react to all radicals in a stereotyped fashion, to lump them together and write them off."

"Why?" Every once in a while when he got bored or irritated Parke would start doing that, keep asking Wein to explain himself and Wein fell for it every time, struggling to define his terms into finer and finer clearness.

"The answer to that is what I want to discuss here, the mechanism through which the oppressing class turns the workers against their potential allies, and what we can do to combat it. Okay?" Wein flushed whenever he was questioned, he stood back from Parke to see him better. "Anything more you want to know?"

"Why," said Parke, "are you standing up again?"

Parke always acted like there was some big joke he was in on that no one else knew. When he was told Hobie came from West Virginia he said no shit and laughed like it was the funniest thing he'd heard all day. "We got em coming from every whichway folks," he said to no one in particular, "they're pourin in from the four corners of the earth. From the cool Atlantic Ocean to the wide Pacific shore, from Bangor to Biloxi, from Providence to Pasadena, from the ridges and grasslands of the heart of the heart of the country. Just goes to show you, fans, revolution isn't just a dirty word in the back of some discontented cellardweller's brain, it's the National fucking Pastime. It's as American as apple pie and vanilla ice cream, as wholesome as Sandra Dee's left dimple. Take this one here, I bet he spent his barefoot years chucking rocks at a target on the side of a barn, pretending it was Jumpin John Mitchell up there in front of the Justice Department. Sharpening up the old control, working on that *smooth* delivery. And here he is, up to the city for a crack at the big time, the Bakunin of the Backwoods." He grabbed Hobie's hand and pumped it in greeting. "Welcome to the Revolution, kid."

"He didn't come to join us," said Sarah. "He just needs a place to stay for a while."

"On the run, huh? A track man! Well, just remember what Trotsky said down in the Mexican League before they stuck the high hard one in his ear. 'I never look behind me,' he said, 'something might be catching up.' Words to live by kid." He winked and poked Sarah in the belly. "See she doesn't talk you into anything subversive."

"He's serious sometimes," Sarah said later, "maybe he's serious most of the time. But he's not about to let you know just when."

"I think this whole business of attaching a stigma to students can be carried to extremes." A boy Hobie knew only as Smallwood was talking. "Historically, students have played an important role in revolutionary movements, and I think it would be a mistake to exclude them from our own because they've had a lot of bad press lately. They seem like the ideal people to enlist as allies — they've got little to lose, they have a sense of adventure, they're relatively ideal —"

"That's exactly why we *don't* want strong ties with them." Wein was sitting down again. "You're giving us all of the basic RYM-Weatherman arguments, claiming that 'youth,' whatever that is, can be a legitimate and self-sufficient oppressed class of their own. The fact is that working-class people don't trust them, *we* don't trust them, precisely be*cause* they have little to lose, be*cause* they have a sense of, as you put it, 'adventure.' They're not in it because they *need* to be, the fact that they're still in school, still students, is the perfect indication of that."

"But when they sacrifice their own concerns for those of working people, like with the GE recruiter at BU, I don't think we should —"

"That's an entirely different question. That's what we're trying to get at, whether this particular *ac*tion by students should be supported or not."

"If we support the action aren't we supporting the actors?" Smallwood was about the only one of the younger kids who questioned Schenk during Revisionist History session. And he was the only one who asked for a reason behind the exercises King had them do during Martial Arts. King called him The Professor and gave him extra attack forms to work on.

It was Miriam who sat Hobie down next to King, saying, "King this is Hobie. His old man is in the coal mines." She turned to Hobie. "King's old man was in steel mills till it killed him." She walked away as if that were all the common ground they could possibly ask for.

"Hey."

King nodded. He had a middle-linebacker's face. Dented nose, high cheekbones and slanty eyes, pale skin with a rash of red zits on his neck.

"They tell me you teach karate stuff."

"Sort of." They were sitting next to each other on the radiator in the group-session room. "They said you're from West Virginia."

"Yuh." Hobie thought maybe he was supposed to ask something about steel mills, but he couldn't imagine what it would be. They sat. The radiator was cold.

"How'd you, uh, learn, you know, fighting like that? I mean they don't teach karate in school."

"I started by copying the moves they did on this television show they used to have —"

"You mean *I Spy*."

"You got that? In West Virginia?"

"Sure. We got everything, least we did once the coal company put up this antenna on this big mountain by us. Yeah, I used to watch that all the time, *I Spy*."

"The fighting on that wasn't totally right, not once I started getting into it and recognizing all the techniques, but it was pretty real. A hell of a lot better than something like *The Man from Uncle*."

"Stunk to high heaven."

"Well, the first year it wasn't so bad, but then it went right downhill. The pits."

"Like the *Twilight Zone*s were real good when they first come out and then they weren't so good."

"Yeah, right." King was smiling a bit, a crooked smile that showed a row of chipped front teeth. King seemed to be the only one in the group who had bad teeth, as bad as Hobie's own. "You remember the one where they had this guy with a ventriloquist dummy who starts talking all on its own?"

"And then it starts walking round till at the end the dummy is a ventriloquist and the ventriloquist has turned into a wooden dummy?"

"Right, right! You ever see the one where Lee Marvin plays this fight manager in the future —"

"When all the boxers are robots —"

"But his breaks down and he's too broke to fix it —"

"So he has to go in the ring against this steel robot himself?"

"Fantastic! That was a great one!"

They talked about old *Twilight Zone*s and then got into *Way*

[127]

Out and *The Outer Limits* and *Chiller* and then got into westerns, into *Gunsmoke* and *Have Gun, Will Travel* and *Wyatt Earp* and *The Rifleman.* It turned out that they were both just old enough to remember Steve McQueen in *Wanted: Dead or Alive* and Nick Adams in *The Rebel,* that they both remembered all the words to the singing ads for Bosco and for Bardahl and for Bactine and that they had both been watching the fight of the week the night Emile Griffith stopped Benny Kid Paret. They sat on the radiator and talked and it turned out they had more in common than Miriam had probably imagined.

"On the surface, denying a GE recruiter access to the campus and demanding the university boycott all GE goods —"
"Unscrew all their light bulbs —"
"— until the strike is settled seems to be the perfect kind of action. Students supporting workers."
"Instead of crying over their courses not being relevant and their lives not being meaningful," said Mark Remington.
"*But,* if more closely examined, their action appears extremely shortsighted. Who is it that GE is out to recruit? What jobs is their man trying to fill?"
"Bosses."
"Exactly. Computer technicians, engineers, managers, all the types who consider themselves 'professionals' and who are on the other side in this strike. By limiting their ban on the GE recruiter to the duration of the strike, aren't they indulging in a hollow symbolism? Aren't they tacitly stating their belief in the legitimacy of the enforced subclassification of workers into professionals and general laborers? Or else why not reject the GE recruiters and their counterparts from other companies all year round?"
"Cause they can't stay on the fucking *case* that long," called Parke. "They've got their classes and their midterms and their football games, they got Thanksgiving vacation coming, they got other things to *do.*"
"They've got the press coverage though," said Remington.
"Who wants it?" Schenk cut in. "It's typical of the enemy's press to give front-page space when a handful of college boys and girls sit down in some professor's office, at the same time they run

*may*be one article a week about the nationwide strike, back in the human-interest section or some bullshit like that. It's almost a rule, the more space they give it the more dubious it probably is."

"And then there's the question of exactly what effect the BU action is having on the progress of the strike and the consciousness of the strikers. What the men on the picket lines think about it." Wein pushed his glasses off his nose. "I think we ought to apply ourselves to that problem."

"I think we ought to apply ourselves," said Miriam, "to the problem that the men on the picket line are a bunch of pigs. I went up to Lynn there, to the factory, to talk to those guys and all I got was honey this and honey that and three suggestions that I spread my legs for worker solidarity."

"You take that stuff too seriously," said Parke. "When I was on the line that was just about all you heard, but they didn't mean anything by it."

"That's bullshit, Grant. People usually act twice as bad as they talk. I ask a guy if he needs any help out there picketing and he tells me he hasn't had a good blow job in a while, you call that not meaning it?"

"We're getting off the track here, people." Wein raised his hand to draw their attention. "I think we all agree that sexism is a divisive aspect of working-class consciousness. But to push it as an issue here, in what is basically a trade-union battle, would be even more divisive. I think if we concentrate on the major economic contradiction the rest of these secondary characteristics like racism and sexism will fall into place. My analysis of the feminist error —"

"Listen, just because the workers are indoctrinated with the enemy's ideas doesn't mean we have to condone them. Trade unionism in the narrow sense it exists in today isn't what we're supposed to be interested in at all, is it?" Miriam was pissed, she had her Dead End Kid look on. "We're using it as a starting point to involve ourselves in the workers' struggle but we're opposed to its limited and self-serving goals, right? Which means we have to educate while we help organize. And as for your analysis of the feminist error, Wein, I've heard it before and it sucks a big dog's dick."

When Miriam first came over to look him up and down Hobie got elevator stomach the way he used to in cold-weather spring baseball tryout when you knew you'd probably only get seven or eight swings to prove you could hit before the first big cut. "This is Miriam," Sarah said, "she's our most successful work-placement so far. She's been winning us a lot of friends at a stitching factory downtown." Miriam wore a brown leather jacket cracking with age, wore her black hair long and frizzy.

Miriam said hello and began to put questions to him.

She asked why he had left West Virginia. He said something about looking for his brother. She asked what he did back home. He said he went to school. Used to go. She asked what his father did for a living. He said a coal miner. When Miriam talked she looked, stared, directly into his eyes. She asked what his mother did. He said she was dead.

"What did she use to do? Before she died?"

"Nothin much. Pray."

"You mean she did housework?"

"Mostly she was sick."

"But before she was sick?"

"I don't remember then."

Hobie felt he was doing all right with Miriam though she didn't react to his answers one way or the other. His nervous stomach began to go away.

"Do you have any idea what you want to do now you're out of school?"

Hobie realized he hadn't thought much about it. "Get a job, I guess."

"Did you have a girlfriend back there?"

"Uh — yeah. I suppose." Sarah was still with them, listening close the way she did. "I used to."

"Is she still in school?"

"Yuh."

"And what does she want to do?"

"Be married."

Miriam gave a little laugh through her nose. "Is that all? She must want to do something more than that."

Hobie thought a moment. "Go to Heaven."

Miriam smiled then. "You ought to stick around with us a

couple days," she said, "see what we're into. We might even be able to help you with a job if you're interested."

Miriam backed off then and Hobie relaxed, feeling like he'd made the team. But he wasn't so crazy about the way she'd put him up for judgment like that. He had never liked playing defense.

"Her grandmother worked with Emma Goldman," Sarah told him later. Hobie began to make an impressed face, but it was only Sarah there, so he asked. She explained as if it were perfectly all right not to know who Emma Goldman was.

Miriam was a funny one, all right, but he kind of liked her. The other night, in a less organized meeting, they were going over household problems and someone mentioned how the two rear burners on the gas stove weren't working. They got into a debate about who should call the gas company and whether they should refuse to pay the service charge if it turned out to be faulty equipment or if they should hit up on the landlord for whatever it cost even though the less they had to do with *that* pig the better and Miriam drifted out of the room. A little later Hobie left to take a leak and had to pass through the kitchen. Miriam was on the floor with stove parts spread on newspaper before her. "You know anything about these things?" she asked.

"Nope. We had natural out of a tank back home but the stove never went wrong. Do you?"

"Not yet." She was peering down the end of a long piece of blackened tubing. "You hand me that broom over there? Thanks. The pilots on both of these burners are working but the units don't light. I figure it's something clogged up somewheres."

Hobie squatted by her. "You remember how to put all that back together?"

"Uh-huh."

"Do you do most of the fixing around here?"

"If it looks like no one else is going to."

Miriam reminded him a little of Darwin, the way Dar got to be after the Army set him loose. Always seemed to be something going on, something extra in his head, that he wasn't letting to the surface. Before the Army he'd only been real bad that way after a long rib-thumping afternoon at fullback, not wanting to show how much it hurt to move. But after — it was like Miriam, like something hurting him all the time but covered up. Like a holler tree fulla hornets, they'd say back home. Might look nice and peaceful sometimes but don't you give it a whack.

Miriam had Hobie take garbage-bag twist-ties from under the sink and peel the paper off them, then twist several of the little wires together to make a single stiff one. She took the burner heads off and poked down into each hole, reaming little grits of black out onto the newspaper. When Hobie returned from the bathroom Miriam already had one of the heads on with a blue circle of flame shooting out from it.

"If you can get a word in," she said, "tell them we fixed the stove."

"Now the usual pattern of campus movements," said Wein, "is that support from the school population only becomes general when there is a strong uniting issue, a matter of self-interest. Like the Berkeley Free Speech thing or all the black admissions sit-ins. Which is the why you have to give some weight to PL's criticism of the viability of youth as a revolutionary class." Wein always sounded like he was reading off something when he talked, but it came directly from his head. "The basic drift has been to do their most serious fighting to establish pockets of separate peacefulness away from the so-called adult world, to make their schools into youth states where they can hang loose, free from draft hassles and grade pressures and all that. The same way the hippies try to create a self-indulgent subculture to live in. But all that kind of activity boils down to is the same kind of bourgeois nationalism PL accuses the Panthers of, only it's a country of the young they're after, not of blacks. However, I think the action at BU transcends the usual pattern in a positive way, which is a development we should support. For students to risk their asses for somebody else, especially for workers —"

"PL has got their fingers in it. You've got to figure that, Ira."

"PL has got their fingers in *everything*. But if they didn't have the student interest they couldn't have swung that thing Tuesday."

"I agree that we should publicly support it. The students have always been willing to fight, it's only been a matter of lack of direction holding them back," said Joel Pinkstaff. Pinkstaff reminded Hobie of Ford Eccles, who everyone on the team called Echo. Echo played cornerback and wasn't bad as a gang-tackler, in fact he was always getting penalties for piling-on after the whistle. But he never made the first hit himself. "Now it looks like they're coming around." said Pinkstaff, "and the workers' movement needs their —"

"Whoa now!" Miriam thumped the floor beside her. "Needs? Workers movement *needs* the students? You got things assbackwards there, this isn't some street fight we're talking about, couple extra bodies tossing rocks gonna make some big difference. This is the mechanics of a certain phase of dialectical materialism we're dealing with. The workers don't *need* anything from anybody, they're the majority, they're the *peo*ple. And eventually the natural contradictions in the system will make conditions intolerable and the workers will take care of business, students or no students. It's an inevitability, that's why it's called dia*lec*tical. Now if you're talking about a timetable, whether outside forces can speed up or slow down the inevitable showdown, then you've got some ground to stand on, but —"

"I think that's an awfully vulgar analysis of the situation." Wein's smile was pitying, like the one Coach put on sometimes when the third string was in and tripping over their shoelaces. "You're totally ignoring the effect of culture on the people's motivation to act. You're ignoring all the socialization, all the brainwashing and training that workers have been subjected to by the enemy. You seem unaware of how successful massive conditioning can be in blinding the people to those natural contradictions you're so fond of, how cradle-to-grave conditioning can —"

"*My* analysis is vulgar! You sit there coming on like B.F.-fucking-Skinner with all this behavior-modification horseshit, then you tell me my analysis is vulgar."

"I'm not defending it, I'm stating that it exists. If you can't face the facts of the matter there's nothing I can do!"

"Listen —"

"Hold it, *hold* it!" Mark Remington raised his arms like a referee from the floor. "Could we please get back on the immediate subject? I know this is a tough issue to deal with clearly, but

[133]

we aren't getting very far with this kind of generalizing. I think it might be possible that this is one of those areas where our overall position will have to come out of practice rather than conscious planning, will only reveal its overall shape to us through the accumulation of spe*cifi*c stands we take along the way."

Schenk cleared his throat from the back of the room. "With that in mind," he said, voice cutting through, trying to take control, "I've already prepared a position piece for the paper on this BU thing. If you all can just listen for a minute while I read it, maybe we can talk it over in detail and come up with something we can all be comfortable with. I think having something more concrete to react to will be helpful."

Some of them turned slightly toward Schenk to hear better. He held a sheet of yellow notebook paper in his lap.

" 'Workers Lead the Way,' " he began. "That's the headline. It sets our priorities right off." He read in a slightly deeper tone. " 'In a recent disturbance on the Boston University campus, students and other supporters of striking General Electric workers joined to demonstrate their solidarity with the men on the picket lines by demanding that the university ban all GE job recruiters from the campus until the strike is settled. The university had previously gained a court order prohibiting any such demonstration, a subtler but more effective tactic than their usual fascist reliance on violent confrontation, taking their cue no doubt —' "

"Schenk —"

" '— taking their cue from the common practice of management and the courts using the tool of injunction to suppress the workers' right to strike.' "

"Schenk, one point." Mark Remington spoke up. "Your use of the word *fascist*. Don't you think that's a little out of control?"

"Well what are they?"

"I'm not arguing the correctness of its application, I'm worried about its effect in our paper. Nobody uses *fascist* that way but the CP. And one thing we can't have the workers reading in our paper is a lot of old-style Communist rhetoric —"

"Well what are we?"

"We're trying to keep it a very small *c*. We're trying to get back closer to the original meaning of the word."

"*Maybe* we don't agree on that meaning. Where's the dictionary?"

Tracy Anne shifted her position, bumping her thigh lightly against Hobie's knee. She was sitting by him again. In the last few days she always ended up next to him, they always turned out to be partners for mirror drill in Martial Arts. She had been bumping more and more, though other than that she didn't seem too clumsy. Tracy Anne always asked Hobie what he thought about the lesson after class, as if it weren't complete without his reaction. She listened carefully like Sarah did, but seemed like she was agreed with him before he got to the point, that the asking was more important than the answering.

"I used to be, you know, really into drugs and all that," she had told him. "The whole decadent hippie thing." Tracy Anne was sixteen-and-a-half and came from Natick. "My friends just got wrecked all the time and complained how dull everything was, which was a major drag. Major — *drag.* Then this one time I was in New York with my girlfriend cause she knew this guy played with the Fugs — well he didn't play, he helped with the equipment and all, a techie — and we were going to see them but it was right when Columbia happened and we went over there and my girlfriend met this guy she's living with now and got hit with a beer bottle by some jock and the whole thing just blew me away. Blew — me — *away.* And I sort of, you know, got turned on by the Revolution. I mean it's a hell of a lot better than sitting around getting wrecked and feeling sorry for yourself. You're doing something to help other people. I used to think I wanted to be in the Peace Corps to do that, help other people in Africa or something, but the Peace Corps has been exposed for its imperialist cover operations now, so it's revolution or nothing I guess. You have to be really committed." Tracy Anne was kind of short and not exactly thin. Not exactly fat either, just baby fat. She wore overalls every day and was almost pretty. The kind of girl Verl Biggins back home would say, "She won't win any contests but I wouldn't kick her outa bed." Of course Verl was a lot of noise, probably never had the chance to do any kicking, but that was the kind of girl she was. Not so pretty you'd have daydreams about her, but not so bad. The less pretty they are, Verl and the rest always said, the *eas*ier they are. It did seem to be sort of true, from what he'd seen. Like Terry Blankenship's sister, who was just downright *ugly*. Tracy Anne wasn't bad, though. Maybe — He'd only had that one time with Lettie Blankenship so fast and nervous he couldn't hardly remember what it felt like and then two-and-a-half years above Delia's waist. Delia rubbing close just to know he was hard then getting all pale and tight-lipped when he wandered onto private property. Knowing how pretty she was, knowing how many guys wanted to have her.

Tracy Anne wasn't bad, but she wasn't so pretty she could afford to be so — *diff*icult. Maybe she even liked, *want*ed to. Lettie Blankenship couldn't be the only one who was that way. Not if even a fraction of what all the fellas said was true. Tracy Anne wasn't bad at all. And she kept *bump*ing him.

Hobie fixed his eyes on Schenk, who was quoting from the dictionary, and let his foot slowly splay out till it rested lightly against her leg. He held it there a moment then eased it off. Tracy Anne leaned back on her elbows, letting her forearm brush the side of his thigh. Could be an accident, the floor was full of bodies. Hobie pulled his legs up and wrapped his arms around his knees, touching her hair with the back of his hand in the movement, enough so she would feel it but not enough so that it couldn't be another accident. She had long blond hair so straight it looked ironed, just like Delia's. It was the only way they reminded him of each other. Hobie waited for an answer, feeling the exact amount of space between them, his whole right side listening for a touch. Was she interested? Schenk and Mark Remington were both smiling just a little the way they did when they were pissed but didn't want a fight. Wein had the floor, dulling the tension with a stream of precedent-setting actions he remembered from his study of the rural Spanish anarchists. Tracy Anne rolled over to lie on her side, not settling into position till her bottom had twice nudged Hobie's ankle. She was. There was too much for it to be just accidents, she must be. Hobie relaxed his right side and tried to tune back in to the meeting. She was. He would bear that in mind.

"The Indians took Alcatraz," said Grant Parke suddenly. "What?"

"The Indians took Alcatraz. Went out there on a boat and liberated it."

"C'mon Parke, don't fuck around, we're trying to get down to something here."

"I'm not fucking around, it's true. You're talking about the effectiveness of vanguard action, right? Here's a perfect example. I read it in the *Globe* tonight. I meant to tell you all at the beginning of the meeting but I forgot."

"What Indians?"

"The Cleveland Indians. How do I know? They didn't say what tribe or anything, the paper just said Indians. They figure the government has boosted so much of their land they ought to boost some back."

"Did they free the prisoners?"

"There's none left. They shut the prison down a couple years back and moved everybody off."

"So what are they doing there?"

"Setting up headquarters. Waiting to see how the Feds react. Isn't that a gas? Fuckin Indians take over Alcatraz. Stormed the beach and set up business."

"Fan*tas*tic!"

"Red Power!"

"Ellis Island should be next —"

"Walpole!"

"America for the Americans!"

"Not bad," said Miriam, "if you're interested in a cold rock out in the ocean." People quieted. "Let them try to get the Black Hills back and see how they do."

"The propriety of vanguard activism depends, in large part," continued Ira Wein, "on the previously demonstrated efficiency of your base-building operation. I don't think you can divorce the two. I think any action is doomed to failure unless you have at least the foundation of the mass support you want already laid."

"But one of the ways you *get* people interested enough to join your base," said Schenk, "is by doing what everyone else would love to do but doesn't dare. Tapping the collective subconscious, if you like. And one of the quickest methods of attracting support in numbers is through the dynamic of militant action by a vanguard and the ensuing mass identification. Look at Columbia."

"What if you take a faulty reading from the collective subconscious?"

Mark Remington raised his voice slightly to enter the discussion again. "What if your action turns out *not* to be something everyone is dying to do? You end up alienating all the potential supporters you intended to attract, you end up looking like some pain-in-the-ass street gang, a bunch of kids. Look at the Days of Rage."

"That was an error in tactics, not in philosophy." The edge was growing sharper in Schenk's voice. "The Weathermen couldn't plan a Tupperware party, much less a successful street action in Chicago. They didn't involve other people outside the Movement in the show, it was just them and the pigs, and you *know* who's gonna come off on the bloody end of the stick in that situation. They aren't *in*terested in a base anymore, they just want to get a few more notches on their skulls. Heroes. They all want to be fucking heroes. Okay, so the Weathermen are off on their own violence trip, so what? That doesn't say *any*thing about the value of vanguard action. The fact remains, consciousness is changed through action."

"I'm not saying it isn't valuable," said Remington, "of *course* it is. I'm saying that you better have a pretty good foundation before you stick your neck out. Consciousness is also changed by patience and education. And to accomplish that kind of steady, long-lasting consciousness raising you have to stay in business, which means stay in the community and the factories and out of the *joint*. Which means sometimes you have to lay low even when the enemy's guard is down and you could get a good shot in, means you have to roll with the punches sometimes instead of punching back. You fight them the wrong way it just ends up in more repression."

"But our job isn't to *avoid* repression!" Schenk and Remington weren't facing each other but they weren't exactly addressing the group in a general way, either. "We can always do that, we can always make nice and be ineffectual so the enemy won't consider us a threat. If the enemy isn't worrying about you, isn't trying to lock you up, then you're probably wasting your time."

"I don't think we should have to rely on the cops to know whether we're wasting our time or not."

"And *I* don't think we're going to build much of a base unless the people see we've got the *balls* to back up our beliefs."

"Those who have to show their balls all the time," said Remington, "are called exhibitionists. People don't take them very seriously."

"Those who have no balls to show," said Schenk, lowering his voice to a more personal level, "are called eunuchs. People don't take them seriously at all."

It was silent for a moment, the group waiting for the next move. They usually didn't come out and disagree so directly, Schenk and Mark Remington, they usually sat to one side and let their opinions be known through hints or through someone else's mouth. Miriam usually argued for Schenk, or King would when he felt like talking and sometimes lately even Smallwood or one of the other kids would argue a line they'd heard in Schenk's class, all the while aware of him listening from the rear of the room. Joel Pinkstaff talked for Remington, and Grant Parke and sometimes Wein did, if you could make out what exactly he was supporting. And sometimes Sarah did, though mostly she tried to talk for herself.

"There's this beautiful quote, it's from Trotsky I think, when he heard that Nechayev had died in prison," said Ira Wein. "I wish I could remember it, it sums up our little impasse here perfectly. Well, anyhow, to get us unstuck, I don't think the positions you two are taking are mutually exclusive. Maybe if we could define exactly what we mean by an adequate base, we could —"

Mark Remington was sleeping with Sarah. Hobie had never seen them together that way or anything and they didn't do any special touching of each other in public but he could tell. The way you could always tell those things if you hung around for a while and got to know people. The way they talked to each other, not having to fill in details, finishing each other's thoughts. The way Mark flirted with the other girls in the house but not with Sarah, the way he had of idly picking food off her plate at meals. You could almost always tell when people were sleeping with each other.

Remington was better-looking than most all of the other fellas, dark and built in the right sizes all over like guys who did gymnastics on the TV. Somebody said he'd been an all-state wrestler in high school. He didn't have to talk so loud as the others to get attention during group and it wasn't just his looks. He knew how to talk. It was like a movie where the first time they open their mouths you knew which one was the main character. They said that Remington had been big in SDS around Boston when he was starting graduate school but had quit after the big split at the June convention, had come back from Chicago to form Third Way. He had started from scratch and gotten it on its feet in just a few months.

He was extra friendly when he was first introduced to Hobie, almost flirting like he did with the girls but in a different way. He had been nice ever since. Mark was with SNCC in Alabama, they told him. Mark was busted in Chicago in '68, Mark was at the Pentagon, Mark was in Harvard Yard in April. To hear them talk about it Mark had been in on just about every important student protest of the sixties and had the scars and police record to prove it. But he never talked about anything he had done before Third Way.

"There's the PL, who are hard-line Maoists and like to think they're reaching the workers," he explained to Hobie the first night. "But actually their politics are too extremely purist to attract many reasonable people. Then there's the Weathermen, who you've heard of, who have sort of written off the American working class as being in cahoots with the imperialists in ripping off the rest of the world. So they figure they're a vanguard group of the world revolution, that their job is to set up a battlefront right here in the U.S."

"Two, three, many Vietnams," said Sarah.

"Right. But the world isn't quite as ripe as they think, so what they're mostly doing now is losing a lot of sympathy for the left and making it hot for the rest of us. Since the factional split there hasn't been much to choose between two dead-end bunches. That's why we started the Third Way, that's where the name came from. PL is pretty much running the SDS now and it's forcing them to be a lot more action-oriented than they used to be, just to keep the students interested, and the Weathermen affinity groups are all cruising around for their big blazing showdowns. When the smoke clears we figure that we'll be the only ones left standing. You probably know from the mines how these things work. Like the early union movement, the way it was weak, then strong, then weak, almost disappearing, then strong again with all kinds of triumphs and defections and shooting wars and right- and left-wing crazies, but through it all there was a dedicated core of people who kept the thing alive, so that today you've got the UMW. We want to be that kind of core of people."

Mark explained the group a little without even hinting that Hobie should join. He said to stay as long as was needed. He always said "How's it goin?" and gave Hobie big-brother pats on the shoulder when they met around the house. He loaned some of his own socks till Hobie's had a chance to be dried out. Hobie didn't trust him as far as he could kick him.

Sometimes in the movies, if the hero was someone like Joel McRae or Alan Ladd or Audie Murphy and the girl was somebody good, Tuesday Weld maybe, Hobie found himself rooting for the bad guys.

"— and so what you probably have to accept is the existence of an immediate base, the people in the real world who will support pretty much everything you do, the auxiliary base, those who can be rallied for certain specific actions like antiwar or a union fight, and the prospective base, the people who can only be expected to join us once the big-picture revolution is well under way. So in any discussion of possible vanguard action we have to be well aware of which particular base we're trying to impress or involve. And in that respect, proper timing seems extra important. I think it was Kerensky who said —"

Wein quoted Kerensky. Wein quoted Brecht and Bukharin and Rosa Luxemburg. And Kautsky and Freud and Max Weber. Hobie knew who Freud was. Miriam gave a report on her progress interesting her fellow stitchers, mostly Spanish-speaking women, in the Third Way. Smallwood requested a discussion and vote on a new name for the group but nobody was interested at the moment. Grant Parke told a story about his last trip to the unemployment office, about having to explain to them how he only paid ten dollars rent a month. Sarah brought up a few household matters that were sliding and asked for more help with the newspaper distribution. Pinkstaff and Smallwood got into an argument over whether pumping two bullets through the door of the Cambridge police headquarters, as twenty-three SDS members had been accused of conspiring to do, was a responsible revolutionary action or not. Miriam told them all to wrap their toothbrushes in paper towel at night, as the roaches in the house were getting out of hand and were especially attracted to moisture. They debated about whether to send a delegation to walk the GE picket line in Lynn.

And all the while Hobie felt Schenk sitting back by the door, watching. Lately when he was alone in a room the feeling would creep up that Schenk was there somewhere. Watching. His eyes that never seemed to blink behind the wire-rimmed glasses, his way of talking to you like you were partners together in some life-or-death business, the things he told you to think about or to do that weren't quite orders and weren't quite suggestions.

"So what do you think about this?"

Hobie had been at the house almost three days, out of the rain, and had hoped no one would ask him that. "It's a nice house."

Schenk shook his head. "I mean what do you think of *us*."

"You all seem to get on real well together. A whole lot of people like you got, that's not so easy."

"Our politics. What do you make of our politics? That's what we're here for." Those eyes on him, unblinking. Unavoidable.

"Well, from what I can see, and I only been here a couple days —"

"Don't qualify yourself so much, you sound like Wein. What do you think?"

"I think a lot of what you're trying to do, to get done, is good. It's real important. I really haven't seen enough of your — uh — *meth*ods, to make any kind of, you know, final *judg*ment or anything. It's a complicated kind of —"

[142]

"Make one."

"Huh?"

"Make a judgment. You can put it off but you can't escape it forever. Make a judgment. And don't pretend things are more pluralistic — *comp*licated — than they are. We have to learn to think crudely."

"Well —"

"Hobie, you're either part of the solution or part of the problem." Schenk caught his eyes and held them. "For us, or against us. Either you're for the people, for workers having control over their lives, for life, or you're with the enemy. On the side of death. Make a choice."

The group argued and debated while Schenk sat back by the door like a Holiness preacher, stern and judging, a nag at the back of each member's head. They talked among themselves of the way Schenk put them under pressure, but they also talked about how he was three times as tough on himself, how he worked for sixteen or more hours a day with no letup. They talked about how he treated them all, even the youngest and least experienced, as if he *expect*ed them to act well. As if he took their dedication and bravery as a matter of course, as if he felt he couldn't ask for better people to work with. Coach acted that same way with the first string and it made guys do more for him than you'd expect they had in them. But Coach was interested in nothing beyond a football game, and the further down the bench you got the less inspiring his treatment of you became.

"Is there any more business?" asked Mark Remington.

The shock troops held their breaths. There was a moment of silence. Hobie's neck was stiff, his bottom had fallen asleep. "My ears are hoarse," he used to say when he was a little kid and his mother would have some big-voiced preacher over for dinner. Dar and Daddy would laugh at the expression but they knew what he meant. Hobie's ears had been hoarse ever since he'd first crashed with these people, they were nearly raw tonight.

"I want to talk about the harassment we're getting from neighborhood people," said Smallwood.

There was a weary, almost-in-unison sigh from the shock troops.

"I want us to clear up our stand on Israel," said Joel Pinkstaff.

"And I don't think we quite settled the BU issue," said Wein. "I don't think we should pack it in with that still hanging over our heads."

It would go on. There was no telling for how long, no telling what direction it would take. Hobie squirmed on the floor, lightly bumping Tracy Anne, and tried to get some blood moving below his waist.

"It's not the Commonists, it's the boogies."

Dominic was fooling with the new hot sheet, trying to tape it down smooth on the dashboard, and Vinnie was driving. He kept it slow and tight to the curb down Tremont, being visible, trying to make eye contact.

"The boogies are their heroes," said Dominic. "It's like you go to the movies, Jesse James gets all the good lines, he gets the girl, he gets to die slow and say his last words instead of just falling off a roof like some stiff from the posse. That's who they think the boogies are, the kids, they think they're Jesse James. The Panthers and the whatsit — who are those guys over —"

"De Mau Mau," said Vinnie.

"Yeah, the De Mau Mau. The kids see them out there with their guns and their motching around — they held up the state capital in California you know — the kids see that and they think it's like outlaws in the Old West. They think it's an adventure story, they get a big hod-on for the boogies. They want to be like them, join up with them."

Vinnie sighed. "Listen, Dawm, you want to take a peek at the sidewalk once in a while? That's what we're out here for."

"Huh? Oh, the sidewalk. Hey, there's nothin going *on*, it's a slow night. It's a Monday, they're all fucked-out from the weekend."

"Good it's a slow night, let's keep it that way. Pay some attention."

"Sure. No prawblem. Don't get your balls in an upraw." Dominic looked out at the people hanging on Tremont for a block and a half, then turned back to Vinnie. "But the boogs don't want any pot of em. What they want is the kids should mine their own business. It's like — you ever hear of a guy name Ambrose Bierce?"

"Nope."

"He was this guy, I was readin about him the other day, he was a writer. Stories and newspaper otticles and a lot of political commentary. A real cynical guy, like that Brinkley from Huntley-Brinkley, only even more. He was in the eighteen-hundreds, Bierce, till around the turn of the century. And even though he was a cynical guy, and pretty well equipped upstairs, he got a hod-on for Pancho Villa. You member Pancho Villa?"

"How could I forget?"

"Wise-ass. They give me a wise-ass, I gotta ride with all night."

"Tell the story, Dawm."

"Okay, so he thinks Pancho Villa is the bee's knees, right, and he goes down there to folla him around, write some otticles and ride with the banditos. There was a lot of stuff around about how Villa was for a revolution, that's what sucked Bierce in, but actually he was just another wise guy went around knocking over banks. Like they said Jesse James gave his money from the train rawbries to poor people. A lot of bullshit. So Ambrose Bierce goes down Mexico, finds Villa, and he joins up. They let him on but they don't trust him an inch, see, cause he's a gringo and the U.S. Calvary has been chasin Villa's ass both sides of the bawder. If I got this straight, now, I read it a while back."

"Back when you were going for your PhD."

"You're a scream, Doggerty, you oughta be on TV. Anyhow, it don't take long before Bierce stots to see what is really the case down there, and the last things he writes you can tell the honeymoon is over with Pancho. And then he disappears. That's what it said in this thing I was reading, he disappeared, no trace, nobody knows what happened.

"But what I figure," said Dom, "he just couldn't resist giving Villa the needle. He's a real cynical guy, remember, and that's the way he wrote, givin everybody the needle. So one day they're out there, riding around lookin for a savings-and-loan to knock over, *robbo el banko* or whatever they say, and Ambrose Bierce he's hot and sweaty and he's got saddle saws and he just can't resist. 'Hey Pauncho,' he yells out, 'how many banks we gotta hit before we'll be rich enough to stot a revolution?'

"Now they don't have much of a sense of humor, the Spanish. Bullfights, they get a chuckle out of that, and chickens pecking each other's eyes out, but they're not a real humorous people —"

"Must be all that hot food."

Dominic sighed. "They'll give you a summer replacement show, right, taking over for *Laugh-In*, and then they'll have you do guest spots, Johnny Carson, stuff like that. You'll have to change your name though, they're all Jewish, the stand-up comics. Vinnie Kaplan."

"So get to the point."

"So the point is Villa bumped him off. Picked up the machete and whack-whack. Like Humphrey Bogart in that movie. Left him for the vultures and the Gila mawnsters."

"So?"

"So that's what you get, you go kissin ass around people like that. That's what these kids are gonna get, they don't wise up to the Panthers and the Mau Maus. They ought to make it required reading in the schools, about Ambrose Bierce."

Vinnie laughed. "Instead of what's his name — the guy on the sled."

"Huh?"

"Remember? You must of had to read it. He gets paralyzed —"

"Ironsides —"

"*No!* The sled —"

"Ethan Allen!"

"Ethan *Frome*."

"Right. Yeah, we had to read that. Ridiculous, the big lesson is that if you want to take yourself out of the picture, don't do it by running a sled into a tree. That's gonna come in real handy in later life. They should make them read Ambrose Bierce instead."

Vinnie slowed the patrol car almost to a stop as they neared West Springfield Street. "Some heavy traffic goin down here," he said. "Captain says to look extra careful, there's a lot of coke around."

Four black men leaned against a building and dead-eyed back at them. One of them smiled and stuck his tongue out.

"What we ought to do," said Dominic, "is we ought to walk in the Rainbow Lounge over there, have everybody empty their pockets on the table. We could open our own phomaceutical house."

"You do that, Dawm. I'll keep the motor runnin."

"You would. I go in there alone, you come back a week later I'd be on the menu. Right after the bobbacue ribs and the hog jowls."

"Hogs got jowls?"

"Sure. They get a little older, too much pasta, not enough exercise —"

"And I'm the one he says should be on TV."

"Lookit em out there." Dom nodded back at the men against the building. "The minute we turn around it stots up all over again. Sellin shit, selling women —"

"So what can we do? Lock em all up?"

"Hey," said Dominic, "you hear about Kilbride?"

"I heard he got transferred to the Nawth End."

"You hear why?"

"Nope. I figured he asked for it."

"No way. It's his daughter. She got Black Fever."

"That like the plague or something?"

"Naw, it's not a medical disease. It's in your head. Black Fever is when a girl, a white girl, she gets this thing in her head she's got to have a black guy. It's like an obsession with them, nothin can stand in their way."

"Yeah, I seen cases."

"Well, Kilbride's daughter, she's fifteen, she's got it."

"You're kiddin."

"No lie. I got this from Phil, they been ridin the same car a couple years, on and off. Kilbride's got a weakness for the tea, he's off duty, sometimes he gets loose and he talks about it. To Phil, you know, he and Phil are real tight.

"So his daughter, she's run off twice, they pick her up in New Yawk City she's with some black guy. Second time the guy was in his thirties, they could have burned him for statutory, Kilbride called them off. Didn't want her to testify, it was too embarrassing. And now she's back, he can't control her, she stays out all night, comes home and tells them she's been fucking boogies. Try and stop her, she says. Won't look at a white boy. So Kilbride, he's too proud, he can't control her but he won't bring her to family cawt or anything, won't go for help. He's stuck. It's stotted gettin to him, you know, he's got boogies on the brain.

"So they had a couple incidents down here, Kilbride leaning a lot hodder than he should have under the circumstances, and Phil, he's scared some kid is gonna get wasted down here, he says the wrong thing or gets caught with a white girl and Kilbride is in on it. So he talks to the Captain, explains things, and they put Jim up to the Nawth End. No boogies up there, just the *paesans*. He's a good officer, Kilbride, no reason to let him get into trouble."

"I didn't know any of that."

"Yeah, she got the Black Fever and there's nothing he can do."

"You wonder how it happens," said Vinnie. He turned left up Washington.

"It's like a disease. Like an addiction, they get hooked on black."

"Yeah. And there's that — you know — about them having bigger ones."

"Shit, Vinnie, you an me, we seen enough black meat in shakedowns and whatnot, know that's a lot of noise. They come in all sizes, just like us. And hey, I never seen anything on a boog compares with Kolodny."

Vinnie laughed. "You got a point. First time I ever seen Kolodny with his shawts off in the locker, I like to fainted dead away. I asked him if he had a license to carry that thing."

"Fuckin ten-pound salami he's got there, don't have to pack a nightstick."

"Maybe Kilbride should get his daughter together with Kolodny, get her off the habit."

"Christ Vinnie, what a thing to say! He wants to cure her, not kill her."

"I guess so. Take a look here, Dawm, see what's doin at the Shanty."

Dominic wiped the breath-frost off his side window to see. It was turning cold.

"The usual. There's what's his name, Wee Willie. Hustling them numbers. Nigger pennies."

"They're not like you, got twenty dollars to blow on the Pats."

"What can I say? I thought it would be closer, Vin. They looked good last week but I thought they'd just squeak this one out. The Bills have got O.J. there, and I figure —"

"He's just a rookie, Dawm."

"So he's a rookie. You seen him all last year, the college, the fucker run em ragged."

"That was college, Dawm, it's a whole different spawt. He'll maybe hang on with the Bills, O.J., they're pretty desperate, but he's never gonna be the big name he was. He's not gonna be like Sayers or somebody."

"Sayers. Jesus he was beautiful to watch."

"Poetry in motion."

"I dropped two hundred on the Bears-Packers once, didn't hodly notice, he put on such a fuckin show."

"I was a fifteen-year-old girl," said Vinnie, "I seen him out there reversing field and going eighty-five for the scaw, I'd have Black Fever too."

Dom laughed. "Well that's different, that's something the guy's actually *do*ing. Black Fever is all in your head, it's a fantasy. It's like imagining they all got telephone poles between their legs. It's not *real*."

"Uh-huh."

"It's just like I was sayin with the kids going round after the Panthers with their tongues hangin out. It's not cause of what they *done*, it's cause of what the kids *think* they done. It's Black Fever just the same, only with the kids it's guns and revolutions, not shacking up and driving your old man bananas."

Vinnie turned the car left on West Newton. "So you dropped twenty."

"Yeah. I had a feeling, but not that strong a feeling. So it was only twenty. You'd of thought I bet my house the way I blew up, the Pats made that last touchdown, wrecked my spread. The wife and I had a big fight about my temper. Just cause I left a stain on the wallpaper, throwin a beer can."

"You got a lousy temper, Dawm."

"I got a shawt fuse is all. I boil over easy. But it's nothin serious, it's mostly a lotta noise. You, you got the temper."

"I keep it under control."

"That's the trouble. You keep it under, keep the lid on. You let things build up, like a pressure cooker, and then all of a sudden outa the blue — kapowie!"

"Tell me one time —"

"Kapowie! That time we were up on Shawmut, the Arab guy gave you a little lip —"

"He was a piece of shit —"

"He was just a small-time fence, watches and rings, and he said something any other time it would of rolled off your back. But you'd had a rough week —"

"I had a horrible week —"

"The Captain was on your ass and that hooker scratched you and your kids were sick —"

"And that fuckin Arab —"

"You went *ape*shit, Vin. I never been so scared in my life. I thought you were gonna kill him with your bare hands."

"He wasn't so greasy, that guy," said Vinnie, turning right up Columbus, "I would of strangled him."

"You're the one's got the temper, Vin."

"Yeah, I suppose I do. When I lose it."

"Which is a good thing you don't do so often. Me, I'm like a crazy man with the six o'clock news. These punks all over taking over college buildings, saying they got the country behind them, 'the people' they call it. When just the other night, you see the results from that poll? Sixty-eight percent he had. Highest ever popularity in history."

"It escapes me." Vinnie shook his head.

"It would. You Irish, you're still in mourning for JFK there. Well he's not comin back, that's too bad. But that's no reason you shouldn't put your weight behind Nixon now he's President."

"I don't trust him. I never have."

"You don't trust anybody don't have a shamrock tattooed over their hot."

"I trust *you*, Dawm."

"I'm your pottner, of course you trust me. You'd be in trouble if you didn't. Hey," Dom pointed out to the walk, "is that what's her name on the cawner there?"

"The redhead?"

"Yeah. One of Slick's girls isn't she? What's her name?"

"Yvonne?"

"Something like that. But Spanishy sounding."

"She's not Spanish."

"Naw, she's a mick like you. But they, you know, change their names. You shook down any two-block area they're workin you'd come up with twenty, twenty-five Jacquelines. It's like a stage name."

"Isabel? Imelda?"

"Inez."

"Right."

"Pull up by her, Vin, I wanna chat."

She was standing back from the curb a little as if she was waiting for someone, shivering in her short, dyed-rabbit jacket. She wore a satiny orange miniskirt and tight black boots up to mid-thigh. She made like she didn't notice the patrol car until Vinnie beeped and Dom waggled his finger to come. She had to stoop over to talk through the window, two young boys checked out her behind as they walked past.

"I help you guys?"

"Hi Inez," said Dominic, "how's tricks?"

"If you need directions I can't help you out. I'm new to this neighborhood."

"Yeah, we noticed."

"How's Slick?" said Vinnie.

"Slick?"

"Slick."

"Slick who?"

"Slick who we're gonna lock up and swallow the key we ever get something on him," said Dom. "That Slick. The coon you hustle for."

"Officer, I don't have the faintest notion what you're gettin at."

"When's the last time we burned you, Inez?"

"You turds couldn't burn a one-eyed shoplifter," said Inez pleasantly, "much less make anything stick on me."

"Slow night?"

"Till you showed up."

[151]

"Scawed yet?"

"If you're referring to what I think you are, that would be in violation of Chapter 273, Section 53 of the General Lawrs of Massachusetts, and I'm a lawr-abiding citizen."

"She's a real shop cookie, this one," said Dom to Vinnie, "I wonder why Slick put her out on the street? Used to be, I remember correctly, she was his number-one piece, never saw fresh air but what she was in the passenger seat of that big El D he drives. Must be some hod times in the cunt racket."

"Dawm —"

"Let me finish, Vin, this is interesting. Now, Inez, to what do you attribute this sudden appearance on our nightly beat? Could it have anything to do with the young lady of Oriental background I seen cruising about town with your sponsor there? Slick got a new main lady?"

The woman's eyes went dead. "Go roll in it, buddy."

"Can I believe my ears? An officer of the lawr subjected to crude language on the very streets of our city? What would you think, Inez, we pinched you for public disturbance and took you out of business for a night? Wouldn't follow up on the chodge, just give you a night on the city. What would you tell Slick when you come up empty? Think he'd take it out of your hide?"

"Listen," said Inez wearily, "you're gonna run me in, run me in. It's freezin out here, I can't be standin here talkin shit with you all night. And since when did you make the vice squad?"

"We come around this block again," said Dom, beginning to roll his window up, "you better be gone. Got it sister?"

Vinnie checked the rearview mirror as they pulled away. "She give us the finger."

"We give her five minutes, come back here and bust her ass if she's not gone."

"Jesus, Dawm, what's with you? She's just a hooker. Why you want to lean on her like that?"

"She's protecting that black motherfucker Slick is why. Out pounding the pavement so's he can flash that smile of his at us, get a diamond set into one of his front teeth, and sit back in his white-on-white El Dorado. That's why. Her I'm not mad at personally. In fact I think she's cute. Freckles. Who'd ever think of a hooker having freckles? And she's tall. I like tall ones."

[152]

"I know you do." Vinnie turned right up Appleton, heading for Tremont.

"More fuck for your buck."

"So why didn't you ask for her phone number, you think she's so cute?"

"Wise-ass. Now there was a perfect example. Black Fever. That's what it leads to. Inez there, not too long ago she was somebody's fifteen-year-old daughter, stayin out all night and chasin after the boogs. Know what I'd like to see? Like to get Kilbride back down here, off duty, you know, put him on Slick's case. Tell him Slick's been after his girl, gonna turn her out. Would that be a show?"

"Don't even kid about it."

"Be nothin left but some pearly white teeth, a two-tone alligator shoe and the hood awnament from a Cadillac. That I would surely like to see."

"Dawminic," said Vinnie, "you're a dangerous man."

"But what about Israel?" The meeting was finally breaking up, people rising from the floor and stretching, drifting off to different parts of the house.

"What about Israel?" Joel Pinkstaff called to them. "We were going to discuss our position on Israel." But Schenk was gone and Mark Remington was headed out the door and Wein had talked himself hoarse.

"Meir Kahane is speaking in Boston this Sunday and we don't have a thing out about it." The kids were all hurrying away, afraid they'd be caught if a discussion flared up. Hobie toured the room emptying cigarette butts from the scattered tuna-fish cans and picking up candy wrappers. It was his week for Garbage Detail. He was left alone in the room with Pinkstaff and Miriam, he collected the remains of a trip to McDonalds and ate a couple of cold french fries.

"What about Israel?"

"What the fuck about it, Joel?" Miriam stopped at the door.

"I don't think our position on it should be so fuzzy."

"Nobody gives a shit about Israel."

"I do."

"Well that's *your* hang-up."

[153]

"That's not true. It's something important that's happening in world politics. And if that's too international for our concern, then what about Kahane coming to talk in Boston? Shouldn't we have some sort of policy toward him and the JDL?"

"Policy? What's there to talk about? They're a bunch of racists and that's all there is to it."

"What's racist about wanting to defend yourself?"

Miriam sighed. "A lot of old ladies in Mattapan worried the *shvartzehs* are out to rape them. It's racist. It's the same kind of crap went down between the teachers and the people in Bed-Stuy. Racism."

"How can you call it racism when a real threat exists? Did you see the latest *Black Panther* that Paris Green brought over? At least three different poems and articles that have some mention of 'offing Goldberg' or 'wasting the kikes.' How can you compare a neighborhood association of old people to that kind of blatant anti-Semitism?"

"The Panthers have their reasons for it. If you don't understand *that* by now —"

"*Rea*sons, big deal, reasons! That doesn't mean you just stand by and let it happen. They stood by in Germany in the thirties and —"

"Don't start that holocaust routine."

"It's true! It's right in front of your eyes, Miriam, if you of all people can't —"

"Me of all people? What the fuck you mean by that?"

"You know. With our — background — if we can't —"

"Oh Christ, Pinkstaff, you're such a fucking *Jew* it's ridiculous."

Hobie tossed the trash into a small can and went into the printing room next door. The oil and ink smell hit him at once, he breathed deep. The only artificial high in the house, Grant Parke said of it. Hobie just liked the smell. He'd been sleeping in with the machine for a while now, the floor of the main rack-out room was too crowded with other kids. He didn't like being stepped on at night. And then, too, the only night he spent up there the business in the next bag got so hot and heavy he felt like an intruder even with his back turned to it.

Hobie plopped down on the big puffy sleeping bag they'd

loaned him and closed his eyes. He couldn't help but hear Pink-staff and Miriam through the wall.

"*I'm* a Jew? Hah! Whose mother still sends her little boxes of carrot cake for Purim? Whose mother called college the beginning of every first semester so her daughter shouldn't be out demonstrating on Rosh Hashanah?" Joel and Miriam had gone to socialist summer camp together, it seemed, had attended Brandeis at the same time. "Whose mother talks to her little doggie companion, her little Schatzie, in fucking *Yid*dish?"

"That's my mother's problem, not mine."

"*I'm* such a *Jew!* My father went Unitarian years ago and lately my mother is sniffing around the Ethical Society and *I'm* such a Jew."

"You are. At heart, Pinkstaff, that's just what you are."

"Okay. Wonderful. I'm a Jew. Big deal. What, I'm supposed to be a*shamed* of it? Are *you* ashamed of it?"

"I really don't feel one way or the other about it."

"Don't hand me that."

"Listen, I wouldn't give a shit if the whole fucking imperialist state of Israel slid into the fucking Mediterranean and was never heard from again. I wouldn't care if Nasser ate it for *break*fast. If you've got some big hang-up about it that's too bad, you can have a tree planted in your name or go pick fucking *grape*fruit on a kibbutz for all I care. Just don't come at me with any of your Zionist-Fascist this-land-is-mine bullshit. Okay?"

They were done then. Hobie heard Miriam stalk out, then Pinkstaff quietly follow. He had never been in a place where people argued so much, where argument seemed to be the language they spoke. The only time everybody seemed to move in the same direction was during drills in Martial Arts or when they watched Nixon on TV together.

Somebody else was in the room. The bench for the mimeograph machine loomed above him, he couldn't see to the door.

"Who's that?"

"Hobie?"

It was Tracy Anne.

"Yuh?"

"Can I ask you a question?"

"Sure. C'mon in."

Tracy Anne peeked around the bench, then came to stand by Hobie's feet. "It took me a while to find you. I was going to try the basement next."

"It's quiet in here."

"Mmn."

"What did you want to ask?"

"Huh? Oh, yeah, Smallwood and Billy and Jennifer and a couple of the others were having this argument over food stamps and we figured you'd know the answer."

"Oh."

She sat by his feet. "Smallwood said they're for people who have jobs and the others said it's just for people on welfare."

"It's for both. Least where I come from it is. It's based on how much of your income you spend for food or something like that."

"Are there a lot of people on stamps where you come from?" Her eyes had widened and there was a little extra tone of sympathy in her voice.

"I suppose. Lots of folks can't do without em."

"Were you ever on?"

"My father don't believe in it, so even when he was laid off we just made do with savings and odd jobs and like that. Some of my friends, their families been on, but we never."

"It must be awful." Tracy Anne shifted so that she was sitting up nearer to his head.

"Food is food, I guess."

"But to have to go through all the red tape there must be, it has to be demeaning. When I see the way the people around here get treated by the social-service flunkies, I mean it just tears me apart. Tears — me — a*part*. And then your people, if they're not on stamps with the government they're probably tied up in debt to the company store."

"We don't have that."

"No?" She sounded disappointed.

"Most of the companies cut that business out years ago. Cheaper to let the government worry about it, people get behind and start missin meals."

Tracy Anne casually stretched out on her side by him, rustling the blue nylon of the sleeping bag. She propped her head up

[156]

on her arm and looked into his eyes. "Do many people starve?"

"Well, starve isn't exactly the way I'd put it. Like I said, they miss a couple meals now an then. For the welfare ones there's canned goods from the surplus which are okay but for the meat, so no one really starves. There's some, what you call it, malnutrition. There's that. Mostly the hill people, don't know about diet or nothin."

"You're not hill people?"

"Well, we live around hills, but we aren't hill people. Not the ones live out away from town and try to make it huntin and farmin. Land's no good to farm, never was much, and the huntin gets worst every year. They don't make out so well."

"Like the Hatfields and McCoys."

Hobie smiled. "Not my part of the state. They're over by the Kentucky border. Mingo County."

"You do have black lung though?"

"Yeah, we do have that, the fellas who go down. My father's got a little touch himself."

"Hobie, that's awful!" She put her hand on his arm. "Is it serious?" She kept the hand there.

"It's always serious," he told her, "it's mostly a question of whether it slows you down enough you can't work or not. He's just got a taste, I think, it hasn't been named by a doctor or nothin. You got to wait till you've got a real strong case before you take it before the doctors, you're lible to lose your job for nothin if you push it too fast. They only just started to recognize it as a disease."

"Really?"

"The companies and the UMW and the insurance people, they didn't want to bother with it, so they acted for years like it didn't exist. Nobody got a dime of compensation less they could come up with some other kind of ailment would show on an X-ray picture. But finally a couple honest doctors and this local politician, fella name of Ken Hechler, and some of those Ralph Nader people started makin noise about it and the men worked in the mines they picked up on that and went out and the bunch of them put enough heat on to force the people in charge to put some laws through. So now you're supposed to get compensated."

"It's under control."

"Oh, the disease is still around, the black lung, but you can get some sort of pay if it puts you out of work."

"That's good."

Her grip on his arm loosened a little. She smiled and shifted as if she might be getting up to leave.

"And then there's mine disasters."

She tightened around his arm and leaned a little closer, as if for protection.

"Cave-ins and explosions and whatnot. With them you don't worry so much about compensation as you do about survival."

"Do they happen all the time?"

"Now and then. The danger's always there, it's almost surprising there aren't more disasters. Had a big one back in '68, up to Farmington. One of Consolidation's holes. Men buried, some killed right off, others you don't know, there was but a few brung back up alive —" Tracy Anne was stroking his arm lightly, as if to comfort him. "It's always the same when one goes, people blaming each other, the television bunch flockin round, the women drinking coffee and crying all night while they dig." Her leg was against his now, her face inches away. Hobie watched her lips as she talked.

"Was it ever some of your kin?"

He would only have to lean over a bit to kiss her. Maybe there would be an opening soon. And if it turned out he had guessed wrong — well, it wasn't like home or school where you had to stay around and be embarrassed by your mistake day after day. Hobie was sticking out, he brought his knees up to hide it. "My what?"

"Kin. You know. Relatives."

"Oh, no. Never any relatives. But you never know with the mines, it's like skatin on thin ice every day. The slightest little spark can set things off, and then you can't stop it, it's just out of control."

Maybe if there was an opening he would kiss her.

"Hobie?"

And if she acted like it was okay, like maybe she was glad he had done it, he would keep coming, kissing her and touching her in the places that were supposed to get them excited, kissing her and touching her and then undressing her in such a rush that she wouldn't have time to stop being excited, to think, to reconsider the way Delia always did. He wished that Tracy Anne wasn't wearing overalls.

Catch em off guard, the fellas always said, come at em like a freight train and don't listen to any ifs ands or buts and you got it made. Specially the real young ones, don't know what's what. They'll thank you for it later. If only there'd be the right opening, if he could get her off mine stuff and onto personal talk. He could feel her breath on his cheek.

"Yuh?"

"You wanna ball me?"

Hobie didn't answer at first, the words took a moment to register. Sure, he said then, sure, and she was all over him. It felt nice, her breath and her tongue so warm, the two of them squirming on the cushiony down bag, fingers buried in each other's hair. It felt nicer with the overalls off, just a workshirt and underwear, big soft handfuls of her to grab and suck into his mouth. She had big breasts, real pillows compared to Delia's, and a rounded little tummy with blond hairs peeking over the waistband, with blue fuzz in the navel that he blew away before he started kissing. It felt nice, knowing she had already said the words, that he wouldn't be stopped just when he was most excited, that he didn't have to venture each new move like a raised poker hand. He had already won, it was just for enjoying. They could take their time.

Tracy Anne took her tongue out of his ear and whispered, "Do you have any rubbers?"

He hadn't thought of that one.

She was still on top of him, still kissing, running her hands over his chest. He had figured girls who said things like you wanna ball me would be on birth control or something. "No. I'm all out." He had had a rubber once, he and Fred Spicer had bought one apiece from the machine in the bathroom of the Blue Star so they could practice putting them on in the dark, which they heard was a big obstacle to your success with girls. They were thirteen or so. They sat under the back stairs of the hardware store one summer night with their rubbers and a flashlight and one of Dar's adventure magazines. They closed their eyes and rolled the rubbers on time after time, shining the flashlight at the She-Devils of Amazon Island whenever further inspiration was needed. They practiced till the rubbers were all stretched out and wouldn't roll up anymore, then filled them with water and tied them off and snuck to the Blankenship's yard to hang them from the handlebars of Lettie's bike.

"Sorry," he said.

"That's okay. I've got some upstairs. You wanna come up there with me?"

There would be the others up there, and even though they turned away politely and pretended not to notice, they would know. And Sarah, Sarah was always up and walking around at six in the morning, set to go down to the Red Line to pamphlet the factory people on their way to work. She'd see them together and she would know.

"It's awful nice down here," said Hobie. "I think it stays warmer."

"Okay. I'll go get them." She was up and out of his arms before he could protest, heading for the door. She turned the light out as she went. "Back in a flash."

"Damn." Hobie slowly took the rest of his clothes off and burrowed under the bag. He went soft. She had escaped, the momentum was all gone and he'd see her tomorrow morning and she'd make some noise about she couldn't find any and then would be careful never to get caught alone with him again. He could kiss it good-bye, the minute she got out the door. Who ever heard of a sixteen-year-old girl owning rubbers?

She bumped into the mimeograph bench in the dark. "Here," she said pressing it into his palm, still wrapped. "I brought a couple. You don't mind, do you?"

"It's better without em." He wrestled with the foil underneath the bag. "But it's okay if you have to."

"Oh good." She slid on top of him and continued where they had left off. It was really happening. She was naked against him with her legs wrapped around his thigh and her hand wrapped around his pecker and *no*body had ever done that, not even Lettie Blankenship that one time, she just lay there with her legs apart waiting for the next one in and when it was time for Hobie she hardly closed them around him, just lay there wide open and wet from the others and when he started thinking about that, about him being in there sloshing in everybody else's come, it was a wonder that he managed to empty out before it shrunk down with distaste. Just lay there like it had nothing to do with her, the same way she couldn't seem to understand why none of them except Hobie and maybe Ardell Higgins who didn't know *any*thing would be seen talking to her in the halls. Like it wasn't even connected to her. But here was Tracy Anne all over him and breathing hard, all her warm skin slipping against him under the cool nylon, making his stomach tingle inside, Tracy Anne humping his thigh and sucking hard on the side of his neck and taking the rubber to roll it on him and it was really *happening*. He had his hand in her, a couple fingers anyway, right inside her and it was wet but only from her being excited and she took his hand at the wrist and moved it around till she found a place and tightened, gasping in air, then let it out in a rush and smiled and gave him a big tongue-wrestling kiss. "I want you to fuck me," she said, squeezing his pecker so hard he thought the head might pop right out of the rubber. "I want you to."

She turned on her belly, then raised her bottom up in the air with her knees. "Come behind and fuck me."

Hobie got up on his knees behind her and held himself and tried to find the right opening, the wet one.

"Fuck me like they do back home," said Tracy Anne, "fuck me like the hill people do."

He hunched and squirmed and pushed till Tracy Anne reached back to start the head into her. It fit, it fit so perfect, oh so hot and perfect around him, why didn't people do this all day long?

"Fuck me like they do in the hills," she said, "fuck me like a *mule*."

He'd have to explain to her about mules tomorrow.

14

The receptionist ducked her head in before him and said, "Mr. McNatt to see you, sir." The office had wall-to-wall carpet and phony wood paneling. A plastic nameplate on the man's desk said MR. ARNOLD.

"Have a seat," he said without looking up from his book.

Hunter sat, pulling his shoulders back so the wrinkles in his good jacket wouldn't show so much.

"Only got another paragraph to go here, be right with you," said Mr. Arnold.

There was a dramatic oil painting of a goal-line stand hanging on the wall behind Mr. Arnold, the players all mud and grim black brushstrokes. From across the room Hunter had thought it was a thunderstorm at sea. The wall to the left was filled with bowling trophies and pictures of Mr. Arnold with different men. In the ones where he had the most hair and the least paunch he was usually in front of a blast furnace wearing coveralls. Later black-and-white pictures had him in suits and ties and the most recent were in color. Either he had grown into the suits or he'd started getting them tailored. There was a bowling shirt pinned up at the end of the wall and beneath it a picture of a bunch of fellas wearing the same kind. It said CAPT. over one pocket of the shirt and *Gus*, in script, over the other. The whole wall looked like a museum display about some fella who'd died a while back.

"So, Mr. McNatt. What can I do for you?" Mr. Arnold was wearing a sort of chocolate-colored jacket with a pink shirt and a brown and red tie. He had the kind of glasses that went smoky if you were in the sun or strong light. You could almost but not quite see into his eyes.

"I called in a couple days ago," said Hunter. "I'm a friend of Ray Wilcox."

"Who?"

"Ray — well the thing is, Ray was in the service with your brother —"

"Which one?"

"Mitchell."

"Mitch. Right. I remember now, the girl told me something about it. Mitch sent you over here?"

"He didn't send me, exactly. I got into town and my friend Ray had wrote here to Mitchell saying I might call, and I did. And Mitchell, he said I should come straight to you."

"He did, huh? So what's on your mind?"

"I need a job." Hunter had no idea why it made him feel so funny when he said it. It made him feel like when he had to get the extra female pads for Molly and couldn't find them on the shelf. Having to ask the girl at the register.

"You need a job so my brother Mitchell sends you here." Mr. Arnold gave a little smile and shook his head. "You start moving up in the union, people think you're like a councilman or something, you got so many jobs you can hand out. They think you hold all the aces when it comes to hiring, like you call the shots."

"You don't have anything to do with hiring?"

Mr. Arnold smiled more broadly. "Now I didn't say that, did I?"

"Cause I don't mean to go over anybody's head," said Hunter. "I'm willing to start out with everyone else, personnel office or whatever, if that's the way you do it."

"Personnel. Hah. You could pitch camp in the personnel office, move your family in there, it wouldn't do you any good. They don't have any jobs, personnel. They're lucky they keep their own jobs, shuffling paper. Jobs are tight, my friend."

"They always been. I'm not lookin for any handout."

Mr. Arnold smiled. "I'm sure you're not. But there's a lot of people who are. You want the reason jobs are tight? It's all this equal-opportunity jazz. The management people tell us they got to hire those clowns off the street, they got no experience, they got no work record, they got no *apt*itude, but there's a quota has to be filled. That's what the management people tell us, it's not their fault, it's a federal regulation. When actually it's them in

[163]

cahoots with the government to break up the union. You know what I mean?"

"Not exactly."

"I mean the dinges figure they got the federal government in their corner, what do they need us for? We're forced to let them into the union and they got no sense of it, they vote against our interests every time."

"Oh."

"Yeah," said Mr. Arnold. "Jobs are tight. But if you want someone to blame it's the dinges, lookin for a soft ride."

"I'm not lookin for no soft ride."

"Of course you're not. What are you, laid off?"

"I had to leave my last job. Personal reasons."

"Personal reasons, huh? You can't get back on?"

"It was in West Virginia. I got to be here."

"Steel?"

"No, I'm a miner. I was."

"No shit. Dark as a dungeon, damp as the dew, right?" Mr. Arnold looked him up and down. "They tell me that's a bitch, mining. They tell me that's about as hard as it comes."

"Hard enough."

"Were you ever with the Steelworkers before? We got some miners affiliated."

"No. I been UMW since I was workin."

"Uh-huh."

"I got an application the woman there had me fill out if you —"

"Naw, don't bother with that. That's what we got instead of magazines out there, the girl gives you a form to fill out. Keep you busy while you're waiting."

The phone buzzed then and Mr. Arnold answered. He said a lot of yeahs and uh-huhs into it and picked his nose. Hunter looked around the room again.

"We were Massachusetts champions in '57," said Mr. Arnold when he hung up the phone. He nodded toward the trophies. "You bowl?"

"No."

"Neither do I, not anymore. I used to roll a pretty good string, the old days, carried a 230 average. Now I play golf. The guys here, they play, so I took it up. It's quiet, you know,

[164]

walk around outside, green grass, nice, get your exercise. But the weather up here, New England — you know. We go to Vegas, I'm gonna work on my game."

Hunter shifted in his chair and wondered how he could get the subject back to jobs. He wasn't sure yet whether this fella could help him or not.

"My brother Mitch, you talked to him, he's still in the leagues. He carries 190, 195, he's stuck around there. He's with the civil service, Mitch. Licensing. He got in there right after the war with your friend, he's gone up the pay scale on schedule but it's still the same job. He's stuck. Now a guy in his position, licensing for the state, could make a nice little thing for himself. If you catch my meaning. But Mitch, he's the kind of guy, an opportunity of a certain kind could trot up and bite him on the ass and he wouldn't take it. Even though everybody's into the thing, cuttin off a little hunk for themselves, it's so widespread they probably allow for it in your salary like tips for cabdrivers, but still it's no dice. He's a fuckin choirboy, Mitch, he don't want any part of it. Which is why he's stuck.

"See, Mitch and me," said Gus Arnold, "we don't hit it off so great these days."

"That's too bad." Hunter wondered if Mr. Arnold was saying that the interview was over. That any friend of Mitchell's wasn't a friend of his. "I'm a pretty good worker," said Hunter, "and I'm willin to start pretty low —"

"Of course you're a good worker." Mr. Arnold smiled again. When he smiled he started out showing all his teeth, a couple of which were gray-colored, then remembered and pulled his lip down over them. It looked like he'd been working a lot on his smile lately. "The world is full of em, good workers. At the moment, to level with you, I'm overstocked with good workers, I got them comin out my ears. My boss's nephew, been outa school a year now, needs something steady, he's a good worker. Shop steward in East Boston, got a brother just been laid off his fishing boat. All kinds of people, they know somebody he's a good worker, they come to me, say, Gus can you get him on? See what you can do. I even got a guy, his old man is just over on the boat, wants me to take care of him."

"And you don't have anything to do with it."

"Directly, no. But all these people coming to me, it's not for nothing."

"You *do* have something to do with it."

"Well, you can go to personnel at one of the plants with your application form there if you want to, but they don't move unless *we* clear it. But it's tough. I got all these other people on my back, they need jobs, and you walk in off the street, the friend of a friend to the guy who don't get along so well with his brother who is medium-heavy at union headquarters —."

Hunter began to rise from his chair, to offer his apologies.

"Whoa, don't get me wrong. Relax." Hunter sat back down. "I mean it's not that I'm without *in*fluence around here. I wouldn't of spent ten minutes jerking your chain if I couldn't — couldn't per*suade* certain people to see things my way. It's just that it's liable to take a *lot* of persuasion, if you know what I mean."

"What kind of persuasion?"

Mr. Arnold shook his head. "It's not a question of what *kind*, my friend. It's the same kind as always, the kind makes the world go round. No, it's not a question of what kind but of how *much*."

"Oh." Hunter let that sit between them for a moment, looked at Arnold and tried to get past the smoked lenses. He stood. "You want a kickback."

"No wonder Mitch sent you over, he thought my day wouldn't be complete. Listen, hold on a second, let me explain how things work here. You might learn something." Arnold picked up the book he'd been reading when Hunter came in and turned the cover toward him. *Winning at Blackjack*, it said, written in poker chips across a king of spades and an eight of diamonds. "You ever been to Vegas, McNatt?"

Hunter said no.

"What am I sayin, of course you haven't. You been down where the rain never falls and the sun never shines, right? Well I never been to Vegas neither, I never could of afforded it, but now some of the guys work here they got his charter flight, I'm gonna be along with them. Used to be I played the horses now and then, up to Suffolk tearin tickets and getting beer spilled over my shoes. I played the football for the limit every week, cards on the weekends, Monday nights, I played baseball, point spread on the Celts in the playoffs, I played Stinky Pinky with the

[166]

guys on the floor every payday lunch hour, I even played the fuckin *num*ber, like I'm some dinge don't know any better. The Office, they must of fuckin *loved* me. They must of lit candles for me Sundays, I wouldn't get sick and stop handin over half my paycheck to them every week. Here and there, a nickel and a dime. I was strictly small change, you know? Playin it careful, always trying to get even. That was then. Now, I'm getting up a little in the union, I can see above the clouds. I see what a jerk I was. You don't play to get *even*, you play to get *ahead*. Vegas, that's big money if you play it right, but you can't go in there you got no balls. To make money, you *spend* money. So I been saving up, I been studying, I'm ready. I get off the plane I march straight to the big money and I lay five hundred on the table. And that, that's only the beginning I figure, that is only my entrance fee to the big-money game. I kiss it good-bye. To make, you gotta spend. And I figure that amount, five hundred, is about what it would cost to get somebody, he's got no experience or real connections, to get him a sympathetic ear he comes off the street talking about jobs."

"I don't gamble," said Hunter.

Arnold laid the book down. "I can see that. You don't, you're not a gambling man. Okay. Maybe that wasn't the best example. Cause you get on with us, money-wise it's not a gamble. You got kids, right? I can tell, you got kids, I know how much it takes, groceries these days, and school. They all want to go to college, so they can be overeducated, look down on the old man. I know. And our guys, they make out pretty fuckin good. In fact, you get on with us, you're golden. *Golden.*

"No, it's not a gamble, it's an investment. You heard of capital investment? That's how you should look at this. You're a fisherman you gotta buy your tackle, rent your boat, pay for gas, all that, right? You're a fruit vendor hawkin lopes and strawberries down the Haymarket you gotta put out for the produce before you take anything in, you gotta pay for your *spot* there. See what I'm gettin at? You got to lay out first before you can operate.

"Why should a spot with us, clear the kind of take-home, the kind of overtime and benefits we got, why should that be any different? I mean you'd make it back in a couple of months, you'd be taking home one, two weeks from now, soon as you get your X-rays and physical out of the way. It's like your union dues, only they come beforehand, right? You get what I'm saying?" Arnold smiled and waited for Hunter to sit.

"I don't think I'd best take up any more of your time," said Hunter. "If I'd knowed how it worked I wouldn't have come." He turned to the door.

"Yeah, well, you try it your way," Arnold called after him. "See how far you get. I come back from Vegas the day after New Years. You change your mind, I'll still be here."

A bunch of young women, office temporary workers from what they said to each other, sat across from Hunter for his trip back from Quincy on the Red Line. Their long coats fell to the side when they sat, showing off their legs. They wore short dresses and were made up real careful. When they talked it sounded ridiculous, but so did everybody else in Boston.

Hunter made a mental note about the X-rays. Arnold had reminded him of that, he hadn't even considered it when he decided he should get work so he could stay longer to look for Hobie. He would send to Doc Early, the company physician, and it would be no problem. Doc's X-ray machine was famous for its blindness to any form of lung trouble. "You could inhale a sack of iron filings," Cletus Spicer used to say, "swaller a crowbar and a radium-handed watch and Doc Early'd still give you a clean bill of health. Hell, you walk in there with but one lung and Doc's pictures would give you two, and both in perfect shape." The X-rays wouldn't be a problem. Finding a job — he'd have to remember to write to Ray and some of the others about Arnold, about how it wasn't only the Mine Workers had crooked people, it was all over you could find them. Five hundred dollars.

Not that he didn't have the money. In fact he had all his six-hundred-fifty right in his pocket. Mrs. Hanrahan had said how the fella who'd taken his room before was a drinker, he'd come home loaded and kicked the door in so many times the lock was bust. And if a tenant wanted it fixed, it was for the tenant to fix it. He didn't like carrying all his cash along with him and the banks wouldn't talk to you unless you had a job or a state driver's license. Couldn't even open a checking account. So he'd have to get to a hardware store, he'd have to pick something up.

One of the Kelly Girls, the tall one in the middle, was especially nice-looking. She had some natural color to her cheek and wasn't made-up so much as the others. Her knees were red from the cold, the same glowing red as her cheeks.

It had been so long.

Hobie. It wasn't going to be so easy looking for him, it was going to take longer than he'd planned on to do the city and be reasonably sure he'd tried everything possible. It was a big city, it spread out more than you saw at first look, plus there was that Cambridge across the river. And there were so many young ones. Mrs. Hanrahan's was a savings over the Courier, but he'd have to get some kind of work if he was to hang on and make a thorough search of it. He would have to go up and try to find Darwin in New Hampshire, just in case, and that would take a rented car. Money. The steel thing would have been perfect, it paid a lot and he could have looked in all his spare time. Even with the five hundred gone right off the bat he would have made it up in no time and been set up fine. Not that he'd ever pay a bribe to work.

He thought he saw a boy in an Army jacket at the Broadway station platform, but the girls were in the way. By the time he'd slid over to see out the window the jacket was gone.

They got off ahead of him at Washington and went for the stairs instead of the tunnel to the Orange Line. Hunter watched them walking away, laughing and pushing each other. A long time.

He'd call Mulcahy from a pay phone when he got back. Mrs. Hanrahan sat right by when you used hers and he didn't want her in on all his business. Maybe he'd try the Common again in the afternoon, just check out the kids till dark. He'd have to pick something up for the door.

The car got crowded and he offered his seat to a woman in a fake-leather coat. She had boots on that were the same material and a perfect line of white scalp where her long dark hair parted. She smiled up at him as she sat.

The ads lining the car above the metal straps said to join the new Action Army, to learn to be an auto mechanic, to give to the Jimmy Fund. The Coppertone girl lay on her side, teeth flashing bright white from her face, bikini flashing brighter white from her body. He could turn and watch the fake-leather girl in her window-reflection till the train came above ground and the light ruined it.

Hobie.

He wondered if Hobie was somewhere sheltered, what with all the rain and now the cold. He wondered if Hobie was with people he'd met or all alone. Lucille had sent a little bit of a letter from Delia Cutlip along with her own. Wishing him luck and Godspeed. She'd actually written that, Godspeed, and said your son instead of Hobie. *Ray's back is about the same,* Luce had written, *and he wonders about how you are even if he don't get around to a letter. The fellas in that club you started (you know what I mean) aren't doing so well. Some slate fell and Curt Lockly cracked a vertebrae —*

There were nurses walking ahead of him on Worcester when he got down to the street, returning to Boston City from their lunch hour. Their legs looked strange, all stockinged in white like that, and they weren't so full of horseplay as the Kelly girls had been. But one of the women, it was impossible to tell which from behind, had a deep rich voice when she laughed. It was sort of like Lucille's, strong but no doubt that it was a woman's. He hadn't been with a woman to talk and laugh and just be easy with since the last time he'd seen Ray and Luce, catching that bus at the Blue Star. They seemed so far away.

He watched the nurses walking and felt a bulge in his pocket. The money, the six-fifty. He turned into Mrs. Hanrahan's just as the woman laughed again. He shifted the bulge and made a mental note. He'd have to pick something up.

15

Liberals. Whenever something important got going in the Movement they'd slither in with their prechewed version and it wasn't long before the original idea wasn't worth shit anymore. Like the whole antiwar thing, this New Mobe crap they were doing in Washington. "Peace" marching as if peace were the point of it all. Another example of liberals sapping the energy of the Left.

PEOPLE'S WAR REPRESSED BY BIG BUSINESS, GOVERNMENT
AMERICANS MARCH AGAINST DEATH IN D.C.

Schenk smacked the keys extra hard on paragraph headings. Big business was a nice touch, always try to get big business in there somewhere. Good for a gut reaction. He would have to try to keep mention of the New Mobe crowd out of the article, no use in taking them on one way or the other. Not that they shouldn't be run over the coals, but it had come up in group and the word was hands-off for now. Keep away from ideological squabbles, it makes you look power hungry. Just concentrate on the war as the primary contradiction in the country today, on its effect on the working class. *La clase obrera.* Schenk didn't speak Spanish but had seen his articles in translation enough that he could immediately visualize all the catch phrases.

La Guerra en Vietnam es Para Sujetar a las Pueblas

It was tempting, just to see what the others would say when they reviewed it in group, to blow the whole New Mobe bunch out of the ballpark. Tell the people it was time to purge the liberals from the antiwar movement, to put an end to all this symbolic cat-and-mouse crap with the government and meet power with power. Get rid of the Spocks and McCarthys who were making it safe, making it sanctioned and "legitimate," like it was some fucking debating-society question. Like it wasn't a killing situation.

The phone rang and Mark Remington got it. Incredibly, no matter where he was in the room, Remington always seemed to get to the phone first.

"Hello?" he said. "Yes, this is Third Way. Well, we'll see what we can do."

Going on in that sappy, solicitous voice, like he was some you've-got-a-friend insurance salesman or some public-relations asshole.

"No, we're not connected to the city, m'am, but maybe we could help get the city to respond to your problem."

Grant Parke had stopped his typing to listen in like he always did, and Wein was mumbling to himself about zeitgeist. Schenk typed harder to try to block out the phone conversation.

"Yes m'am. No m'am. No m'am, we're not connected to the Communist Party in any way. There's not a whole lot we agree with them about."

Schenk went at the typewriter till the tips of his fingers went numb, then paused to scowl at what he'd written. They would have to read it and criticize and revise in group, and Remington would shoot down anything not bland enough to go out as the mass line. We need the liberals, he'd say, the people we work with, the welfare and unemployment cases, respect some of them. They're still in the clutches of Saint Bobby and we don't dare blaspheme, still suckers for a handout and a soft word. Remington, sitting there on the phone with some lady with a landlord beef, being calm and reasonable like some fucking social worker. Sure, build a base in the community, get their trust, but tell the lady something about the basic contradiction of private property, don't send her to the Housing Authority. Light the fire, don't help douse it out. *Let* her get her heat shut off, let her freeze a little. Let her find out once and for all who the enemy is. But no, here's Mr. Social Worker Remington sending her to the liberals so they can smooth it over and win a friend for life. No, don't fuck with the liberals, the people look up to them. Got to go with the soft line in public.

Of course, you could go too hard. Over at Progressive Labor they'd have him cranking out diatribes against Castro and Debray.

FIDEL BETRAYS WORKERS!

REVISIONISM STIFLES CUBAN PEOPLE

It made him crazy over there, before they gave him the boot, all the time wondering who was left in the Left after they dismissed the CP, the Socialists, the Weathermen, Cuba, Algeria and everything in Europe except Albania. Albania for christsake. You could come on too hard, like PL, and nobody would go near you.

Schenk typed. The struggle of the people. *La Lucha del pueblo.* He poked through the photos of the first day's marching that they'd torn from the *Globe,* but it was just a lot of students. Schenk didn't like to put even the word *student* in the paper. The people didn't trust students, and rightfully so. Who with any conscience could stay in a school now, when it was all coming down around them, when the time was so ripe? Who was it, one of the original big marchers, who said that the only study for an honorable man was revolution? He'd have to ask Wein, Wein knew that kind of stuff.

Without turning around he could tell what Wein was doing. Squeezed in his little corner desk overlining passages from at least three different books in yellow marker. *The Phenomenology of Mind,* maybe, *The Grundrisse* and *History and Class Consciousness.* Wein was into Georg Lukacs lately. Muttering to himself, shaking his head and sighing with exasperation or admiration, sometimes even giggling and saying, "Yes, *yes.*" Desk buried under scribbled notes and overdue notices from the library. Coming at the problem from every angle, subjecting the technique of Marxist analysis to Marxist analysis, scrutinizing the arguments on both sides of every issue like a chess player pitting his right hand against his left and making sure neither side won too easily. Schenk had tried chess with Wein and it was impossible, he took half an hour deliberating every move and Schenk

[173]

found himself playing recklessly just to bring the game to a head. Chess was the perfect game for Wein, it was highly structured, sedentary, drenched in theory and precedent.

Not that theory was irrelevant. You had to have an ideological base, had to have a solid line to call on when the shit hit the fan. Theory was important. But Wein never did any *work*. He never organized, he never leafleted, he never helped with the dishes now that the women weren't doing them. He wrote, but only dry political critiques that weren't meant to go beyond the group. And even among them it didn't do much good. The kids, the shock troops, were barely literate and few of the others had made it all the way to graduate school. They were no match for Wein's bad writing and barrage of abstract ideas.

ON AESTHETICS AND HISTORICAL MATERIALISM
THE DIALECTICS OF POPULAR CULTURE

Now Wein's buddy there, Parke, could write a little. It wasn't going to set the world on fire but Parke could put words together in a clear, simple way and the people could grasp it. That's why he was at the far end of the basement with the other typewriter. The electric one, they shot fingers and Parke won again. Doing his average-Joe pieces. Parke wrote like a fucking sports editor.

ANOTHER DEPRESSION BREWING?

That was always a good one, it appeared every other issue, the Left's version of "Rebuilding Year for Sox" in the *Globe*. And they had gone and given the GE strike article to Parke too.

BOSSES HIT ELECTRICAL WORKERS

Schenk had asked for the GE instead of this New Mobe bullshit, but no. Antiwar was a delicate issue with the people, whereas a strike, well, you just rooted for workers and dumped on management. The Bosses. "Let's Go Sox!," that's what you'd get from Grant Parke. Nothing to tie the struggle to the contradiction of monopoly capitalism, nothing to help workers become aware of their common class struggle. Just go along with the boys, that's all he'd do, write a piece you could find verbatim in the IUE house organ. Parke had worked in a candy factory in East Cambridge for a month before he was laid off and now he figured he was one of the boys. He'd learned to swear and how to play the football cards and now everything he said was prefaced with "Back in the factory" or "On the line." Co-opted by trade unionism.

We are the vanguard of the world revolution,

sang Grant Parke —

For every problem we have one great solution,

He sang and marched his feet as he typed his story over —

We have the answer that will save every nation,
Send Richard Nixon on a ten-year vacation.

"Could we do without the musical interlude?" said Schenk.

"But it's a rousing fight song. It's good for our morale. The cadre that sings together clings together."

"I'm trying to get this written. It's important."

"So's my article. Singing helps me do it."

"I think I'd like it quiet, too," said Wein. "It's hard to concentrate with the pounding upstairs."

"The pitter-patter of little subversives. Schenk's just roped-off cause he doesn't have a voice."

"Grant," said Mark Remington calmly, "give us a break, okay?"

You had to *lead*, not follow. Be an example, not a poor imitation. When the workers in France went to the barricades last May it could have come to something important if the Left had been ready to lead. But no, they were along for the ride, out to see what happened next. Or worse, they were students.

There was always the danger, though, of becoming so cynical that you ignored the mood of the workers. Couldn't lose your faith in the people. After all, if you didn't believe the people had

[175]

it in them to rise up as a class, to "seize the banners of Marxism-Leninism and carry them forward" as they were fond of saying over at PL, then you might as well pack up your granola and move to Vermont. Faith in the people. Without it you got frustrated and tried to bring the whole thing down yourself, like those dudes in New York got busted for the bombing. Schenk's other assignment.

MISGUIDED "RADICAL LEADERS" JAILED IN N.Y.

Sam Melville, Jane Alpert, Aughey and Demmerle. He'd met Demmerle once, in the East Village, and wasn't too impressed. Something fishy about the guy. You had to admire their rocks though, fucking with explosives and the kind of prison time that went with them. Lotta rocks, taking on the dragon like that. But they got caught. Whoever planned the thing, Melville from all indications, didn't do much of a job. You could pull those things off with some patience and good planning. Unless somebody ratted. Oh yes, planting bombs took a lot of rocks, you had to admire that. But not in print. The people weren't quite ready for open terrorism yet, he'd have to bad-mouth the New York people a little. *Irresponsible.* Always a good word, if you didn't want to come right out and condemn somebody's motives.

IRRESPONSIBLE TERRORISM AIDS RULERS

Miriam could pull that kind of stuff off, Miriam was a good member. Make a great assassin if it came to that. Out pamphleting with Sarah, or heading off to work in the morning, you'd never figure her for the things she was capable of. Like the GE thing she was helping to set up on the side for Schenk. Just took care of business, Miriam.

And then there was King, upstairs drilling the shock troops, you could hear them through the ceiling, kicking in unison. King would crawl up the dragon's ass if you handled him right. He was a certifiable mindfuck and you had to keep him on a tight leash, but that wasn't so important. You needed a lot of fucked-up people to make a revolution.

[176]

There was that word again. Schenk rapped asterisks over it. Remington had prohibited use of the word for the mass line. So they put out a Marxist-Leninist revolutionary paper without ever saying *Marxism-Leninism* or *revolution* in print. It almost made him long for the PL style again, where *dictatorship of the proletariat* popped up every third line. But no, Remington had persuaded the group, the people weren't ready for that. They were afraid of the words. So everything came out sugarcoated, seductive. Opportunist. That was the sorry fact of it, and the people could smell it a mile away. They'd been schooled in it by their ward and union politicians, by the liberals and social workers, by all the people who pretended to serve them. Even the group's name was a seduction, a compromise to the omnipotence of the enemy's thinking. Third Way. You asked someone cold on the street and they'd say it must be some religious charity fund. How could you pretend to be helping workers face the reality of their oppression when you hid the reality of your politics from them?

Not that you couldn't go overboard with the honesty-above-all bit. Schenk typed in *vital changes* after the asterisks. Like Progressive Labor with their political puritanism, their sectarianism. Their fucking revolutionary discipline above all, killing initiative, expelling him from the party for what would have proved to be in the long run a great leap forward.

"Okay, sports fans," called Grant Parke, "here's today's question. What does the word *reactionary* conjure up to you? I want to be sure of the effect it has before I use it in this sentence."

"It all depends on what time period you're referring to," said Wein. "*Reactionary* has been applied to many different sorts of groups in many different eras. Now, if you were talking about the nineteenth century, then —"

"BZZZZZT! Time's up, Contestant Number One. I want this in ten words or less, we don't have time for a lecture."

"A reactionary to me," said Remington, "is anyone who fights the dialectic flow of history. Anyone who refuses to accept the inevitability of a classless society."

"A little broad, but not bad. Contestant Number Three?"

Schenk fixed him with his coldest glare. "A reactionary is

[177]

someone who stands about five-foot-ten, has a slightly broken nose, a weakness for athletic metaphors, a dim comprehension of theory and an extremely confused set of priorities."

Parke giggled. Giggled. "You forgot to mention his lilting tenor voice. *We are the vanguard of the world revolution* —"

Now discipline, not PL's mindless subservience or Wein's rational-analysis bullshit, but real discipline, self-discipline, was essential if you were going to serve the people. Mental, ideological, even physical discipline. Exactly what someone like, say, Joel Pinkstaff was lacking. Pinkstaff showed zero mental discipline, always needing to be nudged, gently, back on the track by his friends. Always being stuck up for, like a popular dimwit kid in the neighborhood, don't blame him, he didn't really mean it. It was enough to make you sick, carrying deadweight like that, when the plain fact was that Pinkstaff was a liberal at heart. Nothing less.

Self-discipline guarded you against individualism. It kept you from dumb heroics like the New York bombings. And when members had no self-discipline or were politically naive it was the responsibility of the more experienced and knowledgeable members to guide them. Schenk spent as much time working on the shock troops as he could. They were shaping up, with a few reservations. He'd have to watch the new kid Sarah brought in closely for a while. From West Virginia to Third Way headquarters in Dorchester was a sizable culture shock. Schenk tried to imagine how the whole scene might appear to someone so totally outside the Movement — twenty-five people living in one house, studying, training, going out to work in the shops, cranking out literature in the basement. And not an ounce of grass on the premises. He was a tough one to peg right away, McNatt. Politically naive, definitely, but it was hard to tell about his class consciousness. He came from a worker's background, but that alone was no free ride. He'd have to prove himself. It was possible he was quiet but intelligent, and could be brought along with reading and discussion. It was also possible he just wasn't too swift, who knows what the inbreeding and malnutrition up there might result in, but that was okay too. You needed a lot of stupid people to make a revolution.

They were practicing falls upstairs now, thudding en masse,

making the bare lightbulbs flicker under the water pipes. Schenk sat back and watched legs splashing past through the basement window. The fucking rain was holding everything back, the November Action Coalition up in Cambridge couldn't raise much of a crowd outdoors and were all on the brink of pneumonia. Their time was running out, it would soon be Thanksgiving vacation and all their students would disappear. Students. Remington was on the phone with some housing flunkie and Grant Parke was reading his own article and chuckling like an idiot. Wein was wrestling with Hegel. It was almost four, time for the cooking to begin. Tonight it would be Pinkstaff and a couple of the younger kids upstairs. Some rice-and-pork-sausage nonsense again. King said he ate better at the Roslindale lockup and you couldn't doubt him. Miriam was about the only one who could really cook and she was at the stitching factory all day and was exempted.

EL IMPERIALISMO DEL TÍO SAM

Remington called it "winning the masses to our line." The line didn't have much shape to it yet, but that was always hard. Nothing valuable would come easy, there were so many errors you could make, in both directions, so many thin lines you had to walk. You couldn't be too sectarian or too opportunistic. Your line couldn't be too hard or too soft, your activities couldn't be totally rearguard or too aggressively vanguard. You had to steer between co-option by and alienation from the people, between subservience and individualism.

It was what Schenk had always imagined surfing to be like. If you went too fast or too slow, leaned too hard to the right or left, you weren't on top of it anymore. And soon, very soon, it would be like riding a tidal wave. All the signs were there, the emergence of the Third World, the growing repression at home, the decadence all around — it was all coming down. All about to be swept away by the historical tide of the people. And only the strongest, the most agile, wouldn't go under. It would be sooner than almost anyone thought.

Schenk imagined how it must have seemed to the debris of the Russian Left in the fall of 1917, to the smug revolutionary socialists who got up for their morning tea thinking the revolution was safely, indefinitely on a back burner. Plenty of time to do their little power-struggle numbers, to water down the people's will. How it must have felt to wake up in a new world. Schenk would never be caught in that position, never be left at the gate, be swept with the rest of the obsessive base-builders and reform socialists into — who was it, who named it? — the dustbin of history. He would have to ask Wein who said it, it was where Wein would most likely end up, along with people like Mark Remington. People who, given their position and responsibilities, were even worse than liberals.

POWER SHIFT AT THIRD WAY
PRAGMATIC ACTIVISM WEEDS OUT ENEMIES OF THE PEOPLE

16

Get-down time in the Combat Zone and Inez was waiting to draw first blood. She hung on the corner of Washington and Essex, watching the flow, watching the peepers and the cruisers, college boys and brown-baggers, the tourists and natives. Wind moaned down Essex and climbed up her dress to numb her thighs. She felt the men and boys looking at her, felt a moment of panic. It had been too long. She had no sense of it anymore, no idea of who the plainclothes might be, how fast the track was, whether she still had the heart to keep up her game out on the hoof. The call-book life had spoiled her.

It was too cold. Body have to be stuck with a mean case of horniness to even *think* about it in this weather, much less *do* anything about it. Have to be a stone come-freak. Inez considered going over to the White Tower or on down to the Greyhound cafeteria to sit with some coffee. Maybe boost a wallet, she could find somebody drunk enough. But Slick might be out checking up, or one of these chumps out here on the set might rat on her to him. People were always jealous when you got something good together.

"I see you again," Slick had told her, "it better be behind a pile of dead Presidents. Take a load of Jacksons and Grants get you off my shit list, girl." And all because of this Dragon Lady bitch. Got her out here in the Zone again, land of the Eternal Hard-on, and she wasn't ready for it. Was not *ready*.

They wandered down Washington in twos and threes, browsing by the glossies pinned in front of the topless joints, stopping to shiver at the box-office windows and nudge each other's desire.

"You wanna go in?"

"Ida know, what's it cost?"

"Askim."

"You askim, you're the one wants to go."

"*Me?* Guy's tongue hangin out on the sidewalk, I'm the one wants to go."

"I think maybe I seen it before."

"You don't *know?*"

"Hey, I can't remember. The titles, I never remember the titles."

"Oh."

"So you want to go in or what? Fuckin freezin out here."

Hands in their pockets, eyes flicking sideways not to miss a thing, minds working overtime trying to b*elieve*.

PEEKABOO ROOM

TAKE YOUR OWN PHOTOS — LIVE MODELS!

DANISH DELIGHTS!!

!!! 15 GIRLS 15 !!!

Pinball parlors and peepshows, Joe and Nemo's red-plastic hot dogs, iron-grated off-the-rack clothes stores and every rubber specialty item you could hope to imagine. The Fantasy Farm, Slick always called it, the Kingdom of False Promise. There was too much light on the set as usual, too harsh, making her eyes run. She needed her eyes to survive, to keep ahead of the tricks. Their faces turning color with each new blast of neon, whistling and wincing at the boobs in the snapshots, comparing Sandy

Beach with Betsy Wetzel or Georgia Peach with Angina Pec-
toralus and her Grecian Gyrations —

And the buck stopped with Inez. They took whatever they
built up in a night's worth of teasing and pumped it into her. The
men and boys walked past her in twos and threes, gawking back
over their shoulders and breaking into horselaughs over some
dark comment. But no one approached her. Out on the rack
nearly an hour and a half and she still hadn't broke luck. She'd
seen Jacqui get hit on, and Bernice and Natalie from Fleetwood
Mack's stable both hop into passing cars, and even Simple Simon's
little girl, one of the most nothin-ass bitches ever turned out in
the history of the Life, even she had got the nod already.

She didn't want to go hang in the bars. Have all the players and
working girls smiling on her, lapping up the news that Inez been
put out on the block again, handed over her little black book and
gone back in *har*ness. Cold or no cold, she'd have to make it
outside with only the tricks for an audience.

The bitch just wandered out of Chinatown one day, pretty the
way Orientals could be but nothing special, calling herself
Dragon Lady. Choosing Slick out of all the available talent.
Inez didn't think anything of it at first, Slick always had a lot of
women on his case but his shit was together, he was cold-blooded
as they came and he wouldn't look at you less there was a profit
in it someplace. Pullin in a new bitch, he'd said, which was fine,
help keep the rags on his back and the gators on his feet. Wasn't
any big thing, any big threat. From the story she give out, this
Dragon Lady was hooked up with some chump on the West
Coast had to beat her ass and fuck her head up behind all kinds of
blow to turn her out, some chump she just tripped on away from
the minute she got bus fare. She'd tried to play it square in
Chinatown awhile, live with some relatives and try to get her
U.S. papers together. But shoveling fried rice and bean sprouts to
the tourists didn't make it after you'd got a taste of the sweet
ride, and they didn't have *any*thing come up to *Slick* in Chinatown. Slick was all sugar, didn't go messin his girls up with drugs
or whuppin up on them. At least he never had before.

So she come across with enough green up front for Slick to let
her on. "This here Dragon Lady," he'd said introducing her. "She
a little rough round the edges but I got a feelin she learn *fast*."

Back then it was all sugar for Inez, she had the apartment in Back Bay and the call book and she had Slick driving her all over town at his side, showing her off. He'd stroke her hair and push her gently to the middle of the room so the other players could take a good look. "My redhead," he'd say. "My big stallion." He liked to dress her in black velvet, like the whiskey ad, sleeveless black velvet dresses with a black ribbon around her neck. Said how it set off her skin and her hair, said how it made her look like a real high-class lady. Walk into any hotel in the city, front entrance, right past the doorman, desk clerk, whoever, and make her date. "This lady," Slick would say to the players, "this lady worth her weight in gold. She can bring it *in*. You look at any dude out here got a real strong game together like I do, it's cause they got theyself a strong lady like this one. Got theyself a woman knows what she is *about*."

She made Slick so proud to have her, and what with the money flowing so fast and free she was able to put a little aside, to cookie-jar a hundred or two a week for the day when she and Slick were ready to buy that restaurant. Ready to trade up from the Life.

A trick she had hardly noticed before passed Inez for the second time. He was walking slowly but not really looking at the pictures of the girls plastering the bar windows, not really eating up the scene. It was like he wasn't sure he was in the right place. He was nothing special, the kind of guy you always saw with their metal lunchpail and old green workclothes on the Orange Line. Beer drinkers. Guys like her father. There were a million of them.

The trick passed her a third time, then caught her eye and came over smiling like he was going to ask where the T station was.

"Hey."

"Hey."

He waited for a moment then. If he thought she was gonna spell it out for him he was in for a long night. Even Simple Simon's bitches knew enough not to do the plainclothes' job for them.

"You waitin for somebody?"

He talked different, out-of-town. Maybe off a ship. She'd have to make sure to use the rubber if it panned out.

"Yes and no," said Inez.

"How's that?"

"Well, I'm waitin for *some*body, but not anybody in par*ticu*-lar."

"Oh."

His were the worst kind. The lunchpails. The beer. White socks and sleeveless T-shirts all the way down the line. She'd had a nice vacation from them in the apartment, with the call book. You didn't have to bother with these nickel-and-dime straight-date factory turds, these tricks who you could tell their whole crummy future cause it looked just like their whole crummy past. Dockworkers or welders or machinists or pump jockeys, garbage-chuckers, heavy machinery like her father, whatever. It didn't make any difference. They were hardly worth the walk upstairs.

"Uh, listen," said the lunchpail, the trick, "I'm new in town, see —"

"I gathered that."

"Yeah, and I don't know, see, uh — how much — what things *are*."

If you're not a cop, buddy, they just went up five dollars. "Depends on what you have in mind," said Inez.

He looked down Washington then, thinking, looked down away from the light of the Zone. He shook his head. "I sure could use the company," he said almost to himself. "You nearby?"

"Near enough. C'mon." she started left down Essex.

"What's your name?"

"Inez."

"Mine's Hunter."

If his name was really Hunter she was the last of the Mohicans. They walked side by side, hands in pockets, shoulders hunched against the cold. It was almost ten o'clock. At this rate she'd be lucky to pull a hundred-fifty for the night. She'd let Slick down again.

"Bitch," he said the day he took her book away, "you gotten to be one lazy-ass sack a shit layin back in this room, makin telephone calls. You must think you playin me for some kind of *fool*, think I don't see what'd comin down here, you gettin all sidity on me, think you too good to be out peddlin your butt on the street. Think you runnin some shit past me, bitch, but you *wrong*. You just not pullin you weight an you know it and I know it and the only way you gonna show me you is for *real* is you go down there like you did when I first turn you out, git down with the workin gals an bring home that bacon. Cause bitch, you been makin me your chump for too damn long!"

It wasn't true. She loved Slick. She did. She'd show him, she'd prove it. She'd still be around when this Dragon Lady was long gone. And Slick would want her again the way he had before, want all of her.

"Baby," he always said, "most the men in the world, they see you walkin down the street, they rap with you, they get you down in *bed* even, they thinkin bout just one thing. That hole you got tween you legs. And what's a hole? It's a zero, nothin. All that there is to you, baby, and they thinkin all the time on the least part. On a hole. A piece of swiss cheese got a hundred of em. You can make one with your fist, it's just as good and a whole lot cheaper. But that's *all* they want from you. Now me, I want the whole thing. Anything Inez got, I want it to be mine. I want your body, your mind, your *soul*, baby.

"Other men, they want you to be weak, to be negative, be a *hole*. I wants you strong as you can be, cause that make *me* stronger, see? I don't want no weak woman under me, she's gonna stumble and bring me down with her.

"You give some trick that hole, that aint shit, you givin him nothin. But you give me your whole self, that's beautiful, that's man and woman the way they sposed to be. You find somebody out there on the street wants you like I do, baby, and you welcome to go off with him. Good luck. But till then, you *mine*."

The doorway was squeezed between an adult bookstore and a diner that had closed down months ago. Eddy sat just inside the door, half asleep in his chair. Eddy had the world's-champion case of liver spots. He looked like the kind of bananas Inez's mother used to buy ten-cents-a-pound. Yellow mottled with brown and all soft on top.

"Number five or number seven," said Eddy, "others are full up. And shut that door fore I catch pneumonia." He'd be a lot of help if this lunchpail turned ugly, he could barely get out of the chair much less climb up a flight and tangle with somebody.

"Five," said Inez and led the way up.

At first she figured she'd play it open-and-shut, bring him off and charge him twenty for a fifteen-dollar straight without dropping anything but her panties. Though it might be nice to get her feet out of these damn worthless vinyl boots and under some warm covers for a minute. The trick was breathing hard and making little coughing sounds like he'd just run the four-minute mile. It was only one flight up, he must have a bad ticker.

She was going to ask for the cash up front but then he started with the heavy breathing and got this look on him, meeting her eyes the way they almost never did, and she reconsidered. Maybe he was going to be a talk trick, the kind you could make nice with and guilt a couple extra bills from. Say your man would whup up on you if you didn't turn a fifty or some bullshit like that. That would be nice to bring to Slick, he always admired it when you could get your money and not put out a thing. She patted the bed, gently, so as not to raise dust. "Have a seat."

They sat by each other. It was very warm in the room. The trick made her feel creepy. Not totally in control. She wished it was somebody other than Eddy downstairs. There had been that girl, one of the Fleetwood Macks, who had been thrown out the window and died about a year back. And the stories the older girls told about when the Strangler was loose, how scared they all were. Who would miss her if anything did happen? Her father? She didn't exist for him anymore. You're dead, he'd told her, I tell people you're dead. Friends? Friends were all the people laughing at her, gloating over this Dragon Lady business. Slick. Slick would miss her. He didn't know how *much*.

The trick was talking, holding her hand no less, sitting by her on the bed and talking.

"It's not that I never been to a city before, see. I've *been*. But I never tried to — set up, you know, work and live in one. It's different. The people, the way they treat you is different. Back home — I'm from West Virginia — back there people are all in the same boat mostly, which is not doing so good. It's sinkin, is what. So the people, they got a feelin for each other, they been

[186]

through the same hard times and they knowed how it is. Not that everybody is bosom buddies, you know, there's contention and jealousy and all, but you feel like you're *known*, like people see you. Here, even when you're with folks in the same exact fix that you are, they won't hardly look at you. Like down in the subway cars, where even if they look they don't *see*. Makes you feel — makes you need to do somethin, just so's you feel like you're still there."

Inez unzipped and kicked out of her boots while he talked. He talked about how he missed his friends. About how he was so used to working hard that it felt funny to be out on the streets all the time, during the day. Inez nodded and yessed whenever she thought it was expected. It took her a second to be out of her clothes and under the covers. At least she'd be warm while he went on.

He told her how he was looking for his boy. She said maybe the kid was old enough to be on his own, that maybe he was wasting his time.

"No," said the trick. "See, I'm his *fath*er."

As if that explained it, as if that was all there was to it.

Finally he wrestled his clothes off and slid in next to her. It had taken too long already, all this tripping down and chitchat was dead time. Inez had brought guys off before her panties got past her knees and here she was tucking in with this lunchpail like Mr. and Mrs. America.

"I wonder if I could — I'd like to just touch some first."

She began to quote him a price but didn't. It wasn't fear now, it was the tension of the game. It felt like the wrong time for prices with this one. He was strange, he was a pisser. He didn't know what he wanted and that was the worst kind, because until you knew that you weren't totally in the driver's seat.

"Go ahead."

"Just a minute." He was pressing his hands between his thighs. A new kind of freak for her collection? He smiled at her. "They still a bit icy from outside," he explained. "Don't want to make you jump."

He was touching Inez then, softer than you'd expect from a lunchpail, more like one of those executive-suite smoothies just read the *Kama Sutra* and want to practice before they hit on their secretary. Inez shifted to help him get at her and wondered if she'd be able to make it on the street like she had before.

"You got nice hair," said the trick kissing a handful of it. "Beautiful."

Slick had gotten her beyond the whole body thing when he first turned her out. It was all in the head he told her, and he was right. He arranged a date with a priest, one she had received Communion from before her Confirmation. He now had one of the wealthiest parishes in the city.

A priest.

"You just a little Cathlict mindfuck," said Slick. "This'll get you past all that. You'll see how any kind of morals you got that's holdin you back got no found*a*tion, cause the people set up those morals, they is a *lie*. Cause baby, the whole *world* is a trick."

The priest asked for around-the-world service and enjoyed every minute of it. Then he got all depressed and guilt-talking and promised to say prayers for them both. It started with that, Inez getting wise, schooling herself on the street, learning how people really were. How they were so full of lies and playacting about themselves, till she saw that Slick was the only for-real person she'd ever met.

"I'm a pimp," he'd say proudly. "P-I-M-P. I sell ass. I don't do diddley shit unless there's some coin connected to it and that's all they is *to* it. Right up front, people, take it or leave it."

The trick kept talking while he ran his hands over her. He told her how he usually didn't say so much, but he hadn't slept at all the night before and had been out all day looking and it made him a little punchy. He apologized for rattling on.

"I can imagine what you must think about me," he said.

Inez let it go past.

"I mean, the way you must get to see people. Men. At their worst and all. Fellas when they're desperate and — you know — shamed."

Inez shrugged.

"There's a story I remember hearin when I's a kid. Back when just everbody had outdoor plumbin. Bout these two little bugs, they live down there at the bottom of the *hole*, see. Don't never get out of there to see anything else. And the story is, this one bug looks up to the top of the hole and he says to the othern, he says, 'People sure are a lot of assholes.' "

Inez didn't laugh.

"You probly hear a lot of dirty stories, don't you? I didn't mean no offense, I was just trying to show my point about how the way you meet people affects the opinion you have of them. You must get to see their worst side, never get to know what they're really like."

If what she saw of men wasn't what they were really like then what the fuck was? "C'mon, honey," said Inez, "let's get to it."

She rolled the thing on him and he climbed aboard and started, and again it was clear he didn't know what he wanted. For a twenty-dollar trick you couldn't expect any of the moaning and ooh babys a call-book date could, but here was this guy looking her in the eye like he wanted something more than to pop his rocks. Usually they looked at the wall, lunchpails, or had you do the dog so it wasn't a problem. But not this guy, he was looking right at her, giving her the creeps. And worse, she was starting to feel him a bit, a little warning tickle. She'd have to watch that.

Back before Slick, when she was chambermaiding at the Malar Inn and putting out for free she used to bust her nut all the time. Didn't matter who the guy was, whether he liked her or she liked him or whatever, it would just happen. Just plain hit-and-run sex. But the job was such a drag, emptying people's ashtrays, wiping up after their dirty habits, worse even than the mailroom or the dictaphone pool she had done before, it was so suffocating that anything that could bring her above it for even a second or two was a gift. So she gave herself out like candy.

Then she started noticing the girls who worked the Inn, talking with some of them, envying their style and their clothes and their soft touch and it led straight to Slick. Led to the Zone. At first she'd bust her nut with some of the tricks and she hated that, it made *her* into the trick and besides, it was something she wanted to save for her man. You had to save something. But by the time he gave her the book and the apartment she had it under control, only coming with Slick. Only Slick.

Lately though, even before he's put her back on her feet, she'd gone numb to him. Nothing. She kept up the show, the act, oh Daddy, yes, nobody but you, oh *yes*, whip it to me Daddy, *yes*, but it was like with the call-book men. It was like he was just another trick. The whole world *was* a trick and the trick was on Inez, laying under this lunchpail with an hour wasted for his little twenty bucks and starting to feel down there for the first time in months. It didn't make any sense, it wasn't fair.

Inez fought it back. She pictured Dragon Lady in her mind. She thought about Slick finding her cookie jar, her savings, not believing when she said she wasn't holding out, it was for *them*, for life after the Life. Then the beating. Inez fought it, fought it back and won.

He held out a long time, like one of those damn little spics who thought it was the Boston fuckin *Mar*athon, and when he came it was with a sigh, it was *like* a sigh, no little spurts but one long sad unloading into her. He lay next to her and wanted to hold and looked very tired. Inez made her decision.

Pussy power. "These dudes come up to me, these Black Power freaks, and they be talkin bout guns and go-rilla tactics and runnin upside the man's head." It was one of Slick's favorite lessons, he'd give it whenever enough audience was together to make it worthwhile.

"You like a backrub, honey?" said Inez. The trick smiled and nodded and rolled onto his stomach.

"Now that's just suicide they talkin," Slick would say, "that's just some *cra*zy shit. Go up against the Man when he's got tanks and heelicopters and fighter jets and paratroops an all that? For*get* it, sucker. When Roxbury get the atom bomb, then maybe you come back to me with this armed-struggle number. Cause I don't need no *gun* to fight the white man with."

Inez pressed and kneaded each bunch of muscle till it went slack. There was an awful lot of scars on his back, on his arm which didn't unbend all the way. There was a little gray coming up in his hair. Inez rubbed his neck and his temples. She checked out where all the clothes were lying in the room.

"See, I got all the weapon I need in this lady." He would lift her chin to them so they could see. "You got a white woman, a real stallion like Nez here, that's all you need to fight the world. Cause you got control of the one thing all their power can't give them. Pussy power. That's what I got. An this lady worth more than a company a them Green Be*rets*. This lady is *over*kill."

He was asleep. The trick, the lunchpail, Mr. Poor-boy-and-a-long-way-from-home was asleep. He made throat noises like he had some kind of asthma.

Inez eased away, covering him lightly and tiptoeing to pull on her clothes. She held the vinyl boots under her arm, she'd wait till she was down with Eddy to put them on. She found the wallet. Over six hundred dollars. A lunchpail with that much. Must be an awful slow track where he comes from, they don't believe in banks. She considered for a moment only taking two hundred. Must be all his money. Then she looked at him, lying there fucked-out and snoring the way her father used to snore, back from his heavy machinery and laid-out on the couch so they couldn't turn on the TV or play above a whisper without him hollering he'd break their necks. Inez left the door slightly open. She couldn't wait to show Slick. To show him what she could do, to show him how she loved him. She'd make up a better story, make it sound harder what she did, put maybe fifty aside for them and hand over the rest. And he'd see, he'd know. He'd know that Inez was for *real*.

17

They sat circled on the floor around the one operating speaker of Grant Parke's stereo, tuned to FM. Hobie was there, Grant and Sarah, Tracy Anne and King and Smallwood and some of the other younger kids. Billy was fooling with his guitar, an old Gibson spotted with cigarette burns. He'd seen the Stones at the Garden Saturday and was inspired to pull it out of mothballs, he sat quietly figuring out the progression for *Street Fighting Man*. Schenk and Wein and Mark Remington were in the basement trying to collaborate on a feature story about Lieutenant Calley and the Pinkville massacre thing. The speaker crackled softly and distorted the lower tones of the deep-voiced character doing news.

The lottery was scheduled for eight o'clock. They would start at number 1 and pick a date, working up to 366, and you'd know whether the local board would be on your case or not. Smallwood was the only one of them clearly up for grabs. Nineteen years old, no crippling disabilities or police record, and he'd lost his 2-S deferment when he dropped out of Tufts.

"No idea what I'll do if they nail me," he said with a very little smile. "Don't think I'd be much good in jail."

They turned down the news and told General Hershey stories.

"One time General Hershey tried to swim the Potomac but three-quarters of the way across he decided he couldn't make it, so he swam back."

"During World War Two General Hershey was sent to blow up a tank, but he was injured in the attempt."

"What happened?"

"He burnt his lips on the exhaust pipe."

"They had General Hershey do an estimate on how much it would cost to wash all the windows at the Pentagon. 'Five thousand for the second floor,' he said, 'five thousand for the first floor and twenty thousand for the basement windows.' They asked why so much for the basement windows. 'Because it'll cost fifteen thousand,' he said, 'to dig a trench for the ladders.' "

"Listen, these sound an awful lot like Polack jokes."

"With dudes like Hershey around," said Grant Parke, "who needs Polacks?"

"*Number one,*" said the caller on the radio after the program introduction, a convocation prayer by a former Marine chaplain, "*September fourteen.*"

"That's *me!*" cried Tracy Anne. "If I was a man I'd be number one." She seemed pleased by the thought.

Smallwood told them his birthday was August 10 and they all listened for it, tensing whenever the caller said August. December 7 came up, Hobie would have been twelfth on the list if he was old enough.

"*Number twenty,*" said the caller, "*June four. Number twenty-one, August ten.*"

"Oh shit."

[192]

"*No!*"

"Bad *news*, man."

Smallwood put his little smile on and shook his head. He looked pale. Sarah gave him a consoling kiss on the forehead on her way to turn the radio off.

"There but for the grace of a serious knee injury suffered on the lacrosse fields of Hotchkiss, go I," said Grant Parke. "The ball is in your court buddy, what's your play?"

Smallwood shrugged and gave a small laugh. "I didn't think it would hit me like this. I was all mentally prepared to be number one and have to deal with it. But now that it's for real — I feel funny. Numb." Everyone was watching him. He looked around. "What I feel like doing," he said, "is getting wasted."

"No drugs on the premises," said King.

"I didn't mean drugs."

"No house rules against booze," said Grant Parke. "Whaddaya say we help the Chosen One here celebrate his last moments of hassle-free civilian life?"

"A fickle-finger-of-fate party!"

"A help-Smallwood-find-the-way party!"

"A hell-no-we-won't-go party!"

They all looked to Sarah as she sat back down next to Hobie. Getting drunk was considered vaguely antirevolutionary, Schenk was always railing about the conspiracy as evidenced by the state-owned liquor stores in Vermont. Sarah was the oldest there. "I feel like a den mother," she sighed. They waited for her decision.

"If we're quiet and don't bother the guys in the basement," she said, "I don't see why not." She pulled two dollar bills from her jeans pocket and threw them into the middle of the circle. "From each according to their means, and Smallwood doesn't have to chip in. It's his party."

Everyone tossed money in and they sent off the little red-headed kid called Mickey Q., telling him to get whatever was cheap and potent. The wind was roaring around the house outside, he went for his heavy jacket.

They sat waiting, Billy picking his guitar up again, Tracy Anne running to get some Oreos and nut bread from the kitchen, Smallwood explaining the intricacies of the way the draft lottery worked and why it was such an unfair system. It was grave, quiet talking, as if Smallwood would certainly be ducking napalm or dragging a ball and chain the very next morning.

Billy hit a loud chord to get their attention. He smiled. "A little number," he said, "for the unlucky number." He began to play —

> *They want me in the Navy,*
> *They want me in the Corps,*

he sang, to the tune of *The Wabash Cannonball* —

> *They want me in the Infantry*
> *To fight their dirty war.*
>
> *My attitude is lousy,*
> *My aptitude is poor,*
> *But Uncle says he needs at least*
> *A hundred thousand more.*

They smiled and tapped their feet to the chugging bass line, none of them knowing before that Billy could play so well. Parke was always guessing what caliber of machine gun he had in that guitar case —

> *Now some will try Vancouver*
> *And some to Sweden's shore,*
> *And some will travel underground*
> *Till Peace we can restore.*
>
> *A few will get a CO*
> *If they ain't black or poor,*
> *And some will stay as college boys*
> *Till 1984.*

"Ha-haaaaaaaaah!"
"Pick it, Billy, lay it down!"
"Listen tight, Smallwood, this is educational."

> *But if I'm fit and able*
> *I'll hear the fighters roar,*
> *And do a tour of duty midst*
> *The killing and the gore.*

Smallwood was smiling a little wider now, not used to being sung about.

> *Though shootin makes me nervous*
> *And murder I abhor,*
> *I think I'll join the NLF*
> *To even up the score.*

They clapped and whistled at the punch line and joined in shakily as Billy ran the opening verse through to cap off the song.

> *They want me in the Navy,*
> *They want me in the Corps,*
> *They want me in the Infantry.*
> *To fight their dirty waaaaaaaaaar!*

Mickey Q. came shivering back in then with a shopping bag holding five bottles of Crockett Gap Strawberry Wine.

"It's cheap all right," said King. "And if you can force enough down it'll do the job. But did you read the boycott list in the kitchen before you went?"

"I forgot."

"You forgot. I'm pretty sure Crockett Gap is a no-no."

"But it's made of *straw*berries."

"It's the *com*pany we're against, Mickey, not the fruit."

"Listen, it's *freez*ing out there, don't make me take it back! I didn't have my ID and the guy gave me the hairy eyeball all the time I'm in there. Couldn't we make an exception just this once?"

Grant Parke started booing him and the rest took it up, but they were feeling good from the song and Mickey Q. was a nice little kid so it wasn't totally serious.

"You'll be haunted by the ghosts of exploited Chicanos," said

Parke. "Your fingers will turn purple and all your food will taste like it's drowned in Tabasco sauce. On your knees, scab!"

Mickey went along with it and knelt at the center of the group. He pressed his hands together and made a penitent face. "Bless me, Cesar, for I have sinned," he said. "It has been three months since my last confession. These are my sins —"

"I bet he was an altar boy —"

"*Such* a little angel —"

"— I have bought five bottles of scab wine —"

"I didn't know scabs could ferment —"

"— I have partaken of the forbidden fruit. Emperors twice, ribiers once, and I lusted after the muscats when they came into season."

"Venial sins."

"Small potatoes. Let's hear the real dirt, Mickey."

"I have eaten a Welch's fudge bar though I know he helped found the Birch Society. I have allowed the light from GE bulbs to guide my path. I have secretly kept my first-baseman's glove that was made in Taiwan. I've put iceberg lettuce in my BLTs. I own stock in Dow Chemical and invest in U.S. Savings Bonds. I bought a used car from Richard Nixon."

"That's more like it."

"And are you truly sorry for these actions?" asked King.

"I am."

"Then go, my son," said Parke, "and scab no more. Say a good act of sedition, then do five *Viva La Huelga*s and three verses of *Nosotros Venceremos* for penance."

King grabbed an Oreo from the package they'd been sharing and held it over Mickey's head. "Corpus Christi."

"Amen." Mickey Q. received the cookie.

"Once you've had Communion," said Tracy Anne, "the sin is all gone. So we might as well keep the wine."

"You're a Catholic?"

"I was brought up one till it got too ridiculous. Didn't you know that, Mickey?"

"But you're from the suburbs."

"So? There's a law against Catholics in the suburbs?"

"No, of course not, it's just — you don't seem —"

"Listen, I went to Catholic boarding school a whole year."

"Gaaack! *Nuns!* How did you survive?"

"Barely. A full year at St. Mary of the Woods."

"I had a friend went to a school for Catholic golfers," said Parke. "St. Arnie of the Irons."

"Jerk joke."

"That's what finally got me out of the Church for good, that spell at St. Mary's." Tracy Anne shook her head. "It was like maximum security, no escape. We used to kid about digging a tunnel, but some of it wasn't funny at all. Every night the nun who had responsibility for your dorm would come to tuck you in. We had this old bat who made sure your arms were on the outside, then she wedged the blankets real tight under the mattress and came back every couple of hours to see things stayed that way. So you couldn't play with yourself."

"You're shittin me."

"It's true. I remember all the classrooms had these little frosted-glass windows, and whenever someone was in for it the nun in charge of discipline, Sister Gonzaga, would come up and tap on the window with this huge bride-of-Christ ring she wore. Tap. Tap. Tap. God, we all used to die inside when we heard that tap, Sister Gonzaga was just plain *weird* and we were all absolutely petrified of her. Absolutely *pet*rified. The sister teaching class would go open the door a bit, but not enough so you could see Gonzaga, you'd just hear this bullfrog voice of hers calling out a name. You nearly wet your pants waiting to hear if it was you she wanted."

"Sounds like the lottery tonight," said Smallwood. Somehow Tracy Anne had worked her way over next to him. Her knee touched his.

"Close to it. The beginning of the next school year I threw such a big tantrum that my parents decided not to send me back. But my mother made me wear my uniform to public school the whole first week so I'd be reminded and appreciate the sacrifice that was being made for me."

"Unbelievable."

"And after that experience, regular old Sunday church was nothing. They couldn't scare me anymore. It was pretty lame in Natick anyway, the last time my mother dragged me over they were into that whole folk-mass thing, trying to be *rel*evant. I went for a while cause I liked the singing, but the young priests were so with-it and sincere and all I couldn't take it, made you want to puke."

"Do you remember any?" asked Smallwood. "Any of the songs you learned?"

"Sure. How could I forget?" The guitar made its way around the circle to Tracy Anne, in the opposite direction from two open bottles of wine. "Let's see," she tightened the tuners up on the neck, "try to get this key straight."

Hobie held a full gulp of wine in his cheek, then pushed it down quick. He didn't much like wine. Tracy Anne played with each string, her ear down close to the bridge, listening to get them right. After the first time Hobie had been worried that she would hang around him all day and want to hold hands and show people, but she acted like always except that she didn't bump into him anymore. And she didn't come back to sleep with him in the printing room till three nights later. Hobie was worried at first and then mad when he decided she was sleeping with someone else from before, but then when he thought about it everything was fine. It was nice to be able to do it without any other kind of pressure, without saying he loved her or worrying if he was taking advantage of her or not. He only wished she would tell him when she was going to visit and when she wasn't so he wouldn't have to wait up wondering.

Tracy Anne began softly, she tilted her head sideways and sent a sheet of straight blond hair falling to cover her arm. She played even better than Billy —

> *One day when Christ was ramblin*
> *On down the dusty rooooad —*
> *He passed a hill called Calvary*
> *Where martyrs' blood had flowed,*
> *Where martyrs' blood had flowed.*
>
> *The hill was thick with flowers,*
> *With hyacinth and roooose —*
> *His heart was light and joyous*
> *And free from worldly woes,*
> *And free from worldly woes.*

She had a high clear voice, not as strong as it might be, but
pretty. It wasn't anything like the voice she spoke in.

> *He asked the people by the hill,*
> *"Where are the singing birrrrds?"*
> *Up stepped a man named Simon*
> *And answered in these words,*
> *And answered in these words.*

> *"We cut the nesting trees down*
> *And placed where they once stoooood —*
> *One hundred crooked crosses*
> *Hewn from the bitter wood,*
> *Hewn from the bitter wood."*

Hobic tried to connect the Tracy Anne he knew from the
sleeping bag with the one shaking her long blond hair back and
playing guitar so sweetly, but they didn't fit together. In fact
neither of them, the folksinger nor the girl who wanted to be
fucked like a mule, neither seemed totally real on their own.

> *"Up there you'll hear no birdsong,*
> *The wind in mourning bloooows —*
> *The air is rent by widows' grief*
> *And cries of feeding crows,*
> *And cries of feeding crows.*

> *"The soldiers climb Mount Calv'ry,*
> *The people gather rouuuund —*
> *And those who bear a crooked cross*
> *Will soon be in the ground,*
> *Will soon be in the ground."*

> *The story Simon told Him*
> *Lay heavy on Christ's miiiind —*
> *"I'll climb that hill," He said, "before*
> *I leave this world behind,*
> *I leave this world behind."*

Hobie watched Tracy Anne singing and thought of what they did together. All he could summon up were the things he'd never considered, her hair getting in his mouth, wanting to have Kleenex to use after he pulled the rubber off, the little stretch marks that were starting on her breasts. But he'd done it, that was the important thing. He liked the thought of it, of the accomplishment. He wasn't excited by it, though. Not half as excited as he was sitting next to Sarah and brushing her hand each time a bottle passed. Even though there didn't seem to be any chance that Sarah would ever want to sleep with him, it seemed important that he get her to *like* him. Tracy Anne liked him enough to share her body but he didn't have any idea why or how he had earned it. Or how long he would want it.

> "*The King of Jews they'll call me,*
> *With thorns I shall be crowwwwwned —*
> *I'll bear a crooked cross one day*
> *But rest not in the ground,*
> *But rest not in the ground.*"
>
> *So down the road He rambled,*
> *His following to earrrrn —*
> "*I'm gone to find the Soul of Man*
> *And then I shall return,*
> *And then I shall return.*"

"You got a voice like an angel, Trace."

"Back in my day Christ never rambled," said Grant Parke. "He walked. Occasionally he *trod* somewhere, or marched or something, but he never *ram*bled. No wonder the Church is on the ropes, they gotta go the folkie route to attract customers. I mean what's next?"

"Heavy metal at High Mass. Tune in to a little Led Zeppelin before you drop your wafer."

"It's not the music got me," said Tracy Anne, "it was those priests, the hip ones. I mean you take away all the celibacy and mysticism and spookiness that old-time priests had going for them and what do you have left? Just some guy who's probably twice as naive as you'll ever be trying to give you advice on how to run your life. As if they can *help* you."

"I don't know about that," said King. "A priest helped me stay out of the draft."

"How's that?"

"Well, it really doesn't go against what Tracy Anne just said, cause this was an old-fashioned priest. Big beefy guy, red face, prawbly been a heavy drinker for years. Pat O'Brien woulda played him in the movie. Father Hogan, right?" King flashed his crooked smile. "Now Father Hogan was into this whole thing where he liked tough kids. 'I was a tough kid myself,' he was always saying, 'it's good for a kid to be tough. Only they should try to keep on the right side of the lawr.' He used to come over there to Roslindale, the detention center, when I was on ice. They only had me there for minor stuff at first, my mother told the juvenile that she couldn't handle me so they stuck me over to Roslindale till they could figure out what to do. It was nothing big, shoplifting, a couple fights, truancy. Nothin that's gonna keep you out of Nam. Anyhow, I'm in there and this Father Hogan gets on my case. Comes up to me, says, 'I hear you're a pretty tough kid. Hear you're a fighter.' I don't know what he's after, but I'm not gonna give him any opening for a lecture. That's all I get from the parish priests up in Chollistown, my mother makes me go to confession, lectures. Gotta kneel in the fuckin boot, listen to some old guy with bad breath give you lectures. Forget it. Only this Father Hogan, he's after somethin else. 'Ever do any of your fighting inside the rope arena?' That's what he always called it, the boxing ring, he called it the rope arena. He liked the sound of it. Anyways, he gives me this whole rap about street fighting is for punks, your real men they tie the gloves on and go at it, and if I'm so tough why don't I sign up for this boxing clinic he's running? He also hints that if I'm any good with my fists and he takes an interest in me it might be a quick way out of the can. He could be my sponsor, like, and get me out on the streets again. Well there's nothin to do at Roslindale, jerk off all day, you go crazy there, so I decide I'll look into it. And the boxing pot isn't too bad, Father Hogan knows his stuff, sawt of. He's got this picture from his last assignment, some state

[201]

prison out on the West Coast. Him and this guy he refawmed in jail and turned into a professional prizefighter, guy named Victorio Vacio. He's a light-heavy, Vacio, and Father Hogan thinks he's gonna work up to heavyweight and bump Jerry Quarry off out there as the favorite son. In fact, Hogan thinks he's gonna be the next Sonny Liston, which is an indication that he's not totally tuned-in to reality. I mean a Latin heavyweight? Forget it."

"What about the Wild Bull of the Pampas?"

"Grant, you an me both know Firpo was an exception. They're great little fighters, the Latins, but any bigger than middleweight, forget it.

"Anyhow, I went along with it and I could beat the shit out of most everybody my class and he got me out. A regular goddian angel, just said the word and there I was, back on the cawner of Trenton and Bunker Hill with my buddies. He talked my mother into taking another shot at it, talked the headmaster into letting me back in school, talked the juvenile off my back. Beautiful. All I got to do now is show up at this gym a couple times a week, shoot the shit with Father Hogan, tell him how I'm making out, and train for the Golden Gloves. *That's* what Father Hogan was into, he wanted his boys to take the Golden Gloves. Punch their way out of poverty or something like that. So I was pretty good, I could hit and I could move and Father Hogan is talking me up all over town. I get to meet Sam Silverman, the big promoter, I get to meet him personally and he says I'm a prawspect. Big deal, right? Okay, I'm makin out all right on every front, keepin out of trouble and all, and I'm in the quatter finals. I'm gonna fight this kid, Pawto Rican kid from the South End, he's sposed to take the whole thing. I get by him, I'm golden, prawbly I can coast the rest of the way. But first I got to get past this kid, and like I said, in the lighter weights the Latins are dynamite. They're fast.

"So all my friends are out there to watch and Father Hogan is there and there's some spawtswriters there, following this Pawto Rican kid, cause he's such a natural that even though it's only Golden Gloves they figure there might be a story in it. Champion of the Future or something. So it's a whole fuckin mob scene there, even though it's only quatter finals, and what I do is, I figure the guy has been boxing, with gloves and rules and all, for years, and I've just took it up lately, right, and he knows how to work the judges and he's supposed to have this fantastic fast jab and all, so I figure I just got to *chodge* him. Keep coming in, like Smokin Joe Frazier. I mean I hadn't done a whole lot of *box*ing but I had, you know, taken some pretty good shots in my day, I been hit with chains and rocks and fists and one time a baseball bat, a Louisville Slugger in the eye, and I know I can live with the hurt. This kid, this natural boxer, I don't *know* what he's ever been hit with but I figure it can't be much, the priests and the YMCA and all got to him so early that he's got all these junior boxing trophies they keep telling me about. So it's gonna be all-out headhunting from the opening bell, and even if I don't win I won't look like chickenshit in front of my friends."

"What's this got to do with the draft?"

"I'm comin to that, hold your water.

"So the fight stots and it goes pretty much the way I figured. He's got a good jab and he scaws a lot of points while I'm comin in but they got these big pillows you wear, the Golden Gloves, so I don't feel much and I keep comin in and when I get there I hit him. I hit him in the stomach, I hit him in the hot, in the liver, I hit him on the foreoms and the wrists and on the muscle of his shoulder, like he's a rock and I'm gonna punch a hole through it. And when he drops to cover his middle I hit him in the head. The kid doesn't know what to do, he's never been in this kind of fight, he can't get any rhythm together. No matter where he moves I'm right there with him, pumpin away, I'm not even covering my head. Well the folks are up from their seats the whole fight, Golden Gloves is mostly offense anyway, there's so few rounds, but this was more than they were used to. Three steady minutes of banging away, a minute to catch my breath, then back in there and after him. I didn't think about it, I just *did* it, in fact the fight was over and I still thought there was another round. And they had to give it to me, too, the judges, even though it wasn't their idea of a good spawting bout, what I done. But the last round he just covered and backed off and I whacked him in the ribs must of been a hundred times. Kid couldn't stand to be hit in the face, the second round I tagged him a couple good ones on the nose and I think that did it, getting really nailed for the first time in his life like that. Of course he done a job on me with those jabs and he had a pretty good hook to the body so I wasn't in great shape either, coming out of the ring, but I won and that was the point, right? And right away the repawters are all over Father Hogan and he's eating it up. His nose turned a deeper shade of red, he was that happy.

"Later that night, I'm out with my friends, it starts to dawn on me. Actually, what stots to happen is that Pawto Rican kid's jab stots to catch up with me so my left eye is almost completely closed up and my nose is swollen and my ribs are on fire. In the ring you hodly feel it, but after, Christ, it's murder. So we got some beer and we're out there, the street, and no matter how much I drink it still hurts and I figure what for? So Hogan can tell spawtswriters about the next Sonny Liston? So my mother can tell everybody I'm refawmed, I only beat guys up between the bells now? Fuck it, I figure, I'm gettin taken for a ride. Golden Gloves don't pay a penny, they set them up so kids will burn it off in the ring and not make any real trouble. It's, what is it Wein calls it, co-optation by transference. Whatever. It's a rawr deal and I'm aching all over so much I can hodly move but I still got all this adrenaline, all this energy, left over from the fight. I got to *move*. So what you do, you live in Chollistown and you want to move, is you boost a car. These two guys I'm with, one of them knows how to hot-wire so we latch onto this big fuckin Pontiac, this Bonneville, and we're off. We never boosted a luxury car before, mostly around the hill where we hung out you got your basic Chevys and Fords, so I'm not too swift on handling the thing. What we're gonna do, we're gonna get our ass out of Chollistown where all the cops know we don't own no cars and put this boat on cruisomatic over the Mystic River Bridge and up onto the Nawtheast Expressway, then cut over to Revere Beach, hack around awhile, see if we can pick anything up. It's a nice summer night, we figure, why let it go to waste? Brilliant. We'd drunk a shitload of this stuff, this Millers Malt Liquor, it's got more kick than just regular beer and we weren't in the best of mental or physical shape right then. Revere Beach or bust. You gotta understand where my consciousness is at back then, all I know is I feel like I been screwed and when you feel that way you beat on somebody or you boost a car and go honkin.

"We get acrost the Mystic River there, nice, no prawblem at the toll, it's shadowy enough the guy don't see my face all puffed up, and we're onto the Expressway. Only Denny and Kevin, these guys I'm with, they both gotta pee, the Millers, and you can't hack that with the cruisomatic up sixty-five per and all this traffic behind you. So I pull it off, we're in Chelsea, we're lost. You ever *been* to fucking Chelsea? The one-way-street capital of the fucking universe, they got cars driving around there three years, trying to get up to Revere. The place is unbe*lieva*ble. I wouldn't go back there again you paid me, I don't care *how* bad I had to piss. So Denny and Kevin do their business, they're zipping up to get back in the car when this cop pulls right up behind us, big as life. And they're off to the races, those two jumpin over fences with their flies hangin open and here I am fifteen years old and dead broke in this ocean liner, its ac*ces*sories have got accessories this car, with a relief map of Pawto Rico swelling up on my face and this cop getting out of his wagon to look me over. Well, he must of been a patrol supervisor or something, he was riding alone, so the minute he gets by my window I floor the fucker and I'm gone. Only I'm *not* gone, I'm in *Chel*sea. Only town in the world the pigeons fly over completely, it's too dangerous to walk. I'm steering this thing around trying to find the Expressway again and I'm doing most of it on two wheels and not once do I stop to think I should get out and ditch the car and run. It's like my mind is still in the ring, like I got to keep chodging ahead no matter what. I'm going sixty, seventy miles per down these little one-way streets they got, blowing through the few stop signs they've bothered to put up there and my left eye is shut tight with the swelling now so I don't even *see* it when this produce truck hits me at an intersection I was running. I just feel the back end of the car rapidly swinging around to become the *front* end of the car. I hit a phone booth, two light poles and sideswiped a row of double-pocked cars before I finally eased it into the front of this Latin grocery store. Fuckin dried codfish all over the windshield. If the jab don't get you the bacalao will.

"So anyway, to make a long story shawt, it was grand theft and criminal negligence and resisting arrest and all that prawperty damage, which even though I was a minor at the time is enough on my record that Uncle Sam doesn't want me corrupting his blue-eyed boys in the barracks.

"Oh yeah, and when I was back at Roslindale the only thing Father Hogan had to say to me, before they caught on to him, was that in the end I'd proved to be a punk. And if there was one thing God hated worse than a liar or a thief or even a wife-beating heathen, it was a punk.

"So much for religion."

"It's sort of like a conscientious objector thing though, isn't it?" said Tracy Anne. "Only instead of not wanting to fight at all, you wanted to fight too much."

"Not too much, just the wrong people."

"Well, the Lord works in mysterious ways," said Grant Parke. "He's sort of like the CIA in that respect."

"Not too long after this whole story happened they sent Hogan off to this alcoholic priest place they got up in Minnesota somewhere. Dry him out. And the kid they put in his place, all he could come up with was all this 'God is love' business. Couldn't fight a lick."

"God is love."

"All you need is love."

"Love, love, love."

"Love is where it's at."

"Jesus loves you, baby. Peace."

"Peace, love, happiness."

"Toss my *cook*ies."

Grant Parke had the guitar and began to try out Billy's bottleneck on it. "This song actually calls for a pedal steel," he said, "but this here will have to do. This is dedicated to the thousands of Jesus freaks, young and old, throughout our great land. Its title comes from the words of the old pea-picker himself, Cowboy Karl Marx, and it's called *Religion Is the Opium of the People.* Unless of course, you live in San Francisco, in which case *op*ium is the re*lig*ion of the people."

"Jerk joke."

"Do the song, Parke."

Whether staring at the walls in New York City,
Or crying out at night in Tennessee,

Grant sang through his nose in a country-western twang, or what must have passed for one at Hotchkiss —

Take a little Jesus Christ and you'll feel better,
Aaaand you don't need no purscription cause He's free.

He is better than pineapple juice and Sterno.
He is better than a fat and sleepy whore.
You can spread Him with our clever new dispenser,
Aaaand you'll find Him at your nearest grocery store.

It was amazing, he could play *too*. Almost everybody who'd had their hands on the guitar was able to do something that sounded like music with it, Hobie felt like it must be a required course in northern schools or something. After they did it the first night, Tracy Anne had asked him all these names of mountain singers who came from around West Virginia, whether he'd ever seen them perform or knew them personally. He hadn't heard of but a few, and those only cause Mr. Hinkle had brought their recordings into class and had a test on it. And here was Grant Parke bottlenecking long slide notes as the chorus came up —

Take a double dose of Jesus if you're lonely.
Rub your aching life with Christ when you are sad.
Shoot the Savior in your arm when you feel empty,
Heeeee's the cheapest high the world has ever had.

"Yee-hah!"
"Pick it, Cousin Grant, pick it!"

He is every barren woman's smiling baby.
He is every lifelong virgin's loving son.
He's a pal who never asks to borrow money,
Aaaand the fiancé of every blushing nun.
You can feed Him to the minds of starving children,
Or pour Him down the souls of dying men.
If you wear Him on your heart He'll stop the bullets,
Heeee will keep you safe through every lion's den.

You don't have to have no dusty Gideon Bible.
You don't have to search for days or travel far.
If you say His name with faith the Lord will love you,
Heeee's a snake oil that's too big for any jar.

"Work that ax, buddy!"
"Magic fingers."
"Must of escaped from the Grand Ole Opry."

Take a double dose of Jesus if you're lonely.
Rub your aching life with Christ when you are sad.
Shoot the Savior in your arm when you feel empty,
Heeeeeeeeeee's —
The cheapest high the world has ever had!

There wasn't but a single bottle of the Crockett Gap left float-ing around and Hobie couldn't feel his cheeks anymore. He pinched them as hard as he could but felt nothing. Sarah saw him and started to laugh and took a handful to pinch and then, then he felt it. He wished he could sing or play or something for her but he didn't know how. He always just moved his lips in church when they were supposed to sing and there was always so many poor desperate women shouting to Heaven with all they were worth that it didn't make much difference in the volume. Every-body could play the guitar except maybe King, and he could tell stories.

Hobie looked across to Smallwood. The kid was getting pretty wrecked. His cheeks were flushed all pink and his eyes were out of focus behind his glasses. Couldn't blame him. Hobie tried to imagine Smallwood in the Army. Smallwood in Darwin's uni-form. What would Smallwood do, when things like that hap-pened to him? The things Dar went through, things he had to do. Smallwood didn't look much like he'd be able to stand it. What would he do about the hole, about the soldiers? About the bodies underground?

Hobie felt pretty wrecked himself. He couldn't remember when he'd felt lighter. Unless it was that time when he and Dar had found someone's cache of Jim Beam one Saturday afternoon, up where the tree house used to be before it got stripped. They were only in junior high then, didn't know how potent it was and between them forced a whole fifth down in a half-hour's time. He remembered trying to act normal in front of their father, trying to keep those damn frozen peas down until they could get out of his sight. And how even though it was obvious that he knew, he never give them a lecture, just kept doling out more of those peas. Growin boys, he kept saying all night, got to eat hearty.

The bottle and the guitar passed around. Grant sang *If You Ain't Got That Dough-Re-Mi* and *The Battle Hymn of the Republic* and something called *What Made Milwaukee Famous Made a Loser Out of Me*. Mickey Q. sang the English High fight song and Smallwood countered with his prep-school debating team's anthem, a song that rhymed *subtle* with *rebuttal*. The Oreos ran out and everyone shot fingers to see who would go out for more. Parke lost and tried to beg off with his bad knees. Billy sang *Joe Hill* and *Dark as a Dungeon*. Parke came back with Oreos and some barbecue-flavored potato chips. Tracy Anne told a long incoherent story about hitchhiking all the way to somewhere in Connecticut to get Joan Baez's autograph. Then she sang *Thirsty Boots* and *Amazing Grace*. Hobie sang along a bit on that, but not so loud that anyone else would hear him. He was tired of being a guest.

He thought of telling them how his father was trapped under in the cave-in that time. How nobody knew whether he was dead or alive and how it was just luck he got found. But no, that was too personal. He cast about for another story, not so close to home.

"That reminds me," Hobie heard himself saying, "of this old fella we had back home everybody calls Pappy Dan." Sarah's arm was around his neck for a moment, just wine-friendly but nice all the same. "Pappy Dan Radnor. Now this is way, way back, cause Pappy Dan is a really old man and this happened when he wasn't but thirteen or fourteen years old. And he was a preacher. Around where he lived, the coal camps, that wasn't anything unusual, if you knew a little bit of Scripture and got the callin you could consider yourself a preacher and all you had to do was get up and *preach* to the people. Pappy Dan saw all the attention preachers got and the way a lot of women hung around and figured that was for him."

Hobie tried to tell it just like Pappy Dan might, only without the interruptions to spit. Once he was started it didn't seem so bad, talking in front of them all, and he hurried to organize the story in his mind.

"This is back when they were still trying to get the union in, it didn't have but a toehold in the state and things looked bad. There was organizing goin on where Pappy Dan lived at, and wherever there was organizing you'd find the Baldwin-Felts agents, this detective agency that hired its men out to the coal operators. They'd send men and guns and spies into an area and just clean out anyone connected to the union. And the local law either shut its eyes or helped them along. Everybody hated the Baldwins' guts but there wasn't a whole lot they could do.

"Now Pappy Dan's mama was a widow, husband killed in a mine explosion, and Dan was the oldest of seven brothers and sisters. She had to take in boarders, his mama, had to move the whole family into one little room and rent the others out. Of course the coal company, they owned the mortgage on her house, so when they needed a place to put up some of their hired guns she had to take them in. Couple Baldwin-Felts men, one named Hickey and one named Griggs, moved in and took over the house. They were loud and mean and pork-bellied and made no bones about what their business in camp was. People knew that Dan's mama didn't have no say in the matter so they didn't hold it against her.

"It was hell for Dan, though. He had to help with the housework and they were always teasin and bullyin him around, giving him all kinds of grief when they heard he was a preacher, askin him to save their souls and whatnot. Just constant meanness. More than once his mother had to hold him back from going at them with a fire poker or an iron skillet. She knew they could of shot him dead on the spot and gotten away scot free.

"There was another widow in the coal camp, didn't live too far off, name of Bridey Mae. She'd been widowed real young, Bridey, and didn't have any children to keep her busy, so she taken up with men. Lots of men. She wasn't like a — *pro*stitute or anything, but men give her presents all the time. A little dry goods here, a little tinned beef there, a little carpentry around her shack by some of the unmarried men. She made out just fine. The thing was, Bridey Mae just *liked* men. And they liked her back. Always with a smile on her face, doors always open, the joke among the men was that if Bridey ever bore a child she'd have to name it Camp Number Nine.

"At this same time there was this fella in town, young fella, name of Joe Kenehan. To hear him tell it, he was there by accident and spite. Joe was with the Socialists, and he was just about the most good-lookin and nice-mannered fella you'd ever want to meet, full of all kinds of ideas and dreams about the future of the labor movement, the future of the country. He had been working for the Socialists with the railroad people on their strikes, and what happened was that he got too popular. Whenever any other Socialist come into his area with an idea, people would hesitate and say, 'Well, why don't we ask Joe Kenehan first, see what he thinks?' Of course the other Socialists got tired of this and jealous so pretty soon they got together and said, 'We'll fix this bird, we'll stick him down in the mines to organize, where it's death on Socialists.' Next thing Joe Kenehan knows he's plopped down in the middle of a strange fight with nobody to back him up. He's an outsider and a Socialist, the local UMW folks don't trust him and neither do the people in the camp. But the kind of fella he was, Joe Kenehan, pretty soon he'd won everybody over and was in the thick of things, just figured he'd make the best of what he'd been given. Before too long he was right up with the heads of the union organizers, helping to plan strategy and everything.

"Now here it gets complicated. Bridey Mae gets a load of young Joe and she just falls head over heels. Doesn't mention it to anybody, she's always just sat back and had men come to her, like she could take them or leave them, and she's not about to let on anything different. But she's really got a case for Joe, and whenever she runs into him she drops hints all over the place that if Joe should pay her a visit he wouldn't be disappointed. Joe never comes. He's seen this one and that one slippin round Bridey's shack, he's seen the way miners get into fistfights over who she likes best, he's seen the way the men hold grudges and he figures that Bridey belongs to the camp and he'd do nothing but damage if he set himself up as a rival. So when Bridey gets tired of being subtle and sends him a letter that spells out exactly how she feels, Joe writes her a letter back begging off. He knows one sure thing to turn local men angry is outside competition for their women. Which was another reason the Baldwin-Felts agents were hated so much, they were notorious for the way they went after local women.

"In fact Hickey, one of the gunmen at the boarding house Dan's mama was running, Hickey was paying little visits to Bridey Mae himself. Like I said, she just liked men, and here was a new one who'd been to cities and brought her the kind of presents it was hard for a miner to get his hands on. Of course the whole thing was on the sly, and Hickey was also interested in whatever information Bridey could get him from the miners. She didn't suspect a thing, and for the most part she didn't know anything that could be used against the men.

"But every time Hickey mentioned Joe Kenehan, she'd clam up and get all tight, so he figured something was up. He got the whole story in bits and pieces, and he could tell that she'd been really hurt by Joe turning her down. It gave him an idea. A couple months before, the Baldwins had gotten a spy pretty deep in the ranks of the organizers, but he was a drinker and spilled the beans on himself one night, and before the sun rose he was found pumped full of bullets in a crick. You got caught out as a company fink and your life expectancy took a big drop.

"Hickey started feeding Bridey Mae stories he made up, about how Joe Kenehan was bragging all over camp the way she'd chased him, how he was showing around the letter she'd written him and having a big laugh. Bridey wanted to go out and shoot him right then, but Hickey held her back and said why get yourself in trouble? Why not let the men take care of it, like they take care of the rest of your needs? So he got her to go along with his plot.

"What they did was, Hickey got a Baldwin-Felts pay slip and wrote it out to Joe Kenehan, and made up a company identification card and copied Joe's signature off the letter Joe'd sent Bridey Mae. And then he sent Bridey to the men.

"Not to the union organizers, but to some of the real hot-headed miners, the ones were always ready with a rifle when trouble broke out, the ones wanted to blast the owners off the face of the earth. She went to them and she said, 'I hate to tell you this, fellas, but I believe Joe Kenehan is a spy.' She told them how he'd come to her shack all drunk and wanting a woman and she let him in. The miners could all believe that, they'd all done the same more than once themselves. But the problem was that some of the things Joe asked her to do were — were unnatural. He was a Socialist after all, and who knew what kind of strange desires they might have? When she refused, Bridey told them, Joe took hold of her and forced her and called her a whoo-er. She was just a regular old gal. And then, she said, Joe tried to pay her in cash money, like she was some common town tramp, and he was so drunk pulling money from his billfold that some other things fell out too, that he left behind when he staggered away. This check from Baldwin-Felts here, and this identification card with his very own signature on it. Bridey thought she best ought to warn the men, she said, before Joe got too far into their business. The men thanked her and told her to put all thoughts of whoo-ers and unnaturalness out of her pretty little head, that round about midnight the camp would be minus one Socialist. Bridey went back to tell her news to Mr. Hickey.

"Hickey was so pleased with himself that he picked up a couple bottles of the hard stuff and went back to the boarding house to tell Griggs all about his trick. Now it just happened that Dan was cleaning by their door and overheard the whole plot while they were celebrating. But before he could slip off and tell the miners, the two agents crashed out of the room and grabbed hold of Dan for balance and went down to dinner.

"Dan had to serve the dinner his mother cooked for all the boarders so he was stuck there, and he couldn't tell anybody out in the open for fear of how Hickey and Griggs might revenge on his mother. Once when Dan had refused to make them coffee Griggs put a gun to her head and asked if he wanted seven orphans on his conscience. So Dan figured he'd have to get away after dinner.

"The problem with that was that there was a big prayer meeting in camp that night and he was scheduled to be one of the preachers. And when Hickey and Griggs found out they insisted they go with him to catch the show. They were pretty looped, and all through dinner they made fun of Dan and said how if the Lord relied on little shits like him to spread His word they didn't want any truck with Heaven. And as for Hell, well, they'd already been to West Virginia so it would most likely be a step up.

"They weren't hardly done with eating when Hickey clapped his arm around Dan's shoulder and they started off for the church, singing hymns with dirty words stuck in.

"Just about everybody was there, including all the hotheaded miners in to get the Lord's blessing for the night's work. Everybody went dumb when the Baldwin-Felts men staggered in. Dan was in plain sight all the while and couldn't tell anybody for fear of his mother's safety, he had to walk up onto the platform and sit with the other preachers. Knowing all the while that a terrible thing was gonna happen.

"About the only camp people not there was Bridey Mae, who was uncomfortable around all the damnation talk, and Joe Kenehan who was a Socialist and not expected to make an appearance at religious meetings. The preaching always went on deep into the night, each preacher staying up on the platform when he was through, while the men in the audience were expected to drift away as things wore on. The women felt a lot more comfortable about the shouting and rolling and testifying that always ended a big meeting if their men weren't around to watch. Dan was supposed to speak early cause he was so young, the third one up. It looked pretty black for Joe Kenehan.

"But while he was listening to the first couple fellas go at it, Dan got an idea. He figured if there was one thing that local people knew it was their Scripture. Most were like Dan and couldn't read much, but had been told the stories so often they knew them by heart. And Hickey and Griggs had seemed almost *proud* of the fact that they knew nothing at all about the Book. So when his turn come up, Dan was ready to give the folks some *gos*pel.

"Everybody was real tense, they couldn't loosen up to the preachin what with the Baldwin-Felts men sitting at the rear giggling and making fun through everything, guns strapped right out in the open over their fat bellies. And they got worst when Dan stepped up, just about rolling on the floor they thought it was so funny. The miners could hardly hold their tempers, to think Joe Kenehan who they had welcomed into their hearts would betray them to the likes of those two. They could hardly wait for full darkness to go get him.

" 'Friends,' Dan started out, 'I wanna tell you tonight about the *black*ness in the heart of man. An I want to *warn* you' — and here he looked at all the most hotheaded of the miners, stared them straight in the face — 'about the many and devious ways that Satan will hide from us the truth of who our *real* friends are. Warn you of the trickery by which he makes black seem white and good seem evil. An I'm gonna do it with a story from the Patriarchs.' "

"Hickey and Griggs couldn't hardly contain theirselves over that, Dan up on a platform holdin his own before the entire coal camp. But Dan was such a talker that he *could* hold his own, if he wasn't so young and the other preachers so jealous they'd of saved him for the late hours and the real soul-stomping holiness action.

" 'Now we all know about Joseph,' said Dan, 'and how out of all Jacob's twelve children he was the smartest and the smoothest, and how his brothers got so jealous they stripped offen his coat of many colors and thrown him down into a deep pit, and how he was found by some people who sold him into slavery in Egypt. That's where my story begins.

" 'Now Joseph, he wasn't crazy bout being on the auction block, but he seen what hate and bitterness drove his brothers to, and he resolved the same wouldn't happen to him. So when this fella Potiphar bought him for a servant he just smiled and acted as natural as you'd please and vowed if he was gonna be a slave he was gonna be a *good* one. Just makin the best of a bad situation. Well, he put his heart to his work and he was honest and kindly in all his dealins with the other slaves and with the Egyptians and pretty soon everybody liked him. And Potiphar saw how well he done and kept promotin Joseph up the ladder in the household. Joseph didn't take advantage of position though, no, he was extra kind and extra fair with everybody and before you knew it he was *run*nin the household and the fields and just taking care of all of Potiphar's business for him.

" 'The only trouble was Potiphar's wife. She was what you'd

call a loose woman, out foolin round on the sly with other men, but all sugar and innocence when Potiphar was around. When he was gone, though, she just carried *on*. And she had the eye on young Joseph for a long time. He was a good-lookin fella and smart and she said, "Joseph, why don't you come and lie with me?" Joseph didn't want no part of it. He said, "I been good to Potiphar and he's been good right back to me, how can I go slippin round with his wife? Don't you tempt me, woman." '

"At this point Dan looked at the Baldwins to see if they'd caught on at all. But they'd brought some liquor into the church with them and were passing it back and forth makin loud comments about how did a fourteen-year-old boy know so much about loose women unless he'd picked it up from firsthand example. From his *ma*ma maybe.

"Well, it was clear they didn't know a Bible story from a hole in the ground, so Dan began to fool around with the details a little bit.

" 'Also in Potiphar's employ at this time is a couple spies from one of his enemies. They can plainly see the wanton lust of his wife and they also see how it would be good for their purposes to get young Joseph out of the way. So they come to Potiphar's wife with tales of how Joseph is tellin everbody in Egypt the word on her, and you know how it is, Hell hath no fury like a woman scorned. These two spies and Potiphar's wife work up a plan against Joseph.

" 'One day the wife gets Joseph alone and she grabs hold of his garment and tries to pull him down with her, but Joseph breaks loose and runs off. She calls out for Potiphar then like she's been attacked and he comes runnin in and she says, "Joseph, your servant," she says, "he come in here and tried to make me lie with him. Only when I called out he fled, leavin this here garment as evidence. And not only that, while he was here he told me how he's been stealin you blind and plotting with your enemies, how he wants to take over the household and have you killed." '

"This last bit was new to everybody in the church, all the preachers and people in the aisles were scratching their heads over what Dan was saying, but he just stared to the two agents horsing around in the back and kept on.

" 'Potiphar was out*raged* over all of this,' he said, 'he had no reason to misbelieve his wife, and after all, Joseph *was* a slave, a foreigner, and you could never trust them too much. Potiphar vowed to have revenge on his servant that very night. He gathered all his slaves and household workers together and told them of Joseph's treachery and they joined him in arms and they went and they slew Joseph dead. Cut him from gut to gizzard and left him bleedin in a stream. And lo, they never learned of the lies Potiphar's wife had told, and they all went to their Maker *unrepentant*, with innocent blood on their hands!'

"That wasn't at all the way the story was supposed to end, and the people rolled it over in their minds. Most couldn't figure it out, but the miners who'd been with Bridey Mae that afternoon began to see the light of what Dan was up to. Speaking to them in a parable.

"'And that is only an early ex*amp*le,' said Dan, 'of Satan's nefarious double-dealin. The same kind of thing goes on to this very day, with the same tragical results. And in the eyes of the Lord the husbands and servants that do the bloodshed, even though they been hoodwinked, they just as guilty as the folks who laid the plot. Draw your own conclusions.' And with that he walked across the platform and sat down. There wasn't a peep out of the whole congregation but for Hickey and Griggs giggling from the rear. That and the sound of people puttin two an two together.

"The Baldwins got bored pretty soon and staggered out, but the men, especially the real hotheads among them, stayed the whole meetin and come up in the final rush shoutin thanks to Jesus for makin the scales drop from their eyes.

"And the next day Joe Kenehan got stopped every ten feet by somebody who wanted to slap his back and say good morning, he couldn't understand how everybody seemed *so* glad to see him. Come noon his back was red and his shaking-hand swollen up from friendliness. He wondered if there wasn't something to this revival-meeting business after all."

Hobie stopped and looked around. Sarah was beaming. "That's a great story," she said.

"What happened to Hickey and Griggs?"

"Oh, nothin much. They were pretty careful fellas, always had their guns on and stayed in a group."

"And what about Bridey Mae?"

"She got a note told her it would be wise to move on. Word was that she went up to Charleston and turned professional for good. Decided she didn't like men so much anymore."

"And Joe Kenehan?"

"Well that was sad. They finally got him. Found with a bullet in the back of the head, and whoever done it took his blood and painted *Red* on his back. None of the Baldwins were ever brought to trial for that. In fact, they succeeded in busting up the union in those parts for a while, it was a good fifteen years before things began to stir again. Miners wired the Socialists to see if they wanted Joe's body, but they never answered."

They were quiet for a moment. The wine had run out. Sarah had the guitar in her lap and was plunking the A-string aimlessly.

"I got shot by a Baldwin-Felts once," she said.

"What?"

"Huh?"

"In a play. I was in a play about the Ludlow massacre and I was this Welsh woman, Mary Thomas, who was a great singer and an organizer and at the end she's wounded by this company agent."

"Didn't know you could sing."

"I can't much. But I could act some. I was going to be an actress, for a career."

"No shit."

"Sarah Bernhardt in our very midst."

"Can you *imag*ine? It seems like ages ago but it wasn't really so long." Sarah laughed. "I remember the very moment I gave it up too. I was at this huge cattle-call, hundreds of summer-stock producers doing a regional audition, they rented the Wilbur for three days and every aspiring theater freak in the Northeast came to show their stuff. You got five minutes, to the second, and you were supposed to do two pieces. I remember, I was gonna do this decadent-aristocrat bit from *Miss Julie* and then this tough old cowgirl speech from a new play called *Yucca Flats*. Versatility, right? I was scared shitless. But I thought I really wanted to be an actress.

"You have to have resumés printed up for every producer, right, with a big smiling picture of yourself either stapled or offset-printed on the back of it. So they remember your face when they review their notes on you. I had these big glossies, flashing all thirty-two teeth like a quiz-show announcer. If I ever make the Ten Most Wanted list I just *know* the FBI will circulate one of those pictures.

"Anyhow, I'm backstage at the Wilbur, going over my lines in my head, worrying about whether I'm dressed right and waiting for my number to be called. They don't waste a second, you're up, five minutes of material, and you're off watching the next guy suffer. They call my number. I'm like peeing in my pants. Walking upstage to give my name, trying to think myself into Miss Julie, and I hear this giant *rust*ling sound from the audience and I look out. And I *freeze*. The rustling is the sound of hundreds, *hun*dreds of producers picking up my resumé and on the back of them I'm facing hundreds of smiling Sarah's flashing thirty-two hundreds of pearly-white teeth at me. A packed audience of my own glossy self.

"Well, somehow I got through the audition, I went so fast the five minutes I'd planned so carefully came out to four-and-a-quarter and there was this long awkward moment before the timekeeper realized I'd finished. But I didn't *care* that nobody wanted me for summer stock, I was finished. It brought home to me perfectly the kind of total — self-absorption that you need to have to be an actress. It's inescapable. And when I thought about it, about the few really positive experiences I'd had in the theater like playing Mary Thomas, I realized it was always the *part*, the person, that excited me, not the actressing. I wanted to be like Mary Thomas for *real*, not be somebody who might get a chance to pretend her life. So I got out."

"Sing something."

Sarah smiled and shook her head. "I told you, I can't sing."

"Much. You can sing some. C'mon. It's your turn."

"It's pretty late. The guys downstairs —"

"Never mind them." Smallwood was sprawled across Tracy Anne's lap, a sloppy grin on his face. "Would you deny the request of a young Amurrican boy on the eve of his departure to make the world safe for democracy?"

"All of a sudden it's the USO here."

"Please Sarah. Sing something. Sing one of your Mary Thomas things."

Sarah sighed and hoisted the guitar up into playing position. "Okay. But don't expect any miracles. And after this we should probably turn it in." She fiddled with the tuning. "This is what the whole cast came out to sing at the end of the play, the grand finale. I did some research for the part, and found that the story's not a hundred percent accurate, but it's still a great song." She took a deep breath. "Help me on the chorus. Here goes."

She began to stomp out the beat with her foot, stomp, stomp, stomp, *stomp*, then brought in the guitar, then began to sing —

> *Ah, the year of 1914*
> *Brewed a deadly union fight,*
> *In the Colorado coalfields*
> *To relieve the miners' plight.*
> *Thirteen thousand men in all,*
> *When they heard their brothers' call*
> *Lay their picks down in a challenge to the greedy*
> *owners' might.*
>
> *To the mining town of Ludlow*
> *Pitching tents they came to strike,*
> *While the Baldwin-Felts detectives*
> *Called them hunkie, wop and kike.*
> *Though they came from many lands,*
> *By the callus on their hands*
> *They could tell that in his labor every worker is alike.*

She had a surprisingly deep, scratchy voice, but very strong. The song sounded to Hobie like it should be somebody's national anthem, the chorus belted out by a thousand marching patriots —

> *We will sing our song where Liberty lies sleeping.*
> *We will lift each rippling voice into a wave.*
> *Out of factory and field*
> *We will make the bosses yield*
> *And we'll raise Her up in glory from the grave!*

Sarah acted the song as much as she sang it and Hobie ached to reach over and touch her. Sometimes daydreaming he thought about what it would be like to have his arm around her, or to have hers around him, about small things like that like he and Delia had done. With Tracy Anne all he ever thought about was doing it. Fucking. And though he thought about how that might be with Sarah too, it was always calmer, warmer somehow —

In the week that followed Easter
The militia planned a rout.
They would show these bootless miners
What a fight was all about.
On that fatal April day
They swept down in full array
Bearing torches crost the battlefield to burn the strikers out.

Now the miners' families scattered,
From the deadly shot they fled.
But a few were forced to shelter
In a storage pit instead.
They were trapped beneath the ground,
When the smoke cleared they were found,
Two young mothers suffocated and eleven children dead.

It reminded him of a dozen similar stories his father and Pappy Dan and Mr. Hinkle and others had told him. It reminded him of *They Died with Their Boots On.* It reminded him of the thing Darwin had done —

We will sing our song where Liberty lies sleeping.

They were joining her on the chorus now, every one of them, stomping their feet to the beat and touching each other to complete the circle. Hobie felt them all pressed together in the wine and the singing and he had never felt this way about a group of people before, not even the team on a bus back from a winning game, he'd never sung right out loud like this before and been thrilled by the feel of it in his throat —

We will lift each rippling voice into a wave!
Out of factory and field

We will make the bosses yield
And we'll raise Her up in glory from the grave!

Sarah sang the next verse soft and slow at first, then snapped the ending —

In the aftermath of Ludlow
Mother Jones come forth to weep
O'er the cruelly murdered victims
Huddled smold'ring in a heap.
Then she rose up with a roar,
"We must press the fight once more!
Cause Liberty is not dead, She is merely fast asleep!"

They could hear them coming up the stairs then, Wein and Mark Remington and Schenk, clomping up from their genocide debate and suddenly everyone was conscious of the scene they made, a summercamp singing-circle strewn with Oreo crumbs and empty scab-wine bottles. But Sarah kept playing, kept singing it through and brought them back to her —

"Can we wake Her?" is the question
That we ask through bitter tears,
"Or will Liberty be absent
As the final battle nears?
Can She lead us on ahead?
Or has Liberty been dead
In a pit in bloody Ludlow all these long frustrating years?"

We
Will
Sing our song where Liberty lies sleeping!
We will lift each rippling voice into a wave!

And they all joined to sing it out, stomping and pounding the floor in time and holding each other's eyes and shouting it, as much in defiance of the three sober ones entering the room as of the exploiters of the world, stomping and shouting it out for the simple lung-busting joy of their own voices.

OUT OF FACTORY AND FIELD
WE WILL MAKE THE BOSSES YIELD!
AND WE'LL RAISE HER UP IN GLORY
FROM THE GRAVE!

18

It hurt to breathe first. Not just shortness of breath like always, this was different, this was taking in air that was too hot, that had the burn of acid to it. It would start with blackness and burnt lungs and then the trapped feeling, the walls on each side. His palms sizzling as he pushed against them, knowing he was scorching them, knowing he had to climb out or die. Then sensing someone above working against his climb. Pouring molten lead down the sides of the hole to sear over his wrists. *Hell-hole.* That one word in his head all the while as the heat grew and the panic and the pain. Hell-hole. And then, worse than anything before, the knowing. Knowing without seeing that it was Dar who was up there pouring down, Dar who was burning him to death in the Hell-hole.

Hunter woke then as he always did from the dream, wet and out of breath, not knowing where he was, afraid for Molly and Hobie and Dar. Afraid for himself.

He sat up and held his head and let the pieces come slowly. He was looking for Hobie. He was in Boston, living at Mrs. Hanrahan's. And something was wrong. Something else. He was broke. That was it. He was broke and had to take a job, he was starting in the morning. In a few hours.

PACKER
No exp. necc. gen. duties, some heavy lift., union shop. Apply Porchetta Packing Co., 500 Msgr O'Brien H'way, Camb. btween 7-12, M., Tues.

Hunter had circled twenty-five ads in the General Help Wanted of the Sunday *Globe*. He would owe Mrs. Hanrahan rent in two weeks and he had lost all but fifteen dollars of his money. Stupid. Porchetta was one of the first places he'd gone but it didn't look very promising. The woman in the personnel office just had you fill out an application. When he asked she sighed and said there were four openings and almost two hundred had applied already. He told her his phone situation and said it would be best if he called them instead of the other way around. She said that would be fine, to try Monday. Of all the personnel secretaries he met that week she was just about the nicest.

By the time he got to most of the offices the jobs had already been filled. He was told he was too old for a few of them. Some said they would send him a card if he got it.

When he called on Monday the personnel woman sounded tired.

"Yes, the jobs are still open. Two of them, anyway. McNatt, you said? Let me pull it. Let's see — oh yes, West Virginia. Listen, Mr. McNatt, before this drives me crazy, do you have any back trouble?"

"No." It was sore a lot but nothing serious like Ray's.

"Can you start anytime?"

"Sure."

"Wonderful. If you'd come down here as soon as possible and clear up some paperwork I think we can get you by. You ever have two-hundred-fifty equally qualified people breathing down your neck?"

When he got there she told him two of the jobs had been filled by relatives of present employees and that her boss had left the other two in her hands. "You were the first person to call me. If you'd had a home phone I would have closed my eyes and picked two at random."

He was starting a job tomorrow. He might not make the rent. Forty-five years old and he was flat broke and homeless.

Hunter lay back and tried to keep his mind on finances as he fell into sleep. He'd had the Hell-hole at least once a week right after Dar came back and told him the whole thing, then it had tapered off and disappeared. He didn't like it coming back to worry him.

Hunter lay back and wished it was warm enough to open a window in his little furnished room. It was hard to breathe. It was hard to breathe, that always came first.

19

Hobie was cleaning the basement room when Schenk found him. Hobie didn't like being down in the cellar, didn't like cellars in general, but he was glad he was busy when Schenk came on him. Something about the fella always made you feel guilty, like you were an enemy of the people if you weren't constantly grinding away at work.

"When you were in West Virginia," said Schenk, "did you hear much about union politics?"

Schenk never said hey or eased into talking, he just got right to it.

"Heard some." Hobie kept cleaning, mopping the floor while Schenk sat on his desk.

"There much talk about this guy Yablonski?"

"Some."

"What do you think of him?"

Hobie never talked with his father about work or the union or anything. He heard from other people though, he couldn't help but hear.

"I don't know the fella personally. I never seen him talk."

"That's no reason not to take a position." Schenk would wait him out till he had a commitment. Schenk could wait anybody out.

Hobie squatted to reach the mop under a desk. "He seems like a right enough fella. Don't really hear a whole lot about him. The local papers are all for the operators, which means that Boyle is fine with them. And the *UMW Journal* there, well, that's run by the people that's in power. They not about to go advertising the opposition."

"Your father is in the union, right?"

"Yuh."

"How does he feel about it?"

"Don't know for sure. I imagine he'd be for Yablonski though."

"Why?"

Hobie stood to wring out the mop. "He just seems like he would. Yablonski isn't saying a whole lot that other miners haven't been saying for years. Just he's doing it right out in public. He's sticking his neck out."

"You admire that."

Hobie shrugged. "And what do you think of him?"

Schenk gave a little smile. "I think he's an evolutionist. A co-opter. I think you people are being taken in by a dime-store liberal."

Hobie slapped the floor with the mop and pushed away from Schenk. You people.

"It's always easier," said Schenk, "to follow a charismatic leader up the wrong tree than to have the balls to shake the whole thing down on your own. That's why trade unionism has become the dead end it is."

Hobie swished water across the floor. There was only a couple desks and typewriters and a phone on a bare cement floor but Schenk had a thing about keeping it ordered and clean.

"Hobie," he said, "what do you think about the GE thing?"

They had argued the GE thing for two nights in a row. Whether to take the action or scrap it. Whether to swipe the televisions. It was clear that the only reason it hadn't come to a vote yet was because neither Schenk or Mark Remington were sure of enough votes for their side to win.

"Depends on what the group decides."

"What do *you* think, Hobie?"

King had planned the action one day when he and Hobie were out leafleting. They'd both thought it was funny in a way and King had brought it to group almost as a joke. It had turned into a big fight.

"I think it could be good if you done it right and don't get caught."

"By Remington?"

"By the police. It doesn't hurt any people, just things."

"We're doing it."

Hobie stopped mopping then and turned to Schenk. "Without going through group?"

"It's been through group, Hobie. Nothing happened. Nothing more is going to happen. The situation needs a catalyst."

"What will you tell the others?"

"Once it's done, done right, we won't need to tell them much of anything. They'll recognize their mistake. Are you with us?"

He would have liked to be able to tell Schenk to go fuck himself. But something about his way, his cold stare, made it impossible. "Who's going?"

"King, Miriam, Smallwood. Tracy Anne, Billy, a couple of the kids."

"You sound like you got enough."

Schenk laughed through his nose. "King tells me you're a runner," he said. "That you're fast."

"I guess."

"We need you to do it. We need somebody who can run fast. And somebody the cops can't connect us with. Just in case. Which will take a lot of balls if there's a slipup. Think you can handle it?"

"I suppose I could. If I decided to go along." He'd show the fucker. You people.

"We need you, Hobie," said Schenk, levelly, looking directly into his eyes. "We can't do it without you."

Hobie wondered what Sarah would say.

20

Hunter liked wax-dipping. It was a nice way to start the morning. Gave you time to wake up. He held the stick out away from his body, the salamettos wobbling on their strings and bumping each other, he lowered them gently into the trough, held for a second, lifted and held for another second to let them drip, then hung the stick on the second-to-bottom level of the coaster rack.

The wax was amber-colored in the trough but flaked white when Hunter thumbnailed the drippings off his rubbers and coveralls. It made the salamettos shine and look redder but didn't add any to their firmness like it did with the stale pepperoni. The salamettos were like fat bullets the size of grapefruit, you could fit five levels in on the rack. Hunter took another stick, spread the salamettos apart so they wouldn't mold together, and dipped into the hot wax.

Hunter heard someone running up the stairs. He grabbed two sticks instead of one and sped up the rhythm of his work a bit. It was the foreman, Puglisi.

Puglisi walked over, glaring and chewing his mustache. He stood directly behind Hunter, his chin about shoulder level, and watched. Hunter kept his rhythm steady. Puglisi watched for eight sticks, then nudged Hunter out of the way and grabbed two. He flopped them into the wax, swung them onto the rack spraying droplets across the floor and grabbed two more sticks. "You too slow," he said as he jerked the sticks around. "You take all morning you move like these. You gotta move fest! *Fest!*"

He filled the whole third level, then stopped. "You got it?"

Hunter nodded.

"Where Jeemy is?"

"Don't know. Haven't seen him. Maybe he's back in the cold room."

Puglisi showed his teeth and kicked the wax trough. "You fockin guys. Focking play with yourself up here."

He stalked into the locker room over to the right and started slamming metal. Hunter took two sticks at a time but went back to his own pace. He would wait till Puglisi left to do the third level over again so they looked half decent.

"Jeemy! *Jeemy!*" From the sound Puglisi was pounding on the toilet stall. "You in there, Jeemy?"

"Hold your water, Puglisi."

"What you do?"

"I'm takin a dump, all right? The contract says you gotta take a dump, it's okay, right? So quit poundin on the door."

"You not. You up here playing with youself."

"Listen, you don't believe me, I'll throw a piece over. Ready? This is a big one now, you don't catch it you got to clean —"

"I don' wanna fine you in here *again*, Jeemy!"

"Then stay the fuck out. This is for workers here, you're not supposed to come in."

"Worker my ess. I hope you *die*." He gave the stall a last bang and came to stand in the locker-room doorway. "You too!" he called to Hunter. He hustled down the stairs.

Puglisi didn't like Hunter's looks. That must be it. He'd started in the first day down in the basement room and hadn't let up since.

"Get the junior man to do it," Nick had said that morning. Nick looked to be about twenty. He had a tattoo of a rat on his forearm.

"But *ee's* junior men!" Puglisi pointed at Hunter. "I need experience men, I tell them, I get *these*." They stood by a metal table full of small uncooked hams and a pile of net bags. Nick had his arms folded in front of him and Puglisi had his waving in the air. "I gotta have these done fest, I can' fock a*roun* with these guy!"

"Hey, I got other things to do," said Nick. "I'm supposed to go help Gianni with the roast-beef glazing. He's waitin, I'm supposed to be there now."

"Suppose! You suppose to do what you told! I'm tell you to do these job here."

"And I'm tellin you it says in the contract that any job, nobody wants it, you're supposed to have the junior man in the shop take it. This guy here, first day, he's junior man."

"No. I gotta have these done. I say you gotta do, then you gotta *do*."

"Okay, look. You get Joey D. down here, tell him I got a grievance."

"What grievings? You do the job. I tell you to."

"Get Joey D. down here. I don't lift a finger till we settle it with him."

"Don' fock me up, Nick, I'm tell you —"

"Get him."

"*You!*"

"Huh?" Hunter had been leaning against the wall, waiting for them to work it out, waiting for instructions.

"What you do?"

"Huh?"

"You *hens!* Get em outa you pocket. I don' care what you do with, jus you nev' let me catch you with hens in you pocket. Got it?"

Hunter nodded and took his hands out of his pockets. Puglisi ran off to find Joey D. Hunter put them back in. It was cold, he wasn't used to the cold everywhere yet.

"Relax buddy," said Nick, sitting down and crossing his legs in front of him. "Joey aint the easiest guy to find."

"He the boss?"

"Shop steward."

"Oh. Should we start doing this thing? What is it?"

"You got to put the hams in the net bags. Naw, we sit back, take a blow. No reason to kill ourselves."

"The other fella don't need you?"

"Gianni? Naw, he can handle that himself. See, what it is, is Puglisi tries to be a big ballbuster. He tries to have us do everything double-time so's we get ahead of production, the management can send us home early on Friday. Puglisi gets a pat on the head, they save a couple hours payroll, we get the shaft. So you got to slow him down when you can."

"Is he always so — ex*cit*ed like that?"

"He's outa control is what he is. Fuckin *hyp*er. What you wanna do is stay out of his way the first couple weeks, till you get into the union. Then you can tell him to go shove it."

They sat until Puglisi came back with Joey D. Hunter stood and took his hands out of his pockets when he heard them.

"So what's the beef?" Joey D. didn't look much older than Nick. He wore a black nylon jacket and street clothes instead of the white coveralls and white hard hats everyone else had.

"The beef is he's trying to hook me into this shit job, he won't use the junior man."

Joey D. grimaced. "Heyyyy, is that all? What's the big deal? You can't handle it?"

"I can handle, I just don't want to. I'm supposed to be with Gianni, helpin with the glaze. That's my job."

"Gianni'll survive. Jesus, Nick, what you want to make trouble for? It's fuckin Monday morning, already you're hollerin grievance and drag me all the way down here for nothin."

"It's the rules, Joey."

"I know it's the rules, but he says he needs this done fast, he says he needs an experienced man on it."

"For this? A monkey could do it."

"Right, so it shouldn't take you any time at all to finish. Don't be a pain in the butt."

"Okay, but you leave the guy here, help me with it."

"Yeah, sure Nick, we'll leave the guy here."

"You an your fra kin grievings," said Puglisi as they left.

Hunter had stuffed four or five net bags when Puglisi stuck his head in and snapped his fingers. "You," he said to Hunter. "Come."

Hunter followed him upstairs, leaving Nick swearing alone with the job.

Jimmy came out of the locker room with the sports section of the *Herald* folded under his arm.

"I swear that guy is gonna give himself a hot attack one a these days." Jimmy was about the same height and build as Puglisi, but he was pink-skinned instead of olive. He was a little older than Hunter. "Not to mention what it's gonna do to me, I got to run

[231]

in the crapper every time I hear him coming. How you doing?"

"Okay. Got a ways to go on the lot but I can hurry it up some."

"You're doin fine, Hunt, don't listen to him. He wants to run himself into the grave it's his business. Besides, he does shitty work, he always has. You better dip that whole level over again."

"I was just gonna."

"Yeah. So anyway, this job, they want the whole lot down there, should take you till the nine-fifteen buzzer. You watch the clock up there, stretch it a little if you have to. Remember, we got the big ones comin up after first break, hang em up. We wanna be rested."

"Right."

"You seen the Hunk?"

"He just brung all that pepperoni down to the slicing room."

"Good. He comes back up, tell him to check in with me. I'm gonna go back the locker, finish this." He waved his newspaper. "Take it light."

Jimmy was in charge of all the upstairs curing rooms. Puglisi was officially the foreman, but he was usually busy down on the manufacturing floor, so Jimmy got to pretty much call his own shots. There was only the three of them, Jimmy and Hunter and Essenyi. Essenyi was a Hungarian, Jimmy called him the Hunk. He understood enough English to work but never spoke. Most of the other men in the factory spoke Italian and had only a little English. The foremen in the cold-packing and slicing rooms and younger guys like Nick and Joey D. spoke just enough Italian to explain a simple job. Nobody spoke Hungarian but Essenyi.

"An American," said Jimmy the first day Hunter had been sent upstairs. "How'd you sneak in?"

Hunter told him about the personnel woman and how it was just luck.

"Well don't you let the ghinzos know that. They all prawbly think you're related to somebody in management, someone in the cawporation. They can understand that. But hiring an American right off the streets — no wonder Puglisi wants your scalp."

Puglisi had chased Hunter around the manufacturing floor for the entire week, then on Friday afternoon had said, "I'm seek a look at you. Go upstays, ask for Jeemy. Tell him I say put you to work."

"He wants to fire you, buddy," said Jimmy. "That's as plain as day. But if he thinks I'm gonna let somebody speaks American out of my hands up here he's gettin soft. It's like solitary on this floor, the Hunk just sits there, don't say a thing, can't answer if you ask him something. I get better response from the sausage. Grown man, fawty-seven years old, talking to a rack of capocollo. No buddy, you got nothin to worry about. I been askin for a third man since we lost our kid up here when school stotted up, they ignored me. I'll put the word in with Joey D., I wanna keep you here. Puglisi can't go over Joey D., the management is more afraid of the union than they are of one a his temper tantrums. What's your name?"

"Hunter McNatt."

"Jimmy Kearney. Put er there, Hunt. You're on for the duration."

Hunter had stayed up on the curing floor after that. Puglisi came up now and then and rushed him, made him come down to manufacturing for short jobs if he didn't look busy enough, but it was nothing like before. And he wasn't fired like the other three fellas who'd started with him were.

Essenyi came back up. When the door of the freight elevator opened Hunter could hear the racket from the manufacturing floor, then it was shut off. He told Essenyi that Jimmy wanted to see him and the Hungarian went straight to the locker room.

When Hunter had three racks done he wheeled them over by the weighing hook and went to the rear storage area for three more. The rear storage area was at the other end of the building, down a couple hundred yards on steel and concrete hallway with the various curing rooms running off to the sides. The storage area was just a large open room, like a parking garage, kept at the regular forty degrees. Several rows of racks filled with different kinds of sausage stood in the middle of it. One of the government inspectors was poking through them, checking things off on his clipboard.

"Good morning," he said to Hunter.

"Mornin." They weren't like the mine inspectors. They weren't so tight with the owners and they were present just about all the time instead of visits. They did their job, at least as far as the meat being clean went.

Hunter paced himself through the early morning, dipping the sticks of salametto, daydreaming a bit. He liked the sound they made when they broke the surface of the wax, a sound like a hook and fly hitting a still pond. He filled the racks.

When he had seven racks full Hunter got the cards and a pencil out from Jimmy's desk. The rack said *125* on it. He wrote it down on the card. He counted sticks. Fifty-eight. Ten pieces per stick, 580 pieces. He wrote it down. Forty-six wooden sticks, 2 pounds apiece, 92 pounds, 4 of the new aluminum sticks, pound and a half, 6 more pounds, 98 total for sticks. He pushed the Down button of the hydraulic hook till it lowered enough from the ceiling to fit through the metal loop on the rack. He clamped it shut and hit the Up button. The lift brayed and jerked the rack off the ground a few inches, then Hunter froze it. The scale above the hook read 1,416 gross. Minus 125 minus 98 made 1,193 piece-weight. Hunter let the rack down, filled out one card for Jimmy and one to tie on the rack. He hooked the next one up.

Jimmy came out to watch him. Hunter wasn't supposed to weigh, but Jimmy had said not to listen to Puglisi. "Might's well learn it," he said. "Who knows, you might end up here twenty years like me."

"I don't think so."

"Oh, don't be too sure, don't be too sure. I first came here after the war, it was just a couple of months, till my brother-in-lawr could get me on the trucks. It's over twenty years later, here I am."

"I don't think so," Hunter told him. "I really don't think so."

He had most of the racks weighed and recorded when the buzzer for the first break went off.

The men came up the stairs from manufacturing and filed into the locker room. They sat on the wooden benches, smoking and staring at the floor. It was only a fifteen-minute break. Hardly anyone spoke. No one ate but Ugo Struffo, who was the widest man Hunter had ever seen. Ugo had one eye that wandered sideways and arms that hung down past his knees. He made little satisfied grunting sounds as he ate. It was the only sound in the room but for the loud ticking of the wall clock.

It was different in the locker room before work started.

"Buon giorno, buon giorno miei amici!" the little one called Fausto would call as he hurried into the room. "Che cosa dice, Lei?"

"Diciamo che tu sei il lavoratore piú brutto del fabbrica."

"L'Orsa Minore, Fausto."

"All same you guys," Fausto would say, "alla time jayloose." He was a hairy, bowlegged little man.

"Lotsa box today!" Clemente would sing out. "Make lotsa box today a Porchetta! Lotsa salsicce!"

"Ehi! Clemente! Clementino!"

"What you wan?"

"Fock you."

"Fock me?"

"At's ride."

"Non fock me, fock youself."

"Gente, gente! Prego. Watch you mout." Sebastiano wore a Virgin Mary medal around his neck and crossed himself whenever they heard a siren pass outside. "Ee hear evvating you say."

"Chi? Puglisi?"

"No, Eem!" Sebastiano pointed toward the ceiling.

"Wha? Somebody onna roof?"

"Si, Santa Close."

"Babbo Natale. Ee's listen us from a roof."

"Ee know when you been sleepy, ee known when you been wake —"

"Ee know when you been good o bad, so be good for good nut's ache."

"Fuckin ghinnies," said Gianni Greco, who was in his twenties and had been born in the States. "Fuckin singin songs, seven a clock the morning."

"Andiamo, amici! Abbiamo cinque minuti fino il ronzio. Presto!"

Hunter couldn't make out much of what they shouted, but the spirit was familiar. The men joked and insulted and knocked each

[235]

other's hard hats off every morning before work started. They mostly seemed glad to see each other. Jimmy Kearney always blew in a couple minutes late so Hunter dressed alone, the jokes and insults flying over his head. He smiled when they smiled, but not as much.

No one spoke during the fifteen-minute break. It was a long haul to lunch, they were saving themselves. Ugo stuck his face into his big brown bag to see what he had left. The buzzer went off.

Hunter helped Jimmy and Essenyi bring the salamettos down to the shipping floor and by the time they were finished the ten-pounders were all racked and ready to come up. It took them five trips on the elevator, shoving the white-cased bombs of salami on, riding up, Hunter and Essenyi teaming like mules to push the racks up the slight incline to the big empty curing room. They paused and shook the knots out of their thighs with twelve racks parked in the hallway, ready for hanging.

"Don't strain yourselfs, guys," said Jimmy Kearney, and left to fill the slicing-room orders.

There was a row of stalls coming out from each long wall of the rectangular room. The stalls were about twenty feet deep, made of iron brackets five levels high and spaced so that the four-foot sticks spanned them tightly. Each stick had five or six of the ten-pounders strung on it. Hunter hoisted a stick off the rack and walked it sideways to Essenyi, who met him halfway into the stall, turned, and hung it up. He started against the wall and worked out, staggering the sticks on three levels so more could be fit in. The Hunk didn't talk, he rolled his sleeves back over his biceps and kept his back perfectly straight as he lifted. The salamis were still soft inside, they would cook and harden within the casing while they hung. They worked for a while, then switched jobs. Hunter had to use the little stepladder to reach the top level, he had to push up on his toes on the side where his arm didn't unbend all the way. The weight of the sticks felt good against his muscles, they set up an easy, steady rhythm. It was very quiet and very warm in the room. The first stall looked solid white when it was full. Hanging was Hunter's favorite job in the factory.

There wasn't anything as satisfying as hanging down on the manufacturing floor. Down in the pit, Jimmy called it. Puglisi had bounced Hunter from task to task his first week there and whenever he didn't know what else to do with him it was straight to the cold-pack room. It was mostly the older Italian fellas who worked on the packing line, filling plastic supermarket trays and small cardboard boxes with the freezing, still-wet raw sausages. Lined on both sides of the rotary belt, raking piles onto their metal tables, then packing, six Italian-hot per tray till the stacks of trays built up and you turned to lay them in the slots of the belt that carried them to be wrapped and weighed and labeled for the stores. Or the boxes, three layers of the little-finger-thick American breakfast separated by wax paper and a sprinkling of *Porchetta Packing Co.* tags, the sausages flowing constantly, spilling over, your fingers racing to keep ahead of them. A steady stream of sausage and Hunter was always put at the end of the line, responsible to see that none fell on the floor or were mangled where the belt turned under. The other fellas talked and laughed with each other, hardly looking at their flicking hands, they called out advice and insults and Clemente sang American show tunes with Italian words. He tried to sing opera sometimes but everyone whistled and made fart noises till he switched back. They hummed along with him.

> *A sailor went to the Queen of Spain,*
> *His name was Chris Columbo*

sang Clem from his spot on the line —

> *And every day to pave his way*
> *He'd stick it up her bumbo.*

> *He knew the world was round-o*
> *He sailed and then he found-o,*
> *So now we got America*
> *You sonofabitch Columbo.*

Hunter listened but kept his eyes on the meat and hustled to keep up. You could see your breath in the room and the sausage

[237]

was even colder than the air. Hunter's fingers stiffened and refused to bend, they ached in every joint and he could no longer feel the difference between them and the sausage. It kept coming, spewing out of the machine that tied and cut the links and whenever it would seem to be thinning out or a different kind was about to be packed Puglisi would be there behind him.

"You," he would say rapping Hunter on the shoulder and pointing up to the head of the line, "go shove. Fest!"

Hunter would hustle up to the feeder where Raf Scalogna worked. The feeder was like a small cement mixer, meat was packed down into it then pressed hydraulically out through a hose of whatever gauge was needed, hosing out and picking up its casing ready to be hooked into the linker mechanism. Hunter picked up the shiny stainless-steel shovel and began hefting meat up into the feeder. The meat was wheeled into stainless-steel boxes that looked like small coal cars. Hunter shoveled meat up into the feeder hole and Raf stamped it down till it was packed solid. By the time he got back to the end of the line the sausage was rolling down toward him.

The first day on the cold-pack line, after an hour of scrambling not to be totally swamped, Hunter started to lose it. He raked a pile and went to work on it but then another pile came down and another and there was no one beyond him to take any of it and his table was overflowing and there was no more room to stack the trays that he finished and he was sweating, heart beating fast, and when he looked up to see how the others were handling it they were laughing at him. It was his initiation. He smiled and raised his hands in surrender. They came and bailed him out.

Hunter's fingers were always numb when Puglisi came to yank him off the line to fill a spot in the main stuffing room. They couldn't coordinate to make the tiny knots to string the mortadella, they were too slow to pull the loops over the stick and rack it before more bolognas thudded down. Once when they were turning out abruzzese the linker mechanism broke, causing Puglisi to panic, biting his hand and screaming at poor Caesare Capodilupo who only fed the machine and couldn't possibly have broken it, causing Mr. Taylor to come all the way over from the corporation office and borrow a white coat to stand and watch the mechanic fiddle with the works. In the meanwhile the men from the cold-packing room appeared with jackknives and balls of twine. They tied the sausage off into lengths as fast as the feeder could shoot it out, faster even than the linking mechanism went, so that Hunter was hard pressed to stay ahead twining the abruzzese around the sticks. He had never seen hands move so fast, it was like Pappy Dan's stories of when he was a boy straddling the coal belt, sorting out the chunks without breaking any fingers.

"Old time here," Caesare said to him, "no macchina. Joost hen. Evvating by hen. Nowdays, *tutto macchinale.*"

The hardest thing Puglisi put him to was fitting the intestines. They floated white and slippery in a great tangled mass in a bucket of warm water next to the feeder outlet. You had to dip in and pull one free, find the opening with your fingers, lift it out and fit the opening over the metal pipe, then roll a few feet of the gut onto the pipe before the next stream of meat came hosing out. Ideally the meat would catch onto the slack intestine and pull the rest along with it. The intestines slipped through Hunter's packing-numb fingers like wet cornstarch, they were like five-foot-long rubbers, Trojans for some fantastic animal, and Hunter couldn't get the hang of them. Caesare worked on the other side of the bench from him and had to do three intestines to every one of Hunter's to keep them up with the feeder. A few times Hunter was caught still fumbling with the gut when the stream shot out, the meat flopping uncased on the bench like a dead snake. They would have to scoop it up to hide it from Puglisi till there was a chance to sneak it back in the feeder or into one of the little boxcars. Puglisi was worse about the intestines than any other job, literally breathing down Hunter's neck, yelling *pronto, pronto, pronto!* and scowling at Caesare when he helped out too much. Hunter had to keep reminding himself how much he needed the money.

"Don' mine eem," Caesare said one time, "ee try to break you ball. You don' make trob, get inna Yoon, the Yoon take care." He nodded his head reassuringly. "The Yoon take care."

The rails were the most dangerous thing in the factory. You hung sticks across them like on the racks, but they were suspended on tracks bolted to the ceiling. The rails went all over the factory, you had to pull ropes to switch tracks and change direction. It was possible, if you weren't looking ahead careful enough, to pull a rail holding a half ton of meat through an open switch and down on top of yourself.

The only nice job on the manufacturing floor was helping Highland out in the spice room. Highland was a big blond kid who Jimmy said was related to someone over in the corporation office, maybe even Mr. Taylor himself. He had let his hair and mustache grow out all over and wore extra-thick glasses that made his eyes big and fuzzy. He usually had the spice room all to himself, smiling absently and taking in the smells, the barrels of ground pepper and nutmeg and sage, the sugar and salt, the crocks of wine and vinegar. Cayenne, garlic, coriander, oregano, sweet basil, peppercorns, blending or taking over depending on where you stood in the room. Hunter got to help in the spice room only twice, when there were rush orders that had to be mixed, but it was quiet and nice. Highland smiled constantly and giggled to himself and hummed snatches of songs as he worked. There was another smell in the spice room that was sweet, though more like something was burning. Hunter was never able to track it down.

Mostly Puglisi yanked him from one job to the next, through all the different stages of manufacturing, through all the machine noise. Belts humming, feeders whining, clack and chop of the linker mechanisms, rails screeching overhead and in the center of it all Puglisi, the veins sticking out in his neck, eyes bugging, Puglisi screaming for more speed, more speed, more speed —

Hunter lay the last stick of the last rack across the brackets. His arm and chest muscles, the backs of his legs, were all pumped full and ached pleasantly. It was quiet and the stalls were full, hundreds of long white bombs hanging to cure. The Hunk came back with Jimmy. He smiled at the room.

"Very nice," he said, nodding his head slowly, "very nice work. You guys just moved over four tons of meat. It's almost lunchtime, you take a blow. Sit in here and if Puglisi comes I'll make a racket."

You had to go down to the shipping floor to punch out on the time clock for lunch hour whether you left the building or not.

Most of the Italians from the manufacturing floor went back up to the locker room to eat, though there was a lunchroom with tables and a few vending machines downstairs. Jimmy stayed down, pulling up his seat at the daily poker game with Joey D. and Nick and the foreman from the shipping floor who was another Irish.

The work didn't build up the appetite that mining had, and Hunter was trying to save as much money as fast as he could. He sat without a lunch on the wooden benches of the locker room, resting his eyes and thinking. The Italians sat all around him, rooting through their paper sacks, drinking strong-smelling thermos coffee and chattering to each other. They ate sandwiches made of small white loaves cut open and stuffed with peppers or cheese or some kind of meat without mustard or mayonnaise. They would hold a tomato in the other hand and alternate bites.

"Non mangiare, Il Cacciatore. Niente."

Hunter knew they were talking about him, as they did from time to time with idle curiosity. Several had tried to pronounce his name when he first came but it came out all grunts. So they had asked Gianni Greco for a translation and that's how they knew him. Il Cacciatore.

"Non mangiare, come vivere?" said Caesare.

"Chi sai?"

"Mangia forse la salsiccia?"

"Non posso tollerano, gli Americani," said Fausto. "È troppo piccante."

"Egli hai l'aspetto d'un asmatico."

"Aqua e pane," Ugo Struffo would chant through a mouthful of egg-and-pepper, shaking his head sadly, "vita da cane."

When they were done eating Caesare and Clem and Fausto and Raf Scalogna would turn over a trash barrel and start a card game that Hunter could never figure out the rules to. Whenever a pattern started to show itself Raf would begin to shout and rap his knuckles on the cards and everything would change. It was clear though that Raf lost most of the time. They didn't play for money like Jimmy and the fellas downstairs but they hollered a lot more.

The only time the men spoke English was when Gianni Greco

would come in and joke with them or when they discussed something they had seen on television.

"Gianni," they would say when he swaggered in to get his lunch from his locker, "show us you treek."

"Trick?" He would pretend not to know what they were getting at. "What trick?"

"You *treek*. With you head."

"Oh, *that* trick. You mean practice." He would smile around the room and wink at Hunter and pat the side of the metal locker. "This is my practice pad here. Karate." He would take his hardhat off and make an invisible X on the side of the locker then bull his neck and *whang!* — butt his forehead into the metal. There would be a big dent and Gianni would bow and smile and leave the room.

"Pazzo," the Italians would say, crossing their eyes and circling their temples with their fingers, "tutto pazzo."

"Ehi, Fausto," Caesare would say, "you watch a news less nigh?"

"I watch. Why?"

"You see what a Presiden say?"

"I don' rememb."

"Presiden Neex, ee say soon no mo gazoline. No mo automobile. Evvabody buy sick."

"Che?"

"Buy *sick*. Bicicletta. Lei capisce?"

"That so?"

"Ee said eemself. Alla price go up. Evvating coast too much. Groun beef, dolar a poun. Fo*get* it."

"Where you go to buy?"

"Stope anna Shope."

"You go to Gran Yoon, is jus as good."

"Not what they say onna TV."

"You gonna bleeve evvating they say? Listen a me, I'm go to Gran Yoon five, seex year now. Jus as good. Nice low price."

"Maybe I try."

"Ehi, you see after the news, Fausto? I Bruni?"

"Tony Esposito, eh? Make the het treek. Tree goal, beautiful!"

Hunter liked to hear them talking around him, whatever language. He liked the way they almost sang when they called out to each other, the way they could argue at the top of their lungs but not stay mad for too long. He sat with his eyes closed, letting their talk wash around him, and planned on what neighborhoods he would try for Hobie. He was running out of ideas, running out of places and people to try. The buzzer went off and they rose to go punch in.

In the afternoon the just-cooked pepperoni began to come onto the rails and the raw abruzzese on racks. Jimmy put Essenyi on the pepperoni while he and Hunter hung the 'bruzzese. It was wet, slimy-feeling sausage, fresh from the feeder and gut-bucket, strung like a bow to make it harden in a C-shape. That made the sticks clumsy to handle and caused more meat than usual to hit the floor. They would wait till they had a pile of drops, then bring them out and run them under the steam hose and string them back up. If Puglisi saw anything lying on the floor he would throw a fit, so they hid the drops under Jimmy's hardhat, which he never wore.

"He'll get all hot an bothered about a little thing like that," said Jimmy, "when *he's* cutting every corner in the book. Twice since I been here he's broke the freight elevator, overloading it. Awdered guys to put in as much as double the load of meat that it says is capacity. The second time he done it a couple kids almost got hurt, guys from the shipping floor. But he told them they prawbly lose their jobs if it come out so nothin happened."

"They couldn't bring a grievance against him?"

"Well, Hunt, it's like this. The Meatpackers, the national organization, is a pretty good bunch. Sometimes they get into politics, they don't belong, they come on a little too radical for my blood. But all in all they come through for the workers. It's a good union, the national. The prawblem is the local. This used to be a one-man operation, Porchetta, used to belong to this guy Rocco, Rocco the Nip we called him onaconna his eyes were these little slits. He brought all these guys over, just about, he'd hire a guy and then say, hey, write your cousin, the old country, we got an opening. He had a temper, Rocco, but he was up-front with the guys and they trusted him. When he saw everything was unions he didn't fight it. He *controlled* it. He helped set up the union local and made sure the guys got to be officers weren't any boat-rockers. And it hasn't changed much since. You know, workers breed workers, owners breed owners, and union officials breed union officials. These guys we got in there now, only a couple ever worked onna floor here. Mostly they come from other locals, the union office, you know, and from schools. Joey D., he's shop steward, his old man used to be with the local."

"He don't seem to do much."

"Joey? Hey, Joey's a good kid. I like Joey. It's not true he doesn't do much, he does a lot. He's hustlin all over the fuckin place. Not a whole lot of the stuff he's doin is union business, I grant you that, but he's a very busy guy, Joey. Any bet that comes out of this factory, he's got a piece of it. There's what, three, four floors to cover, the drivers, the maintenance guys, the night cleanup people on Friday — hey, it's a lot to juggle. But he's not a bad guy, Joey. Lots of times he's carried me two, three months, I get behind. He's got the capital, he can let you ride on the cuff a little while. If only I could pick em."

"I mean he don't do much about bein steward."

"Well, first, all this hustlin he's got to do don't leave a lot of time. Plus you got to understand the way he sees his job. Which is no trouble. You got trouble, you got a problem, he don't want to hear about it. That's how he handles grievances, Joey D., he ignores them till they go away. Everybody's got his own method, and that's his."

"So there's nothin you can do about Puglisi."

"Yes and no. Officially, there's not a thing we can do. Joey gets along with Puglisi, he figures everybody else should too. The cawporation loves Puglisi's ass, he squeezes every drop of production he can out of us. He turns up the speed on the belts a little every day till someone gets wise and has Joey come down with the stopwatch and they have to call in the mechanic. The same game he's been playing for years. So officially he's in like Flynn. But on the other hand — well, you just watch some time, when he flies off the handle at one of the guys who's in the union five, ten years or more, one of the old-time ghinzos. He screams and he spits and he swears, but alla time he's backing *up*. You watch careful sometime, you'll see. There's an unwritten code what the guys will accept and what they won't. These are some pretty tough boys, these old ghinzos, and some of the younger ones too.

"Gianni, right, Johnny Greek? Big smile, nice kid, happy-go-lucky, the whole thing. He's fuckin crazy. I don't know if you noticed. He's a karate guy, he's got a couple knuckles on each hand, they're like walnuts. All the better to bust your skull with. He used to work for this place, Gianni, the Amiable Loan Company. No shit, that was really the name of it. And they're amiable all right, amiable right up to the time you can't keep up with the vig and they send Gianni over to bust your legs. It was piecework Gianni was on, a hundred per leg. But he's a nice kid, right?

"And Caesare, another guy with the smiles. Helluva nice guy, Chez, give you the shirt off his back. Only you see him with his shirt off, you stot to wonder. Looks like somebody played tic-tac-toe with a broken bottle. You want to see the smile disappear off Chez's face ask him about *i neri*. The blacks. He was in the war, right, only on the other side. Fighter pilot for Mussolini and that bunch. He had to bail out over Ethiopia there, parachute down, and the natives got hold of him.

"Couple years ago he catches this kid, black kid, onna trolley, couldn't of been more than fawteen or so, catches him with his hand in some lady's pocketbook, and he busts it. Just takes hold of the kid's hand and squeezes so hard all the little bones in there stot to snap, crackle and pop. The kid's screamin bloody murder, big crowd gathers, they got to get a cop, have him tap Chez back of the neck with the stick to make him let go. Chez. They see a colored guy on the street, his wife takes his om and steers him in the other direction. He's just one of those guys, you never make him lose his temper if you know what's good for you. And Puglisi knows it. There's other guys too, they're capable of some hod boggins. That's why old Rocco knew not to fight it when it looked like they wanted the union."

"But it's better than it was?"

"Some ways yes, some ways no. You had to work hodder then. Rocco would come and chew you out personally. The whole works was on the same floor and everybody did a little bit of everything. It was hand-stuffing then, you had a pile of meat, some casings, a knife, string and a stick. You stuffed, tied off, cut, looped, strung, and when you had a full stick you racked it or packed it yourself. There wasn't so many pots to it then, it wasn't like an assembly line. Then when the cawporation, Taylor and all them, when they bought Rocco out it changed. Everybody had one specific job, one pot of the process. That's why I like it up here. You still got a feeling for the product, you do everything yourself and there's always something a little different to do, the different steps of curing. Yeah, I suppose it's better now, the money and the security and all, but they give me a funny feeling, the cawporation people. Like if you hung me from the hook out there all they'd see is a hundred fifty pounds of meat."

"You miss Rocco?"

Jimmy was clinging two brackets up the stall in the first dry room, arranging the highest row of abruzzese. He spat for the floor drain and hit it dead center. "I don't want he should come back from the dead, no. He was one scary old ghinzo. But what I miss, is when things are fucked-up and I can't take it no more and I go lookin for somebody to blame. Used to be I could point straight to Rocco, it was *his* factory. Things were easier then, clearer. You knew where to aim. Now, hey, it's not even totally Puglisi's fault. I'm sure they got him scared shitless he's gonna be out on the breadlines if they have to pay us overtime this week to fill their awders. He's just over his head is all, he can't handle it. He should have stayed a worker and gotten his pat on the back every year for never missing a day. And Joey D., it's the same. There's trouble, there's a strike or maybe the company goes out of business and he's out of commission. The word he gets from the local is keep those ghinzos under control. We call the shots, not them. And the cawporation aren't even *peo*ple, for Christ sakes, we had a guy over from the local once to explain. They just supervise the thing for the stockholders of another company that owns another company that owns *us*. So if something goes wrong, say, with the glass business in Toledo, it's liable to mean we don't get a Christmas bonus this year. At least that's how they explain it. And hey, most these guys don't even speak fuckin *Eng*lish, much less have a degree in business economics. Half of em prawbly think old Rocco the Nip is still in the background somewhere, pullin all the strings. But you learn to live with it.

"Hunt," said Jimmy, climbing down from the stall, "There's three ways you can play it. And the way you are and the way you play is what decides whether you can hack it here or not.

"Number one, you can play it like Puglisi. Scream and hustle and clawr and ass-kiss your way up the ladder, make a few extra bucks a year, make people hate you and develop an ulcer.

"You can be like the Hunk there. A machine. He's like something Taylor put in to speed up production, he just does whatever you point him at. I never asked, but he don't seem like a real happy guy, the Hunk.

"Or you can be like me."

"I figured that was comin up."

"Don't laugh, my friend, don't laugh. I been here over twenty years, never had any trouble I couldn't handle. Number three. You do what work you have to, get out of what work you can avoid, look for the angles and don't get caught makin waves. You keep all that in mind, be like me, and you'll survive. That's the impawtant thing, you gotta survive."

It took them till the 2:15 break and beyond to hang all the abruzzese. Then Jimmy and Essenyi took turns sitting down while the other filled the slicing-room orders. Hunter washed pepperoni. If the product wasn't moving fast enough the older lots of sausage would develop a fuzzy blue-green mold. The mold wasn't harmful but it looked like hell and had to be washed off before a lot could go out for sale. Hunter loaded racks from Lot F and wheeled them to the open floor space just outside of the locker room. He set the water to slightly below body temperature and knelt to turn the big hose on the pepperoni. You could control the hardness of the stream with the lever-grip. Hunter kept it hard enough to blast the mold off but not so hard it would knock the sausages off their sticks. He knelt and sprayed, turning the racks to get at all four sides. It was easy, calming work. Now and then he would have to stand and rub his knees, but that was no big problem.

Joey D. came up and looked around, then leaned in to ask if anyone was in the locker room. He had some business to attend to and didn't want to be disturbed. Hunter told him to call at the doorway so Jimmy wouldn't have to run for the toilet.

The work was pretty easy all around. It was four dollars an hour, only a little less than what mining paid with none of the danger. The people were nice enough and it was only a half hour, forty-five minutes away on the subway trains. There wasn't a whole lot to complain about, except for Puglisi.

Puglisi came up twice to stand behind Hunter and shake his head, then grab the hose away like he always did. He waved the nozzle around a lot more than Hunter did, but the pepperoni didn't get any cleaner or get done any quicker. Hunter stood and waited to be given the hose again. It was all he could think to do.

He finished the lot with a half hour left to work and went to report to Jimmy. Jimmy said there was nothing left to do, to fake it till quitting time but be careful.

Hunter could hear cleanup starting downstairs. Steel cars and machine pieces banging together, steam hoses hissing. If Puglisi came up and found him idle he'd have to go down and help. It wasn't the extra work, it was having the foreman on his tail the whole time.

The whole manufacturing floor had to be steamed clean every night, Hunter was given a hose and a wire brush the first week when he was down there. The meat boxes, the shovels, the benches and cowling and walls and floors had to be scoured and blasted with the scalding-hot water. You couldn't see five feet through the steam in the big cleanup bay when it got going. Only the junior men were left, Hunter and Gianni Greco and Sebastiano and a few others, with Puglisi shouting orders. Hunter's hands were raw from the hot water and slivers of steel wool, he fought to breathe in the steam. Once Gianni appeared next to him and asked if he knew what it meant to frag. They could hear but not see Puglisi screaming somewhere over to the left.

"It's an Army term," said Gianni. "*To frag.* I frag, you frag, he frags, we frag, they frag."

"What's it mean?"

"Watch."

Gianni turned to the direction of Puglisi's voice. He held the stream of water down and away from him for a moment, listening careful, then whipped it up for a long burst at the voice.

There was a scream and they both hurried back into the steam. "*To frag*," said Gianni. " 'A spirited demonstration of lack of confidence in or respect for a leader. From the Latin, *Fragmentation grenade*.' And don't let him see that smile on your face."

Hunter took the hose off the wall and ran a little water on the floor. He squeegeed it down the drain. Then he ran some more, trying to fill the puddles that usually formed not too far from the drain. He hung the hose up. He took the squeegee pole and stood behind a puddle, leaning a bit so that the moment he heard steps coming up the stairs or down the hall he could complete the stroke toward the drain, as if he were just finishing up the job. He could see the clock from where he posed, twenty minutes to kill. It was the worst part of the day. He hated faking work, he hated having to stand doing nothing. He would rather have heavy lifting to do, anything, but that would mean starting a job one day and finishing it the next morning and the factory didn't operate that way. He watched the second hand go round for a while, but that seemed to slow it down. He thought about what he would put together for dinner. He figured out how much money he would have in the bank after he got paid Friday, whether it was time to rent the car or not. Time to go see Darwin. He thought about what a nice job it would be if only Puglisi were gone.

Someone began to run up the stairs and Hunter swept for the drain.

21

Boston Garden was dark at the end of Canal Street. The Celts and the Bruins were both out of town. Miriam eased the old station wagon ahead, toward where the street T-boned into the Garden and North Station above it. The Green Line elevated rose behind the buildings on their right. Hobie was squashed on the right side of the rear. It reminded him of riding to day labor, only he was a lot more nervous. The big ball-top streetlights were on, the front of a little ticket agency was lit enough so that he could see some of the fight posters inside.

"On the left, on the corner," said Miriam.

Two streetlights glared off the big front window, glinted off the dozens of glass chandeliers hanging inside, off the chrome and bronze and steel. Electrical appliances.

"Time?"

"Eleven twenty-two and thirty-five seconds," said Smallwood.

"Good. I'll hang a left up here in front of the Garden and we'll drift in from the back. Everybody set?"

No one answered. The back seat had been folded down for more room. Hobie was crammed in with Mickey Q. and Jeff and Tracy Anne and Steve and Jennifer and the new kid they called Monk. On account of how he'd shaved almost all of his hair off when Schenk asked him to get a trim. Smallwood sat with Rit DeRusso and Miriam in the front. They had considered asking Grant Parke along, knowing he'd get off on the action, but Schenk said no. Schenk was back at the house refining the Manson Family article and waiting.

Miriam drove along the front of the Garden, then turned left up Friend, parallel to Canal. She slowed near the beginning of Traverse.

"Smallwood?"

"Eleven twenty-nine and fifteen seconds."

The station wagon rolled to a stop. The street was empty. "Okay, children," said Miriam, "the lot is just up here to your right. He'll be waiting. See you in five."

Mickey Q. let the tailgate down and they hopped out in the order they'd practiced beforehand. No pushing or crowding, just fast and smooth. Everything would be fast and smooth.

They walked quickly up Traverse as Miriam pulled away. Billy was waiting with the stolen panel truck parked alongside the loading dock, engine and lights off. There were other back lots around them, no dangerous windows.

Rit walked to the metal sliding door and gave it three quiet raps. They waited, crouched in the shelter of the truck. King had checked the place out. He would try to hide in an empty refrigerator crate that he'd spotted in their storage room. If he hadn't been caught and prevented from calling to warn them he would be inside now.

The metal door began to rise slowly, so as not to rattle or screech. King stood exposed in the opening for a moment, then motioned them to come. Nobody spoke. They formed their prearranged passing-chain into the building. Hobie was deepest in, first to receive each set from King. King had had most of the evening free to wander and pick out the GEs. Only the GEs.

Hobie heard a noise from the outside. Maybe the sets going into the truck. It seemed to be taking forever, though they had rehearsed it to be slightly under three minutes. It seemed to be taking forever and he was trapped, all the way inside now.

Televisions.

"It was the first time I took serious that I might really die. It was right there upon me. And it was when I got the whole thing figured out."

Darwin at home for good, they thought, that summer. Alive, unwounded, quiet like always but in a different way. And then talking all of a sudden, talking nonstop for a day and a night, desperate to make them see how it was. To understand.

"We were watchin television. We were down in this bunker, dug into the ground so's the artillery fragments'll just blow over, out at the forward camp. It's the second night I been up there from the base camp. And they got television over there, they got some way they can pipe it out to you, I don't understand the electronics of it, but they have it, old taped American TV shows. We were watchin *Bonanza*, that was a big favorite. And the Arvins are up on the ground sleeping or guarding the perimeter. Both at the same time probly. Our C/O is back at base camp and that means our top dog is this second lieutenant, fella bout my age, and he's hunkered down right next to us watchin Hoss and Little Joe and all. And we hear it. Just poppin at first, kind of far off and scattered, like you hear up on the ridge the first day of deer season. And this second lieutenant speaks up and says it's snipers again, had em every night for a week and the Arvin commander knows how to handle it. Only right then it isn't far off anymore, it's rifle and machine-gun fire all around us and you can hear them jabberin their heads off and bawling bloody murder when they take a hit. There's so many rounds in the air it's like the night is *scream*ing, like all you have to do is stick your head out in that air and you're an automatic goner. Might's well crawl in the plastic bag and shoot yourself, save somebody a lot of trouble.

"We're on our feet and we got our weapons, some of us, and the second lieutenant asks what everybody thinks we should do. *He's* not about to make any decisions. Nobody says a thing, but nobody's movin toward the door neither. We just sort of all decide in our heads that we'll wait down under and see what happens. Now I'm really *scared*. This is it, I figure. There's somebody just outside who's been hit, in the throat it sounds like, cause every time he screeches we hear this gurgling too. This is it. We been overrun, we hear all this fighting all around us and there's people racing over the *roof*, we hear their footsteps, and we're all huddled together where just one little grenade could zap the whole lot and all the while the Cartwrights are havin a gunfight of their own on the television. That's when it all come to me, about the war. I was watching the television as much as I was listening to the fight up above. And I figure, if you can be watching *Bonanza* and people run in to shoot you dead then there's no rules, anything can happen. One way is just as good as another, cause in the end neither of them matters. And I said to myself, if I get out of this, which didn't look too likely at the time, there won't be any rules gonna stand between me and staying alive. Cause whether you die a hero or a coward it don't make any difference, you're dead. Whether it's for some freedom idea somebody sold you or for an old rerun TV show. You're dead. That's what I thought when I was trapped inside there.

"Well the shooting died down and there was a knock on the trapdoor to the bunker and we all just about blew the thing fulla holes, we were so jumpy. It was the Arvin commander. He said we'd been overrun for about a minute but his people drove them back and now everything was secure. The lieutenant went out to check around and call in a report and the rest of us we took our turns up at the latrine trenches then come back down out of the heat to talk about what had happened and watch the rest of the show."

"Seventeen and eighteen," said King, handing Hobie two portables. He picked up two more and nodded to the outside. "Let's do it."

Billy met them and added the sets to the pile on the truck floor. The others had already scattered. Each had a pickup point arranged with Miriam. Like a football play, thought Hobie, fullback at three play-action pass. Everybody with their own job on separate parts of the field, basic blocking, fullback faking through the three hole, tight end squaring across, split end on a deep post and the flanker, Hobie, slanting out into the flats. They always tried to get the ball to him in the flats.

Billy waited till King and Hobie were a full minute's walk up Canal before he turned the key and headed in the opposite direction.

They got in the front seat with Miriam since they were last to be picked up. "About two and a half," said King. "Very nice."

The point was to have the bunch of them connected with the televisions and the boosted panel truck for the least possible amount of time, to cut down the chance of a major bust. Billy was in the truck because Schenk said he had the best sense. But nobody would get busted. It would all be smooth and fast, it had been planned too well to fuck up.

"Smallwood?"

"Eleven forty."

"Okay children, one at a time."

They were on Beacon Hill. Miriam let them off in ones and twos. They had ten minutes to regroup in the shadows of City Hall and meet Jeff.

It was a fairly warm night for December. Clear. Schenk had pushed the action ahead a week to beat the snow. Hobie tried to walk as if he were just on his way to the Government Center T station, just on his way home. The bad part was over. Being inside. On this part of it you could run if something went bad.

It *was* a little crazy, but it was just TVs, they weren't hurting anybody. Except maybe the insurance company, and they could handle the loss. Schenk had come to him personally, and, well, if they really *need*ed him —

City Hall looked like a mammoth internal-combustion engine of brick and concrete. It sat at the back of an open, brick-floored plaza, a three-quarters circle of stairs and sloping levels lit with short ball-top lamps. The opening for the Government Center T bulged up to the front right as Hobie faced it. Beyond that, a couple hundred feet from the building, stood three aluminum flagpoles. And at their base rose a twenty-foot-square air vent for the Blue Line subway, a shoulder-high brick structure that made a natural pyre, a high point for better display and the air from underneath to feed the flames. Hobie crossed the street and walked slowly toward the T station. No one was waiting outside. The faretaker inside sat with his eyes closed, dozing behind his glass panel. Hobie walked out of his sight around the side of the station. The plaza was deserted.

The panel truck appeared on Court Street to the right, hopped the low curb to the plaza brick and rolled toward the air vent. The others immediately swarmed out from the shadows of City Hall and the buildings surrounding Government Center, running under control to meet Billy.

He had the side door open already when Hobie reached the spot, the others were bucket-brigading the TV sets up on top of the air vent. Hobie grabbed the five-gallon can of gas from the front seat and climbed the vent. He sloshed gas over the televisions. King and Mickey Q. were shinnying up adjacent flagpoles, each holding an end of the banner they had decided on.

SUPPORT THE STRIKE!
BOYCOTT G.E. PRODUCTS!!!
The Friends of the People

Hanging from the center of it on a piece of wire was a broken lightbulb.

All the sets were piled. They hurried back into the shadows, back to their second pickup points. Billy sped away to ditch the panel truck. Hobie was left alone, pouring gasoline onto twenty General Electric TV sets in the middle of City Hall Plaza. But at

[254]

least he was in the open. He could always run. He tried not to spill too much gas down the vent, not knowing what was at its bottom. He felt for the book of matches in his pocket.

"They built these tunnels, the villagers did," Darwin had told them, "they dug down under the ground like woodchucks. Door under a mat right inside the hootch. They stored things under there, rice and guns, and then a lot of times it was people. Charlie would get under in those holes and he'd wait till you were on your way out of the village and then he'd up and blast you from behind. So you have to look for it, you have to check every damn hootch, even if its been burned to the ground. Cause maybe Charlie is down in a hole. Or maybe just some villagers scared of you from what Charlie has told them or from all the bombs been dropped on their heads. You don't know.

"I'd been field-promoted to corporal after we'd lost a couple of officers in an ambush, and then up to sergeant after we lost a couple more. I had the experience by this time, I guess. They said after this last patrol was over and new orders come in they'd put me up another grade, like that meant anything to me.

"So I'm the head of this patrol and we have to go through this little village after the spotter planes say they seen some suspicious activity. They throw a couple rounds in from the air, some gunner thought he saw a flash, but there's nothing definite.

"We go through fast, on a run almost, hootch to hootch, bustin in and checking each place out. It's just Americans, the Arvins refused to go out to the villages in this area. We been taking a lot of sniping from the villages so the guys just want to get in and get out. But in one of the hootches we find one of these holes hidden under the floormat. And you can tell that there's been people down in it from the smell. They go there if there's bombing, see, and the little ones get pretty scared.

"What they said in training for this situation was first to try to talk them out of the hole. If you get no answer you send one of your little fellas down there, cause the holes are so narrow, pushing his gun in front of him and blasting hell out of anything that don't look friendly. People pretty much ignored that part of it after a while. Awful lot of small fellas gettin blown away in

[255]

holes, most of em Puerta Ricans cause of how they don't grow so big, and it got to be a thing where the officers knew they best not order any more people down. We were losin as many officers from behind as we were from the enemy.

"So the procedure that got worked out was to send a little smoke down there, wait, throw a little heat down, wait, and *then* you think about either sending the fella in to see if it's a closed bottom pit or a connecting tunnel, or else you just decide in your head there's nothing down there and go your way. The little fellas, they still don't like it much, but there's a real good chance if you done all the rest without flushing anyone out that the thing is empty.

"We get some old fella, a villager who's too old and too slow to run away and hide, and we try to make him understand what we want him to say. Come on out and you won't get hurt. The old guy yells something down into the hole, but there's no answer. So then we get ready with our rifles and we toss a smoke grenade down in there and when it goes off we cover the hole back up with the floormat for a minute or two. Nothin. We wait for the smoke to clear out a bit. By now we figure it's either empty or it's Cong for sure. Civilians couldn't take that smoke, we figure, but sometimes Charlie had got himself a gas mask from the Chinese or the Russians. So it's my move, I'm in charge of the patrol. We got this fella Weasel, little Eyetalian kid, real popular, who is supposed to be our tunnel man. I look at him and he says no way. No damn way you're gonna get me down there. And I look around and it's every one of the fellas shakin their heads. They seen too many friends get blown away, and they all been in-country long enough to know the same as I do. There's no rules. There's just you and your life.

" 'Probably empty,' I say.

" 'Maybe not,' says Weasel. 'Might be somebody down there to shoot us in the back, we start to leave here.'

"I know what they want to do, and I know that they don't really want to have to come out and say it. 'There might still be civilians down there.'

" 'So what?'

"That's just what I'm thinkin, 'so what.' There isn't any rules. There isn't any such thing as a civilian.

[256]

"We take another smoke grenade and we give that one more try and there's still not a peep. So Weasel ups and he's got a phosphorus grenade and we thrown matting and all the flammables we could find in and then we all lie flat while he tosses that down. Anything left alive in that hole is not human. It's burnin like crazy and we got to back away from the heat.

"We're coming out of the hootch when this villager, this woman, she come high-ballin acrost the fields towards us, screamin to wake the dead. She flies past and into the hootch and she's trying to climb down into the hole, smoke and flames and everything. Her children are down there, they were left with the oldest but she wasn't only seven. The old man tells us best as he can, from what she's yelling. She told the oldest if there was trouble to take the little ones and to go in the hole and not make a sound no matter what.

"She come after us then, clawing at us and trying to bite and Weasel, he wanted to shoot her and the old man too but I said there wasn't any reason for it. Not that there had to be a reason. We tied her down in one of the empty hootches and left her for the villagers to care for when they snuck back in.

"Weasel took it like a big joke and was giggling about crispy critters and like that and I really couldn't get mad with him. We killed them children, but at the time I just didn't care. You got to understand how it was. You got to know about the rules.

"I don't think I care even now.

"Oh yeah, they offered the grade when we come back. Said I done right about the hole. I told them I didn't want the decisions, didn't want their grade or their sergeant or their corporal. Just call me Pfc."

Hobie spilled a wide trail of gasoline as he climbed down and backed away from the vent. The banner swung over his head in the slight breeze. He tossed the near-empty can up onto the pile of TVs and waved his hands in the air to let the gas evaporate. He turned his back to the pyre, lit a match and held it to the gas trail, then took off from a crouch.

He was running, accelerating into his stride toward Congress Street when there was the huge coughing sound and the blast of heat from behind and he could see the leaping flame reflected in the windows of the surrounding buildings he was racing for and and he hit stride, leaning forward slightly, fire at his back. Fast and smooth across the open plaza, going all the way with it out in the flats, leaving the burning behind.

22

Mrs. Hanrahan sat across from Hunter in her dim parlor, her good eye swiveling sideways to see him like a big bird. The phone call excited him, there were so few people who knew where he was.

"Mr. McNatt?"

"Yes?"

"This is Soggint Mulcahy from Missing Persons. I spoke with you at the station?"

"Yes. I remember."

Hunter held his breath.

"We've located your son."

"Yes?"

"Your older one."

Darwin. "Where? In Boston?"

"He's in New Hampshire, like those people told you. Just on a hunch I checked with the unemployment people there. Took them a while to run it through, they're not so computerized up there, but they come out with your boy's name."

"Unemployment?"

"Yeah. I figure he just wandered up, there's never much work in New Hampshire this time of year, he might be collecting. There's a big winter layoff, the construction closes down. Sure enough, he's drawrin a check."

"Oh."

Mrs. Hanrahan tilted her head sideways to listen in better. Sergeant Mulcahy gave Hunter an address, said they didn't have a phone number on it and that Dar wasn't listed in the book up there. He said there hadn't been anything on Hobie. He'd keep on him but that was all for now.

He thanked Mulcahy. He thanked Mrs. Hanrahan for the use of the phone and she told him that somebody had been using too much hot water. That the water bills were killing her, that a woman alone had to watch out for everything. He thanked her again and excused himself.

Hunter climbed to his room. He'd found Darwin. Maybe Hobie was up staying with him. Maybe Dar had changed back, maybe it could be good between them again. He would have to go see Dar. Hunter took out the little hotplate he'd snuck past Mrs. Hanrahan, took out a can of baked beans and a chunk of onion and a couple of slices of warm cheese, and, with hands shaking slightly, made himself a meal.

23

Hunter sat trying to drink himself numb in Riordan's on East Eighth near L Street in South Boston. Jimmy Kearney had suggested after work that Hunter should get out and around, should get some fresh air. It wasn't but old men at Mrs. Hanrahan's, they kept to themselves and watched TV and banged on the radiator for more heat. There was only one bathroom on each floor and you could never find a roll of paper in it. You'd listen for a flush and the door opening, then stick your head out in the hall and there would be three or four old men leaning out of their doorways with rolls of toilet paper clutched in their hands, waiting to dart in and turn the lock.

"Why go back there?" Jimmy had said. "Hey, it's Friday, you got your pay, got the whole weekend to look for the boy. I'll ride you over by my place, nice bar right down the street, have a coupla pops, live a little, right? All work and no play makes Jack a fuckin basket case."

Riordan's was the darkest bar Hunter had ever been in. The only light came from the little TV set up in the corner. The TV was playing *Gilligan's Island* and there was something the matter with the sound, it rattled and rasped like an old man's voice. No one was watching it but no one suggested that Riordan turn it off. They would be in pitch-blackness.

Riordan himself was tending bar. Riordan was nearly deaf. The fellas raised their hands and waved them like kids in a schoolroom whenever they wanted another. Riordan looked a lot like the fella used to be in silent pictures. Keaton, Buster Keaton. Never changed expression, even when he pulled the Schlitz tap too long and ran foam all over his hand. Mostly he sat on a high chair under the TV, going over his books. Every once in a great while he would sigh and take a couple nibbles of his red pencil.

There had used to be a big, fancy-edged mirror on the wall behind the bar. You could tell from where the paint was faded and where it wasn't. There was some magazine pictures of sports heroes clipped out and tacked up here and there, Hunter recognized Ted Williams and Lou Boudreau and thought that the fella in the Boston Braves uniform looked like Warren Spahn. There had used to be pinball machines, you could see where the legs had dug holes in the floor. There was a piano pushed into the far corner, keys to the wall.

There was a couple of younger fellas, in their late thirties maybe, sitting in the one booth. Jimmy had nodded to them when he came in and mumbled that they were a couple of bad characters, that whatever they were up to in that booth it would come to no good.

Sitting at the bar was Jimmy and Hunter and Jimmy's best friend, Francis X. Coughlin. Francis X. had little pointed teeth and though he talked Boston like the rest of them his voice put Hunter in mind of the radio fella. Walter Winchell. And then there was the fella who joined them, who they called Old Flynn. It was obvious he was old but they called him it to keep him straight with young Flynn from the shipyard and Father Flynn from the next parish and Representative Flynn who you saw on all the posters. Old Flynn had a lot of hair and it was as chalky white as his skin, he had pupils so pale-blue that sometimes he looked like a blind man rolling his eyes. His only color was the red pinpricks on his nose and along his cheekbones. He was wearing a black armband.

"Let me guess," said Francis X., cocking one eye at the armband. "Tom McManus?"

"Saw him this morning."

"Fogarty's old man?"

"A good five years left in him."

"Donny Madden there, with the bad lungs?"

"Goin strong."

"I surrender. Who is it?"

"This band," said Old Flynn, "is for the founder. For poor Joe Kennedy, God rest his soul."

"He's been dead two weeks."

"And I've been wearing this two weeks."

"No kiddin? I guess it's that more often than not when I see you, you got one on for somebody. It's hod to keep them straight."

"This is for poor Joe."

"Poor is hodly the word I'd use," said Jimmy. "Dead, for sure, but poor and Kennedy don't mix."

"He came from poor," said Old Flynn. "He came up out of East Boston, back before the Eye-tralians took it over. It was poor times then, poor people."

"He did all right for himself, Joe."

"I'm not denyin that. But I'm sorry to see his passing. He came by his money honestly."

"That's a matter of definition there, old man. What he stot with, Francis, movie theayters?"

"Orpheums, wasn't it?"

"Something like that. And then he made a lot from the booze." Francis X. showed his pointed teeth in a smile. "A subject close to my hot. Somebody see if they could get Riordan out of his trance long enough to give me a refill here. Riordan!"

"Don't shout, Francis, it's a waste of breath. Tap on the bar with your glass a bit, maybe the vibrations will reach him."

Francis X. was buying whiskey-and-water now. Hunter had moved on to bourbon and Jimmy had stuck with the beer.

"I never touch the hod stuff before dinner," he said. "It kills the taste bulbs."

"And in my case," said Francis, "that's a merciful death. When the Lord handed out cookbooks my wife was taking a nap. A disgrace to Irish cue-zeen."

"She's not that bad, Francis."

"Only woman I know can't boil a potato. Riordan!"

Jimmy caught Riordan's eye by waving a handkerchief and the bartender hit them all again. Old Flynn was having Wild Turkey on ice.

"Just before they repealed the Eighteenth he cawnered the mocket on Gawdon's and a few of the other finer labels," he said. "When they opened the bar, poor Joe was ready. He cleaned up. A man of fawsight."

"Certain political connections didn't hurt any either."

"As I said, a man of fawsight. Why do you think he bought the Presidency?"

"For poor Jack."

"*No*, not *that* Presidency. There was only one President as far as I'm concerned, and that was Franklin Delano Roosevelt, God rest his soul."

"That's right, he backed Roosevelt, Joe."

"He bought him the job," said Flynn.

"Well, hey, he threw in a lot of money there, but there was a few other people involved."

"He bought his way into politics."

"He sawt of married his way in, too, didn't he? Rose's father there, he was a mayor. Fitzgerald."

"Honey Fitz."

"Right."

"He bought his way in," said Old Flynn. "There's no shame in that. Just good business sense. That's politics, you get what you pay for. Some people pay with influence, some with favors, some with votes. Poor Joe, he paid cash on the barrelhead. He got Roosevelt into the '32 convention and backed him till he won it."

"That was a rough one, that convention, wasn't it?" said Francis X. "I remember, I'm just a kid, listening on the radio. It was the first one I ever heard to pay attention to."

"That was a convention. Not like the last sideshow. We come to Chicago for politics, not for shenanigans in the streets."

"You were there?"

"I was workin for Bill Twomey at the time, God rest his soul, and he went for the Massachusetts delegation. I ran messages on the floor. It was a great experience." Old Flynn took a long pull of his whiskey and made a face. "Of coss they were for the other man."

"Who?"

"The delegation. The governor had control of them and of coss Al Smith was a great favorite here."

"Al Smith, right. I remember hearing. God, that guy could talk."

"Come right out of his head and through his hot," said Old Flynn. "None of your ghostwriters for Al Smith. He was a great one, but there was no way the rest of the country would have him. Catholic. And the people that was here then couldn't admit it. So only the Mayor was left to pull for FDR."

"Honey Fitz."

"*No!* There was only one mayor of Boston as far as I'm concerned," said Old Flynn, "and that was James Michael Curley. God rest his immawtal soul."

"He bucked the delegation, huh?"

"He wasn't in office at the time, or they would have taken his viewpoint into greater consideration. The governor and that bunch turned the rest against him, so that he couldn't even get a seat on the delegation."

"They froze him out."

"Not entirely. He attended the convention as a delegate from Pawto Rico."

"Curley? That must of taken some heavy wheeling and dealing."

"He had a friend in the right place. He did something for the friend and the friend returned the favor. He had a lot of friends."

"It cost him some time in the joint, his kind of friends."

"A political conspiracy by small men. The great ones are all plagued by small men."

Riordan pulled out what looked to be a cigar box full of slugs and went to the jukebox. Tony Bennett began to sing *I Gotta Be Me*.

"A real music lover, Riordan."

"He does the same thing every day this time. Thinks he's primin the pump, that everybody else is gonna rush to play some songs. Of coss he's allowed to use his private stock there, everybody else needs the real coin."

"Does it work?"

"The sad fact is, Hunt, they empty the bucket out Saturday night, everything's got a picture of Ott Linkletter on it. It's free music, enjoy it."

"Great men," said Old Flynn. "There was a number of them behind FDR that convention. There was the Mayor, there was Huey Long, there was Boss Pendergast of Kansas City, may God rest their souls. There was your namesake, Francis. Father Charles Coughlin."

"The radio priest."

"Coming to you from Detroit's Church of the Little Flower," said Francis X. "I remember my mother tuned into that all the time."

"Great men. And on the other side there was Al Smith and Sam Rayburn and Cactus Jack Garner and far in the background, pulling a few impawtant strings from Califawnia, Mr. William Randolph Hearst. The Mayor helped out with him though, and he came around eventually. It was a regular free-for-all. Repeal was the big issue on the platform and that set the blood to boiling. And there were favorite sons and dock hawses coming out of the woodwork. Will Rogers even got a few votes on the second ballot. Great men, great men. They don't have the like of them anymore." Old Flynn scowled. "Hubert Humphrey my royal Irish ass."

"This all must be goin right past you, Hunt," said Jimmy.

"Pardon?"

"The names. They're prawbly all before your time."

"Oh, I known most of em."

"You're a boy," said Old Flynn. "You've got your best years ahead of you."

"I hope to God they ain't behind me."

The men laughed. Old Flynn began to muse again.

[264]

"The great men that were gathered for that one occasion. It staggers the imagination."

"And you were there, Flynn?"

"Me and Bill Twomey, God rest his soul. He didn't last much longer after that. The booze."

"It's ruined many a good man."

"And helped a lot of bad ones on their way, too."

"Gets holt of you when you're young and never lets go."

"My brother-in-law, Timmy Quinn," said Francis X., "he wasn't but a young man, thirty-seven, thirty-eight years old when it did him."

"There was a man who lived for his tea."

"That he did. He was already a prisoner of it when my father-in-law got him on the foss. I'm surprised he lasted as long as he did."

"He was with the police?" said Hunter.

"An officer of the lawr. They used to come over in the morning with black coffee, his friends on the foss, and walk him around a bit to get him in shape to repawt for duty. He was in the car then, only the veterans got their own foot beat. He'd sleep most of the day away in the back seat. Finally it got so not even his friends would pottner with him, too unreliable. The captain tucked him away on a traffic job, crossing the grammar school kids for lunch. Figured being out in the cold air might keep him straight. The school principal called, said one of your men is passed out in a snowbank here, creating an attraction. The captain let him resign so he wouldn't lose all his pension."

"Right there," said Jimmy, pointing to the stool directly across from Riordan and his books. "He sat right there and committed suicide."

"Took him five hod years on the tea but he did the job."

"And how is Helen making out these days?" asked Old Flynn.

"Oh, as well as can be expected. She's a good strong girl, my sister, but it's a hod deal she's been given. She might be droppin in a bit later, as a matter of fact." Francis tried to wink around Hunter's back, but he caught it.

"It touches everybody, the booze," said Jimmy. "It's a curse. My own father, had a hot condition most of his later years, he couldn't stay away from it. I remember it was running battle between him and the mother, every Saturday when we'd go out. You'd go from place to place, the whole family, have maybe one beer and then move on. Before the Saturday was over you'd have crossed paths with everybody you knew, makin the same circuit. Mother, she kept a careful eye, made sure he stayed with the brew, no hod stuff, and went light on it at that. I remember it was in a place that's gone now, was over on West Broadway. The old man goes in the back room for a minute, he comes out and his face is all flushed. Mother is right on top of him. 'Dan Kearney,' she says, 'did you have a shot back there?' 'Would I ever?' he says. 'Answer my question and don't beat around the bush.' 'Carmel,' he says raising his om in the air, 'if I had a shot back there may the Lord strike me dead.' And within the minute he fell out on the floor with a hot attack."

"God rest his soul."

Francis X. flagged Riordan down on his way to the jukebox with another slug and they went for a fresh round. Hunter's teeth and tongue were gone but he could still feel his cheeks when he pinched them hard. He had a ways to go.

"He was a printer, your dad, wasn't he?"

"In a small way. He did a lot of printing for the local parishes. In fact he knew Cushing when he was only a buck private in the cloth."

"In my opinion," said Old Flynn, "there was only one religious man worth his salt. Richard Cardinal Cushing."

"He's still alive, Flynn."

"He'll be going back soon enough, though. He said the honors at poor Joe's planting."

"There was a man who could talk for you. And the face on him, scare the sin right out of your soul."

"The only face I ever seen could match it," said Old Flynn, "for strength and fearsomeness, belonged to Mr. John L. Lewis."

"That's your old boss, int he Hunt?"

"I suppose." Hunter shrugged. "He went out this past June."

"God rest his soul," said Old Flynn. "He was a great one. I remember we burned him in effigy, my VFW post, during the war. Took his miners out on strike right while our boys on the line needed all the coal they could get."

"The miners was hurtin, war or no war," said Hunter.

"I'm sure they were, and that Mr. Lewis was a sincere man. It was a matter of priorities, and in our minds at the post he chose the wrong one. Even the great ones can make a mistake."

"That's true enough."

"They're only human. You cut them and they bleed, just like anyone else. The great powers of the world are no more infallible than the four of us sitting at this bar. They're just men."

They stared into their glasses for a moment. Frank Sinatra sang *My Way*. Finally Jimmy spoke.

"Old Flynn, my friend," he said, "that is a frightening thought."

Hunter looked the room over and there were no edges left. He liked the darkness now, it was like swimming under water at night, everything slow and thick and gray. Even the noise from the jukebox was like it was wrapped in cotton. Nothing sharp, nothing that could hurt. Francis X. and Old Flynn went on trading stories about Curley. The Mayor.

"I ever tell you about the last time I sawr the Mayor?" said Old Flynn. "It was in '54, not too many years before he passed away, God rest him. I'm in a cab, on the way to visit friends, and it's a rainstawm. We're up in what used to be the West End, heading down Cambridge Street, when the driver jams on his brakes to take on another passenger. I don't mind now, I know the tricks of the trade, he won't have to call in the extra fare and he'll get to clip the whole thing for himself. And it *is* raining, I'd want him to do the same for me, I was out there getting soaked.

"Only when the man slides in next to me it's none other than James Michael Curley himself. It was quite a shock, I was used to seeing him at official functions, with the limousine and the driver and all, and had never considered he might have cause to use a more common method of transpawtation.

"Now the Mayor had seen me around during all of his various terms in office, I was with the Public Works for one stretch, then with the Collecting Division where I finished out. But in all that time he'd only spoken personally to me once, and that was at the '32 convention I mentioned earlier. There were a few of us who wanted him to know we were behind him, even if we were there under the governor that day, and Bill Twomey chose me to bring him a letter to that effect.

[267]

"I was only just thirty, a young man for the Potty in those days, and oh was I nervous to be standing there in the presence of the Mayor. He reads the note and he smiles and thanks me. And then he asks if I might do him a favor, a couple messages he needed delivered around the convention floor. Only it was impawtant that no outsiders know it was Curley sending the message, he couldn't use any of his regular runners who might be recognized. 'Delicate negotiations,' he said. Well I can tell you I was flattered, but I was there with Bill Twomey and Bill was there at the suffrance of the governor, and I didn't want to get Bill into trouble. Politics. So I made a bad excuse, said I had hurt my leg, twisted it running up some stairs earlier in the day. Well, it wasn't much of a lie and the Mayor knew it, but he just went on.

" 'Flynn,' he said, 'Flynn? No relation to Edward Flynn are you?'

" 'Why yes, that's my uncle,' I say.

" 'How's he getting along?'

" 'Not so well,' I say, 'his firm went under last July, it's hod times in the building trades.'

" 'Now that's a shame,' says Curley, 'good solid Democrat like Ed Flynn out of a job. That's a crime is what it is. But you know, I bet if he was to drop by the Public Works, talk to my friend Matt Thomas, they might have something for him. Always happy to put in a word for a good Democrat.'

"Well, I was with Public Works at the time and I'd struck out for my uncle long before I even got close to Matt Thomas. 'Now about these messages,' he says, and continues as if he hadn't heard anything about a hurt leg. Well the long and the shot of it is that I spent most of that afternoon running messages for the Mayor, and sure enough after the convention my uncle goes to see Matt Thomas and there's a nice position waiting for him. He was an able man, my uncle Edward, it was no featherbed, but the streets were full of able men without jobs in those days.

"So that was in '32 and that was the only time I ever spoke to him personally. I was never in a situation that close to the center of power in my years with the city. So when the Mayor slides into the cab and doesn't recognize me, I can make allowances.

We ride together quite a while, there's a bit of a traffic jam, and he hodly looks up from his newspaper the whole time. He must have been nearly eighty then, and I figure his memory, all the people he's had to keep track of in his day, it's no surprise he wouldn't recall a small potatoes employee like myself. It's a terrible thing to lose your memory, I'm what, only sixty-nine and already I've begun to develop gaps.

"Anyhow, we get to the address on Joy Street he'd asked for, and he pays the driver and climbs out. But then, at the last second before he slams the door, he leans in with a twinkle in his eye and he says, 'You take care of that bad leg, now, Flynn.' The last time I sawr him."

Old Flynn sighed and rattled the ice in his glass.

"After all those years," said Francis X.

"The system worked back then," said Old Flynn. "You gave something, you were sure of getting something in return. It was all done up front, you scratch my back, I'll scratch yours. If a man didn't deliver for his people, they'd vote him out the first chance they got. It was pure, above-bawd patronage politics and no bones about it. It made sense back then."

"It's still going on, I'd say."

"Not the way it was. The kind of people they have nowadays. I don't even bother to vote most of the time."

"I've always voted for the winning candidate in a Presidential election," Jimmy announced.

"That's pretty good luck."

"Luck had nothing to do with it. I wait until the last minute, see who seems to have it in the bag, and he's my man. My one vote is not gonna make the difference, right? So I figure why disenfranchise myself. You voted for the wrong man, the winner owes you nothing, see, you're disenfranchised. You got no say in the government. The only time I had second thoughts was Dewey-Truman. It looked closer than most of the newspapers thought, so I voted for both."

"How'd you manage that?"

"You'd be surprised, Hunt, how many names are on the rolls who never made it past their tenth year. A lot of dead men and women are resurrected every November."

"Sounds like Mingo County back home."

"The next one for mayor could be interesting," said Francis. "Mrs. Hicks is thinking of going up against White."

"She doesn't have a prayer."

"And if she doesn't," said Old Flynn, his face taking on a little more color, "it's because of the Eye-tralians and the Spanish and the niggers. They've taken over and he's stooped to get their vote."

"They got a right to vote like anyone else," said Hunter.

"But they all *want* something. They pull the lever and they expect to have the city handed to them on a silver platter. It isn't honest. It's pandering, is what, he's pandering to the lower elements to stay in power."

"It's a shame," said Jimmy.

"The whole thing is going to Hell in a handbasket," said Francis. "You see that thing in California with those degenerates? Those Mansons?"

"What has that got to do with the city here?"

"Everything, Jimmy, everything. It's the breakdown of everything that used to hold life together. The patronage, the Church, the family, it's all going back to seed. Man reverting to his worst. Even the Kennedys, there's a perfect example. You stotted with Joe and he was a great one, like you said Flynn. Then there was Joe Jr., from all repawts he should have been President, he didn't get killed during the war. Then Jack, he was okay, had some funny ideas, Hovvid and all that, but basically a pretty good top man. Bobby, to my mind, was always somewhat of a punk. I don't mean to speak disrespect of the dead, but he just didn't have it. He had to push too hod, it didn't come natural. And Ted, killed that girl, problems with his home life — it's like, what do they call them? The genes — retroactive —"

"Regressive."

"You got one of the world's great memories, James. You heard that one day in grade school, right, and thirty years later out it pops. Regressive genes. The greatness in the family has passed, they're going in the other direction now. And at the very bottom of that other direction you got your Mansons."

"It's the drugs," said Old Flynn. "It makes them crazy. It

makes everything crazy. I can't understand it anymore. You know Mike O'Dwyer, don't you? His boy, the oldest. Dead. The drugs. And old Philly Dolan, ran the newsstand, stabbed to death. Some dope fiend murders him for a pocketful of small change. I don't understand it, it's a proven fact they kill you, they turn your brain wrong, and yet people continue to take them. It's crazy." Old Flynn shook his head in wonder, then waved to Riordan for another round.

"It's all in the way they're used, Flynn," said Jimmy. "It's like anything else, like the patronage, it depends on how you use it whether it's good or bad. Now I'm sure your poor Joe was full of some kind of drugs right up to the end."

"But he was a sick man." Old Flynn sighed. "Had a stroke and was paralyzed not long after young Jack was elected. Left speechless in a wheelchair. But the mind, the mind went on for a good seven years. He had to sit there and witness the horrible things that came to pass in the world, came to pass in his family, and him not able to lift a finger, to speak a word to protest. Poor Joe. I know just how he feels. An old man with the world out of his grip, the frustration. I feel just like that sometimes, like I been struck dumb and paralyzed and my Hell is to hang onto life and be fossed to see it all fall apot."

"Nothing lasts forever, old man," said Jimmy. "There are very few things stay constant. There's death, there's taxes, there's —"

"There's the booze."

"— and there's the booze, for sure. To your health, gentlemen."

They drank.

Francis X.'s sister Helen came in then and somehow she ended up sitting between Francis and Hunter. She looked about forty and was still slim. She wore very red lipstick and some kind of scent, she seemed overdressed for either Riordan's bar or the telephone-company job she said she was headed for.

"They've got me on a kind of split schedule now," she said to Francis after he'd introduced her to Hunter and reintroduced her to Old Flynn, who forgot the last time they'd met. "I go in at seven in the evening three times a week and at eleven the other two. It's terrible on my sleep, but it's the only way they say they can keep me on nights. I don't have any seniority there to complain."

"Helen was widowed a few years back, she's had to make out for herself."

"Right," said Hunter. "I think you mentioned that."

"And I have children," said Helen, turning to him, "two girls." It sounded like an apology.

"That must be nice."

"Oh, it is, but sometimes it can be a lot of work." She had a very nice smile. If only she didn't use that kind of lipstick, made her look straight out of the forties. "I leave them at their aunt's when I work nights," she said, "but in the day and when I'm not working we live alone."

"You do a fine job, Helen Quinn," said Jimmy. "Those are two of the nicest little daughters you could ask for."

"Thank you." Helen sipped at her beer and left red on the glass.

"It's a sacred trust," said Old Flynn. "Parenthood. The good Lord knows I tried to be the best father I possibly could to my sons, God rest their souls. Whenever I could get a moment away I'd take them into the great outdoors. Made them into regular little spawtsmen, by the time they reached their early teens they were the equal of their old man with the rod and the gun. It was a great thing to be a father, a sacred trust."

"Didn't you have girls too, Flynn?"

The old man nodded. "Three. Their ma, God rest her immawtal soul, took care of that."

"That reminds me, Hunter," said Jimmy, "do you shoot?"

"Pardon?"

"Shoot. Go for deer. *Hunt*. We been thinkin, maybe we'll get up a little safari in a week or so, catch the end of the season. Up to the Vermont–New Hampshire bawder area there."

"Anywhere near Orford?"

"Yeah, as a matter of fact it is. You know that territory?"

"Not exactly." It was where Mulcahy had located Darwin. Collecting unemployment.

"I got an old thirty-ought-six you can tote around, you don't have your own rifle up here."

"I'll tell you," said Hunter after considering a moment, "I

don't think I want in on the shootin, but I would appreciate a ride up that way."

"You know someone up there?"

"I got a boy."

"Another one?"

"Yuh."

"Oh," said Helen, beaming, "you have children?"

"Yuh."

"Hunter's been a widower for some years now," said Jimmy, "he raised them up himself."

"How nice for you," said Helen. "To have the boys, I mean. They must be a great comfort."

"Yuh."

Helen left a little beer in her glass when she rose to go. Hunter noticed her legs sliding off the stool. Nice for a woman her age. "I'm sorry to drink and run," she said, "but the Bell System waits for nobody. Very nice to meet you Mr. McNatt."

"Same here."

"And how come we never see you down here anymore, Helen, now that Quinn is gone?" Jimmy winked at her. "Are you too good for us now?"

"I have better things to do," she teased, smiling her nice smile, "than hang out in this graveyod with a bunch of drunken Irish."

All of a sudden Hunter wanted to say that he had better things to do too, but she was out the door. All of a sudden he wasn't so numb anymore, at least not in his stomach. He tried to take deep easy breaths.

"A fine woman," said Jimmy when she was gone. "A fine woman."

"It's a terrible thing to be alone in the world. My poor little sister."

Old Flynn raised his glass in the air. "To the ladies."

"Go on, Flynn. You got nothin at all to do with the ladies, your age."

"A man can remember, can't he?"

"Depends on if he's got anything worth remembering."

"You don't know the first thing about it. I have a great store of memories to call on. Do you know what I like to do?"

"No, and I'm afraid to ask."

"Around two thirty, three o'clock the schools let out. I like to go out on the sidewalks —"

"Must be the only sunlight he ever gets —"

"Be still now. I like to go out on the sidewalk and watch the little Catholic schoolgirls walk past. They don't wear pants, you know."

"On the other side of France. What do you mean they don't wear pants?"

"Pants. Like they let the girls do now in public school. The sisters won't allow it. So they come by in their little plaid uniform dresses, with dark stockings underneath, and those shoes, they're two colors —"

"Saddle shoes."

"Yes, their saddle shoes and their white blouses, I watch them come by —"

"I think you'd better be off tellin this to a priest in the confessional, Flynn."

"It's not that kind of thing at all!" Old Flynn reddened. "What I feel, when I see them walking by, is a very tender sawt of thing. I feel — pro*tec*tive."

"Like a wolf feels protective of little lambs."

"You're a cynical man, Jimmy Kearney." Old Flynn eased himself off his stool, then grabbed it to hold steady. When he had his balance he stepped out and took a pose, one foot in front of the other, chin lifted, eyes closed reverently, one hand spread over his frail chest and the other held ready to gesture before him.

"Uh-oh," said Jimmy. "Here it comes again. Casey at the Bat."

"It's no such thing," said Old Flynn, not opening his eyes. "Be still and listen now."

They swiveled around to watch the old man recite.

The woman was not taken

he began —

> *From Adam's head you know,*
> *So she must not command him,*
> *Tis evidently so.*

[274]

The woman was not taken
From Adam's feet you see,
So he must not abuse her,
The meaning seems to be.

The woman she was taken
From under Adam's om,
Which shows he must protect her
From injury and hom.

"And the manner in which a man lives up to that," he said, climbing back on his stool, "is the measure of the man."

"Well I've been a failure, then," said Francis X. "Not a total one, not all at one time, but by and lodge over the long run I've been a failure."

"We've all been," said Jimmy. "All of us. If things are in the shape they're in, pot of the blame is on us, for not holding out. For not being firm enough, for not being strong enough."

Old Flynn raised his glass. "To failure."

Hunter couldn't breathe. *Hogan's Heroes* was on the TV, buzzing and gurgling and Dennis Day was wailing something about his mother over the jukebox and the numbness had gone to Hunter's lungs, it felt like he was breathing in some kind of syrup. He was drowning, it felt like, and they were all as deaf as Riordan to his struggling. Hunter pushed off his stool and swam his way over to the door, to the street. To fresh air.

24

Grant Parke III settling in at his ringside seat for the action, lips turning up slightly in that familiar smile of humorous detachment, that warning sign of dark and acid wit that most surely, if they only knew about it, would have long since made his name a household word among the tube-addicted masses. A crossbreed of Hunter Thompson, H. L. Mencken and Howard Cosell. Yes fans, Grant Parke III perched high above the field of combat on a stone-cold radiator, sharpening his mind to skewer every knock-down and nuance of the main event.

On paper it looks like no contest. Because the challenger is none other than Paris Green, weighing in at a hundred-seventy pounds of lean Black Power, stepping confidently from his corner in a shiny-slick, black-leather knee-length jacket with the belt ends hanging down in the back. He's got Panther Power packed in his left lead and martyrdom coiled and ready in the right. Cause they gone and shot Freddy Hampton *dead*, folks. We all remember Brother Hampton from the Illinois branch, a young man who could do it *all*, offense and defense. Had that something *ex*tra the great ones seem to possess. What a future he had in store for him, what a loss to the game and to us all, sports fans. Cause in the latest Pigs-vs.-Panthers tilt Fred and Brother Mark Clark were sidelined permanently by the heavy hand of Fate and the even heavier hand of Hizzonner Richard Daley's finest. So here's Paris Green, sent over from Roxbury by the local bloods to invite the Third Way to join them and the cosponsoring Weathermen in City Hall Plaza tomorrow for a little rage-and-recrimination. Yes, the very same Weathermen who were labeled by the very same late lamented Fred Hampton (not long before his own heroic Last Stand) as irresponsibly "Custeristic." But there is a kind of universal hatchet-burying that takes place whenever one of the potential Great Ones bows out, when a promising career is nipped in its bud, so the Weathermen are along for the ride with an open invitation to their version of the smart-lad-betimes-to-slip-away routine.

Perhaps "invitation" is the wrong way to put it, as Paris Green indicates with his opening words to the assembled members of the Third Way —

"Dig it — the pigs offed Freddy Hampton in Chicago yesterday, and their campaign against the people is just gettin up *steam*." Comes out smokin at you, Paris, nothing cute or jab-and-peddle about his style. "This is the way it's gonna *be* from now on. So tomorrow we gonna do this thang, it's called Students Against Fascism, see, to show the Man he can't go vampin on the

*peo*ple without somebody calls his *hand*. Show him that any hoss-
tile actions on his part is gonna have some ser-yuss *con*sequences.
We got the Weathermen comin in on it and some of you other
white groups that's fed up with the way thangs bein run in this
country and we want everybody that's with us to come *out*. If
you not *with* us you *against* us, right? We got to show we
through gettin pigged and just turning that other cheek. We
done run out of *cheeks*, Jim, this is *war*. You get behind what I'm
sayin?"

Grant Parke III has seen this youngster come up through the
ranks, followed his progress from schoolboy days to the present.
He seems to have all the essentials, Paris Green, to be a serious
contender. But the game has changed an awful lot since those
early days and the big question is whether Paris has changed
enough to keep up with it. The surface indications are there, the
standard Do, big and bad and kinking out from all angles of his
head, look like one of those evil-ass weeds grows its way up
through the pavement and then just hangs *out*. He's got the black-
leather Gestapo-pimp jacket, the rock and rhythm of his ghet-toe
(accent on the *toe*) jivetalk with its sprinkling of no-bullshit-
mufucker Maoisms, it's all there folks. But is it all, pardon the
pun, *nat*ural?

Cause Grant Parke III remembers Green from the hardwood
courts of Phillips Exeter, from the Eastern Preppie League, when
his was often the only black body to be found on the floor or in
the stands, back when leather was for whitetrash townie dropouts
and all Parls's shirts had a crocodile on the left tit. The days of
overt co-optation and a-credit-to-his-race. Shanghaied off a street
corner on the strength of a high IQ test and a higher shooting
percentage for his ninth-grade five, fixed up with a minority-
athletic scholarship, a battery of tutors and a summer-in-the-
country boarding program to instill a taste for the good life, Paris
was a fox in the henhouse. It was days of sit-ins and Freedom
Riders, when SNCC was still salt-and-pepper, days of the first
push for voter registration down in Darkest Alabama and if you
were one of the chosen ones, one of the lucky knee-grow win-
ners in the Great White-Liberal Guilt Sweepstakes you could do
no *wrong*. Of course shooting a righteous game of hoop just
when the sport was swinging into popularity didn't hurt any

either. It wasn't long before the only touch of Roxbury left to Paris was his basketball style, the triple-pump joy he brought to the ham'n'eggs pick-and-pattern dullness the coaches and fans were used to. His conversation was soon loaded with "brew" and "beevo," with talk of "hometown honeys" and things being "gross." As in "that's really *gross*, man." And except for a few dirty looks from the townies and envy too guilt-laden ever to be expressed, he was *loved*. *Adored*. Grant Parke remembers the ball games, how even the kids on the team who had to play against Paris could come up with nothing more slurring than "those guys." As in "those guys sure can *jump*." And Grant Parke remembers the interchangeable string of pretty blond-headed girls, the succession of Dresden dolls Paris always had cheering for him from the stands, waiting for him after the game. Grant could always pick them out in the bleachers during a time-out, each one with hair to her waist, blue-eyed, looking like a surfer's wet dream sitting alone and cheering for Paris Green. Getting tingles in her wee-wee at the mere *thought* of his beautiful black self and all the status that went with being his girl. Each black-on-white sliding of skin made all the more electric by its political and social statement. Paris's color was worth a good half hour of come-on at any mixer, what liberal preppie folk-junkie young girl could risk giving the icy eyeball to a symbol of oppression without seeming an oppressor? What young girl could totally resist the curiosity factor, the what-would-it-be-like?

So Paris Green was well on his way at Phillips Exeter, well along in the great tradition of crumbs-to-Cadillacs established back at the turn when Jack Johnson was dispatching the likes of Sam "The Boston Tarbaby" Langford and a succession of over-fed Great White Hopes and *cop*pin, Jim, coppin the Man's game and his money and his women, coppin left and right and givin the poor fokes stuck back in the pea patches and coldwater rattraps something to dream on. Well on his *way*.

But answer this one, sports fans — What Ever Happened to Paris Green?

"The only thing the pigs have for an ex*cuse* in any one of these murders they been up to, bustin in on Panthers, is that the brothers was storin up some *weap*ons. Like that gives em some kinda reason, some kinda *right*, to go blowin people away in their beds.

Like it isn't spelt out there in the fuckin Constitution about the right to bear arms. The pigs, they is a *lie*. It's got to the point where every Panther knows he's got to be ready to *die*, it's gotten to be a life-or-death thang, see, and the way we look at it, if we can't have any kind of meaningful *life* in this system, maybe we can have a meaningful *death* bringing it *down*."

He even *looks* blacker, as if a new shade came with the style, some kind of Pinocchio number where you darken every time you say "up against the wall." Clean Paris Green must of had one *shit*load of changes to go through after he blew his freshman year at Providence, partied his way off the basketball team and landed back on his black ass in Roxbury. All those hours parroting after the Berlitz records — "Keep the faith, baby — now repeat — keep the *faith* —" All the physical therapy to relearn the walk, to train the ear away from Gerry Mulligan and Dave Brubeck and that whole pseudo-intellectual cool jazz thing and into Otis and Aretha and Brother J.B. And maybe it was a natural process, the real Paris Green coming out from behind that all-American token niggerhood. Maybe he really *was* an African deep in his soul and those Jungian tribal drums were finally starting to beat, the man approaching his essence.

But maybe, just maybe, it was a bit of a *hustle*. Maybe Paris was no colonized African at all, but just another preppie thug. A sobering thought. Was he, like Grant Parke III, *slumming?* Working a show for the folks in the cheap seats? And did he ever recognize the fact, be wise to himself, and go on with it just the same? Schizo City if that was the case, with Africa, America and Phillips Exeter all pulling in different directions. Did he ever long for the days of blond-headed girls and white puppylove from the bleachers the way that Grant Parke sometimes longed for the uncomplicated life of lacrosse and rugby and hou-bro beevo parties, of happily hugging the toilet all night long with your barf buddies after draining a half-keg for no special occasion? Was Paris trapped in his Bad Panther bag the way Grant felt trapped sometimes in his detachment and cynicism? In fact was it possible that the original superstars, that Lenin and Trots and Nechayev and Patrice and Fidel and Che, all those screaming-Red Hall-of-Famers, did they ever feel trapped the same way, wonder how the fuck did I get stuck in this revolutionary number with the fate of the yearning masses hanging on my every breath and no way I can retire to the ranch and work on my stamp collection? Were they all Schizo City too, or were they like Schenk, a one-way street, a closed set?

Of course the game hadn't changed *to*tally, it never does. There was Tracy Anne and Jennifer, sitting up front there, Pinkstaff and Debbie and Smallwood all gobbling up every holy word Paris was laying down, spreading their ideological legs for his rhetoric because it came straight from the Panther's mouth, from the very man out there taking slugs in the street. Drinking it all in like amateur jocks flocked around a flesh-and-blood Sunday-hero pro*fes*sional, the real *thing*, fans, fresh off the front lines. Giving Paris all that power-to-the-people automatic empathy you know he ex*pects* from a bunch of lefty kids. His appearance here is a mere formality, what self-respecting underground outfit could possibly pass up anything the Panthers actually in*vit*ed ofays to join in, what upright member of the community of conscience could miss such a juicy chance to renounce his or her white-skin privilege?

"Have you ever been shot at?"

But hold onto your seats, sports fans —

"I mean *you*, you know, in the flesh —"

There are some new wrinkles after all, cause here's Miriam Katz up with that no-bullshit tone, that hint of challenge in her voice, wanting to inspect the stigmata —

"Well, not myself *per*sonally," and oh the psychic open-fly of that admission, the little twinge of shame for never having ducked a bullet, "*but*," try to get it back Paris, you're losing momentum, "as a Panther I have to live constantly with the probability of that happening."

Almost is no cigar, Paris, got to watch your semantics. *Cer*tainty is what these children want to hear, none of this probability shit. Every kid who ever caught a whiff of tear gas in some Young Democrat peace-and-freedom park bust was stone sure in his head of the probability that they'd be catching lead from the National Guard next. Shouldn't let on that you've still got your amateur status when they're all set to believe any six-gun shoot-out story you care to hand them.

And here's Sarah, who no doubt was somebody's Civil Rights

Sweetheart six or seven years back, Sarah raising a question —
"Isn't this whole idea of stocking up on guns to protect yourself from the police, doesn't it, possibly, begin to be like the Cold
War thing back in the fifties? I mean when you lay in all that
hardware it's bound to come down on you. They've got you
outnumbered and outgunned and I don't really think there's
much chance of winning somebody's respect by trading shots
with them."
What's this? Feedback from the Freedom Riders? Is the game
changing rules again or is this Third Way bunch gotten so deep
into their working-class trip that they all gone redneck?
"You got to understand," says Paris Green, "that this isn't only
a question of firepower, but a question of national morale. The
morale of the colonized black nation trapped in America." Paris
avoids looking directly at the women when he addresses them,
instead searching out the eyes of Schenk and Remington and Joel
Pinkstaff as if to say what *gives* with you turkeys, let your
bitches run off at the mouth like that? How you spect to get
your revolution thing together you can't even keep some women
in line? "The thang is," he answers, staring at Mark Remington,
"we figure the time hasn't come where we got to worry bout
winnin the white man's r*espect,* so we might's well settle for his
fear."
Eyes like cold yellow stone at Mark, a regular Sonny Liston
prefight hoodoo glare that would sizzle your average bleeding-
heart radical's nuggets to a crisp. But it's a different kind of
crowd here tonight, these folks want *blood* and here's Miriam
jumping back in to ask about the Panther women.
"The Panther women," says Paris Green to Schenk, "realize
that their place in this stage of the struggle is to support their
men. Anything else would be counterrevolutionary."
Yes, it looked like no contest on paper, but not to the seasoned
eyes of Grant Parke III. He could sense the Caucasian in the
woodpile. None of your tell us what we can do to promote the
Ten Point Plan and Free Huey Newton this evening, fans, cause
in the other corner all night long has been Kid Machiavelli himself, a hardrocks little Jew packing enough ideology and balls that
he is far beyond honkie-baiting and suburban-whiteboy guilt
trips, beyond the promised glory of dying in the streets at your

grateful black brothers' side. Schenk has got himself and his people primed, has got his act to*geth*er, and if the Panthers think they can hook Third Way into their left-fascist death trip by sending one hardeyed street rapper over to state the case and cash in the chips they are sadly mis*ta*ken.

Not that the bout is over, oh no, far from it. Mark Remington is still the official tacit-consensus captain of this squad and he smells paydirt in the Students Against Fascism gig. The Weathermen, the Panthers, a safe enough spot for the Third Way to make its public debut, to show its numbers? You're a pretty together fella yourself, Markie, but you can't hide that hard-on you've got for the cameras. Plus there's that score left to settle over the GE-television-burning thing, that little practice action Schenk circumvented group procedure to set up. Got to reestablish your *cre*dence, Mark, can't let the blood go back to his people saying there's a new man in the driver's seat over to Third Way. Got to smile and sound reasonable and slug it out with Schenk.

"We sympathize with the loss of one of your key members, but I'm afraid if we attended this rally it would seem we were admitting to agreement with your overall policies," says Schenk.

"I don't see why groups of differing — tactics — can't get together on major issues in which they have a common stake," says Mark Remington.

"What the fuck you people *talk*in bout?" says Paris Green.

Schenk says he wants to put it to a vote right away and Remington says he wants to debate it in group first and Paris Green looks like he wants to go back to '62 when you could tell the racists without a scorecard. Schenk leads with a bourgeois nationalism to the midsection, then closes in with a mindless-activism–left-revisionist combination. Remington is ducking and backpedaling, counterpunching with a little solidarity of youth, some unity in the face of repression. Racist, goes Paris Green, fascist. Typical-bullshit-white-liberal. All those old surefire knockout punches, wham-wham-*wham*, but nobody is even staggered by them. What gives? Throw your best shots and nothing, like they're not even in the same ring with you.

Paris has got a sniff of what's in the air now and he wants no part of it, all of a sudden he feels like a referee and who ever heard of a blood in whistle and stripes? So he backs off, disengages, he's still just *scout*ing the Third Way to bring back a report, he says, getting their reactions so the brothers can caucus and decide whether they *want* to invite Third Way or not. He really doesn't have any authority to do any inviting *personally* see, so don't call us we'll call you and he's out the door. Just like that. Old Paris was always *light*nin on the fast break.

Scratch Paris Green folks, but the card isn't over yet. Schenk has missed his shot at having the heavyweight-title showdown tonight but he can at least flex his muscles a little. He gives the nod to his second, and Smallwood takes the floor.

"Now that our friend has gone to reconsider his attitude toward us," says Smallwood, "I think it might be the right time to bring up something that's been festering for quite a while. Which is the ha*rass*ment that many of our members have been subjected to by certain elements in the community."

You mean by the jungle-bunnies, dontcha Smallwood? I mean the color line has been *brok*en, they're dominating the sport. No need for that "certain elements" runaround. You sound like Ira Wein.

"There's no reason we should have to run a gauntlet every time we go to or from Columbia Station, there's no reason we should be hassled getting groceries at the corner store. Our women being constantly propositioned and our men openly challenged. I mean, do they think we're some kind of in*tru*ders?"

Does Johnny Unitas go to the air on third-and-fifteen? Does Muhammad Ali own a mirror? What do you ex*pect* is gonna happen when a bunch of honkie political-freaks plop themselves down in the middle of blood territory and start walking the streets like they own them? Welcome Wagon? You decide to play on the asphalt court and you got to count on some bad hops now and then.

"I think it's time we established our presence here. I mean how many of you in this room have been hassled at least once, for clearly racist reasons? Let me see hands."

Remington doesn't raise his because he doesn't believe this is happening. Schenk doesn't raise *his* because he needs both of them to pull the strings. There are a lot of hands in the air.

"Right. It's been going on since we moved here and the longer

[283]

we pretend it doesn't exist and put up with it the worse it's going to get. I think we should consider some kind of *act*ion to make it clear that Dorchester is our home too and that we will protect our own. Like the man said, if people won't give you their respect, you may have to settle for their fear."

"Whoa now," says Mark Remington, "don't you think —"

"A vote on the need for an action!" King, barking it out from the rear.

"— that maybe you're overstating the case —"

"All in favor?"

"— just a little bit? I mean slow down for a —"

"*Hai!*"

The shock troops karate-chop the air in unison with their vote. It's an awesome sight, fans, the power and precision of the Big Red Machine. They are more than half the group now, and with Schenk and Miriam and King it is an unbeatable combination. It's all over but the shouting folks, an incredible turn of events. Schenk has all the marbles he needs to take over the game, the old bloodless-coup TKO in the tenth round.

But he doesn't want official victory to hang on this issue, not on a racial ticket. Make him seem too antispade, which is not the point at *all*. This is *poli*tics, not some street gang deciding to rumble with the local color or not, and Schenk wants his to be a *poli*tical victory. So he gives it a rain check.

"It's pretty late," he says. "I think we'd be better off considering exactly what form the action will take tomorrow, in group. Don't you?"

"Wait," says Mark Remington but Schenk is already walking out of the room and all his people are following him. *His people.* Like a halftime drill team, they're actually lined up in twos on their way out.

It's over that quickly. People turning around with their change from the hotdog vendor, ready to settle in for the action and it's *over*. Like a Patterson-Johansson bout, like one of those second-and-a-half sumo-wrestler bellybumps. The promoters shaking their heads in the wings, vowing never to book *that* bum again, the box-office window slamming with finality. No refunds, folks, we never promised it would go the distance. Oh, the thrill of victory and the agony of defeat, ladies and gents, the vagaries and vicissitudes of the sporting life. The way the ball *bounces*. Grant Parke III here, high above the action, wondering whether to stay and cover the solemn human interest of dashed hopes, the sour funk of we-wuz-robbed and wait'll-next-year, or to go down the hall for popping corks, flashing teeth and we're-number-one.

Sitting half-dazed in the room, they try to pick up the pieces and to instant-replay the touchdown bomb, the knockout uppercut, the grand slammer that has turned the tables so suddenly. Mark Remington and Wein and Pinkstaff and Sarah, all stunned on their asses, Hillbilly Hobie McNatt playing out his option by the door, torn in both directions. And Grant Parke III, who saw it coming all the way folks, who had a feeling back in his preseason forecasts, who views the bruised spirits and broken egos and thanks the deities of radical sensibility for his detachment, for his seat in the pressbox of life. Cause from that well-protected vantage, from that revolution-for-the-hell-of-it perspective, it matters not whether you win or lose, my friends, but how you play the game.

25

Norman stood and shivered in front of the Common on Boylston Street, stood in front of the little graveyard with the old stones. It was the worst kind of cold, the kind where the wind cut through your clothes no matter what you wore. Like the cold that came off the Lake back in Detroit. It was keeping people indoors, Norman had only a quarter to show for the whole morning of panhandling. The wind cut through his thin khaki pants, cut through the oversized Army jacket he'd boosted from the Goodwill the other day. He hadn't eaten since he swiped the oranges at Haymarket yesterday noon, the cold only made him hungrier.

A guy wandered toward him from the Boylston Station entrance, a guy in sort of un-Sunday-looking clothes and workshoes. A guy around the old man's age but not so beefy. Norman considered putting the bite on but was warned by something about the way the guy was looking at him, looking right at him. Another creepy-drawers, probably. Another old fag. It was cold and he was hungry and he just didn't need that routine again. Two already this morning, a gooser and a guy who offered him a place to sleep, who said he had a special feeling for young boys on the run. They gave him the willies and he just didn't need it right now.

So he let the guy pass though he was the first warm body to go by in ten minutes. Boston wasn't bad so far but it was a real morgue on Sundays. He should have stayed back up in the Square in Cambridge, even with all the competition. Norman had lasted a month now since he turned rabbit on the old man, had done Boston on no dollars a day, but things were getting thin. He had no idea what would happen when Christmas vacation came and the colleges closed up. It would be nice to get something to eat before he had to worry about it.

The guy in the workshoes doubled back and came toward him. It was probably no picnic to be out cruising for ass, either.

"Hey," said the guy.

"Hey."

"You just hangin out here?"

"What does it look like?"

The guy smiled. He was nervous. The nervous ones were better than the slick ones, they gave up easier. "I don't mean to bother you or nothin." The guy talked funny. Not funny like Boston, funny like the hillbillies came up to try to work at the Ford. "I'm lookin for somebody."

I'll just bet you are. Didn't know they bred fairies in the hills.

"Lookin for my boy."

"I'm not him, mister."

Again the smile. The guy pulled something out of his pocket. "I know that. This is who."

It was a picture. A kid holding somebody's hand, but the photograph had been folded back so you couldn't see who it was.

"You seen anybody looks like this around here?"

There were millions of kids hanging around Boston. With just the other rabbits he'd met in a month there could be a dozen would look like the kid in the photo, you cut their hair and cleaned up their act a little. "Nope," said Norman. "I don't think I have."

The guy looked a little disappointed. Maybe he was straight, maybe he was really looking for his kid.

"You live around here?"

And maybe not. "Yeah. Right around the corner."

"What street?"

Norman considered a couple snappy comebacks, then answered the first name that came into his head. "Dunster."

The guy shook his head. "Dunster is off Harvard Square. Up in Cambridge."

How did the shitkicker know that? Something was very fishy. "So what if it is?"

"I'm not with the police or nothin," said the guy, "so don't worry. But you run off from home, didn't you?"

Whenever somebody tells you they're not with the police, Kid Kilo always said, watch your ass. Either they're lying or they want you for some kind of monkey business. Kid Kilo was only sixteen but he'd survived on the streets for a good five years, three of them before he started dealing. He undersold most of the competition around the Square and wouldn't burn you unless you looked extra stupid. He sold mediocre grass for ten dollars a lid, coke for fifty a gram when you could get it and a hit of windowpane acid for two bucks. Advice he handed out for free.

If you're on the field, he always said, you might as well play the game. Just make sure that you set the rules.

"Yeah," said Norman. "I took off."

"How you doing?"

"Wonderful. That's why I'm out here begging small change in this weather."

The guy considered for a moment, then offered to buy Norman lunch. They could talk where it was warmer. Norman said okay.

Just play the game for a while. And maybe if he worked it right he could get fed for nothing. For nothing at all.

They went to a Burger King not too far away. It was early yet, they weren't doing much business.

"Order what you like," said the guy. "I think I can handle it."

Norman ordered a Whopper and french fries and a chocolate shake. The guy got a coffee and paid. They sat at one of the plastic booths, Norman choosing one close to the door. Their knees bumped under the table. Norman realized he'd been holding in a leak for a long time. He had been eating snow all morning to make his belly feel full and shivering and now he was nervous. That always made it worse, being nervous, and straight or not, taking food from this guy gave him the willies.

"So," said the guy, "how old are you?"

That was always one of their favorite questions, a real icebreaker. The younger you said the better they liked it.

"Fifteen," said Norman. He took a big hunk of the hamburger. He could feel it sliding all the way down his throat to his stomach, feel it press on his bladder when it got there. He took a swallow of chocolate shake to lubricate but that only added to the pressure.

"How long you been on the road?"

That was another one. When they knew how long you'd been out they could guess how hungry you'd be. How willing.

"Month or so. I done it before though. Coupla times. They sent me back."

"You don't get along with your folks?"

"Only got a father. We don't get along."

"Why?"

Why does rain fall? Why does Wiley Coyote chase the Roadrunner? Why does anything happen? It just was. Norman shrugged. "We don't have much in common, I guess. We don't see eye to eye."

"About what?" The guy seemed real interested, like it was important what went on between him and the old man.

"You name it, we don't agree on it."

"But what in particular? School? Your friends? Girlfriends?"

Sure, girlfriends. They always got around to that. Do you like the girls? they'd ask. I bet you got them falling all over you.

Good-lookin young boy like you. "Just everything. We don't like each other much."

"Did you use to? Like each other?"

You had to admit it was a pretty original line. The whole looking-for-your-kid routine, complete with the picture. A great icebreaker, you could walk up to any rabbit on a street corner and start into it. And the guy wasn't a bad actor, Norman was tempted to believe him. But a father coming all the way from the hill country to look for a kid who from the picture must be sixteen or seventeen — it was too much to swallow.

"He wasn't around. He works."

"Do you think he's worried about you?"

"He's worried about how it looks to the neighbors, he can't control his kid. Other than that he doesn't give a rat's ass."

"You sure? I mean sometimes things between parents and their — sometimes everything doesn't get said. Parents worry more than they show. And sometimes they can change about things, change their minds."

"You run into my old man," said Norman, "you can tell him that. See where it gets you."

The guy smiled his nervous smile. "You're really packin it in. You must have been pretty hungry."

Norman grunted.

"You get regular to eat you're probably a pretty stocky fella."

That bit. They always got around to how much you weighed. Just to get the subject onto bodies. The old let-me-feel-that-biceps routine. Though usually they did it through asking whether you played football or something.

"Where you from?"

"Michigan. Just outside of Detroit."

"You play sports there?"

Damn him. Norman had forced half the hamburger down and a couple gulps of milkshake but the nervous made it like he was going to bust.

"Scuse me," he said, "I gotta go to the bathroom."

"Yeah," said the guy. "I think I got some business to do myself."

It figured. But there was no backing out now. Norman hurried

[289]

and beat the guy to the men's room by a couple of steps, jumped into the one empty stall and got the door locked. If the guy wanted a look he'd have to get a stepladder.

Norman sat and relieved himself with a high sharp hiss. He couldn't help but notice the wall decorations. *If you have nine inches*, they said, *you're my kind of man*. HAVE BUNS WILL TRAVEL. *I suck black cock. If you are young and hung meet me here Thursday, 11:30 a.m.* GIRLS ARE DIRTY. *4 B.J.* try BPL *mns rm, sat. eve*. And, in red marker just under the coat hook on the stall door, DEATH TO FAGGITS.

The guy was pissing in a urinal just a few feet away. It seemed to take forever, it sounded like a garden hose spraying into a trash can, loud and echoing. If you think I'm impressed, pal, you got another thing coming. Norman waited him out, waited till the heavy workshoes clomped past and the door swung shut.

There are two ways you can play it with the fruits, Kid Kilo would always say. Muscle or hustle. You're big and bad enough you can play them along and get them alone and pow! There's a couple dudes around making a living from fag-bagging but you don't last long. The word gets around and the fruits protect their own. And of course then there's hustle. A lot more dudes make ends meet, if you'll pardon the pun, by doin what comes unnaturally.

Norman was tired. He was still hungry and still cold and he sat and remembered the one time he had tried it. Thumbing around the Lakes in a storm, colder and hungrier than he was now, thinking what the hell, a mouth was a mouth. Closing his eyes. And then losing it, pummeling and yelling let me out, let me out at the first scratch of beard on his tender parts. The memory made him piss some more.

Norman cracked the men's room door and peeked out. The guy was sitting there. The rest of the Whopper and the french fries and the shake were sitting there. The guy was playing with a bill, Norman strained to see. A ten-dollar bill.

Somebody cops your joint, Kid Kilo would always say, it's ten bills. The Kid could quote you the going rate on anything.

Sure Mister, looking for your boy. Just want to buy a poor rabbit some lunch. Sure.

Norman eased out of the men's room and slipped behind the

[290]

counter, into the kitchen. It was slim pickings outside, but he wasn't that hungry yet. He didn't think he'd ever be that hungry again. He'd have to spend his quarter to get back up to the Square. The kids in their hairnets and paper hats stared as Norman rushed out through the sizzling meat to the back door.

26

Hunter had to get up at five in the morning and call a cab to take him back to Mrs. Hanrahan's to wait for Jimmy Kearney to pick him up for the Vermont trip. Jimmy lived only a block and a half from Helen's, but neither she nor Hunter was ready for it to be out in public about them. Not yet. Helen had left the girls at their Aunt Agnes's overnight, telling them she had to work an extra shift at the company.

Helen got up with him though he'd told her she shouldn't bother, that she needed her sleep. They both had wrinkle marks on their faces from the bedding and looked just awful. Helen put the second pillow back in the linen closet.

"They're pretty shop, my girls," she said. "Never know what they're gonna catch on to."

Helen put on a flannel nightgown but he could still feel the warmth coming off of her, still smell her when she was close. She smelled a little like him, like them, but that was all right too.

Helen checked through the bedroom and bathroom to make sure he didn't leave any traces behind.

"The girls and Francis and Jimmy and all the rest will know soon enough," she said. "If there's any need for them to. And if things work out that they *don't* ever need to, well there's no hom done is there?" Helen was a very practical woman. "The only one who suspects, I think, is Aunt Agnes. But then Quinn *was* her favorite nephew. She suspected something on our wedding day."

Helen made sandwiches for the trip though he'd told her not to bother. She made a very professional-looking sandwich, cutting the bread diagonally in half and wrapping neater than he'd ever seen someone wrap.

"I used to make lunch for the brothers and sisters for school," she said. "There were nine of us and that was my permanent job. One time Francis got tired of sterilizing the baby bottles every night so we switched. Nobody would eat his sandwiches, we had to go back to the old way. I was the oldest girl, so I had to be a bit of a mother."

Hunter led her back to the bedroom and she slipped under the covers. He knelt by the side of the bed and they touched and rested together till the cab honked outside. Hunter said good-bye and that he would call when he got back. She wished him luck with Darwin. Hunter hurried out to the cab thinking how nice it was to have someone to say good-bye to, someone to miss.

It was very dark out and the streets were deserted. The cab-driver looked tired, like he'd put in a long night. It was surprisingly warm.

Hunter crept as quiet as he could past Mrs. Hanrahan's door. He was sure she was aware of the two times he hadn't come home all night and he didn't want to start her ugly little dog yapping so she'd have an excuse to bring the matter up. The carpet on the stairs smelled like dog pee and old men. He had lived in a boarding house once before, right when he came back from the Army, but it was nothing like this. Lucille Wilcox's grandmother had run it and she was a nice old woman in her eighties who was used to miners and cared only that you were quiet and a union member.

Hunter used the shower in the bathroom, not accustomed to having it to himself for so long. Usually if you took your time the old men would all turn on the water in the sinks in their rooms and your shower would go freezing. Hunter changed his clothes and waited on the front steps.

Jimmy pulled up in his Rambler with Francis X. They asked if he had gotten a good sleep. The backseat was full of gear, Hunter had to shift it around to make himself a space. They were only going up for the day, but there were backpacks, canteens, binoculars, rifles mounted on a rack and on the floor, Swiss Army knives, ponchos, a tube of Indian Guide Buck Lure, heavy combat boots, an ice chest full of beer and a battery-operated chain saw.

"That's for field-dressing our buck when we take im," said Francis X.

Francis was wearing at least three layers of thermal cotton and down-filled nylon. His only concession to the warm morning and the car heater being on was to leave his boots off.

"You have pretty good luck usually?"

"Well," said Jimmy, "we have good luck *see*ing the fuckers. I mean they're up there, no question about that. And we get a piece of one every once in a while, don't we Francis? But as far as actually bringin one down —"

"It isn't whether you scaw or not," said Francis, "it's the spawt of the thing. The great outdaws."

"But we have gotten our licks in."

"You've wounded ones that you haven't taken?"

"Oh sure. Coupla times. At least we're pretty sure we did. I mean you know how it is with shooting, you line up a nice one and let it rip and you just *know* you got a piece, even if the fucker don't fall down or bleed or nothin. And they run away so fast you don't get a chance to see where it was you got em."

"And there's always the chance it was somethin wrong with the bullet. Some of em got imperfections, they got machined wrong at the plant and they don't fly true."

"Yuh."

"But this time, Hunter, I got a feelin, there's a buck out there with our names on it."

"See, we go halvesies, Jimmy and me. Only Jimmy has the big-game license, that's why we pack the Marlin .22 there, we run into a game wodden he'll believe I'm just out for rabbit. But we can both go for the deer when nobody's around."

"I got a feelin, pottner, this is gonna be the one. I'll bet them deers are just hanging around shakin in their tracks, they sense that we're comin for em."

"I'll bet," said Hunter.

"I remember the last time you had a feelin. That time we blew the leg right off the buck."

"And you didn't take him?"

"Strange as it may seem, Hunter, we didn't. We were comin around a bend in this little path, middle a the fuckin forest, and we just about bump heads with this old buck. Thing must of been so old it was deaf, walk right into us like that. So many points I couldn't count em, and besides everything happened too fast to take a survey. Francis ups with his Remington-pump and he would of nailed him right in the old snot-locker, only we're in these thick woods and the barrel snags on a branch and the fucker goes off halfway up. It blows the old buck's front leg off right at the knee. Shears it right off.

"The blood is like steam coming out and that buck he goes crashin through the trees on three legs like it's nothin. I'll tell you, we had brought that sumbitch in you couldn't of eaten him, he'd of been like leather all the way through. *Tough*. We were so stottled, Francis an me, we didn't know what the fuck to do. It's gettin dock, right, we were heading back to the car, we gotta get on our way home. We're in the woods so it's docker still. We can't hodly see the blood on the snow or the branches where he's tore through em. But we figure how far can he get on three legs, right? So we stot off after him, whack him out for keeps. Francis picks up the leg, it's still wom, and off we go.

"Branches snappin in our face, snow all deep, it's coldern a sumbitch out there and we can hodly see. The flashlight's in the car, naturally. We followed a good quattah mile and still we didn't find the thing. You magine that? Run that far with a leg shot off at the knee?"

"So what happened?"

"What happened? We went home. It was too dock."

"You left him out there?"

"Oh, he bled to death soon enough. And the poachers, the woods are full of poachers at night up there, they must have got him after we left. Save em a bullet."

"I was thinkin of having the leg mounted," said Francis X., "but I figured it would look too funny."

"So actually we *do* have a deer to our credit. We just didn't get to eat him."

"I'll be sure to invite you to dine with us, Hunter, if Jimmy's notion here pans out. I hear venison is a real treat."

"It's not bad," said Hunter.

"It's a date then. And I'll see if my sister is available. She's prawbly never had any either."

Hunter was silent.

"You're so damn subtle, Francis." Jimmy shook his head at the wheel. "It's just like going through the woods with you, like there's a brass band motchin ahead saying here comes Francis X. Coughlin loaded for bear."

"Well can it hurt to help something along? There's a lot of fires that went out cause they weren't tended prawperly."

They talked as if Hunter wasn't there. "You haven't seen the spock," said Jimmy, "and you're throwin on the heavy logs. These things take time."

"She's been widowed five years, how much time does she need?"

"Hasn't seen the first puff a smoke," said Jimmy, "and the man calls in the fire depottment."

Jimmy and Francis X. each had a beer for breakfast then and they continued up Interstate 93 to Manchester. The sun rose and it was a warm, clear morning. Hunter took over driving and the other two dozed off for a while.

Hunter rubbed his beard stubble with the back of his hand. He would have to start razor-shaving it before he saw Helen. It irritated her face, left the skin red and scraped-looking. Hunter had been using an electric for years, a straight-razor shaved too close and left his face sensitive to all the sweat and coal dust on the continuous miner, he was always breaking out with pimples or rashes. The cold at Porchetta wouldn't be too bad for it though.

Forty-five years old and worried about his complexion.

"Well, here it is," said Helen when she came out of the bathroom undressed the first time. It's not much but I call it home."

"It's nice." He was sitting on the edge of her bed with his shirt and shoes off.

"Thank you. At first look it's so-so, but it grows on you."

"You must of been real pretty when you were a girl. I mean, not that you're not —"

"I know what you mean." She smiled. "I wasn't though. I was a notch below plain. I'm a hell of a lot better looking forty-year-old than I was a twenty-year-old. A lot of the competition had faded and I hung in there. My mother used to give me that whole ugly-duckling-into-a-beautiful-swan story. She never told me I'd have to wait till I was older than she was for it to stot coming true." She sat down next to him just like she had clothes on. "I think I'm going to be embarrassed," she said, "if you don't hurry and take your pants off."

Her breasts hung down loose but were smooth and full around the nipples, there were stretch marks on the sides of them, and on her middle from having the girls. She had a little roll and those lumpy fat-things on her bottom, which was big and firm. The skin on her face was coarse, dry like she had spent a lot of time out in the sun, though she hadn't. She was strong all over though and he liked to feel her muscles tense when she was excited. Liked the way her neck muscles stood out from her breastbone when she arched and bucked and the way all of her seemed to concentrate wherever he was touching her with his hands or his lips, as if she could put all of her mind and her self into a breast or a palmful of skin, liked the way her lips swolled up thick and took on a deeper color, the way little strands of hair stuck to the sweat beading her forehead and neck and the way she clutched onto his back and shoulders and looked right at him to tell with her eyes what she was feeling. He liked the way she held his cock inside her, tight and wet-warm, how she hugged and wrung it in her, the blood and muscle-tension lighting her face till it was beautiful like a statue face, frozen in some emotion, all her muscles standing out taut in her flesh till it broke and ran down through her to collect between her legs for the strong sweet milking. When they made love everything seemed tighter on her, skin, muscle, everything. Seemed younger. And knowing that all that was there, that she could be like that for him, made him see her different all the time. He couldn't notice her breasts or her bottom or her lips even when she was dressed and made-up without thinking of how they were in bed, without being a little excited just to be around her.

"No need for that," she had said the first time, when he pulled the foil-wrapped rubber from his pocket. "I'm all set."

"You on the Pill?"

"Never tried it. Never used one of *them*, either. Quinn had a prejudice against those things, said they ruined your performance."

"They're no picnic."

"Right. The thing is, I was a good Catholic wife."

"So?"

"So, I had Michelle and Donna within eleven months and had another on the way against doctor's orders when complications set in. I lost it and had to have a hysterectomy."

"That's too bad."

She shrugged and smiled at him and lay back on the bed. "Took the crib and left the playpen," she said. "It's easier this way."

What he liked best was waking at night and finding her next to him. Warm. It was the most seductive thing about her, the way she made it warm all around her, made it so easy to go back to sleep. Hunter remembered the time he and Dar were out scaring up rabbit for the table and they found the hibernating bears. An adult and two cubs curled in a little root-cave in one of the back hollers. At first you could only see a big mass of bearflesh, moving ever so slightly in breath-rhythm, and then you could make out the parts of the three separate animals. But the most striking thing was the smell and the heat that came off the bears together, one a part of the other like woodsmoke, a gamey mammal heat like a small furnace in the cave. It was dead of winter, bitter cold, and there was the slight urge to crawl in and join them, to surrender to bear-sleep. Helen had that kind of warmth and lure to her in bed, it made it hard to leave her early in the morning.

Sarah woke in the dark and couldn't force herself to sleep. Everyone else was out cold, wasted from the arguing at the marathon group meetings the last two nights. Arguing over the high-school action. The confrontations, the accusations. Some of the members seemed to thrive on it. Schenk, Miriam, Wein, Mark when he was winning. Mark had slept restless all night, he had walked himself over into the corner, his back flat to the wall. She had tried to comfort him but he wouldn't stay put.

Sarah lay holding her stomach for a while then crawled off the mattress and onto her feet. She pulled on a sweater of Mark's, the one she'd given him way back in college, and padded out of their little room.

There were members scattered all over the floor in the hallway. Darkness was their only privacy, Sarah waited a bit for her eyes to adjust before she picked her way through them.

Tracy Anne lay curled next to Billy under a sleeping bag. She was a mouth breather, making little noises with the knuckle of her thumb held in her lips. Sarah knelt to see better. Trace had a fine fuzzy down of blond on her cheek and neck, Sarah wanted to stroke it, to tell her how nice she was relaxed like this. Not so hyper like she was awake, so hungry. Sarah rose and moved on.

Smallwood slept flat on his back on the bare floor. He looked lost with his glasses off, squinting even in his sleep. He looked like somebody's little boy.

Sarah walked through them as quiet as possible, Joel and Rit and Jennifer and Mickey Q. and Debbie Ellenbogen, through all of them. Sprawlers and cuddlers, pillow huggers, moaners and snorers. She took her time and tried not to disturb them.

She had done a children's theater tour once, playing Wendy in *Peter Pan*. It was an uncomfortable role, an uncomfortable tour. Most all of the men were gay including the boy playing Peter, who had developed some inexplicable hatred for her. The bunch of them made her feel like a nasty den mother. And at the end of the play, when she was supposed to have broken her vow to Peter and gone ahead and grown up, she always felt the strongest sense of betrayal, felt the resentment coming up from the audience and cast. All the little boys surrounding her, accusing her. It was one of the reasons she'd given up on theater, taking everything personally like that.

Sarah came to the hall's dead end. Schenk's room. He had hung a blanket across the door, had moved his books and even a little furniture in, had made it clear that no one else was invited to share all the space. Nobody had said a word, not in group or out of it. The fact was accepted, like the roaches that had taken up residence in the kitchen. A thick gray blanket, nailed to the top of the doorsill.

She turned down the stairs, itching under her arms a little. Mark's sweater was starting to chafe on her. Only King and Hobie McNatt had set up on the second floor. Hobie was in with the printing press and King was on the mats in the martial-arts room. King always smelled slightly of sweat. The ground floor was left empty and only Monk racked in the basement, though she'd never actually seen him sleeping. He just went down there every night. Monk gave her the creeps a little.

Miriam was already up for work and in the kitchen when Sarah got there. She was sitting at the table in her leather jacket with her head held in her hands.

"You look awful," said Sarah. She didn't know why she said it, she usually didn't feel very comfortable with Miriam, and almost never comfortable enough to joke. But Miriam really did look awful.

"Thanks," said Miriam. "So do you."

Sarah sat across the table from her. "I couldn't sleep."

"You worried about something?"

"The action." It was true. She had started worrying about the high-school thing when it was first suggested and it hadn't been off her mind since.

Miriam gave a short laugh. "You're not even going on it."

"I might be less worried if I did."

Miriam put her head back in her hands.

"Would you like some cocoa?"

Miriam peeked over her fingers. "I don't need a mother."

"You're not getting one." Sarah crossed to get milk. "I thought you might like some. I'm making some for myself."

Miriam squeezed in on her temples. "I'm sorry," she said. "I'd like a cup, thanks. I feel like shit in the morning."

Sarah measured out two servings of milk into the pot. "You don't sleep?"

"Naw. I sleep fine. It's the job."

"I thought you liked it there."

Miriam grunted. "I hate punching in." Her voice almost broke, like it was hard to get the words out. "I hate the work. I hate always coming in as an outsider, never being totally trusted by the people. I wake up every weekday sick to my stomach."

Sarah wished that Miriam could be her friend. She was the only woman near her age in the group, she had been in the Movement since the Freedom Rider days. Longer, she was born into the Movement. Sarah had tried to approach her before, tried

[299]

several times to make the bond, but no dice. Miriam wasn't interested. Sarah wished she could rub her back or play with her hair or something to make her feel better, to make the stitching factory easier to face. "You could ask for work in another area."

Miriam shrugged, stood to get the box of Hershey's from the pantry. "You do what you have to. You do what you can. I can organize factories."

Sarah nodded. "And I can make cocoa."

Miriam smiled to her then, cracked her morning face into a laugh and Sarah felt a little less scared.

"I seen where they been having a little contest in your old outfit," said Jimmy.

"Huh?"

"The Mineworkers. I read about the election, it was in the papers, what, Wednesday morning. That guy Yablonski poppin off."

"Mmn."

"I mean hey, you lose an election, it's not really even close, you concede. You don't go on with this sour grapes, this vote fraud stuff. I mean what good is that gonna do for the miners?"

"There might be somethin to it."

"You mean Boyle cheating? Well, hey, it's a tough racket. Look at Hoffa, he's in the joint, look at what's his name, Auto Workers, got his om blown off. You got to be tough."

"Maybe."

"Were you involved in the politics there? Before you come up?"

"No. Not really."

"I mean I'm not sayin I know all about it, I just read the papers, it's this guy Yablonski bellyachin about the election, says something stinks. Which reminds me, Francis, you bring that odor stuff? That deer musk?"

"Yeah, it's back there somewheres."

"We got to remember to put it on. Last time we forgot, the deers prawbly smelled us and run off."

"Yeah, they thought they were movin the Schlitz brewery to Vermont."

"Speak for yourself."

"I never understood the whole thing, Jimmy. It's supposed to be like a doe in heat, right?"

" 'Hides human scent,' " Jimmy read off the tube, " 'stops big bucks in their tracks and brings them kissing close.' Sounds like you're all set if you don't get caught with your pants down."

"But the mating season's not in winter is it?"

"They don't know that. They're dumb animals, Francis, dumb hawny animals. Guys've come on em humpin holes in deadfall trees. Hey, you know how it is, you get the urge and there's nothin loose around. Any old pawt in a stawm."

"Yeah, you leave your rifle on the rack too long and it gets rusty. I know just how they feel, them bucks. Just how they feel."

Jimmy took the wheel back as they started across New Hampshire on 89 and Hunter stretched out in the back. He closed his eyes and tried to rest his head and thought about what he'd do if Hobie wasn't up there too, if it was just Darwin. The chances were that it would be just him. It made him nervous to think about it.

"It means a lot to you, doesn't it?" Helen had said. "Come all this way on an outside chance of finding him."

"You have to do what you can. Even if it looks like there isn't much hope." The words sounded right but Hunter wasn't so sure how much he still believed them. He had always acted that way, with Molly being sick, in the mine, in the war, and it seemed the only right way to be. But up here — things got complicated. Fuzzy. You didn't know exactly where to aim yourself.

"What's he like?"

"Which?"

"The one you want. Hobie."

Hunter thought on that a moment. "I don't know enough to answer that," he said, "and be sure I'm right. I thought I known him as well as I could, but now — it's the same way with Dar. There was the war with him though, I have that to explain why he turned out to be different than I thought. With Hobie, he just run off and I'm left wondering if I ever knew the first thing about him. I just remember things from when he was little and try to piece something together."

[301]

"Like what? What kind of things?" They were lying in bed in the dark, side to side, talking quiet.

"He used to run all the time, Hobie did. You'd be walkin with him somewheres and he just tear off runnin ahead of you and then run back by your side. Like it was something inside him he had to get out. Like a rabbit he was, scootin around, he run before he could really walk. He wasn't a nervous kid or nothin, in fact when he's runnin he'd get this calm look on his face and go so smooth you'd hardly notice how fast he was moving. Wasn't anybody around could beat him in a footrace by the time he was twelve. I used to watch him and just wonder at it. It was nothin I could ever do when I was young, run fast, but I couldn't help but feel watching him that there must be some part of me that always wanted to, that I passed it on to him. I mean I know about genes and all but that's how I *felt* about it. Let him outside and he just run."

"That's the way I felt about Michelle, my oldest, when she used to make up stories," said Helen. "She'd be playing by herself or in a bubble bath or something and she'd tell herself stories, out loud. A lot of dragons and princesses and things like in kids' books, but just regular people too, her friends and relatives and all. I wish I'd written some of them down, they were so good. She had such an imagination. That's something I never did, I mean I'd daydream things but I'd never put them together into stories. But I know I always wanted to and wished I could."

"She doesn't do it anymore?"

"Well, the age she is now, she's so self-conscious about everything. They have to write a few stories in class, but one of the ones she wrote got her in trouble with the sisters, so she doesn't like it anymore."

"That's too bad."

"You grow up. Hobie prawbly didn't run so much when he got older, did he?"

"For sports he did. But no, not so much for the hell of it anymore."

"That's when the trouble stots," said Helen. "That's when it gets tough to figure them out. When they stot getting like us."

"Darwin was the one always wanted to be like me. Dar was always on my heels, wanted to go down under to work with me, always holdin the hammer or luggin the paint bucket when I did things around the house. I think part of the reason he went into the Army like he done was cause I'd been during the war. But you can't do things over the same like that. Kids can't live their parents' lives over."

"I hope not," said Helen. "God, I hope not."

They crossed the Connecticut River into Vermont and followed alongside it a ways northward. The day was starting to cloud just the slightest bit but it was getting even warmer. Jimmy turned off the exit and brought Hunter the three miles into Orford Center.

"Good hunting," he told them when they dropped him in the center of town.

"Same to you," said Jimmy. "We'll pick you up here around eight, eight-thirty. Hope you'll have another passenger for us."

"Yeah. Thanks."

There was a hardware store that looked open and Hunter went in to check out the address Mulcahy had gotten from the unemployment people. The man by the register squinted at the slip of paper.

"What you want with them?"

"Visit somebody."

"You know Fazzone?"

"Nope. Somebody stayin with him, I guess."

"It's about three miles further north, just over the river and up a mountain a ways."

Hunter asked for directions and while the man was drawing a map another man, a customer, came up to say he'd heard a friend of his was going to be driving up there. They called him on the phone.

"Mason Hadwick," he said when he pulled up in his Ford pickup.

"Hunter McNatt."

"You're welcome to come along," he said, "you don't mind a few stops on the way."

"That's fine."

It turned out that Mason worked for the people on the moun-

[303]

tain where Dar was supposed to be. They were from New Jersey and ran a construction outfit and the pickup belonged to the company. But Mason got to drive it to and from work cause he was a foreman, got to use it on weekends. In payment he had to do hauling jobs whenever they called him, which was why he was going up today. He was a thick-built man with knuckles like pine knots and a gray bristle on his face. He never said anything but what it was a grumble.

"I don't ask questions," he said. "I just *do*. They tell me come up, I come up. They tell me to build one way, that's the way I build. It's their money. It's their truck. Got no union up here, just them and you. You ask questions it only makes things wuss. What do you want up there?"

"My boy is spose to be up there."

"What's he called?"

"Darwin."

"Never hud of him."

"He's kind of medium height but real solid, dark, don't talk much —"

"He in the war?"

"Huh?"

"Vietnam. Was he there?"

"Yuh. He was in the Army —"

"You'll find im then. Call him Pfc."

"You know him?"

"He tried the job once. Lasted two days, couldn't take awders."

"Sounds like it could be him, all right."

They stopped at a drugstore where a lot of young kids were hanging out. Mason went in and came back with a young boy who he introduced as Enoch. Enoch jumped into the rear and they headed out of town.

"He yours?"

"Nope. They said to bring im. Didn't say why. He wucks at the job. Snake crew. Nice boy, nothin wrong with him a few more points of IQ wouldn't fix."

"Huh?"

"Slow. Not quite an idjit or crazy, just slow."

They drove on blacktop for a while, crossed the river and

began to climb, then turned off on a newly plowed dirt road still rutted with Caterpillar tracks. They came to a bulldozed clearing in the woods where two clusters of condominiums squatted on the frozen mud. One cluster was the kind with roofs that came nearly to the ground and the other was supposed to look like old English or something, all tan with dark brown trimming. They were putting up some of the same kind along the road to Charleston.

"Won't take a minute," said Mason Hardwick, getting out of the pickup. "Just give it a check."

He walked around looking over the heavy equipment, testing the locks on the trailer and the Sani-Port, tightening a tarpaulin thrown over a stack of two-by-fours. He picked something up and brought it to the truck. It was a sign. MASHAPAUG PARK, it said, A NEW CONCEPT IN LIVING. It was riddled with holes, especially around and in the o in CONCEPT. Somebody had been taking BB practice.

"Vandals," said Mason and tossed it in the back with Enoch.

The road began to climb steeply, it was potholed and shoulderless. The day was still warm but getting overcast.

"Boy name Jackie owns the house," said Mason, nodding up the mountain. "He's our head fawman. His uncle is in chodge of the site and his father owns it. Least that's the story they tell."

"You don't believe it?"

"Don't matter one way or the other. Money's just as green. There is a story though, that suttin gentlemen down in Providence are behind it. Italian gentlemen. It's only a story though, some believe it, some don't."

"You mean like the Mafia?"

"We get up there, you'll meet em. Draw your own conclusions."

"How is it workin for them?"

"Best pay around this area. Pert near the only pay around."

"You like the building?"

"You saw it. No building to it. Assembling, that's all. All the wood comes in even lengths, everything standard. If you have to cut a bawd most likely someone's made a mistake."

"But you like the carpentry part?"

"Spent this week inside with an ax and stepladder. Got exposed beams inside, I've got to chew em up so's they look authentic, then restain. One of Jackie's ideas."

"You had to do that?"

"Jackie said. You say no, he goes to Condo."

"Condo?"

"His uncle. The boss-man. They call him that cause of condominiums and cause of this Westun movie. *Hondo*. John Wayne. He wears a gun and holster at the job."

Hobie turned down Marginal Street in East Boston, hunting for signatures. It was the same old antiwar petition they'd been pushing since he'd come to Third Way, and it was clear that Schenk would soon have the votes to phase out petitioning as a tactic. It was a miserable cold day, the wind whipping off the harbor to cut through his thin Army jacket and do numbers up and down his spine. But Remington was into the project still and Sarah had personally asked Hobie to cover this area. People in East Boston didn't seem too interested. It was mostly older people who spoke only Italian, home in the middle of the day, or young men out of work hanging around their little tube-and-pool-table social clubs.

He passed a tall old brick building, tall for East Boston anyway, that had HOME FOR IMMIGRANTS carved on its cornice. Must have been a clearing house for people just off the boat. The harbor was directly to the right of Hobie as he walked down the street, Pier Number One stretching out into the water. He paused to look at the unloading ships. There was a huge one being worked on, the *African Neptune*, under a Liberian flag. Hobie had been into ships once when he was a kid, right after his dinosaur period. He had read *Treasure Island* and *Two Years Before the Mast* and *Typhoon* and the Classic Comic Book version of *Moby Dick* and had read everything he could find about Jack London.

He could take off. He could hit the road. He was nervous about tonight, about the game. It was still possible for him to just split, the possibility was endless. Hitch to the West Coast or down south, up to Canada maybe, all kinds of places he'd never seen, never dreamed he'd be able to see when he was back home.

It would be getting pretty bare on the hills now. Piles of dead slippery leaves for the little kids to chute down on, branches clawing up naked at the sky. Plenty of deer and rabbit to shoot if you were into that. It would be basketball season.

The game. Tonight.

A huge crane swung boxcar-sized containers off the deck of the ship to the pier. King had explained to him how it had become cheaper for the shipping lines to containerize everything, how once the Longshoremen got a strong union together they priced a good third or more of their membership out of work. Explained how horny and dumb the sailors who came ashore seemed to be, what a drag the life sounded like. Hobie continued down Marginal.

He had covered over half of East Boston with only twelve signatures to show for it, and eight of those were from the Lefties in the *Community News* office. Hobie came to the end of the street, a blockade at the entrance to the Bethlehem Steel shipworks. A high Page fence with curls of barbed wire at the top, a little turret with a uniformed guard overlooking the gate.

He could split. Dar had done it. Plenty of people had done it.

Hobie turned back, trying to remember where the T station was. A bad smell came up from the old wooden piers that lay beside the new cement one, a rotting. Hobie headed back to Third Way.

They heard gunfire. Hunter picked out three separate sounds. There was a solid, deep sniping, single shots well spaced, of a big-game rifle. There was a high cracking like from a handgun and then, drowning them both, a flat burst Hunter had heard nothing like since the war.

They came on the house from the side. It was a Swiss-style A-frame, stained dark, with a deck on stilts downslope. Hunter could make out three figures crouched at the deck railing. Down the hill from them maybe seventy yards was an old Chevy Impala propped on cinder blocks, a buff and white four-door with big manta-ray fins. What was left of it. The side that faced the A-frame looked like a hunk of meat someone had chewed and spit out and as the rounds kept coming the metal puckered and popped. Mason honked three times and braked out of range. The firing stopped and he drove up next to the deck, parking behind a lime-green Porsche.

They got out and were below the deck when the handgun opened up again. Slivers of metal jumped above and below the front vent window of the car as the bullets whanged in, it was the only solid piece of glass left on it.

"Condo!" somebody yelled from above. The last two shots missed everything.

"Condo! *Con*do! Fastest draw and worst fuckin shot in the East!"

"It's not a fuckin sniperscope," said another, deeper voice.

"Condo, I scoff on your shooting Condo."

"It's made to stop people, not pick fuckin monkeys out of trees."

"Tell me about it."

"Stopping is what counts," said the deeper voice. "It's a defensive weapon."

"Condo the stopper."

"Smart-ass kid."

Mason put his foot on the first step and cleared his throat loudly.

"C'mon up, Mase," said the first voice. "We're reloading."

The voice belonged to a boy in his middle twenties wearing a big sloppy grin and holding his eyelids half shut. He had a headful of curly black hair and held a beautiful light-finished rifle. A man with silver, razor-cut hair and yellow-tinted sunglasses sat next to him on a canvas lawn chair. He was holding a glass of liquor between his knees and feeding shells into a big black revolver. Both men were wearing blaze-orange hunting vests. Behind them, sitting against the wall with what looked like an M-16 across his lap, was Darwin.

Dar was even thinner than when he first came home from the Army. His chest looked like it had gone hollow and you could see the bones in his face. He had grown even more hair and a mean-looking long black mustache, like Fu Manchu's in the old movies. He gave a slight, silent nod when he saw Hunter.

"Heyya, Mase, what's shakin?" said the boy, Jackie. "How they hangin?"

"Said to bring the pickup. I did."

"S'what I like about you, Mase, you're such a live wire. And what we got here?" he said, turning to Enoch. "Looks like a wiftoe to me. Wiftoe, how's it goin Wiftoe?"

The boy blushed and smiled a little at the nickname. Jackie gave him a poke in the belly with the rifle barrel.

"And who's your other friend?"

Mason pointed to Darwin. "His father."

Jackie grinned even wider. "No shit! Pfc.'s old man, outasight! Didn't know you had one, buddy, I thought you were hatched. Like a lizard."

Darwin's expression didn't change. He looked like he had been awake for days and was too tired to speak.

"Well, well, well," said Jackie. "Pfc. Senior, my name's Jackie and this here's my uncle Paul Fazzone, better known as Condo."

The man looked up from his gun and nodded. Hunter said hello.

"And you know m'man Wiftoe, dontcha? One of our native Va-maun-tahs. On the snake crew?"

"Right," said Condo. "Hi kid."

"Beautiful. A regular family reunion. Look at these two, willya? Just like *This Is Your Life*, they rush into each other's arms and start chewin over old times."

Hunter crossed the deck and sat down next to Darwin, who was fiddling with his rifle. Mason and Enoch stayed on the top step. Hunter didn't know what he could say in front of all of them.

Jackie bolted a cartridge into the chamber and shouldered his rifle. He sighted down at the car through the mounted scope. There was a solid report, Jackie's upper body kicking back slightly, and the vent window was gone. Glass, frame, everything.

"Wow," said Enoch.

Jackie kicked the empty off the deck. "How's that grab you Condo?"

"Use a fuckin missile-launcher what do you expect? It's an offensive weapon."

"Binnnnng!" called Jackie to no one in particular. "Liner up and BINNNG! Blower away!"

"Like to see how you'd do if that heap was coming at you sixty per with some maniac behind the wheel," growled Condo. "See how you do if you gotta stop something quick."

"That car never did sixty in its life. Am I right Mase?"

Mason didn't say anything.

Jackie laughed. "We been getting a lot of mileage out of her buddy, moren you ever did. Mase here is the former owner of that shit-on-wheels out there. Couldn't hack the payments, wasn't it Mase?"

"Insurance," said Mason.

Condo stood holding the revolver then, steadying his wrist with his other hand, and opened up trying to hit the rabbit's foot that hung down from the windshield frame. Hunter used the noise as cover to talk.

"How you doin, son?"

"All right." Darwin didn't look up from the M-16. "Why'd you come here?"

"Hobie's run off."

"Yeah?" Still he didn't look up. "Where to?"

"I thought maybe he'd come here."

"He hasn't."

"You haven't heard from him?"

"Nope. You two have a fight?"

"No. Nothin like that. Nothin like — you know — like you and me."

Darwin considered that for a moment. "He just run off?"

"Left a note one day about a month ago. Said he had to, couldn't stay at home no more. I don't know why. I quit at the mine and come up to Boston to look for him, there's been a couple people seen him there. He was lookin for you."

"He's always been the runner in the family," said Darwin, "he'll make out." Darwin met his eyes then, and shook his head slightly. "You should have stayed home."

"I thought he'd be here."

Darwin shrugged. "Sorry you wasted a trip."

The shooting ended.

"Condo! *Con*do! They ever put me against the fuckin wall I want you for my firing squad. You couldn't shoot your thumb off if it was tied to the muzzle."

"It's a defensive weapon."

"A little more practice and a little less bourbon is what you need, Condo. Speakin of which, I forgot to offer you a beer, Mase. We got Heineken's. You want?"

"Nope."

"Pfc. Senior?"

"No thanks," said Hunter.

"What about you, Wiftoe? Have a brew?"

"Sure."

Jackie pointed his rifle to a cooler at the top of the steps with bottles floating in half-melted ice.

"He old enough to drink?"

"I should hope so Condo, I should hope so. Nothin else to do in this fuckin state, at least they can let a kid drink in peace."

"Whatter you, Wiftoe, sixteen, seventeen?"

The boy hesitated a moment. "Seventeen."

"What's that, senior at high school?"

"Tenth grade."

"That right?"

"They left me back."

"Wiftoe, you're kiddin me Wiftoe. Bright kid like you? Piss on it, buddy, they must be crazy. Have a brew."

"Fuckin world comin to," Condo griped, "kid can't shave yet, he's drinkin."

"We're gettin wrecked, buddy, *wrecked!* W-R-E-C-K-E-D! You like to get wrecked Wiftoe?"

The boy blushed and pulled out a beer. He wiped his hand dry.

"That's what I like about m'man Wiftoe, brilliant fuckin conversationalist. Just like Mase must of been at the age, hey Mase?"

"Leave the boy be," said Mason.

"Seventeen, huh?" said Jackie like he hadn't heard. "Seventeen. Pfc., how old was that kid you said you wasted?"

"Thirteen," said Darwin. "Maybe fourteen. It's hard to tell with them."

As if it was nothing. As if it happened every day.

"Over there you're seventeen, you're a man already. You're eligible to get wasted by fuckin animals like Pfc." He raised his hand before Hunter could speak. "No offense, sir, but your son had informed us of his Army experiences. He tells us war stories before we go to bed, that's how he earns his keep around here. Aint that right, Pfc.?"

"Yeah, Jackie. That's right." Darwin went back into his rifle workings.

"How many people you kill over there?"

"Didn't count."

"Didn't count! Is that great? Comes back such a mindfuck he can't remember. Fuckin space cowboy. Ever meet a killer before, Wiftoe? M'man Pfc.! *P — F — Ceeee!* World's champeen monkey-plunker!"

Hunter didn't know what he could say or do. It was Darwin's friends, Darwin's life, and Darwin was just sitting there.

"He looks familiar," said Condo. He was staring at Enoch. "He looks like somebody else."

"What, who, Wiftoe? He ought to, he's a chip off the old block, aint you Wiftoe? His old man in on the crew. His faw-thah."

"Whozat?"

"Parker Fenway?"

"Oh yeah, the whatthefuck, carpenter." Condo was plastered to his deck chair looking like he had just swallowed something acid and was trying to hawk it up.

"Cop-in-tah. This here is the *boss*, Wiftoe, this here is Condo himself. *Con*do!"

"I thought you were boss," said the boy.

"Oh no. Just head foreman. This here is the honcho, this here is *Con*do, King of the Condominiums. The Wizard of Mashapaug Park. Thout him your father and the rest of you people round here would be back sucking sap from the trees come autumn. That right, Mase?"

Mason was sitting on the deck by the stairs. "Not much doing around here. But people suhvived before you came, they'll suhvive when you're gone."

"You're survivin pretty fuckin good on the wages we brought in, buddy."

Darwin slid out and hung his legs over the edge of the deck. Enoch fished for another beer.

"Wasn't for us you'd be up Shit Mountain without a backpack. That right, Condo?"

[312]

"Give it a rest, Jackie." Condo dipped a few solid cubes from the cooler and plunked them in the glass at his feet. He was groping for the bottle of bourbon under his chair when Dar let go with a burst from the M-16. The handle on the front door of the Impala jumped into the air. Ice cubes slid across the deck.

"Fuckin lunatic." Condo bent and tried to zero in on a cube, his face flowing red with the effort. "Fuckin GI Joe. Comes back, goes on the roll, buys a fuckin hot Gatling gun and brings it home. Must of abolished fuckin Section Eight when they let you out. Where that glass go?"

"Wiftoe, you like guns Wiftoe?"

The boy shrugged.

"You like one like this?" Jackie indicated the M-16. "This is the kind you kill Viet Congs with. Ever hunt them?"

"Nope."

"How bout one like mine? Ever see anything like it? This is what you kill lions and tigers with. Beautiful, right?" Jackie loaded, sighted, and blew away the taillight on the car.

"Goodwood! Fuckin .460 Weatherby Mark V!"

The boy worked his jacket zipper up and down. "It's nice."

"Fuckin-A it's nice. Put me out some heavy dust."

"You mean your daddy," said Condo.

"I mean me, juicehead. Every penny. And this, Wiftoe," he said pointing to Condo's revolver, "is a Colt Trooper .357. The kind you stop coons with. A coon-stopper."

Condo crunched ice in his teeth. "Haven't seen one in a month of Sundays. Not that I'm complaining."

"They got but one in the whole state, Condo. Keep him in a museum over to Montpelier. You can buy chitlins at the door and feed him through the bars."

"Fuckin boondocks."

"You ever hunt, Wiftoe?"

"Sometimes. With my father."

"Your father. He don't like to work for us so much, your father, does he?"

Enoch didn't speak.

"Does he?"

"He says you'll be gone pretty soon."

"That so? How does he figure?"

"Won't be any lumber left."

"What's this all around us?" Jackie sounded truly shocked. "No lumber left my ass. State is up to its fuckin *ears* in lumber, thell always be lumber, it grows on *trees*, lumber."

"He thinks we build shit, doesn't he?" asked Condo.

"He never —"

"Of *course* we build shit, kid, everybody builds shit. You'd be crazy not to."

"He says a lot, your father, don't he?"

"You gentlemen don't mind," said Mason, trying to take the heat off Enoch, "let's get on with business. You need the truck or you don't."

"That's just what we're doing now, Mase, getting down to business. With our buddy Wiftoe here."

"Does he ever say, your father," asked Condo, "where he gets the lumber for those private jobs he does? For his weekend moonlights? Seeing that he's so concerned over how scarce lumber is."

"He gets it over to Judge's yard like everybody else."

"He doesn't ever bring home a little from the job, does he? Little fringe benefit?"

"My father doesn't steal."

"Doesn't steal, *everybody* steals!"

"He ever say," asked Jackie, "if he sees other guys ripping off lumber? Or equipment?"

Enoch looked like he was about to cry.

"Did he say if he knows who glommed onto a batch of white pine last week?"

"You want what his father knows, ask his father."

"Cram it, Mase."

"The boy is slow."

"That right, buddy? What he said? You slow?"

"The Groundhogs took it!" Enoch blurted it out and began to cry silently.

"Groundhogs?"

"You know," said Jackie, "the ones got the commune on the mountain, just up the river a bit? Built a log cabin up there and went organic? They wanted to borrow our chain saw that time?"

"Fuckin creeps, you mean," said Condo. "Give up begging for stealing. How you come by that, kid?"

"I saw it."

"Saw them lift it?"

"Saw the lumber. I was up there, this guy is building a frame for his waterbed."

"Waterbed." Condo spit it through his teeth. "My fuckin white pine."

"So it was the Groundhogs?"

"Yuh. Only don't say I told you. Please?"

"Would buddies do that?"

"Please?"

"Wiftoe, you ever shoot a rifle like this?"

Enoch's eyes grew big in his head. He sniffed back his tears. "No."

Jackie put a cartridge in and handed it to the boy. "Set your sights, squeeze it off and binnnnng! You have shot a rifle before?"

"With my father," he said. "Plenty of times."

"Sure, Wiftoe, sure. Why don't you take a crack at the rabbit's foot there?"

Enoch shouldered the rifle and wagged it around a little, then seemed to freeze. They waited. He was breathing slowly, with his one eye squinted it was almost like he was asleep holding the gun.

"You pull the trigger to make it go," said Jackie.

Enoch gasped in a quick breath and fired, the rifle butt smacking his shoulder. The rabbit's foot was gone.

"Holy shit."

"I hit it," said Enoch, almost apologizing.

"I seen that, Chief. That's good, that's wonderful. Now go get it."

"Huh?"

"The rabbit's foot. Go find it. You don't want us to lose our good luck do you?"

"Oh. Sure."

"Attaboy, off you go."

Enoch hurried down the steps and trotted down to the woods beyond the car.

"The boy," said Jackie when he was out of earshot, "is definitely a wiftoe. I hope his old man never gives him a gun of his own. He'd be dangerous."

"Kid's a mess."

"Not one of your mental giants. Don't breed em too quick in these parts. Kid hangs around a lot, he's got a hard-on for the wife."

"What do we do now?" asked Mason.

"Get some more beer. Antoinette!"

"I meant —"

"Toni! Toni!"

"Yeah?" A young woman's voice came irritated through the glass partition.

"Let's have a little brew out here!"

"It's all gone."

"What? You didn't get another case?"

"I forgot. I should of made a list."

"Another one with toys in the attic," said Jackie to the men. "Blends right in with the surroundings." He yelled through the glass, "Then roll us a couple Js and don't spill it all on the fuckin rug! Fuckin vacuum cleaner stays higher than any of us. What Mase?"

"The lumber. What do you want to do? That's why you had me come up, isn't it?"

"Patience, friend, patience. Eventually we are going up and getting it back. Which is why we need the pickup. But for the moment we're going to try to get a little mellower for the drive."

The glass slid open and a young woman in shorts and a T-shirt came onto the deck. She read a magazine folded in one hand and walked on her heels, toes lifted and spread apart to air wet polish. She handed the joints to Jackie without looking up, turned and went back in. The glass slid shut.

"Vacancy on the top floor," said Jackie. He lit both of the joints, big fat Mexican-bandit things, and handed one to Dar. "You like a hit Mase?"

"Nope."

"Pfc. Senior?"

"No thanks." Dar had told Hunter about smoking the stuff when he was in the war. It didn't surprise him so much. He remembered being a soldier, drinking anything he could get his hands on. And it wasn't true it made you crazy. It would have been nice if he could blame it, the smoking, for the way Dar was. But it didn't work that way. Dar pulled smoke deep into his lungs and held as he cleaned the rifle.

"Fuckin hippies," said Condo.

"Nature freaks, they got their log cabin up there, five or six guys, five or six girls, they fuck and dip candles all day long."

"I mean you two. What you see in that stuff."

"This?" said Jackie. "This is good stuff, Condo. And good *for* you. Super-reinforced Wonderhash. Got vitamin B-12 in it, niacin, thiamine, riboflavin, all kinds of goodies. Builds strong bodies three ways."

Schenk and King stood at either side of the blackboard. Only those who had voted to go were there, though no rule had been made keeping the others away. Hobie sat near the door wondering why he was there, why he hadn't just kept going that afternoon. Mark Remington and Wein and Pinkstaff were somewhere else in the house. Sarah had come, though, she stood with her arms folded in front of her, looking sad.

"I want you all to study this and remember it," Schenk said, pointing to the floor plan King had drawn of the high school. "Whatever you do don't copy it down. It could be used as evidence of conspiracy if there's a court action after this. I mean if things should come to a head."

"Come to a head," echoed King, smiling crookedly.

"Memorize all the escape routes. When we first go into the gym, check them out as subtly as you can manage."

"Be cool," said King. "And don't be afraid to run if you're outnumbered or outmatched. The street code recognizes the right to avoid getting creamed. And if you're on top of somebody, if you've got the advantage, remember that this isn't a battle to the death. It's just a way of breaking the ice."

"Not that I want you to go in there looking for a fight." Schenk held up his hands. "The black community is not our enemy, our enemy is the irresponsibility and decadence of the element that has been harassing our people. So all this is just in case something of a violent nature does happen."

"Yeah," said King. "Just in case."

"This isn't the movies. If you get hit it's going to hurt."

"Learn to control the pain," said King, "like I've taught you. Learn to channel the anger."

Hobie crept his eyes sideways to Monk. Monk had kept up shaving his head after the first time, his scalp was a veiny blue. He was wearing pop-top rings from beer cans on the fingers of his right hand, torn off so they were like jagged brass knuckles. If anything happened at the game Hobie wanted to stay clear of Monk.

"Ideally," said Schenk, "this action will lead not to a fight but to a dialogue."

Sarah snorted a laugh.

Hobie shifted away from Monk.

The shock troops leaned forward to study the board.

"Ideally," smiled King.

It was gray and feeling like rain by the time they got going. Condo and Jackie sat up with Hunter, Jackie shouting out instructions and drumming on the dashboard. Dar stretched out in the back. Only Condo brought his gun, strapping on a hand-stitched Western-style rig that rode high over his paunch. The road up to the Groundhogs' was frozen mud-rut and Hunter had a hard time keeping the pickup out of the woods.

He tried to think of what he wanted to say to Darwin. That hadn't been said and settled before. It was like with Molly's mother after she'd finally died, they'd meet and have nothing left to say. It was like they'd be drawing the funeral out.

He tried to plan what he would say to Darwin and found himself thinking about Helen. She seemed more real to him even though Dar was right in the back, was his son.

"If you find Hobie," she had asked the night before, "and get things cleared up with him, do you think you'll go back to West Virginia?"

"I don't know. It's not so bad around here."

"It's really something how you just picked up and moved your life like that. I could never manage it."

"Course you could. If you had good reason."

[318]

"No. There's no way. I'm pretty tied down here. There's the girls, they got their friends and I wouldn't think of pulling them out of St. Brigid's. It's so hod to find a decent school, you stot moving around. Then there's this house, I got the mawgage to keep up with, I got loans out all over the place, along with all of Quinn's debts. He left us in pretty deep. And sometimes the taxi isn't good, I got to help Francis a little for extras. There's my job. The system takes good care of you but you got to stay where they want you. Terrific benefits, good pension, I couldn't leave all that. It's security, the first security I ever had. Then there's all my friends in Southie, my life here. Me, I couldn't move because of me. I'm very set in my ways."

It was true. Helen insisted on wearing her dark red lipstick even when Hunter told her she looked fine without makeup. She crossed herself every time she accidentally swore and went to Confession every Saturday even when she had nothing to confess. She lit candles for her dead husband even though she admitted she didn't like him. Didn't like the memory of him. Helen had played cards with the same three friends almost every Thursday night for the past ten years.

"If you don't find Hobie," she asked, "will you go back to West Virginia?"

"I don't know."

"I mean if you're positive you're not going to find him till he wants to be found. Will you go back then? Is there anything to keep you?"

He didn't catch the hint in her voice, the real question. "I guess not. Not really."

"Thanks."

"Huh?"

"Nothing."

"Oh you mean you and me? Sure, that's —"

"Don't bother —"

"Of course that's something."

"Don't do me any favors, Hunter."

He hadn't wanted to do much talking about them. It was still up in the air about Hobie, and then again something felt wrong with Helen. Not that they weren't married or any of that preacher nonsense, but because he was supposed to be finding his boy and anything else was a distraction, was the wrong path.

"I'm not doing you any favors, I'm —"

"Damn right you're not. I was twenty-eight years old when I got married. For a long time I thought it would never happen. But I made out okay, all those years alone. I did without men. And then for nine years I did all right in spite of the one I was married to. And after he went out I did fine without them again. I might want something, Hunter, it might be nice to have, but I don't *need* it. I don't need you. Remember that."

Jackie had him stop a ways down from the cabin and they walked up an old narrow logging road. The element of surprise, he said. It had gotten very cold and was dark in the woods.

The clearing had been done with an ax from the look of the stumps. Underbrush was growing back in toward the cabin. Off to one side was a little generator, painted bright blue and mounted on the remains of the crate it had come in. There was a rusting VW van with its rear axle up on cinder blocks. LIVE FREE OR DIE, said the license plate.

It wasn't much of a cabin. It looked to Hunter like they hadn't let the logs dry enough before putting them up, so when they shrunk it had left extra-wide chinks. There were a couple shuttered windows and a stone chimney in the back.

Condo led the way in his camouflage duck-hunting hat, his yellow bugeye glasses, blaze-orange vest and plaid pants. Jackie had his hardhat from the job on and the gloves with the knuckle-holes. Darwin carried a crowbar from the pickup.

Someone was rapping with a hammer inside. Condo kicked the door hard, twice. The rapping stopped. A voice called.

"Who is it?"

"The big bad fuckin wolf," yelled Condo. "Open up."

There was scuffling and voices inside. The door opened a crack, a blond, walrus-bearded boy peeped his head out.

"What do you want?"

"Lumber."

"Lumber?"

"Lumbah!" called Jackie, and helped Condo push into the cabin, sending the blond boy back sprawling. Darwin followed and Hunter stood by the door, ready but not quite knowing what he could do.

The room was crowded. It looked like an old-time picture of Santa's Workshop. There was a boy and a girl at an oak table with leather strips laid out in front of them, a girl doing macrame on the floor, polished stones on a card table, a foot-treadle in the corner with plastic bags of clay. There were knee-high barrels along one wall, labeled BARLEY, GROATS, WHOLE WHEAT, RYE, and panels of thick pink fiberglass insulation. The blond boy had threads of pink caught in his beard, he was holding a hammer.

"You sure you've got the right place?"

"We're sure. Who are you?"

"They call me Captain."

"Captain Crunch," said the girl on the floor.

"Wonderful. Okay, Captain, make it easy on yourself. Fork over the wood."

"I don't get it."

"Some white pine? From the job, over Mashapaug? That you creeps ripped off? Sound familiar?"

Captain Crunch shook his head. "No hassles. We don't want any hassles up here. But I think you've got the wrong people."

All the boys in the room had some kind of beard, they mostly wore checked flannel shirts except for Captain Crunch. He had a heavy old Army overcoat on, with a pair of joined silver bars on one shoulder and a big red *A* backed by khaki on the other. The girls wore their hair long and were dressed in heavy clothes. They didn't look much different from the kids in Boston, paler though, and their eyes seemed a little sunken in.

"*Creep*os!" called Jackie, laughing, "Fag*goons!* You ripped off that pine and you fuckin know it. It's right in this cabin."

"Where?"

Hunter had been in worse shacks in the back hollers, only the people there never chose it to be that way. It was the best they could do and whenever they got the money together they'd put it into a trailer or something modern. Hunter couldn't quite understand it, playing poor when it got so cold up here.

" 'Where,' he asks," said Jackie. "Show me the fuckin bedrooms, I'll show you where."

"I really don't know what you're talking about."

"Come off it, creep, the kid told us. You know Wiftoe, he hangs around everywhere, gets under your feet? He blew the whistle on you."

"Wiftoe," said Captain Crunch, directing a glare to the girl sitting at the oak table.

"What can I do?" She threw her hands out defensively. "He likes to visit. He's harmless."

"He said it's wrapped around a waterbed," said Jackie.

"We want it." Condo drew the revolver and one of the girls yelped. Hunter took a few quiet steps into the room. Darwin was just standing, no expression, waiting for what would happen next.

Hunter said to be careful with the gun. Nobody listened.

"No hassles," said Captain Crunch, backing off and sitting on a grain barrel. "Please, no hassles."

"You don't need a gun," said the girl at the oak table. She stood up with her hands out, making little calming motions. She was wearing overalls and thermal underwear. "Nobody here is going to fight you."

"Damn straight they're not, girlie." Condo waved the Colt at Captain Crunch. "What's gonna happen, is this bird here is going to show us where our lumber is. Right?"

The boy rose and led them to a back room that lay behind a blanket hung from the doorsill. In the middle of the room was a waterbed, the mattress full in a frame of stained white pine.

"Ah," said Jackie, "the simple frontier comforts. The old values."

"How do you know it's your lumber?" said Captain Crunch.

"We know."

"But listen, it's all banged together. I made a nice frame, why rip it up?"

"Can you pay for it?"

"Well, not in cash —"

"Right. And what the fuck are we gonna do with a truckload of hand-painted roach clips? Take it apart."

"You've got no right to just barge in here like this."

"Tough titty. You should have thought about rights when you lifted the stuff." Jackie glanced around the room. "We can make things pretty hot for you up here. I see a couple building-code no-

nos right off the bat. Ever try to dig a septic tank in the winter? And then there's possession of a controlled substance, I don't see it but I can smell, there's theft, there's transporting virgin pine across state lines for an immoral purpose —"

"Cough it up, creeps," said Condo. "It was a nice try but you been caught."

"Right, let's get it *on* here."

"I don't see," said the girl in the thermal underwear, "why you can't just *share* it."

Condo's mouth popped open and somebody groaned from the main room.

"I mean you've got so *many* boards down there."

"Sweetheart," said Condo, "up here you maybe share things, but *we* live in the real world. You pay for what you take, cash or kind. You want to come down to the job sometime, share your ass around, then, girlie, maybe we got a deal. Otherwise knock this thing apart and hand over the lumber."

"It's only a couple boards," said Captain Crunch, "I just finished —"

"*No!*" Condo was through discussing. His face was full red, his gun arm tense, his breath coming hard. He stepped to the waterbed and aimed the gun a few inches from the top of the mattress. "Our lumber," he said, "or I shoot."

It was silent. Everyone looked at the waterbed, then at Captain Crunch. "I'm trying to be reasonable," he said. "We can settle this peacefully if you listen to reason."

Condo poked the barrel of the gun into the mattress, a dull circle rippling out from it.

"Wait," said the girl. "No violence." She ran and brought a length of hose. She attached it to the drain on the mattress and ran the hose out through an open chink in the wall. "It says you're not supposed to have it filled without a frame."

The rest of the Groundhogs crowded in to watch the mattress pucker and sink. It didn't take long. Darwin went in with his crowbar and Jackie with his boots and they knocked it apart. Condo marched three of the boys out with armfuls of splintered board to load the pickup. He took a leak on the side of the cabin.

"If I ever see any of you at my site again," he said, holstering his gun and shifting the rig so he could climb into the front seat, "I'll put one between your eyes. Personally."

"See, it's not the stealing so much," he explained on the way back down. "It's construction, everybody steals. We go down to Queechunk, steal some of their cement, they come up here, steal some of our shingles. It's all in the game. It's who *done* the stealing got my blood going. Fuckin creeps onna mountain. Waterbeds."

Jackie sang every verse of *The Ballad of the Green Berets* twice on the way back and shot Condo's revolver out the window at birds. Hunter drove down the mountain and across the river as fast as he could manage.

"What good is it?" said Mason when he saw their haul. "Can't be used at the job, all stained and full of nails. No damn good to anybody this way."

"That's where you're wrong, my friend," said Jackie. "Get your toolbox out of the truck. We got some building to do. Condo, you supervise."

"What the fuck, Jackie?"

"I'm tired of the same old target. Me and m'man Mase are gonna put together a replica of Fort Groundhog there. So's we can practice our search-and-destroy in case push comes to shove with those freaks."

Mason got his tools and went down by the car with Jackie and Condo. Enoch trailed after them carrying a little piece of fluff, what looked to be a rabbit's toe.

Hunter and Darwin sat by each other on the deck. It was cold and so dark they could hardly see the men. Mason was standing to one side, passing a tool now and then, while Jackie and Condo worked.

"You been here long, son?"

"Three or four months."

"You like it?"

"It's a place to stay. It's free. How'd you find me?"

"Through the unemployment."

"Oh."

"You can't find a job?"

Dar nodded down the slope. "I could work for these guys if I wanted. No need to, once I got my case opened at the office. I make enough."

"You know what I think of that."

"And you know I don't give a flying fuck what you think."

They were silent for a while. Hammering echoed up the hill. A breeze came up and Hunter shivered. Finally Darwin spoke.

"So Hobie hit the road?"

"He left right before the Beckley game."

"Hah. Coach must of had shitfits."

"Did he ever talk to you about runnin off? Did he ever say where he'd want to go?"

"We never talked much. We — you know — sports and stuff, but never anything personal. I know he didn't want to be in the mines, but who does? He hung out with them Appalachian Volunteer people, which I never done. Maybe they give him ideas. Maybe he had ideas of his own."

"I never got to know him enough. I never known what he thought about things."

"It's not your fault." Dar smiled. He looked more sickly when he smiled. Hunter wanted to tell him to get himself right, to eat better and to go to work and get away from these people, wanted to tell him so many things but he knew it wasn't his place. Not anymore. "It's not anybody's fault," said Dar. "Things just happen. Not a hell of a lot you can do to change them. Why fight it? Hang loose. Let it happen. It's all the same in the end."

"That how you got here? Just let it happen?"

"I guess. Jackie wanted to be a fighter pilot, he's got this thing about speed. But his head's so messed up with all the stuff he's done, everything in the drugstore, that he couldn't get past the physical. He's a war freak. I been to a war. So he likes to have me around, like a souvenir sword or something."

"And you just put up with all of it?"

Dar smiled again. "You remember the bears? The ones we found sleeping that time?"

"I remember."

"That's what I'm like inside now. There isn't the noise that was in me when I first come back. I lay around here, smoke, sleep. It doesn't even touch me, Jackie and all that. Those bears, they had the right idea."

Hunter shook his head. He felt like crying.

"Go home," said Darwin. "Things are too complicated up here. It's not simple like the mines are, black and white, life and death. They'll fuck with your mind up here, up here on the surface. Forget Hobie. He's part of it now, he doesn't belong to you. Go home."

They came running up the slope then, racing ahead of pea-sized hailstones that tore through the leaves and danced on the roof of the A-frame.

"Just in time!" yelled Jackie, clomping up the steps. "We got her up just in time. The Groundhog Hilton."

They had tacked together a flat facade, a log-cabin imitation with a little fake door. It shook forward and back under the hail.

"Have to wait till tomorrow to take a crack at it. Nice job, huh Mase? Maybe we'll come out from the trailer at the job sometime, give you natives a little carpentry lesson. Shit, that stuff's comin down! See you tomorrow, Mase, Wiftoe. Pfc. Senior, it's been a pleasure. Any time, any fuckin time."

Dar nodded good-bye and joined the others behind the glass partition.

Enoch sat between Hunter and Mason in the truck. Hailstones drumrolled on the metal roof. Mason stopped by the Impala and the mock cabin to collect his tools. He snuck a look up to the A-frame, then pulled something from the rear and hammered at the facade a moment. Hunter wiped the condensation from the inside of the windshield to see. Mason had nailed the sign from the site on the door of the new target.

MASHAPAUG PARK

A NEW CONCEPT IN LIVING

Vinnie and Dominic were cruising Washington Street when they got the call for the Cathedral project. Some lady called in, thought she heard something wrong going on in the apartment downstairs, was afraid to check it out herself. She had called three times.

"Prawbly some boogies havin a potty," said Dom, "lady knows

we're not gonna come if she says that's what it is. Pain in the ass."

"That's what you get paid for, Dawm. You're a public servant. House calls are just pot of the service."

"They better not give me any lip, we get there, that's all. I'm not in the mood."

Vinnie parked by the side door on Harrison, called in their location and that they were leaving the car. The hail had stopped but it had gotten colder with nightfall, they hurried inside.

The lady had said 22A was the problem. There was no music coming from it, no sound at all. Vinnie knocked.

No answer.

He turned the knob but didn't push. It wasn't locked. He rapped on the door again, louder.

"C'mon in." The voice was faint, like it came from a couple rooms away.

Vinnie swung the door open. There was a couch in the center of the room, turned three-quarters toward the door, with three people sitting on it. A very old black woman with a piece of gauze over her left eye, a thin middle-aged black man who Vinnie recognized as Mr. Banks, one of the superintendents at the project, and a very dark-skinned woman in a nurse's uniform. The only light was from a lamp on the floor in front of them. It was spooky, casting weird shadows around their eyes and on the ceiling. Something was wrong.

"C'mon in po-leases," said the far-off-sounding voice. They could just make him out in the darkness behind the couch. Black. Male. Holding some kind of handgun.

"Just ease in and be still, po-leases, and won't nobody get kilt."

"Don't shoot with him," said Mr. Banks, "my God, please don't shoot with him."

Vinnie and Dom moved slowly into the room, leaving the door open behind them.

The gun was pointed at the backs of the three people's heads. The couch lay between the gun and Vinnie and Dom.

"So what we got here?" said Vinnie.

"I just waitin for this lady come crost wif her money she got hid," said the man in the shadows. "I just wants the money, is all. She won't give it me."

"I try to tell him an I try to tell him," said Mr. Banks, looking scared and keeping his head perfectly still, "this old woman *got* no money. He got it in his head she been hidin all kinds of money round this place and I know for a fact she's just one step ahead of the rent payment. He won't listen. Mrs. Watts upstairs calls me, says she aint seen Mrs. Ivey go out to wike yet, maybe she overslep. So I stop by and they say come in and here they are on the couch with him pointin that *gun.* This old woman got no money, she can't even *see.* She got cateracks. I tell him he just wastin his time, I got to go home, Mrs. Ivey here hot to go to wike, but he won't *lis*ten."

"I come out from me bedroom, the mon sittin right theer," said the nurse. She was a West Indian. "Have a gun in him hond, say to sit down and shut me mouth. Nearly give me heart feelure."

"I just wants the money," said the man with the gun. "Don't want to do nobody hurt."

"That's a funny way to come on, you don't want to hurt anybody," said Vinnie. Dom drifted to the left slightly as he spoke. "Comin into people's houses with a gun."

"What's she want wif all that money she got? She too old to spend it. I need it bad, man, you tell her to give it over and I'll just leave. Won't be no trouble."

"What's your prawblem, son?" said Dominic. Vinnie moved to the right, not so much a step as a shifting of weight that left him further away from his partner. "What's got you out botherin these people?"

"I'm sick, man. I got to get some medicine."

"Sick with what?"

"Jones got me. Got me bad."

"Yeah, there's a lot of that goin around."

"I know him," said Mr. Banks, "I know his whole family. That's Junior Wall an he's one them dope addicks. He no good, his whole family no good. I knowed them all my life. No damn good."

"Easy, Pops," said Vinnie. "No point in getting him upset, now, is there?" Dom moved off a little further to the left. There was a good six feet between him and Vinnie now but the couch was still in the line of fire.

[328]

"You tell the old lady for me, tell her I got to have that money quick," said the shadow-man, "tell her I know she got it, she been hidin it round this place for years. Tell her I'm gonna have to get wrong if she don't hand it over."

"You hear that Grandma?" Vinnie could see the gun clearly now. It was a little snub-nosed thing, not too much punch to it probably and hypes weren't known for their marksmanship. But he'd never been hit with anything anywhere and wasn't anxious to find out what it was like.

"Grandma?"

The old woman didn't seem to be paying attention. Her uncovered eye looked kind of glazed.

"She don't hear so well," said Mr. Banks.

"You hurtin, Junior?" asked Dom.

"That's right, po-lease. I'm hurtin bad."

"You think there's any way you're gonna get out of here, get past us and get somewheres you can score, in one piece? I mean we called you in, Junior, there's a couple cars backing us up outside."

"I got the gun, man."

"We got guns too, Junior." As Dominic spoke, waving his hand in the air a bit to draw attention, Vinnie caught Mr. Banks's eyes and motioned for him to slide down. He did, very slowly, head still tensed as if he were expecting a bullet in the brain any second. He slid down till his head was below the back of the couch. Mrs. Ivey eased down next to him. "Both me and my pottner here got guns," said Dom, "and we know how to use them. We don't *want* to, see, but we can. You think you can get either or both of us before we blow you away you're crazy. No *way*, my friend. It's all over, Junior."

Mr. Banks grabbed the old woman's legs and pulled her off the couch. "Who's theer?" she said suddenly, sounding like a parrot. "Who's theer?"

"*Hey!*"

"Eeeeeesy, Junior. No sweat. No prawblem." Vinnie and Dominic both had a hand resting on their revolvers.

"You think you're sick now, Junior, you catch one in the belly and you'll wish you were never bawn."

"It's over, son."

[329]

"It's over."

The gun was still pointed at the back of the couch. Vinnie couldn't see through to the face, but he knew right where it was. There wouldn't be any belly shots if it happened.

"Who's theer?" cried the old woman.

"You come with us, son," said Vinnie, "somebody will take care of you. Take care of Jones."

"That's right, Junior, that's the way it works. The doc will look at you first thing, he sees how sick you are he'll give you a pop."

"Sure he will. They don't want nobody climbin the walls in the lockup. They'll give you something to keep you quiet."

"Real medicine, Junior," said Dom. "Pure. The liquid stuff."

"It's the only way, son."

"And you know how it is, you'll be back on the street in no time."

He was crying. The gun was pointing at the floor and he was crying. "You promise?" he said. "I'm so sick."

"Lay the gun on the floor, Junior."

He dropped it. It glistened in the lamplight, nickel-plated. "I'm so fucking sick."

There was a crowd gathered around the patrol car when Vinnie and Dom brought Junior out in the cuffs. Twenty-five to thirty people, maybe half of them young men. Junior had turned out to be only a kid, fifteen, though his face looked a lot older. They stopped in the doorway.

"Think they come to hail the cawnquering heroes?" said Dominic.

"You ask em, Dawm. I'm goin on my coffee break."

A little girl in a white parka, her hair done in neat corn-rows, pushed up screaming from the crowd.

"That's my bruvva, that's my bruvva!" she shrieked. "You leave my bruvva *go!*"

"Oh shit. I knew it couldn't be that easy." Dom pulled Junior back inside a bit and Vinnie gave the crowd a better look. Somebody tossed out a baseball bat and the little girl lugged it up and went for the car. The people drew back a bit to watch her.

"You leave him *go!* Leave him *go!*" she yelled, and each time she yelled *go* she brought the bat down on the front fender of the patrol car. The bat was almost as big as she was and she couldn't get much behind it but the crowd loved the show.

"That's it, honey," they called, "you give it to em!"

"Take care of *biz*ness, child!"

"Whup em, baby, *whup* em!"

"Whup they *ass*es!"

Vinnie stood in the doorway knowing the worst possible move would be to go after the little girl and Junior was crying let me go, let me go, whether to the cops or the crowd he didn't know and Dom was starting to swear to himself which was always a dangerous sign, when they heard the siren. It was Walsh and Buchanan with the siren on full choke, always good for scattering a crowd for a moment, hopping right up on the sidewalk and screeching to a stop by the door. Dom pushed Junior into the backseat, slammed the door and jumped back as Walsh pulled away, drivin just fast enough so the little girl could chase but not quite catch them, with most of the crowd following. Vinnie and Dom had no trouble getting to their car and making tracks.

"Bee-youtiful!" said Vinnie to Walsh over the radio when they were back on the streets. "You blew in there like the Seventh fuckin Cavalry!"

"Saw the crowd," said Walsh, "thought we'd take a peek. What have we got in the back here?"

"Hype was tryin to take some old lady off. We got his gun."

"He's a wet one."

"Yeah, we talked him down. He's just a kid."

"I'd of put one in his head."

"Yeah, Walsh, you prawbly would have."

"Believe it. Okay, we'll bring Tiny Tears here in and see you guys at the station."

"Right."

Vinnie put the channel back open. "Looked like we might have some hairy action there tonight, didn't it?"

"If it was Walsh there we would have. Old Quick-Draw McGraw. The kid's lucky."

"Right. To get a soft touch like you." Vinnie said it matter-of-fact.

"What's that supposed to mean?"

"Nothin."

"Hey, I haven't used the gun six years now. And that was just a couple wawning shots, the time I did."

"Like I said, you're a soft touch."

"You had that one time, though, didn't you?"

Vinnie nodded. "Yeah. I had that one time." It was clear he didn't want to talk about it.

On the next block they got a Code Three from the Jeremiah Burke High School.

"They gotta be kiddin."

"Natives are restless tonight," said Vinnie. On went the flasher and the siren, he squealed the patrol car into a U-turn and headed down toward Dorchester. "Must be the full moon come early this month."

When they arrived there were already a half-dozen cars parked and flashing out front, but no one in them. There was only Detective Doyle, sitting on the hood of one of the cars wearing his overcoat and gloves. His bulk pushed the nose of the car down like the suspension had been torched.

"Doggerty and Aiello," he called out, "our prayers are answered! The rest of us can fuckin go home."

"What's the story, Doyle?"

"Basketball game, right? Nigger team against a nigger team, the stands look like *Who's Who in Dockest Africa*. In walks this bunch of white kids don't go to the fuckin school, sit down like they own the place. So naturally all pandemonia breaks loose."

"Why? What did they want?"

"It's some political thing. Another bunch tried it at Boston English beginning of October, remember? Weathermen? Think they're gonna win converts. Duke it out and end up best friends like in the movies."

"Christ. What's happening now?"

"Moppin-up operations. We got a couple guys into the gym quick but they cut and run all over the building. Some got away already."

"What are you doin down here?"

"They got me working this student-politics bullshit. Called me out of bed and said get over here. Can you magine that?"

"Yeah, I can imagine. You're laying there with your prick in your hand, the phone rings —"

[332]

"Get your ass in there, Doggerty, they need you."

A couple younger cops they didn't know were covering the exit. It was kind of spooky inside, all the lights turned on and no one in the halls.

"You might try the second floor," said one of the young cops. "It sounds like there's still some up there."

They were a few steps from the second when they heard sharp breathing and a white boy skidded to a halt at the top of the stairs. He was wearing an oversized Army jacket and running shoes with stripes on them. He froze, staring at Vinnie and Dom.

"Come on, sonny," said Dom. "We'll take you home."

The boy paused another second, then whirled and tore off down the hall. Vinnie and Dom were up the steps and right on his tail for a moment but then he hit a gear they didn't have and zipped on away from them around the corner.

They pulled up, both panting.

"Kid runs like a nigger."

"No shit. I think I strained somethin."

"He look familiar to you, Vin?"

"Yeah, but I can't place it."

"Remember, back over a month ago, we rousted that kid in the rain? The one you threw back?"

"The one from Kentucky or something?"

"Right. He said please and thank you and you wanted to give him a medal? That's our boy. Mr. Speed Demon."

"You're right. The jacket."

"What did I tell you at the time? What did I say?"

"You're right, Dawm. You're a fuckin genius. You're an unfallable judge of character. Listen, how does it feel when you pull a hamstring?"

"You wouldn't be standin."

They heard a racket from downstairs then, men's voices shouting and a lot of running around.

"What do you say we give it a rest, Dawm?"

"Sounds good to me."

"Looked like they had enough guys to handle it. Besides, we already earned our pay tonight."

"You ask my opinion," said Dominic, "they should of locked the doors and stood outside. Let the niggers handle it. White kids are that stupid I don't see why we should work up a sweat bailing out their asses."

"Good point, Dawm. Let's find somewhere to sit."

They walked down the hallway past dark classrooms, Vinnie limping slightly, till they heard scuffling. It was coming from the girls' room.

"I always wanted to see what one of these looked like inside," said Dom, "but I never had the balls to peek when I was in school. After you, Vin."

Three black girls had a white girl up against the tile wall, slapping, scratching, pulling hair, punching. The white girl whimpered and tried to cover her face but they kept snatching her hands away, playing with her. Vinnie and Dom watched silently for a moment and then Dom gave a metal trash barrel a loud kick. The black girls jumped back.

"Recess is over, ladies," he said, and stepped aside to let them pass. "Make yourselfs good and scarce." The black girls hurried out.

The white girl knelt on the floor, pulling the collar of her denim jacket around to stop the blood from her nose. She was cut over one eye and on the scalp. She was very young, chubby, with straight blond hair.

"You all right, honey?"

She glared up at them, then looked beyond to the door.

"Don't even *think* about it, sweethot. You've taken enough punishment for one night. *We've* taken enough punishment for one night. Make it easy on both of us, all right?"

They each took one of her elbows and led her away.

Lieutenant Berg was chewing out some young cop when they got outside again.

"Hey, hey, Lieutenant!" Dom called. "What's the word?"

"The word is we fucked up. Shit-for-Brains here left an exit uncovered. They must of cased it ahead of time. They all flew the coop."

"You didn't get *any?*"

"None of the white ones. The others, hey, it's not their fault. Just protecting their own. What you got there?"

"Miss Racial Hominy, 1969. Want her? I mean it's your turf."

"Naw. My guys didn't do nothin, they should get nothin to show for it. She's all yours."

The girl sat in the rear of the car and sulked. She wouldn't tell her name. Vinnie called in their location and mileage the way he always did with female prisoners. No crying hanky-panky later.

"You sure you're all right?" asked Dom.

The girl stared at her knees.

"We're gonna have to book you, honey. Disturbing the peace, fomenting a riot, something like that. If you're a minor it's no sweat. You have the right to remain silent. Anything you say can and will be held against you in a cawt of lawr. You have a right to counsel prior to or during any statement you might care to make. If you can't afford counsel it will be provided to you. Any questions, dear?"

The girl remained silent.

"You know we could of left you with the Lumumba Sisters there. You couldn't recognize yourself, they got through with you."

The girl lifted her chin and looked at him. She had stopped crying.

"You suck," she said.

Sarah laid out the bandages and waited for them to come back. Schenk had acted like they wouldn't be needing bandages, just a display of solidarity he said. A lot of crap. They were going to fight, to bleed and draw blood. That was the point.

Butterfly Band-Aids for over the eyes, tape and gauze, hydrogen peroxide for the cuts you got on the inside of your mouth. Sarah had wanted to go, thinking she might be able to talk them away from it. But no, Schenk said she was too valuable on the outside in case something went wrong, in case the cops interfered, because she knew the whole bail procedure. And Schenk was running the show. Mark was upstairs reading theory, pretending not to sulk.

Don't take it personally. That's what Mark had said to her the first time they had ever really talked, in June of '66 when they and all other whites were officially read out of SNCC. Seeing her crying after the press conference, he had come down from the platform to set her straight. Sarah was so upset she hardly noticed it was Mark Remington talking to her, who she only had seen behind a microphone or at the head of a march, who she had once worked a month to raise bail for in Tupelo, Mississippi. He explained it so well, why the move was absolutely necessary, overdue in fact, why it wasn't any kind of a putdown, why the words sounded so much more antagonistic than they were meant. It made a lot of sense when he explained it, when he answered her personal questions with his political answers. Mark Remington.

Of course at the time she couldn't ask him the ideology behind the way Reuben had suddenly dumped her. Had cut her off. It's a new day said Reuben, and it was. It's time we started takin some pride in the sisters said Reuben, and it was. It's not like I was ever that interested in your ugly gray self said Reuben, you just hook me in. Hook me into thinkin it was some big fuckin big thing to get it on with a white girl, the way you been hookin our men in for centuries, y'dig? So's you could go round thinkin you not just as racist as the rest of them and gettin your piece at the same time. All them word games you done to fuck up my head. All that love-and-respect business, let me tell you girl, it don't mean shit. It *don't mean shit*.

Mark was a comfort though, with his explanations, his rationalizing. But he was too much of a big mover, too much of a *star*, to think about seriously as a possible man for her. She was a gofer and a groupie, part of the women's auxiliary. Chicks up front they'd yell, back when that was any kind of deterrent. But in the dorms and offices it was coffee detail and typing and hoping you'd be picked by one of the big kids, one of the boys who ran the show.

Mark picked her.

It was fine for a while being the first lady of the Left on their campus. Being so close to the center, to the open nerve of action. Mark carried the ball and she led the cheers and if she worried about anything it was the competition from all the bright-faced little girls on his tail, outradicaling each other for a scrap of his attention. She worried whether she was committed enough to deserve him.

Crushed ice in Baggies for swollen knuckles, for busted noses.

A huge pot of stew bubbling on the stove. Fighting and running scared always worked up an appetite.

She followed him to Chicago for the convention with a hang-loose chapter of SDS. See what's coming down and take it from there, Mark's kind of politics. Clubs, mostly, were coming down in their section of the city. Sarah pissed in her jeans and was separated from Mark in the very first charge. She was lost in Chicago without him and couldn't imagine what she was doing there. Someone gave her an armband and suddenly she was a medic, taping gauze over anything that bled, crying half-hysterically the whole time. Managing not to get hit by running, always running from somebody or other, leaping over bodies of the gassed and injured, running with the sure knowledge they were out to kill *her*, Sarah, personally. Then coming back when the heat had cleared to help with the wounded. Something was changing all around her, she sensed it as tangibly as the tear gas hanging in the air. Sensed it mixed among the terror of the McCarthy kids and the indignation of the burned and beaten bystanders. A growing strain of pure joy. It was *real*, they were fighting. *Fight*ing. Eyes glowing, speed-rapping at total strangers, parting their hair to show off each red badge of commitment, all the Dr. Spock babies who had never hit or been hit in anger, riding out their violence high, juiced on action. *I hit a pig in the face with a rock. You shoulda seen it.*

Cool night air and floodlights too bright, colors too brilliant, the cops squeaking with leather and plastic and so big, so real and glass breaking, sirens, everywhere sirens and glass breaking like the anthem of the convention.

It made Sarah sick. She was chickenshit in a fight and that was all there was to it, she admitted it freely. Find the nearest victims and play Clara Barton, the cops tended to leave you alone if you looked like you were there just to nurse.

Mark found her again on the third night of Chicago and was so hopped and horny with the whole thing it was an effort to keep him from climbing on her right in the street. And when they had gone inside, semi-alone, it was awful. Hip-busting the way Reuben used to do every time she had dared to suggest he should go down on her. You want that faggot action get yourself a white boy, hear? Socking into her, bitch, bitch, bitch and walking away when it was done. Leaving her sore and thinking maybe he's right, maybe I *am* subconsciously trying to emasculate him, maybe I am just a tool of white domination. Unable to separate the personal from the political. Feeling like shit.

And here was Mark still battling the Chicago police force in her cunt and it was all breaking glass and sirens to her and it had to stop and for the first time she could recall in their relationship she said no to him. No. Stop. Wait. Listen to me, you make love like you're deaf, dumb and blind. Listen to my body, listen to me, give me the same hearing you'd give the most anonymous face in the crowd at a rally. Sarah had been loose and alone in the Chicago convention riot for three days and she had survived. She didn't need him to survive. She wanted him, yes, but she didn't need him and now it was important to her that he was aware that she knew the difference. Even if it meant them ending together. Changes in the air, as real as the hanging tear gas.

It was a struggle all the way, though Mark denied it was even a problem. Mark explained it politically. You're coming along, he said, that's good. It's about time the women stopped taking shit and started taking responsibility. It was as if Dulles had thanked Castro for taking Cuba off his hands. What took you so long? She showed Mark how to make love with her but it was nothing personal, just the effects of a raised consciousness.

But in terms of their living together it worked, whatever he chose to call it. The minute she began to act like something more than Mark Remington's chick he began, slowly, to treat her like more. He expected to hear her opinion in a meeting now, and listened when she gave it.

Mark listened. He really did, he listened and changed and made it possible for them to stay together. It was one of the things that set him apart from the other bright boys who headed the actions and trotted their wit and wisdom out for the newspeople. It was why he had gotten as far as he had without either ruthlessness or pure luck. He listened to the people around him and then told them what they were feeling in more coherent form. It was his talent. It was probably why he was alone upstairs right now.

Trust the people, he always said. They've got the ideas, the energy, the will. Put the facts before the people and they'll make the right decisions. It's not the people who are the problem, it's the system. But not only did he trust the people, he wanted them, all of them, to follow him. And worse, he wanted them to *like* him. He would never admit it, nothing so personal, oh no, not Mark Remington. But there it was in every move he made. He wouldn't discipline, he wouldn't infight, he wouldn't politic and lie. Not Mark Remington's style. He wanted to fight in the mud and never get his hands dirty, he wanted to let the people be hang-loose and do-your-own-thing and he wanted to build a mass movement with himself as one of the prime movers. He actually believed he could build it with nothing but charm and honesty and intelligence. He trusted the people and they broke his heart time after time.

Nothing personal.

SNCC threw him out and he found a political rationale for that. He lost twenty pounds in the aftermath, in the depression and soul-searching, but he found one. And when SDS ignored all his warnings about base-building and swung into heavy-confrontation politics with only college students in their ranks, when he was outshouted and outpoliticked into obscurity at the national meetings, he explained it away again. These things go in cycles, he said, they'll come back to their senses when it doesn't work. And finally back in Chicago in June at the big split, with PL spinning off in one direction and Weatherman in another and thousands left hanging between them. The revolution purging itself, he said, cleansing out its more destructive elements so it can belong to the people once again. Hanging on with Klonsky and the RYM-2 people till it was clear they were a nongroup, then starting Third Way from scratch. Trusting the people to believe him, to follow him, to like him. Admitting everybody who wanted in, no matter what their political background. They were the people, weren't they?

And leaning on Sarah more and more, needing her energy, her assurances. Not in words, no, on the surface it was all just the blowing winds of politics and he was plotting a steady course. But his lovemaking was all questions now. Am I liked, am I right, am I doing something that touches other people or am I just Mark Remington, ex–Movement-bigshot, jerking off? It's fine, baby, she whispered to him when they made it together, it's good. I'm with you. Do it for me.

Sarah dragged more chairs into the kitchen. They would want to sit together and swap their experiences after the game. The fight. The kitchen felt weird, so empty, the house felt too big. She needed people around her to be with and work with, even if they were thickheaded and impossible and pissed her off. They were her people. It wouldn't do to be with Mark now, he needed time by himself to figure out this latest test of his faith. The loneliness at the top, Mark could get into that.

If it came to a choice between Mark in his exile and the people in the kitchen, what then? Where was she needed most, where did she want to be? Wein was writing a book, *Personality and Politics* he was calling it for the time being. Sarah thought he should dedicate it to Mark. Contradictions within paradoxes within contradictions.

It was during the first big Washington Mobe. Mark was back in the ranks, wanting to get the people's perspective on the whole thing. They had been stalled in a roped formation waiting to march for over an hour, not knowing when the marshals would come to give the green light, standing bored stiff back-to-belly in the midafternoon sun. "Christ almighty," said Mark, as fed up with the good vibes and complacency of the marchers as he was with the wait, "let's get this thing into *gear!* What gives with these turkeys?" Hot, angry, footsore.

An old, tiny woman who'd been dozing off up ahead turned and looked him in the eye. "Young man," she said, "I've been in this line for fifty-eight years. Have a little patience."

That was the way Sarah had to take it. Revolution was a way of life, it was a natural process. Like breathing. It wasn't an event, like Mark made it out to be, a battle you won or lost and then retired from. It was how you *were.*

It had progressed, the deeper into the Movement Sarah went the more her life was tied with Mark's. It was hard to separate them, to evaluate one without the other. But if this thing with Schenk had done as much damage as it seemed to, had turned Mark away from the struggle, she might have to do just that and make her choice. Sarah turned the stew down to simmer.

"Make way for the Rumbling Reds!"

They blew into the kitchen, a gust of cold air following them from outside and fluttering the bandages laid on the table.

"Bring the war home!"

"Did you *see* those fuckers jump out of the stands? Talk about your solidarity —"

"— the look on that pig's face when Miriam —"

"— dudes can fight, some of them. We get their politics on the right track and turn them loose —"

"— think twice before they mess with any of us —"

"Today's pig is tomorrow's bacon!"

Some bleeding noses and lips, puffed eyelids and bruised cheeks. It looked like it had stayed pretty much a bare-knuckle fight. No one sat in the chairs yet, they strutted around Sarah still pumped and panting.

"Did you see King?"

"Did you see Miriam?"

"Did you see fuckin Monk wade into it? Man has got some hard stones on him!"

"Is everybody here?"

"Naw, Jeff and those guys took the long way around, they're a couple minutes back."

"And Tracy Anne lost her cherry."

"What?"

"They got her?"

"They copped it. I saw her with a pair of them when we hit the exit. Wasn't anything I could do."

"And that's her first?"

"Far as I know."

"Got to happen sometime."

"Wild in the *streets*, Mama!"

"Shake and bake!"

"Bring it *down!*"

"— so he says to me, he says what the fuck you people doin in here, man, and I say watchin the *game*, just like you, an he says bullshit and I say no bullshit man, it's a free country, right, an he —"

"Mercurochrome! Who's got the Mercurochrome?"

"— gonna have yourself a bit of a scar there, Jennifer. Give your face some character —"

"— see that big mother with the shaved head? Holy-shit-on-a-shamrock! You don't catch me goin near that fucker with anything less than a fuckin anti*tank* gun, he's —"

"Wash it off first for Christ sake, you wanna get gangrene?"

Schenk was there smiling a little, not even looking winded. King's hands were bleeding badly through the scar tissue, he'd cut them hitting someone with glasses on. Debbie had a broken nose. Sarah had her take a deep breath and thumbed it into what looked like the right position. She gave Debbie two icebags for the bleeding, one for the base of the skull and one for the upper lip. Almost everybody had some sort of souvenir to show but Schenk and Hobie. People were pounding Hobie on the back and calling him The Flash. He offered to help Sarah with the bandaging.

The younger kids didn't want to wash their cuts off right away. Probably should give it some time to clot first, they said, I'll leave it be for a while. They left bright-red droplets on the floor and table, droplets that were soon black smears. King circulated giving pointers. More foot action, he said, you're wasting half of your attack potential. *Snap* those elbows up. Mickey Q. and Smallwood argued over which side had actually thrown the first punch. People ate stew straight from the pot, hardly blowing on it before gulping it down. Grant Parke sat in a corner hugging his ribs, moaning and laughing at them.

Sarah worked quickly, patching them but not responding to their enthusiasm. Hobie handed her things and held the other end when she needed it. He wasn't shouting like the others but seemed excited. He was bumping into her a lot.

The first bunch were just settling when Jeff and the rest of the shock troops began to drift in, starting the energy flow again.

"Pow!"

"Zap!"

"Bam!"

"I wonder if it'll make the papers?"

"I wonder if we'll hear from Green again?"

"I wonder if they know for sure who we are?"

Sure they know, thought Sarah, a bunch of dipshit white punks with no better way to get your rocks off than to get creamed in a fight and pretend it's some kind of political statement. She said nothing. It wouldn't register. Maybe tomorrow, in group, when they evaluated the action she could have her opinion considered, but now it would be drowned in adrenaline.

"— had me down and the two of them start kicking —"

"— pulls out this can opener —"

"— must of been the ring he was wearing that cut —"

"— some of those black girls are tougher than the —"

"— right in the *nuts*."

They got higher and higher on it, retelling each bone-snapping rock-in-the-pocket moment of it a half-dozen times while Sarah bit her lips shut and slapped on tape. She imagined Mark lying upstairs listening to their shouts and chanting. Right in the nuts indeed.

Grant Parke eased over and put his arm around Hobie. He held an inverted Coke bottle like a microphone. "Ladies and gents, I have with me here a leading contender for rookie-of-the-year honors," he said, "a kid you're gonna hear a lotta noise from in the future. I mean none other than The Anti-Fascist Flash himself, Hillbilly Hobie McNatt. Kid, you've proved yourself. In a contest that gave us all a good look at the young blood that's coming up to replace some of our tired old veterans, you illustrated once again that the race goes indeed, to the swift. Hobie, you've got the smarts, you've got the desire, you've got all the moves. Where do you go from here?"

Hobie squirmed under Grant's arm and beamed shyly.

"I guess he's not accustomed to the limelight, fans, and he's had a busy night out on the floor. So let's send you back to Al Derogatis at Revolution Central — Al?"

Hobie was high on it, no doubt about that. Sarah had never seen him so smiling, so open with the other members. He couldn't be still, darting around, getting in her way more than he was helping. It was depressing.

The adrenaline started to turn to fatigue and one by one the street guerrillas headed up to sleep. Debbie's nose had stopped bleeding, Sarah gave her a couple Darvons and a big slug of brandy. Schenk announced that they'd have criticism of the action at noon tomorrow and went off to bed. The stew was all gone and a few people slapped together peanut-butter sandwiches to take up with them.

[343]

The kitchen emptied out. Hobie volunteered to help Sarah clean up a bit.

She wanted to be alone to cool down some, to think. But he was such a sweet boy and you had to encourage cleaning help whenever you could. For someone who had all the moves, though, he had an awful hard time getting around the kitchen without running into her.

Or was it something else? Please no. Not now.

She knew Hobie had a crush on her, thought it was nice, he *was* such a sweet boy. He'd never made her feel uncomfortable because of it. Sarah moved to the table to pick up. Hobie moved to the table. She moved chairs out into the group meeting room. He was right with her moving chairs. She went to the stove. Hobie was at the next burner. He was looking at her almost constantly now.

The new blood replacing the tired veterans. Of course, goddammit, he was thinking with his balls just like the rest of them. Feeling that fight-juice in his veins, thinking now was the perfect time, himself hot off the battlefront and Mark brooding safe in his room. Laying his role in the action at her feet, like a cat offering a dead bird. Thanks but no thanks, buddy.

Sarah turned her back and went to the sink. She ran scalding water into the stewpot and tried to send off her most discouraging don't-mess-with-me vibes but he was there anyway, stroking her shoulder and saying her name softly.

"Sarah?"

It came up from her stomach like bile, the whole night of choked-back rage, all of the nights of sirens and breaking glass, all of the helplessness she felt, all the things she could never express with fist or club, it came up in disgust for the whole bunch of them and poured into Hobie.

"*Listen* — you just get your fuckin hands off me and wipe any romantic fucking notions out of your *head*, buddy." He stepped back wide-eyed and she slammed the stewpot into his arms. "I don't need it at *all* from you right now so just leave me a*lone*, understand?" He just looked at her and she wanted to hurt him, she was sick with wanting to hurt somebody. "You think it's a big fucking deal, don't you? You can go out and get in a fight with somebody, you can get the cops to chase you, you think you're a big fucking man, a fucking *he*ro! You think that's something important, that I'm impressed! Don't you? Well listen, Mister, it doesn't mean shit to me. It doesn't mean *shit*."

And left him, holding the stewpot amid the blood and the bandages.

27

It didn't take long. Hunter first noticed in the morning, the way the Italians were talking all hushed and tight with each other when they passed in the building. Usually they'd yell across the floor, some joke or insult, mostly ending with one of them miming jerking-off and both laughing. But this morning they came and stood by each other in twos and threes, arguing in low voices.

Then Jimmy came up and said there might be some layoffs. The meeting with the union man over the new year's contract was set for after work and Jimmy had gotten the feeling from Joey D. that there would be trouble.

"There's a layoff it's almost sure you'll go, Hunt," said Jimmy. "Sometimes they close the whole thing up for a couple weeks, sometimes they just lay five, ten of the junior men off. You're about third from the top of the list."

"How long do you think?"

"Well, *if* they do it, it's hod to tell. Whatever they tell you, you can count on being out a lot longer. You never know, sometimes around negotiation time they like to stot layoff rumors, so's everybody feels lucky to still have their job and votes for whatever contract they offer. It's hod to tell."

"I'll find out today?"

"Prawbly. Sal's gonna be here from the union, they usually have the union break the bad news. No guts, the company. It happens, you should go right down and open your case after work."

"Huh?"

"The unemployment office. The sooner you file the sooner they pay off. You prawbly been here long enough, made enough, to be eligible for Massachusetts. If you haven't then you can count some of what you made back home, but it takes longer for a two-state claim."

"I couldn't."

"What?"

"I couldn't do it, I never — never been —"

"Hey, come on, buddy, it's no big deal. You must of been on relief or something *some*time, where you're from. I mean it's not like you're takin something doesn't belong to you."

"No. No, I don't think I could."

The rumors got bigger as the day went on. Maybe five or ten men laid off. At least thirty. The whole plant shut down for two days a week. For the next two months, like they did back in '67. A strike. If they went too far this time, it was a sure thing the union would have them strike. There hadn't been one since '52, the last year Rocco the Nip ran the factory.

Puglisi was extra nervous all day. He yelled and prodded, faster, faster, faster as if meat were going out of style and they had to race the clock and empty all the freezer rooms before the four-o'clock buzzer. Everyone tried to stay out of his way.

He grabbed hold of Hunter at 3:30 and sent him down for cleanup. Hunter had been in the union two days now officially but didn't know if he could protest. He hid in the steam and tried to breathe steady.

By the time he got down to the lunchroom all the seats were taken. The men were in their street clothes, coats on their laps. They argued and waved their hands and pounded on the table-tops. Hunter found a place to stand against the wall by the coffee machine.

"Okay, okay, tone it down guys!" Joey D. hurried into the room, followed by two other men. "Mr. Bottolo and Mr. Zimmerman are here from the union, tell you about the new contract, but they gotta get over to the Armour in South Boston, so let's move this thing. You wanna take it, Sal?"

Bartolo stepped forward a bit. He was wearing a blue shirt

with the sleeves rolled up and a loose red tie. "The first thing you got to know," he said, "is that the company is in a lot of trouble. The meat business, the mocket, is bad all over. But this shop here is in even worse trouble. They finished the new wing upstairs, they got that to pay off, they opened up the roast-beef down in the basement, that's still got a while to get on its own feet, they got a lot of back payments to make and then the mocket tightened up and we're sittin on all this meat here. The stuff is gettin soft up in the storage." Bartolo pointed his finger for emphasis almost every sentence. Joey D. stood to one side and looked very nervous. He looked like he was waiting for the men to rise up and jump on him any second.

"So the thing is, they're in the red over here and they asked us for relief. They can't meet our demands and stay in business."

"What that mean?" asked Caesare.

"It means they can't give us everything we ask for, Chez."

"What about a raise?"

"No raise."

"Ow come? I'm get a raise evva year since I'm come to Porchetta. What appen?"

"Maybe that's why they're in trouble, Chez. Maybe they reached their ceiling. You done pretty good, you guys, it's gotten better every year, but maybe that can't go on forever. There's gotta be a ceiling sometime."

"Che avvenite con lo prezzo —"

"Fausto, in *En*glish, Fausto," said Joey D. "We run the meetings in English."

Fausto was upset, he grimaced and thought for a moment to translate.

"What about costaleeve?"

"We didn't get it," said Sal Bartolo. "We got basically the same contract as last year. No cost-of-living, no raise. The company asked for relief."

"I'm ask fo releeve too. Fock the comp."

"Hey, they even let us see the books. They never done that before. They let us look for ourselves, see the hole they're in."

"The comp inna hole, they dug it themself."

"Strike!" yelled Caesare. "They can' do these. We strike!"

[347]

"Sciopero! Sciopero!"

The men were all buzzing in Italian then and Joey D. jumped off the wall looking like he'd wet his pants.

"Hey! Hey! Whatta you, crazy?! Shut up an listen a minute! We strike, I'm tellin you, the company goes *un*der. That's all there is *to* it. Ask Jake, he's our accountant, he's seen the books."

The little man who had been standing to one side looking uncomfortable nodded.

"This company goes under," said Joey D., "what the fuck are you gonna do? Caesare, you, what you gonna do? Guy your age out onna streets. Who's gonna give you a job? There's no Roccos left out there, it's business, they don't hire no old men gonna walk out on a good thing half-assed. Right? Am I right, Chez? What the fuck you know about getting a job out there, you been with this company since you got off the fuckin boat, never had to worry about a thing? Never even have to learn the language, the union take care of you. Am I right? Alla you guys."

They were quiet, watching him. They didn't look happy.

"You guys got it pretty good here, every year it's gotten better, you buy a car, nice, little house up in Somerville, it's been good. So for once it stays the same, it don't go up. You gotta be greedy? The meat business is in bad shape, you gonna walk out when every packing house in the country is in a pinch and expect to find something else?"

They grumbled a little as Joey stepped back, but quieter now, not talking strike.

"There's gonna be a little layoff," said Sal.

The grumbling stopped.

"Don't worry, just a few guys, four or five junior men, just for a while. Get the books balanced. Have it back to a full house in a couple of weeks, no need to sweat. But we got to hurry up and vote this contract through, we're overdue as it is. I know it's tough to swallow, we're not getting the cost-of-living, but we sat with the company, we held out for everything we could for you guys. We got some good new language in there on the retirement, Joey can fill you in if you're interested. But we done what we could."

Bartolo spread his hands wide and fixed them with a sincere look. "Hey, guys, they wanted to *cut* your present rate, they wanted to shut the house for a whole *month*, everybody out runnin up bills they can't pay over Christmas. You talkin strike, we already *threat*ened to strike. That's right, we already tried that on em. Hey, they know you guys, they know you're not gonna lay down for any bullshit. 'Go ahead, strike,' they said. 'We *all* be on the street.' See, it's not just all up to them and us. It's the mocket. The meat. Nobody's buying like they used to."

"Yeah, it's the mocket," said Joey D.

"It's the meat."

The meeting broke up as quickly as it started and someone told Hunter he should see Puglisi in his office. Puglisi's office was in the rear of the spice room, a little desk covered with papers and forms. He gave Hunter two blue forms to sign. One stating that he was officially laid off and one saying that he understood he was no longer covered by Blue Shield. Puglisi didn't say anything the whole time, just pointed to the dotted lines and tore off the company's copies. Hunter took a last deep whiff of fennel and sage.

Fausto and Clemente and Raf Scalogna were sitting across from him on the Green Line until Government Center. They talked among themselves. Hunter caught Fausto staring at the blue forms he was holding, but he didn't say anything. It was like they didn't know each other anymore.

It didn't take long at all.

28

Hobie took his place in the next to the last row. King had given him his seating assignment that morning, pulling him aside to half-whisper it. There was tape on the floor showing two large squares for sitting and an aisle leading between them up to the blackboard. And they had painted the room yesterday, painted off-white over the finger- and footprints, over the squashed roaches and the sign Smallwood had written one morning in red Magic Marker. You could make it out through the new coat though.

```
A     M     E     R     I     K     A
n     o     x     e     m     a     u
t     n     c     a     p     p     t
i     o     r     c     e     i     o
h     l     e     t     r     t     c
u     i     s     i     r     a     r
m     t     c     o     i     l     a
a     h     e     n     a     i     c
n     i     n     a     l     s     y
      c     t     r     i     t
            y     t     s
                        t
```

"The seating will be divided into leadership, secondary leadership and cadre," King had said, "once everything is settled. And everything will be settled after group today."

Ho squatting with the children, Che on his horse and Huey P. Newton in his wicker chair were all missing from the walls. There were no tuna-can ashtrays or newspapers on the floor. The shock troops walked in quietly and found their places in the rows. Schenk sat in front of the blackboard, facing them, smiling. Schenk had been smiling a lot more lately. To one side of him sat Billy and King and Smallwood and Miriam with two thin, dark boys Hobie had never seen before. Miriam whispered to them and pointed to different people around the room.

Schenk began. "An interesting development has come to our attention. In fact, we only confirmed it this morning. They're watching us." His smile broadened. "The Man has decided to get on our case. He's taking note of our activity, which means we must be doing something right."

A small laugh from the seated shock troops and then Mark Remington came in with Pinkstaff. Sarah followed him, and Parke and Ira Wein.

Schenk looked up and nodded at them. "Glad you could make it."

They looked at the neat rows. There was no more room allotted within the tape. They spread out and stood along the back wall.

"We were discussing the fact that we're under surveillance."

"I hope they're being paid well," said Grant Parke. "I mean staking out this bunch would be like watching a day's worth of *Candlepins for Cash.*"

Schenk ignored him. "We first suspected when we decided to pay the bill and try to get our phone service reinstated. Ma Bell was being *awfully* generous. Anyone can get four months behind on a bill, they said, no problem at all. We didn't even have to pay the fine. Very fishy, right? Beware of monopolies bearing gifts.

"So King and I decided to run a little test. King calls me up from a paybooth a couple days ago and we fake a conversation. 'Did you get it?' I say. 'I got it,' says King. 'Is it planted?' I ask. 'It will be.' 'When is it set for?' 'Eleven A.M.' 'How much are you using?' 'Oh, more than enough. That thing'll go up like a rocketship. People in Charlestown gonna get their fireworks on Christmas this year.' 'Beautiful,' I say, 'scratch one historical monument.' And then we hang up. And we wait. We've given them a couple days, enough clues to figure it out. The Bunker Hill Monument, right, cause what else is there worth blowing up in Charlestown? Eleven A.M. Christmas day, this morning. As far as they know that's where our heads are at, bombing statues, like they're trying to stick the Panther 21 with in New York. So King gets over there at nine this morning and it's closed to the public, which maybe it is on Christmas anyway, but parked just around the corner on the hill there is the bomb-squad truck. We've been plugged into the Big Ear."

Hobie had almost forgotten it was Christmas. Back home the company always sponsored a pageant and the Mine Workers' local gave out free candy to the little kids. Most all of the different churches had singing at night and the merchants put up a tree in front of the post office. It had been mostly reorganization and criticism sessions since the basketball game, so he hadn't been out to see the shoppers and all that. It was funny, how you could lose touch with the rest of the world.

"King has rewired one of our radios and we've checked the whole building out for bugs. Nothing so far. But what this means, besides an indication that we're being taken seriously, is that the free-and-easy days are over. We have to be concerned with security. We have to tighten the collective and keep it tight. From now on new members will have to live in separate housing and be excluded from all important strategy meetings until we can check out their background and test their commitment. And each of us already in the collective will be subjected to evaluation and screening in the near future, incorporated with our criticism/self-criticism sessions. There will be a lock-and-buzzer mechanism installed at the front door. All other entrances are to be permanently sealed. We will have a codeword for admission that will change on a regular basis. The phone will be disconnected, we'll use paybooths in the area, only when absolutely necessary. No one is to call parents or former friends on personal business. We have to learn to trust and rely on each other, to completely sever our actual and psychological ties with the enemy. We have to work as a unit. This means an end to the rampant and counter-productive individualism that has for too long characterized this group. This isn't Hippie Heaven we're running here, this is a cadre engaged in world revolution. Do I make myself clear?"

No one spoke. They sat up straight and listened to Schenk. Coach had always said that, in halftime chalk-talks when things had been going bad on the field. He would spell out the possible consequences if everyone continued to play like a bunch of pantywaists and then look them right in the eye and say, "Do I make myself clear?" Schenk was a lot scarier than Coach had ever been, though he wasn't half the size.

"I realize that these developments can only take place after a certain amount of struggle with the way we've all been brainwashed and conditioned by our backgrounds, our inherited class biases. But as the saying goes, 'Dare to struggle, dare to win.' Real learning can only take place through struggle. In essence, we're going to make ourselves into new people. Make this into a totally new group. You change or you die."

Schenk cleared his throat. "Bearing all this in mind, we've decided that the collective should have a new name. To help us gain a fresh start. We've considered the alternatives and have come up with what we think best expresses our present position within the Revolution. 'The National Labor Front.' *National*, because our concerns are with the promotion of people's war within the fascist state of America. *Labor* because we expect our greatest support to be from working people rather than students. *Front*, because it *is* a war and we expect to be in the vanguard of the struggle. The National Labor Front. The similarity of our acronym to that of the Viet Cong is not accidental."

"Don't you think that should be voted on?" Mark Remington spoke from the rear. It was startling to hear his voice again.

Schenk smiled. "Of course. All in favor?"

Hands shot up in the rows.

"I don't think it's necessary to count, do you?"

"It's your show, Schenk."

"And what the *fuck* do you mean by that?"

Mark began to speak but there was a loud knock from the hall. Everyone tensed and looked to the door.

"If it's a bust," said King quietly, "everybody's deaf and dumb until we get the lawyer in to see us." And then loudly, "It's open."

A light-colored black man walked into the room, sniffling his nose, stopping in his tracks when he saw the two divisions of short-haired white kids staring at him.

"What do you want?" asked King.

"If Paris Green sent you," said Miriam, "tell him he can stuff it up and break it off."

"We — uh — we —"

"You come here alone? You with those suckers from the high school the other night?"

"Yeah — uh, no — I'm with —"

"Who sent you?"

"We're from the Full Gospel Missionary Baptist? We been out singin carols in the neighborhood, and they sent me up to see if you people'd like to —"

"Oh *shit*."

"Who left the door open?"

"I don't think we're the audience you had in mind. We're having a meeting."

"Oh. Sorry. I'll show myself out."

"You do that."

The man gave them a nervous grin and ducked out the door. They listened to him going down the stairs.

Schenk signaled Mickey Q. to follow him out. "See if there really are carolers down there," he said. Mickey left. Schenk turned to Mark. "In answer to your insinuation, this is *our* show. The collective. That's how we're going to make decisions from now on, as a collective, that's how we're going to operate. To do it we need security and we need discipline and we need commitment. We can't have people just *liv*ing here, people who are not involved, who are not totally committed to the collective. We have to separate ourselves from that kind of people." He raised his head to take in the group standing in the rear. "Mark?"

It had been coming for a long time. Somehow the thing had changed so quick and quiet that this wasn't even a showdown, Remington was already out and it was only a matter of saying his good-byes. It was going to split up.

Hobie figured he'd probably drift off after it did. Maybe they were right about the security and discipline stuff, and about the other, how nobody was really much for the government and were just waiting to get together to take back control of it. But he'd never liked Schenk that much and Tracy Anne hadn't come by to be with him at night for nearly a week, sitting there eyeballin the two fellas Miriam brung in, and Sarah, Sarah would be going along with Mark. Not that what Sarah did made any difference to him anymore. Besides, he had other things to do —

"Subtlety was never one of your strong points, Schenk." Mark laughed. "Well. It looks like you won't have Remington to kick around anymore."

Nobody even smiled.

"Listen, I don't want to sound bitter. I'm not bitter." He directed his words to the shock troops. "But I think you're being seduced. A little hard-line rhetoric, a little urban guerrilla fun-and-games and he's got you sewed up. I'm disappointed. I thought some of you could think for yourselves."

He shrugged and smiled. "Funny, I've been sitting around expecting this, not knowing how to avoid it, for days now and I'm at a loss for words. Look, try not to get busted or hurt for anything you're not positive you believe in. Dress warm. Good luck." He walked out the door.

Immediately Pinkstaff was in his place, red-faced and shouting. "You just cut your own throats! I hope you realize that." He spat and showed his teeth when he yelled. "You just cut your own fucking *throats!*" He followed Mark.

Everyone looked to Wein next. He was shaking his head slowly. He pushed his glasses up on his nose and took a deep breath. "What we have here," he said, "is the paradox of freedom of thought versus political efficiency. Though in belief Mark rejected the liberal dodge of the so-called pluralistic society, in practice he allowed everybody to voice their own interpretation of ideology, leaving himself wide open for the very kind of factionalism and power struggle that led to the disintegration of SDS. However, the alternative you people seem to have chosen is the kind of doctrinaire restriction of individual thought that tends to stifle any —"

"Write it in a book and mail it to us!" Miriam shouted. "We don't need to listen to your bullshit anymore."

He sighed. He cleared his throat. He took another deep breath.

"Piss or get off the pot, Wein!"

Wein gave them all a pitying look. He walked out.

Grant Parke was giggling to himself.

"Grant?"

"Yes?"

"Do you have anything to tell us?"

"Do I —? Oh. Hey, you know me. I'm with whoever's got the action. I'm afraid we're stuck with each other."

"Think you can handle the discipline?"

"Schenk, old buddy, if *you* can take it, *I* can take it. You're talking to a man who came to *play*." He stepped up the aisle and sat next to Hobie.

"Sarah?" She was the last one standing.

She stood frowning slightly, hands in the pockets of her Levi jacket. She hadn't turned to watch any of her friends go.

"If you make a commitment," she said quietly, "if you make a commitment to something, to some people, you can't go splintering off the minute things don't go your way. That's why the Movement is in the mess it's in, nobody has any patience. You stay and you struggle from within for what you believe. That's your responsibility.

"And if a group claims to hold the people's interests at heart," she said staring at Schenk, "it can't deny anyone the right to work alongside and prove their commitment to that same ideal."

She looked around the room, looked into each face. "Right now, the way I see it, there's not much choice. PL has got their ideology up their assholes and Weatherman is up in Michigan at that War Council, and from the first reports it sounds like it's going to be based on the premise that the Manson Family is the greatest thing since sliced bread, and then everybody else is milling around like a bunch of zombies asking each other whatever became of the New Left." She waved a hand at the seated National Labor Front. "Where else is there to go?"

Schenk smiled. Smallwood and King slid apart to make a seat for her at the head of the room. She ignored them and sat in the back row.

"Well." Schenk rubbed his hands together. "I'm glad we were able to settle that with a minimum of melodrama. We can get on with the *ac*tual purpose of this meeting, which is to discuss our first full-scale action as a collective. Our opening shot, so to speak. Miriam has been working on this for several weeks now, so I'll turn the floor over to her."

Hobie buttoned his Army jacket a little higher. You could see people's breath in the room, the heating had gone out a couple days back when Miriam had been too busy with other things to fix it and they didn't want to involve the landlord. Miriam stood to talk. Hobie watched Sarah from the corner of his eye. She was still with them.

Miriam introduced Jaibo and Esteban. "They work at the factory where I'm a stitcher," she said, "making bras. Jaibo is in the stockroom and Esteban is a clicker operator."

Jaibo and Esteban sat together, not taking their eyes off Miriam.

"Now this bra factory is a regular nineteenth-century operation. Guy name Rudnick owns and runs it, one of the last of the small-time robber barons. And he's got the ideal setup for that kind of thing. Almost all the employees are women, most are Spanish-speaking with little or no English, and a good percentage of those are illegal aliens. The majority of the people either don't know their rights or don't *have* any rights under the immigration laws. Most of them are afraid to go to the doctor or open a bank account, so it's obvious that there's no *way* we're going to be able to organize them in the usual trade-unionist manner. The local Garmentworkers' shops don't seem to be interested and there's a lot of evidence that Rudnick has the fix in with them to stay away from his people. He's paying slave wages, minimum or less, and there's absolutely no benefits or paid holidays, no sick leave, no grievance procedure. Love it or leave it. This is a situation where the people just aren't gonna be able to do it on their own.

"Which is where we come in. I've already got us some connections, some base support within the factory. What our job is, is to *expose* the situation Rudnick has created, to give the people courage and direction, to show them who their enemy is. To be their vanguard in demanding better conditions."

"How?" asked Grant Parke.

"We close it down. The tools of production belong to the workers, it was their labor that paid for them in the first place and that keeps on paying for them. So we liberate the tools. We liberate the whole shop, in the name of the people. When we're in there and have a chance to talk with them, when they see where we're at politically and just how exploited they are, they'll join us. Like Columbia, the mass following the vanguard. Like what almost happened with the workers in France. We can secure the building, I've gone over the floor plan with Jeff and King, and they'll have to lay siege to get us out. This isn't going to be any campus sit-in, this is the real world. We're going to bring the war home to Mr. Rudnick."

"What if there's a big bust?" asked Sarah.

"There probably will be. But it will get Rudnick into court and he won't have a leg to stand on. He's violating so many laws that he'll probably want to settle outside, which means we'll have him over a barrel."

"I mean what if some of the people who work there get busted? Or just checked up on? If the law finds out they're illegal aliens they'll be deported."

"Right." Miriam smiled. "And when they see who's putting them on the boat they'll know who their real enemy is. So that when they get home they'll probably join the Tupemaros."

[357]

"How many people do we have inside?" Tracy Anne was asking Jaibo, flashing her dimples. "I mean how many of you workers are already with us?"

He turned to Miriam. "Que dijó?"

"Dijó que quiere poseer tu cuerpo," she told him. "He doesn't speak English."

"Oh. I'm sorry." Jaibo was smiling back at Tracy Anne.

"In answer to your question," said Miriam, "we have enough. And once we're in there we'll have the rest."

Miriam began to tell them about similar actions in history. Hobie was watching Sarah. She was giving her full attention to Miriam, as if nothing had happened. As if Mark hadn't just been given the boot. Hobie had thought that it was because of Mark that she'd come down on him so hard the other night, but Mark was gone and she was staying. She had apologized to him, saying she had been generally on the rag that night, that she really did like him but just not in "that way." It didn't make him feel any less awkward around her though. If only he hadn't come out and tried it would be fine, it would be like before.

Maybe he'd hang around a bit after all. Not that what Sarah did made much difference. Just hang around to see what would happen next.

Miriam began to explain the details of the action. "The doors open at six-thirty. There are no security guards, just the two floor supervisors. They'll have to be taken care of."

Anyhow, there didn't seem to be any way he could track Darwin. And the fellas at Labor Power said that right after Christmas was real slow for work. He couldn't head back to West Virginia. Might's well hang on here for a while. Where else was there to go?

29

The streets were still flooded on Monday morning, Hunter found it hard to find dry pavement in the half-light. It was over a foot deep in the middle where Tremont met Chandler. The Man Pool office was on Tremont, just around the corner from the Courier, where he'd spent his first night.

There were three men in grubby denim jackets hanging in front of the Man Pool. They looked a bit like the Latins that lived by Mrs. Hanrahan's, dark and all, but there was something different.

"Hey buddy," said the tallest of the men, "think you could help us out?"

"Depends on what you need." Hunter could see beyond the glass front that there was a couple fellas already sitting inside. In case there was trouble.

"What we need, to be honest with you, is twenny-fie cents to make a bottle a wine."

"It's a worthy cause, mister."

"Sorry." He'd never given anything to panhandlers. Never once. "I had money to be buyin people wine I wouldn't be down here."

"Hey, you'd be helpin out a vanishin breed."

"What's that supposed to mean?"

"We're Indians."

That was it. They didn't look so much Spanishy as they looked Indian.

"We're the Needaquattah tribe."

"Never heard of em."

"Sure you have. Every time you see us we need a quattah. Tribe's been on this corner for centuries, bummin change. Hey, when the pilgrims come, John Smith and those guys, my ancestors stood here and hit em up for two bits."

"Be serious, Charlie," said the tall one. "You'll give the man the wrong impression. We *are* Indians, mister. Ever hear of the Mic Macs?"

"Nope."

"Well that's what we are. And we need a little change to get a gallon."

"Why not go in and work a day?"

"We done that before but Charlie got in a fight. We're boycottin."

"Besides, it's beneath the tribal code of honor, work for less than two-fifty an hour. The Great Spirit would shit a brick, he saw us pullin that."

"What is it, mister, you never been down on your luck? You never took a handout?"

Hunter thought about it for a second. He smiled. "What you say you needed?"

Charlie made a face and figured in his head. "Let's see, gallon a Thunderbird, we need — twenty-seven cents."

"You sure you gonna buy wine with it? Not gonna waste it on solid food or a place to sleep or some nonsense like that?"

"Mister, please, do we look like the type?"

He handed thirty cents to the tall one.

"You'll be rewarded in the hereafter, mister. If not sooner."

There were wooden folding chairs facing a counter inside. A man sat behind the counter, half sleeping, half listening to a radio. There wasn't but four or five wino-looking old black men sitting in the chairs.

"Tell you the truth, McNatt," said the man behind the counter when Hunter had finished filling out the forms, "it don't look too good. It's our slow season here. Lot of small businesses that use temporary help close down from Christmas till New Year. And then we got to take care of our regulars first." He nodded toward the old men.

"Whatever you got," said Hunter, "I'm willin to take it on."

He sat by himself in one of the wooden chairs. He closed his eyes and slumped down. It had been nice for a while, sleeping till eight, visiting with Helen while the girls were out at school, but now being without work was starting to bother him. And not just the money problems, not just that he had to make excuses with Helen when she wanted to go out somewhere with him. It was the feeling of being idle, he wasn't used to it. And from what Jimmy said there didn't look to be much chance of him getting back on at Porchetta.

He'd come across a meat job at the Armour in South Boston when he was going through the Help Wanteds. He figured he would have a good shot at it, with his experience and being a union member. Four dollars an hour it said, nearly twice as much as most of the jobs he had been interviewing for. There wasn't much around that didn't take some special skill, and nothing he knew was much good out of a coal mine.

Interviews begin at seven, the ad had said, so he got there at 6:30. Along with over a hundred other people, men and boys and one strong-looking young girl. They huddled out on a loading dock, not speaking to each other, until a fella in a bloodied white apron came out and sighed and told them it was only one job open. Nobody left.

A fella in a suit came down at seven and clucked over their number, then lined them into single file and marched them upstairs to his waiting room. About twenty-five could fit into the room at a time, the rest were lined on the stairs, waiting. Somehow Hunter got in with the first twenty-five. The fella in the suit had one secretary working with him, they handed out pencils and application forms and a few clipboards for a surface to write on. There weren't enough pencils to go around so you had to wait and borrow. The fella went into his office to do interviews but would pop out every couple minutes to yell at the secretary to keep an eye on the pencils and clipboards and make sure she got them all back.

Hunter finished his form and got in the line waiting to be interviewed. No one spoke. It was early and they were out for the same job. He looked at the others and tried to guess which ones had worked in a meat place before. It was impossible to tell in street clothes.

"Did you have a pencil?" asked the fella when Hunter got in and sat down. Hunter told him he'd given it to someone else. The fella read his application and sighed. "To tell you the truth, Mr. McNatt," he said, shaking his head as he looked at the form, "a man your age — we need heavy lifting — somebody to stay with us permanently — sorry."

He'd been hearing a lot of sorrys lately, a lot about being a man his age. There wasn't a job he had applied for that he wasn't sure he could do and do well.

Two of the old black men were called up to the counter. They weren't really so old, not much older than himself. It was just how they looked. Sad and tired. That was it, tired.

MAN POOL, said the red-white-and-blue banner on the wall. THE BEST JOBS FOR THE BEST MEN. There was free coffee bubbling on a hotplate but if it was going to be a long wait he didn't want to be too awake. He could hear cars beginning to move outside, swishing carefully through the flooded streets.

Last Friday Hunter had stood in line at the unemployment for the first time. He felt like everybody was looking at him, though when he glanced around nobody really was. He knew he never could have done it back home, he felt funny enough about it here where nobody knew him. The people in the line were different than he had figured. They didn't look so sorry as he thought they would. He thought he recognized a few from the morning at Armour. There were old people and there were kids just out of school. He wanted to ask each one of them why they were there, especially the ones looked young and healthy enough to work. He wondered if they wanted to ask him the same thing. It wasn't that he was too sorry to work, it was — it was *cir*cumstances.

He didn't get any money yet, he had another week or so before that. But he had to check in at the 9:30 line on Friday mornings, to give in last week's work slip and pick up next week's.

During the week ending December 27, 1969 —

said the slip —

Did you work either for an employer or in self-employment?
No.
Did you look for work with anyone other than your last employer?

[362]

Yes.

Did you refuse any work?

No.

Were you able and willing to accept work on all *full-time* shifts, customary for your occupation?

Yes.

Did the number of your dependent children increase or decrease?

No.

You were supposed to check all the right boxes and hand it in. They didn't ask you anything or challenge what you wrote down. It would be easy to lie. But everything Hunter wrote was true. He was looking. Looking as best he could. He *was*.

Hunter sat with his eyes closed and wondered what they would say back home if they knew. Oh, there was plenty on the rolls back home, but he nor any of his family had ever been among them. He wondered how things were in Number 7. It made him feel a little guilty, being up top when they were down under, being safe when they were in danger. Sitting when they were moving all that coal. He missed it some.

But it seemed so far off. It was good to breathe real air all the time, no coal dust or silica, good not to wake up with his stomach in knots knowing he'd have to go down again and chew at the face, good to be without the acid burps and the aches and the pains and the coughing all the time. That much felt good.

"McNatt."

He shook himself and went up to the counter.

"I've got something here, it's only five hours, but I don't think you're gonna do much better today."

"I'll take it."

"Okay, it's the Cambridge Novelty Company, the Red Line gets you right by it, Vassar Street. Ask for a guy named Gene. Light manufacturing, we send guys out there a lot during the peak season."

"What do they do?"

"Ping-Pong balls," said the man behind the counter. "They make Ping-Pong balls. Try not to strain yourself."

[363]

30

Sarah and Hobie sat, on the first day of the new year, protected from the blizzard by the Lechmere Station awning at the end of the Green Line. Plows had already come twice to clear snow-drifts from the turnaround, but the tracks were instantly buried again in white. Traffic crept stop-and-go over on the Monsignor O'Brien Highway, low beams pushing through the gray morning. Tires spun and whined from the side streets. Sarah and Hobie couldn't even see to the Deran factory through the falling snow. They sat with a box of leaflets in between them.

A three-car train appeared on the hill, eased down and came to a stop under the shed. The doors wheezed open. Sarah worked the front and Hobie the rear. The men and women stepped down silently, eyes red and sticky with sleep, stepped down wearing hooded sweatshirts under their heavy coats and took or did not take an offered leaflet without looking up. The doors rattled shut and the train sparked into its U-turn. The people gathered just inside the edge of the roofing, blowing big clouds of breathing and psyching themselves to go out into the howling gray. A cluster of men by Sarah grumbled in Italian, then lowered their heads and ran out together in the direction of the highway. The rest of the people sighed and shuddered and pulled on their gloves, braced themselves and disappeared into it. Sarah and Hobie stood back in the shelter with pamphlets swirling around their ankles.

Sarah waited for Hobie to pick his side of the box and then sat down next to him. "I probably wouldn't be too interested in reading some political stuff on a morning like this either," she said.

"Mmn."

"Probably a lot of them don't understand English."

"Uhn."

"You warm enough with just that jacket on?"

"Yuh." Hobie closed his eyes like he was still sleepy. They waited. The wind scooped under the awning, Sarah had to put a hunk of pavement she'd found on top of the leaflets to keep them from being sucked up out of the box. The wind got inside her poncho and puffed it out around her, the wind sent bits of icicles stinging against the walls and benches. Sarah covered her face with her gloves.

Another train pulled in. Sarah rose and put on her smile and took a stack of leaflets to meet them. Hobie took a stack of leaflets.

Once again the people looked beyond them to the blizzard outside. Most kept their hands in their pockets. The men wore steel-toed boots and the women wore sneakers or flats with rubbers over them. The wind got in through the open doors of the train and the cars shook where they stood. A big red hand clamped over Sarah's stack of leaflets.

"What we got here, sister?"

It was a cop in his heavy leather and his fur hat, holding one glove under his armpit and pulling the papers from Sarah. She hadn't seen him coming.

"Leaflets."

"Some kind of political garbage?" He didn't bother to turn them upright, cocking his head to glance at the headline.

"Read it."

" 'People's war,' huh? Who you with? SDS?"

"It says on top."

"NLF. I never heard of yuz."

"We just changed our name. We've actually been around for quite a while, we used to be called the —"

"Wonderful. Beautiful. I'm sure it's a fascinating story, but I don't have all morning to listen to how you got your name. Your name'll be mud though, you don't clear out fast. No soliciting on city prawperty."

"We're not soliciting. We're giving them out free."

The papers fluttered in the cop's hand. He pushed them back to Sarah and put his glove on. "Same difference. It's no go, there's a lawr against it."

"Who says?"

The cop stared at the awning and sighed. The train pulled out. Hobie came and stood a few feet from them.

" 'Who says?' she asks me. *I* says, that's who. The guy in the uniform, it says police on the badge. Who the fuck *else* you talkin to here? You an your boyfriend pack up and git."

"I don't think that's a law at all," said Sarah. "The last election the subways were full of council members handing out stuff every morning. I must have run into what's his face, Dapper O'Neill, a half-dozen times. Kissing babies or whatever. If they can do it why can't we?"

"Listen, sweethot, I'm not gonna stand here, the fucking blizzard, an chew the fat with yuz. You wanna go back Hovvid Yod, smoke your dope, hump your little ass off with the college boys that's fine. Just keep your bullshit out of East Cambridge, awright?"

"Watch your mouth."

The cop looked at Hobie like he was a mirage. "What did you say?"

"You heard me."

"I hope I didn't hear you correctly, my friend. What's your name?

"Tony Gramsci."

"Where you from?"

"North End."

"In a pig's gizzard you are. You got any ID?"

"Nope."

"Why aren't you in school?"

"I graduated."

"Where'd you get that jacket?"

"Brother."

"He was in the Army, your brother?"

"Yup."

"In Vietnam?"

"Yup."

"I bet he's real proud a you. Real fuckin proud. You said you graduated?"

"Yup."

"How'd they let a punk like you past the eighth grade?"

Hobie didn't answer. Schenk had told them all to be extra careful, no trouble, no busts. The factory siege was set for the fifth and they would be needing full force.

"What the fuck you doing up here, you're from the Nawth End?"

Hobie shrugged. "Passin the things out."

"Where from in the Nawth End? What street?"

"Prince Street."

"Little fot." The cop shook his head. "Out here, the fuckin Yukon, I'm takin gas from a little fot. Little faggot."

Sarah was holding Hobie's arm, pulling him back a little. "Where does the city property end?"

"What?"

"You said we can't pass our stuff out on city property," she said. "So where does it end, where are we legal?"

"Anywheres under this shed is city as far as I'm concerned." He jerked his head out at the storm around them. "The rest is up for grabs."

"C'mon Hobie." Sarah gave him a tug and then went to grapple with the box of leaflets. Hobie followed her.

"Take my advice girlie," called the cop from behind them, "get on the next train. Freeze your tits off out there."

The wind slapped into them, they had to bend at the knees and wade out across the tracks. Sarah's poncho whipped around her. They stopped on the far side of the turnaround, maybe twenty yards from the station. Hobie kicked a space clear and Sarah laid the box down. Hobie was wearing his low-cut running shoes, with the stripes beginning to peel off the sides.

"We can cover both ways from here," said Sarah. She had to shout though they were only a few feet apart. "You take the ones that head for Deran, I'll get the ones going for the street."

"Uhn." Hobie was wearing a pair of gloves King had loaned him. He covered his ears with them and stomped to get some feeling back in his toes.

"What's the cop doing?" Hobie didn't respond, so Sarah made her way back across the tracks to peer through the blowing snow. She came back. "Drinking coffee. He's in there with the guy who takes your quarter, drinking. Cooping, they call it in the city, in New York. We disturbed his coop. No wonder he was actin like such a prick, it's like a bird protecting his nest. Poor guy probably figured it would look bad if he's in there sitting while we're out here advocating violent overthrow of the government and who knows what else, so he had to get rid of us." Hobie didn't respond. "He's right about one thing though. I *am* going to freeze my tits off out here.

"Hobie?"

"Mmmn?"

"You sure you're warm enough in that thing? I mean this stuff is important to get out, to prepare for the action Monday, but it's not life or death. Can you make it okay?"

"Mmmn."

The wind kept shifting and they turned constantly to keep it at their backs. "It's not that it's really *freez*ing out," said Sarah. "Not temperature-wise. It just feels like it, cause we were sheltered in there and now we're not. It's whatever you're used to. Relative. So all you got to do, see, is you got to *ac*climate yourself."

"Mmnph," said Hobie.

Sarah scooped a handful of snow and waited for him to turn his back against the wind. She stuffed it down his neck.

"Hey!"

"See? It's just snow, it won't kill you. Acclimate yourself to it."

He just looked at her.

"Get used to it. Let it slide down and kind of slush it around back there. You little fot." She mimicked the cop. "You fuckin little fot. Fuckin Tony Gramsci, from the north end of West Virginia."

Sarah laughed and Hobie smiled a little and started walking toward her. He picked up some snow. "You think that's funny, huh?" Sarah backed up. "You think that's funny, you think you're a regular comedian, dontcha? Huh? Dontcha?" He kept coming at her till she backed over the box of leaflets and fell into the snow. "Acclimate yourself to that."

"Aaaaaaack! You prick!" They were both laughing. "Instant frostbite! I'm a goner." Hobie helped her to her feet. "This is ridiculous, you know that? We'll never get across the river alive. It's the siege of Leningrad all over again."

Sarah held her wrist to her forehead and put on a Russian accent. "Pipple frozen in the strit. Killink horses to drink their blodd. Wudka frozen solid in the buttle, houses gotted for fire-vood —"

"Where they get horses in Boston?"

"You got a point. Killink automubbles and drinking the redia-tor fluitt, Budvicer frozen in the can —"

"You shoulda stayed on the stage."

"And you should have stayed in the hill country — leetle fots from Vest Wirchinya, frozen in midair —"

"Cops frozen in their coops."

"You got it, Hobie. It's curtains. The Revolution has been postponed due to a new Ice Age. The ink will freeze in the mimeograph machine and that'll be all she wrote. Sticky Dicky will be a museum piece, like the stegosaurus and the pterodactyl."

Sarah stopped and looked at Hobie for a long moment. He was squinting through the blowing snow and wiping his nose on his sleeve.

"You still mad at me Hobie?"

"Naw." He shrugged it off. "I wasn't ever *mad* at you, I was — you know."

"It's a bitch, isn't it?" Sarah shook her head. "It must be rougher on guys in some ways, always being expected to make the first move."

He stared at his feet. "Wasn't much of a move."

Sarah reached to brush the snow from his hair. "You still like me?"

"I like you a lot."

"Good." Sarah tried to get him to look at her. "I want us to be friends. And I don't want the sex thing to fuck it up, you know?"

"I guess."

"With Mark gone and the way the group is now, you're about the only — only *per*sonal friend that I have left."

"You're not with Mark anymore? On the outside?"

"It would be too hard on both of us. It's best that I be alone, sleep alone for a while now. Time to think. But I need my friends more than ever."

"Everybody likes you. They look up to you sort of. Lean on you."

"That's fine. I'm glad if I'm some help to them, that's why I'm still there. But there isn't anybody I can be — vulnerable with. You know?" They were standing close now, to hear without shouting. "I'm always the one listening to their problems, settling their fights, giving them advice. I feel like a fucking den mother. I need somebody I can just relax with and talk about what's bothering me."

Hobie bent and brushed snow off the leaflets with the side of his hand. "Hell," he said, "you know me. I'll listen to anything."

Sarah smiled. "Hobie, would it bother you if I hugged you? I mean I really want to, it'll make me feel a lot better. I know it might be like — like rubbing it in — I know that. I once had a professor I thought I was madly in love with pat me on the head after I'd made a move on him. Can you imagine? Like a puppy just did a piddle on the rug. I thought it was the cruelest thing anyone had done to me. But all he wanted to say was that he didn't want me to stop liking him just because he didn't want to start an affair with me. I know how it feels. I transferred out of his class and wouldn't answer when he'd say hi to me on campus. I wasn't strong enough to deal with it.

"Hobie?"

He shook his head no, he didn't mind if she hugged him. Their cheeks were icy at first but made a warm spot between them when Sarah pushed tight. Hobie's lower body felt numb against her, but the pressure of her arms seemed to squeeze all the bad feeling out of his chest, all the nervous out of his throat. He was glad to be with her.

They heard another train pulling into the station. Sarah grabbed a handful of leaflets and ran to the gap in the highway. Hobie split off toward the candy factory.

People tottered forward out of the gray with their arms covering their faces, veering away from Hobie as if he were a stop sign or a fence post. He managed to stuff a few into pockets, and ended up chasing after one woman to apologize for scaring her. There weren't so many people as there had been before.

"It's not like you've been totally shut out in the nookie department," said Sarah when the people were gone and they'd come back to the box.

[370]

"Huh?"

"You heard me turkey. You and Tracy Anne."

"You seen us?"

"In a tight group like that you don't need to see to know. Besides, Trace has made the rounds of every other able-bodied male in the house, why would she pass you by?"

"Got a point."

"Not that she wouldn't have been attracted anyway, I mean —"

"Already she's after those Spanish fellas Miriam brung in."

"You come from *Ec*uador?" Sarah pushed dimples into her cheeks with her fingers. "Far out! Far-fucking-out!"

They laughed.

"And then I noticed a little something with you and Jennifer —"

"Only that once —"

"Tell me about it. And Debbie?"

"Nothin's come of that yet."

"But you're working on it, right?"

"She's so serious all the —"

"Hobie, you're making out like a fucking *ban*dit. And here you had me feeling all guilty cause I wasn't —"

"I like you better than them. Even if we don't — I'd rather be with you."

Sarah paused, smiled. "That's a nice thing to say. Thank you. And now what's that cop doing?"

Hobie trotted forward to look. "Still there," he said. "Readin a paper."

"Shit. Don't they have anything to *do*?"

"Maybe we could throw snowballs at him, smoke him out."

"You crazy? That's how the Boston Massacre started."

"Huh?"

"What did they *teach* you up there? You never heard of the Boston Massacre? Crispus Attucks?"

"Not that I remember."

"There's a plaque in the sidewalk where it happened, by the State Street T station. I'll show it to you sometime."

"You can't spit in this city but what you're lible to hit some kind of historical monument."

"So we don't need another one here. The tomb of the Unknown Radical. No snowballs."

"I remember in school a couple years ago, we went on this field trip." Hobie brushed snow from his eyebrows. "A real big deal, clear across to the edge of the state, to Harpers Ferry. Where John Brown was?"

"Yeah, I know. A-mouldrin in the grave and all that."

"Right. Mostly what they got there is floods. All over the place they got lines drawn up on the buildins, saying how in the flood of '28 it was this high, in the flood of '32 it was this high — like that. And wax museums, they're big on those. And there's the firehouse where John Brown and his people got cornered, you push a button and this voice tells you all about it, all about his raid and how he was gonna get guns from the armory and give em to the slaves and go round freeing everybody. But what I remember best is this one plaque, you wouldn't know it's there except that it's right on the way to where they sell ice-cream cones, it's up on the side of this building.

"The plaque is dedicated to a fella named Heyward Sheperd. He was a black freeman and he was the first person killed in the raid. See, he was a railroad guard and he heard people runnin around and he come out to see what was what. It was John Brown, and they killed him dead. So's they could free the slaves, see.

"That stuck with me, that plaque."

They stood and listened to the wind whistling through the awning of the station. There were no cars to be seen on the highway now. The Deran building let out a whoosh of smoke.

"You worried about the action Monday?"

Hobie nodded. "Some."

"It worries me too. I think we might not be well-enough prepared, we might not be totally sure of our base support. But Schenk wants it done before the college kids come back from their vacations, so it's clear to the media people that we're an independent workers' group. I mean you *do* learn through action, I've always believed that. But you might just learn something that you don't want to *know*."

A one-car train pulled in, nearly empty. Sarah ran to catch the people. She came back, shaking her head and shivering.

[372]

"How'd you get into all of this stuff?" said Hobie. "Where you're ready to be stuck in jail for some people don't hardly know you? I mean what started you in it?"

Sarah closed her eyes and took a deep breath. " 'Men have unrealized potential for self-cultivation,' " she said, " 'self-direction, self-understanding and creativity. It is this potential that we regard as crucial and to which we appeal — not to the human potentiality for violence, unreason, and submission to authority.' "

"That from a play?"

She laughed. "It's from a thing called the Port Huron Statement. It was the Movement's version of the Declaration of Independence."

"You got it all memorized?"

"It made a big impression on me. It made me into a radical."

"Don't sound all that radical to me."

"It was at the time, believe me. Now —" She sighed. "Things change. Especially politics, they change faster than you can keep up with them. I'm what, maybe eight years older than you? And it's like we've got a totally different history behind us. How old were you when they shot Kennedy?"

"Sixth grade."

"I was out of college, already into voter registration and all that. Things have polarized, things have escalated — you've got to just hang on and do what you can. I know enough about myself to realize that I have to be in some kind of political group to be at all effective. To have any effect, you know? So here I am freezing. Can you understand that?"

"Nope."

"You got any money?"

"Two dollars."

"In that case," she said, "let's blow this cookie stand and get ourselves some breakfast. I think we owe it to the workers of the world."

They each took an end of the box and headed for shelter.

31

It was a beautiful sunny morning on Chauncy Street. Schenk strolled self-consciously, not taking his eyes off the filthy brown building across the pavement. He had never worn a backpack before, he was sure it was adjusted wrong. It was heavy, canned foods in case they had to hold out for days. He had the slip of paper in his breast pocket, with the numbers where he could reach Smallwood to phone out press releases. King, on the next block, had his tools and phone jack in case the pigs tried to cut off communication once they were inside. The news that came out of the action was just as important as what actually occurred within the factory. If not more.

It could be like Columbia. Bigger even. This was the real world.

NATIONAL LABOR FRONT JOINS WORKERS!
PEOPLE TAKE FACTORY; POLICE, BOSSES LAY SIEGE

It could last for days if they manned the entrances well enough. They'd be afraid to charge, a factory wasn't an administration building, there were machines and goods to hold for ransom, not just some bullshit cumulative files. They wouldn't jeopardize their precious private property. And maybe, if the workers held fast and he could get the story out far enough, it would spread, it would spark a similar action, the way Columbia had. Two, three, many stitching factories. If only the GE people had their shit together, they'd been out ten weeks, picketing and going broke, not even dreaming of *taking* what was rightfully theirs. If only this was the Lynn plant instead of a little robber-baron throwback. If they took Lynn it would spread to the Pittsfield plant, to the Schenectady operation, to the whole GE network and then maybe to the Auto Workers, to the Steel —

Then again, maybe not. This was private property, private business property and they loved that more than their own lives. They might be willing to sacrifice this Rudnick's sewing machines to make an example. There wouldn't be the pretense of nonviolence the colleges tried to keep up. This was the real thing, the real world. You put your ass on the line out here you were liable to get it creamed.

So use it. That was it, if it went bad, went hairy, make the defeat into a victory, an example of the moral swamp of the oppressor's value system. Property over people. Maybe it wouldn't be like Columbia but like the Easter Rebellion. A few tense hours in the buildings, overrun by the pigs and thrown into jail. But living on afterward, a memory and a metaphor of resistance, a point of reference for struggling workers in the future. The Pullman strike of 1910, the Boston police strike of 1919, the Athena Lingerie strike of 1969 —

ATHENA MARTYRS SENTENCED TODAY
WORKERS CRUSHED FOR ASSERTING RIGHTS

They would enter from three directions. Schenk leading one group, King and Grant Parke the others. Swift-walk up the stairs and in, 8:30 synchronized on the dot. The floor supervisors would be together, said Miriam, in their frosted-glass office taking their morning break.

They would walk in with their leather and their hard-toed kicking shoes, ready for gas, glass and clubs, walk in and liberate the building for the workers. Miriam would translate. He felt better with Miriam waiting inside. His heart was rattling his ribs, he had to hold onto his wrist to read the watch.

Thirty-five seconds.

Now or never. It was the only way.

He crossed the street and immediately ten people fell in behind him. A rush, it was a definite high to have them there with him, the numbers, the purpose. Up the stairs, musty, no ventilation, up and through the frosted-glass door to the shop floor. Chattering noise, like a thousand fingers drumming all in different rhythms, bobbins, reels, thread and elastic, shafts and cylinders singing in a

[375]

tangle through the air, the Latin women on high chairs at their machines, sneaking their eyes up suspiciously but not budging from where they sat. Frozen.

Sheep. It would be like stampeding a flock of sheep, in the end the sheep would trample the dragon. Schenk smiled and moved down the center aisle toward the spot where King and Miriam were heading, all his people breaking off behind him to take their positions, to fill their assignments. It was here. It was ripe. The banner was picked up and there was no turning back.

They jumped up on the table where they met, Schenk and King and Miriam in her leather jacket, kicking scraps of cloth out of the way.

"Obreras!" boomed Miriam over the din of the stitching machines, "ésta una huelga! *Huelga!* Libertar la factoría! Solidaridad para si*em*pre!"

LA HUELGA ATHENA

thought Schenk, smiling down at the bewildered brown faces —

EL PROTOTIPO POR LA REVOLUCIÓN

Hunter watched Jimmy push his scrambled eggs around the plate. They looked like they hadn't been cooked enough. It was hard to tell though, the light in the diner wasn't too good.

"So the thing is," said Jimmy, "they laid off the Hunk, I'm all alone up there except for whoever they send that doesn't know the curing, and they expect me to take it layin down. So I figure I take the day off, it's Monday, they get all their big awders in downstairs. Give em a taste of what it is without me. Figure I come downtown here, see some people I know." Jimmy buried the eggs in ketchup.

"You think they'd let you go?"

"Hey, who knows? The Hunk had twelve, thirteen years in, he come over during the Uprising there, the Commonists got on his tail. One of the Freedom Fighters. Thirteen years in and already they're that far up the seniority list. It's spooky, it's like a mawg over there. Nobody's workin. All that new machinery Taylor and them put in, where there used to be guys."

"And the union can't do anything about it?"

"I'll tell you, Hunt, I done some checking around. That new packing operation, does everything but fry the things up and eat them, it's the only one of its kind on the East Coast? It had to be made special. It took a year just to figure out all the specs. So the company had to have awdered it at least a year ago, right? Which shows on the books. And the union, they're up there in the cawporation office looking through those books these days, they knew damn well that thing was coming. The company must of cleared it with them a year ago. All that bullshit about the meat business going wrong and temporary layoffs was just to make it easier to do the changeover."

"They done that in the mines. Aren't half as many fellas workin as there used to be."

"But the ones who are still in are makin out a lot better, right?" Jimmy gave the ketchup bottle a thunk with the flat of his hand. "It's one of those things, you don't get nothin for nothin. The ones inside aren't gonna kick, they're makin the best they ever did, and the ones outside don't have no say, they're out of the union. Jesus, Johnny Greek is gone and Nick from downstairs and Sebastiano, a bunch of the guys on the shipping floor. It's a fuckin ghost town, it feels like. And the old ghinzos, it put the fear a God into em. They ratified that contract so fast that Sal didn't have time to roll his sleeves up. They're scared shitless, those guys."

The waitress came and asked Hunter if he'd like to order. He told her he wasn't eating.

"So did you think about what went over the other night?" asked Jimmy.

"Yuh."

"You gonna do it?"

"It goes against my grain."

"That wasn't the question. You gonna do it?"

Hunter rubbed the stubble on his face. His eyes were smarting from the cooking smoke and the fella in the next room had been up all night coughing. Always the coughing. "What about the loan?"

Jimmy smiled. "I made some phone calls. You want it, I can arrange it."

"What would the interest be?"

"They couldn't give me a figure right off, they want to check you out first. It won't be anything you couldn't clear up in four, five months, you keep your overhead down."

"Four or five months."

"Listen, there's not a bank gonna touch you. These guys, they don't have the security like a bank, they're not federally insured, all that, they got to chodge higher rates. You don't like it, there's still Francis."

"No."

"Like I said, I personally got my own difficulties, couple wrong guesses, couple bum steers, but Francis, he don't play. He just drinks, Francis. Anyhow, I talk to him, explain the situation, I'm positive he'd be overjoyed to help you out. No interest, no problem."

"No," said Hunter. "Not Francis. Half of it would come out of Helen's pocket like it always does with him. And I don't want him to know — you know — about us just yet."

"Hey, he's her brother, he's gotta know sometime."

"Not yet. I can't borrow from Francis."

"You're a proud man, McNatt."

"If I was all that proud," mumbled Hunter, "I wouldn't be thinking of this."

Hunter got change from the waitress and closed himself in the phonebooth. He dialed the number.

"Yeah, I remember you," said Gus Arnold when Hunter got past the receptionist. "Friend of my brother Mitch. What can I do for you?"

"You remember we talked about a job?" said Hunter.

"I remember. You wanted to get on with us. Then you decided you didn't want. So what's up?"

"I guess I changed my mind."

"It's a bitch out there, ain't it, McNatt? Especially if you don't have friends, you don't have nobody to look out for you. You changed your mind. Wonderful. The thing is, I haven't changed my policy. You know that, don't you? You remember my policy?"

"Yeah," said Hunter. "It was five hundred to get on."

Arnold laughed over the phone. "I like a man who gets to the point. It's a funny thing about that, though. You talked to me, it was before I went on vacation. I went to Vegas, see —"

"I remember."

"Sure you do. I went to Vegas, and I went in — they — I took a beatin, to tell you the truth. I got my nuggets handed to me. But it was good, I learned a lesson. I learned something about the value of money, about the value of a good, steady job. I understand, see, how much more — more *val*uable —"

"How much?" said Hunter.

"What?"

"How much?"

"Seven-fifty. And I got to have it up front. Of course if that's a problem, I could make some phone calls, I know some guys, could see clear to take a chance on you, they know you're on with us. It would mean a little interest but nothin you couldn't clear up in a few —"

"Never mind that. When can I start?"

"You can come up and get the paperwork out of the way tomorrow if you want. Don't bring the uh — initiation fee — don't bring that yet. We'll arrange for something. How're your X-rays?"

"Huh?"

"Your X-rays. We got to get you past the physician. See, the slot I can get for you is workin on these ships, over the East Boston pier, and there's, you know, welding and paint being burned off and all. Fumes. We got to be careful, the company don't like to pay out for lung trouble and —"

"They're fine," said Hunter. "I got some recent ones."

He was tired. Tired of the whole thing. The unemployment was only thirty a week and he had to keep switching day-labor places for fear they'd catch up with him. There wasn't much work and what there was always had some fella thought you were another wino had to be treated like a child. He was tired of Mrs. Hanrahan's, tired of single dollar bills over the counter, tired of the red-typed letters the collection agency for the hospital back home kept sending. Tired.

"I'll see you tomorrow," said Hunter. "Early."

"Beautiful. But about this money thing, you gotta be sure you come across. We understand each other, right? No monkey business."

Hunter said that he understood.

"Mr. McNatt, you won't regret it. You get on with us, you're golden."

"So?" asked Jimmy when he got back from the booth. The eggs were gone and he was working on the home fries.

"He says seven-fifty."

"I can still arrange it. Take a little longer to pay off, lose a bit more in vig, but it can be done. You're doin the right thing, Hunt. That steel, that's a tit. In no time I'll be borrowin money off you."

"Yuh."

"I'll get on the loan right away. Oh, there was something else — somethin I saw — Jeez, it slipped my mind. It'll come to me later, I'm on the toilet. That's when I remember things. Where you headed?"

"Try a place over on Beech Street, see if they have any work."

"Okay, buddy, take it light. See you around seven, my place first and then we'll go over. And don't worry, you done the right thing."

When Hunter had gone Jimmy went back to reading the morning *Herald* over his breakfast and immediately knew what it was he had forgotten to tell. The story right on the front page, how they had found the mine-union guy, Yablonski, and his wife and his daughter all shot dead in their house.

Rudnick got the call in the middle of his French toast. It was unbelievable. Why him? What could they be thinking of? His car was in for its tune-up and Ruthie had the Buick. He had to call a cab.

Rudnick tried to think on the way over who the troublemakers might be. That kid, that Esteban maybe. Ecuadorians, you couldn't trust them. And the Puerto Ricans, they were so bold, could come up and down whenever they wanted, it made them reckless. He would have to give the immigration people a couple calls maybe, shake things up. And get Hector to send the word down to some of his people in Florida. Cubans. They'd never pull a stunt like this. They were a stable people, the Cubans. At least the ones up here.

It made his heart jump to look at it. The patrol cars surrounding his building, the people all thronged on the street and watching. Like all his bad dreams about fires. It was good though, to see almost all the girls outside looking on with the rest of the crowd. Chattering away, looking as concerned as he was. Good girls. If it wasn't them, though, who the hell was it? The policeman on the phone had something about a strike. Rudnick pushed through the crowd and looked for the nearest high-ranking officer.

"Kids," said the captain. "Most of your people escaped out a side exit, but the kids are still in there. Our people are inside with them now. They been given instructions to be careful with the machinery, so I wouldn't worry, sir. We've called in men from other districts, it should be under control in no time."

Kids? What could they want? What could they possibly hope to do? It was worse than his nightmares, it made less sense. Rudnick wondered if it was going to affect his insurance rate.

They brought one out, screaming and kicking, a girl. Old leather jacket, frizzy black hair. She was bleeding from the mouth and trying to butt the two officers who pinned her arms behind her back and hustled her down the steps to the sidewalk. Rudnick stepped out toward them. He wanted to talk to her, to ask her why.

She dug her heels in when she saw him in her path. She tried to spit but it just come out blood and hung from her lip.

"Miss," he said, "just tell me one thing. I want to know one —"

"Kike!" she yelled in a surprisingly strong voice. "You fucking big-nosed kike!"

Hobie was stuck in the cellar when it started up. That was his assignment, he and Monk, to stay in the cellar guarding the two floor supervisors. The two Cubans. It wasn't guarding exactly, no guns or ropes, the two were so scared that they weren't needed. Schenk didn't want to let them go out and contact the police till they'd talked strategy with the workers. Schenk was supposed to come down and say when to let them loose but he never did and then it started.

The one who spoke English was named Hector and he kept asking what the whole thing was about. Hobie didn't feel he knew the politics well enough to do any educating like Sarah would, so he just kept saying not to worry, they wouldn't be hurt. Hector didn't seem too reassured, and Monk didn't help any standing there not saying a word with his head all shaved looking like death on a soda cracker, not hardly blinking. Hobie hadn't wanted the assignment in the cellar, and he had extra not wanted it with Monk in the picture, but you took what you were given. Like a football play, you carried out your assignment or the whole thing broke down. Hector and the one who didn't speak English sat whispering in Cuban with their backs against the boiler. You could hardly straighten up without hitting your head on the pipes and there was only the one lightbulb by the metal circular stairs.

It was dark and close and spooky and then they came and Monk went bananas. Scuffling and shouting from above and then screams, fighting sounds, police sounds and then it was Monk screaming, his eyes bugging as he hit with the slash-kneekick-slash attack-form King had taught them and someone upstairs was crying no, please no as something heavy thudded the floor and Hobie spun him and hit him with a straight-punch to the throat. Monk sat down and made choking noises, flopped like a fish. The lightbulb was swinging, making shadows leap and the Cubans were jabbering, looking at him and then to the stairs, debating whether to jump him and it was worse from upstairs, he could tell the crying was Tracy Anne, could hear Schenk screaming and police sounds, deep voices and he was down in a dark hole, trapped, trapped and it was like Ludlow like Nam like a mine must be and that made him want to run, had made him want to run in the first place and he was scrabbling over with Monk trying to clutch his leg, shoving by the Cubans to get at the iron rungs to be first one up, crawling hands and feet toward the fight but away from the cellar, away from the hole.

There were police everywhere and tables tipped and cloth scattered and there was Schenk still standing on top of a chair screaming orders with a rip in his backpack with tin cans thunking out one at a time as King made the kai-ai noise with each thrust taking an armed and helmeted cop, charging straight for him the way you were never supposed to do unless it was hopeless and Grant Parke laughed hysterical somewhere unseen, while Sarah knelt behind a barricade of tables holding the bleeding face, nose flattened, smeared red, of Tracy Anne still crying, Sarah knelt with one arm bracing a tipped desk against the pushing cops holding her ground while it fell out around her, and there were cops, cops all over swinging and trying to grab and he couldn't get to them, had to run, to jump and dodge. It was Debbie, Debbie Ellenbogen catching a club blow in a swirl of cloth, using the machinery and cloth to keep two of them off him, Debbie using everything she could find to back closer to the exit, Debbie who made the screen for Hobie to break loose, duck a grabbing hand and cut off her back like a downfield block and twist away from the one at the door, taking the steps three at a time to the street, head-faking, hip-juking around the two on the sidewalk, feeling their fingers, leaping to break a hold, accelerating past the cluster to the left and hurdling the back of a parked patrol car through the crowd, feeling the power come into his legs, the speed, so good, so good, turning it on to hit daylight, to break clear, to break free —

Vinnie was on the rag. He'd pulled a muscle in his leg again and lost a good bust in court on a chickenshit technicality and then when they reported for work the Captain said they'd have to go an extra four because of all the people out with this flu thing. Ten to ten. And his daughter just came up with root canals which were going to cost an arm and a leg and somebody threw an egg at them outside the Rainbow Lounge and got away and the fucking patrol car kept bucking all the time, some kind of carburetor business again. When Vinnie was in this kind of mood Dom tiptoed around him. He did as much of the driving as possible, steered clear of trouble and tried his best not to break the silence. They hadn't passed a word for three hours when the call for the Chauncy Street thing came in.

"The fuck they want us up there for?" grumbled Vinnie. "Take care of their own fuckin back yod, we'll take care of ours."

"It's a Code Three, Vin."

"I got ears, Dawm. I know what they said. Drive the fuckin car."

There was someone running toward Essex Street. A kid. Army jacket. The shoes. He skidded to a stop a block away when he saw them.

"You make him, Vin?"

"It's him. It's our boy."

"From the direction he's comin he's in on this factory thing. Whatta you say?"

The boy cut right down Oxford.

"Herd him," said Vinnie, getting hold of his stick. "Chase him back up here, left side of the street."

"My left or yours?"

"Yours." Dom stopped at the mouth of Oxford. It was a narrow street, the boy was halfway down already. "I want him," said Vinnie jumping out of the car. "I want that kid."

Dom squealed ahead and around the corner of Harrison. If he stepped on it the kid would never get to Beech Street, he would have to double back.

Vinnie limped down the street a couple yards and tucked himself into a notch out of sight. He pushed a garbage can back to give himself more room. He got a strong grip on the stick. He planted his good leg firmly. He heard tires screeching up at the end of the street.

The kid was so fast, it wouldn't be long. He listened. Running, a car engine behind it. He took off his hat and peeped around the brick. Maybe six strides away. He braced himself. Stride, stride, stride, stride —

Vinnie swung with all his shoulder and back behind it, swung two-handed low and powerful into the forward knee just as it locked stiff into place and felt the rest of the body carry past it.

The boy was lying on his side shrieking when Dom jumped from the car, panting a shriek out with every gasping breath, hands shaking stiffly, uncontrollably in front of his face, looking down in horror at his leg. His leg was broken backwards at the knee, bent almost double in the wrong direction.

[384]

Dom winced and backed toward the car to call the ambulance in.

"Looks like you clipped his wings for good, Vin."

Vinnie's stick lay at his feet, he was bent over a garbage can. He wasn't looking.

It was a beautiful morning as Hunter headed toward Labor Power. He was feeling a little more awake. He heard the sirens ahead and didn't want to get tangled up in anything, he dropped down past Beech to Kneeland and continued along. Maybe it wouldn't be so bad after all. At least he'd be able to bring it to Helen that he was taking the job. She would like that, it would put her more at ease with him knowing how long he was committed to stay, how much he was tied now. And then this evening he'd meet the girls. Casual, dropping in with Jimmy like they just happened to be in the neighborhood. That was how Helen wanted to do it. He wondered if they'd like him. It was so hard to know what to be like, how to act with kids. So hard.

It wouldn't be so bad. A couple months and he'd be clear. He'd be out of the hole. He'd be golden.